THE GOLDEN SPOON

THE GOLDEN SPOON

SADIE & SOPHIE CUFFE

THORNDIKE PRESS
A part of Gale, a Cengage Company

LIBRARY OF CONGRESS CIP DATA ON FILE.
CATALOGUING IN PUBLICATION FOR THIS BOOK
IS AVAILABLE FROM THE LIBRARY OF CONGRESS.

ISBN-13: 978-1-4328-9474-0 (softcover alk. paper)

Published in 2023 by arrangement with Sadie and Sophie Cuffe.

Printed in the USA
1 2 3 4 5   27 26 25 24 23

To Dad — a true son of California, who always loved a good western, and to Mom — a dyed-in-the-wool Maine Yankee, who was born reading.

ACKNOWLEDGMENTS

The internet probably gets more cheers and jeers than it should, but for two rural girls who grew up in the era of the traveling bookmobile — where encyclopedias and grandparents were the source of all knowledge — the amount of information, facts, and factoids available on any subject at the touch of the keyboard is astounding and much appreciated. If we can't learn something while writing a book, there's something seriously wrong with *us*.

A writer's salute to Marc McCutcheon for his timely info, research, and insights concisely gathered in his timeless classic *Everyday Life in the 1800s.*

The book you hold in your hands is a tribute to my meticulous sister, Sophie, who has a much sharper eye and ear than her sibling. She never lets anything leave our office that's only just "okay" or "good enough." Where would the writing team of

S & S Cuffe be, if Mom and Dad hadn't had the perfect type A middle kids to make up for the rest of us?

It's also a tribute to my free-spirited little sister, Sadie, whose imagination has no limit, whose love knows no bounds, and whose words will never end (hopefully!).

And to JV, our sister-in-words. Thanks for your dedication to quality, your investment of time and talent, your fresh set of eyes, invaluable insights and wisdom, and for your friendship. We couldn't do it without you.

GOLDRUSH JARGON

Absquatulate: to take leave; move on
Balderdash: nonsense, foolishness
B'hoy: oh boy, spirited lad
Boodle: a collection, or a large group of people
Bungtown copper: a copper token resembling an English halfpenny
Butter: gold
California toothpick: long knife
Claptrap: absurd or nonsensical talk or ideas
Didoes: get into mischief
Galluses: suspenders
Gum: lies or exaggeration
Hangtown Fry: pull-out-all-the-stops meal
Highfalutin: highbrow, stuck-up
Hullabaloo: commotion, uproar
Jalap powder: an herb known for its purgative effect
Long tom: similar to a sluice; a long, open box set on rockers
Muckle: to grab with force

Peaked: thin or sickly in appearance

Pile: stash of gold

Pile on the agony: add insult to injury

Plank down: pay in cash

Poke: sack used to carry gold

Pony up: pay up

Poor as Job's Turkey: very poor

Sartain: certain

Shut pan: shut up; shut your mouth

Skedaddle: run away, depart quickly

Switchel: concoction of water, apple cider vinegar, and molasses, and ginger; Haymakers Punch.

Twaddle: foolish speech

Whiffletree: mechanism to distribute force evenly through linkages

Whitewash: gloss over one's faults

CHAPTER ONE

Eagle Bar, California, 1850

Cassandra Vincent sidled out the front door of the Golden Spoon and drew in a deep breath of evergreen-scented air. The breeze running down the mountainside was hot for June, but a welcome relief from the acrid press of unwashed bodies mingled with the suffocating scents of baked beans and biscuits. Head spinning, she edged away from the clink of metal spoons on metal plates and the constant rumble of male voices. She hated herself for such weakness. *Just one moment alone.*

Cassie glanced around for any sign of Isaiah, but her friend was blissfully absent from his usual post by the door. A ghost of a smile graced her lips as she slipped around the corner of the plank-and-canvas eatery and crashed straight into a human stone wall. She stumbled and looked up into the bearded, clay-streaked face of a miner. His meaty hand grabbed her upper arm just as she shoved both palms against the rank, filthy shirt stretched across his barrel chest. "Ho there, girly." His teeth were as brown as his beard. He leered down at her, his right eye bugging out a bit more than the left.

She pulled back a step and he released her. She clenched her jaw to ease the trembling and smoothed her skirt to quiet her panic before she shot him a quelling glare. "Pardon me," she said. His face was new to her, but every day more and more strangers crossed her path.

"I came for some vittles, but I could be persuaded to taste what you have to offer." His grin widened before he let fly a stream of tobacco juice.

His unsavory look and vulgar comment were nothing new. Cassie had gotten used to the crudeness that infested the boomtown of Eagle Bar like flies on horse manure. Before she could give the lout a proper set-down, a long-fingered hand grabbed the man's shoulder from behind and spun him around. "That's no way to speak to a lady."

The deep voice hit her ears like a thunder-clap. Cassie looked past the foulmouthed stranger to a mountain of a man. He dwarfed the ruffian by several inches in height and was at least his equal in brawn. There, any comparison ended. He stood like an avenging angel, hair as gold as any ore taken from the river, and his pristine white shirt with dark coat and pants proclaimed him no miner. His dandy appearance was suspicious at best, branding him a confidence man . . . or worse.

Cassie was used to dealing with the miners, even ones as churlish and dirty as the man next to her, but someone in Sunday duds reeked of trouble. She'd had more than her fill of his kind. A fancy man, with eyes as blue as the California sky, here in Eagle Bar, no doubt had intentions as dark as the mountain night.

"May I escort you somewhere, Miss?" The blond-haired gentleman held out his arm and Cassie gaped — not at the rugged jaw and handsome features, but at his fingernails, cleaner than a city-bred lifelong church organist.

She curled her fingers, hiding her stubby stained nails in her palms, wary of the cultured tones and pricked by her own lack of sophistication. She'd been a fool to come out here alone without Isaiah on the watch. Best she could do was brazen it out and nip back inside.

She plucked up her nerve and pasted on a

bright smile, her hospitality coming to the fore. Cassie had discovered that one didn't need courage as much as the ability to keep moving and talking normally, as if everything around you was right as rain. There was nary a shred of normalcy in this low-down boom town, but it was her home for today and no one, bully or saint, was going to push her out of her place in it, least not before she gave them a proper pushback.

From hard-won experience, she slowed her words and dropped her tone, calm as a mill pond in spite of her racing thoughts and skipping heartbeat. "If it's food you want, gentlemen, you're both welcome. The Golden Spoon is open for another few moments." She checked the watch pinned to her bodice. "But you'd best hurry. When the food's gone, we're closed."

The brute barely glanced her way as he brushed by, rounded the corner of the Golden Spoon and disappeared. *One down.* The easy one, she suspected.

Cassie took in the other man through lowered lashes. He was studying her, head slightly tilted, his eyes cooler than the waters of Left Branch Creek. "Dinner can wait," her self-appointed protector said. He extended his large hand toward her and waited. "Matthew Ramsey, at your service,

14

Miss . . . ?"

"Cassandra Vincent." She slipped her hand in his, intending the barest contact, but he engulfed it and held it firm in a warm clasp before he released it. Those were no church organist hands. In spite of their cleanliness, they were as calloused as a working man's, which made her initial suspicions sit not so bread-and-butter plain. In that instant, she raised her guard higher.

"Pleased to make your acquaintance, Miss Vincent." He nodded and smiled, revealing perfectly straight white teeth. "Might I escort you somewhere safe?"

A miner turned gambler? Some sort of confidence man, with his fine manners and flowery speech? Cassie cleared her throat and fought down the jitters. "Thank you for your offer, but I'm perfectly fine here on my own. I'm not far afoot, Mr. Ramsey. This is home."

He leveled a quizzical blue stare at her, as if weighing the truth of her statement. "A woman alone in the gold fields?"

Quick pique squashed any residue of disquiet. She narrowed her eyes and frowned. "We are few and far between, but we do exist," she said, her words sharp at his implication.

"Of course. Truth be told, I hadn't expected to meet someone so lovely upon my arrival in Eagle Bar. I would be pleased if you'd allow me to buy you dinner in this establishment." His stomach growled and he chuckled. Cassie noted the dimples in his clean-shaven cheeks. He raised his blond brows. "I apologize, but I don't think I've had a proper meal since I left San Francisco."

Cassie took a deep breath. Her fresh-air escape was over, ill-fated before it began. Her quest for privacy no longer mattered — the business came first. Regardless of his butter-churned flattery, Matthew Ramsey was a man with an appetite and, from the looks of his clothes, well heeled. He might be willing to spread his gold around as carelessly as his compliments.

She glanced past his rugged shoulders at the lowering sun. "Come along, then." She waited until he matched his step with hers and they strode side-by-side around the corner to the open door of the restaurant.

Isaiah stood outside, blocking the entrance, beefy arms crossed, face dark as a thundercloud. "You ain't gettin' in here unless you take the pledge."

The bearded miner stood toe-to-toe with the powerful black man.

"Isaiah, is there a problem?" Cassie asked.

16

"No, Miss Cassie. I was wonderin' where you'd gotten off to, but now you're here everything's fine . . . 'ceptin' this fool thinkin' he knows the way of things around Eagle Bar. Green as a grasshopper and likely as short on brains."

"You got no right to talk to me that way," the miner growled.

Out of the corner of her eye, Cassie saw Matthew reach out, and she lurched forward to cut off any renewed contact between the men. Mr. Matthew Ramsey might be taking her for a buggy ride, or he might be well intentioned, she had yet to decide. Either way, it appeared he might be as big a fool as any man here; or, as Isaiah put it, "green as a grasshopper." And while hopefully not short on brains, obviously unschooled in the unspoken code of the mining camp.

She'd help him mind his own business today and avoid any unpleasantness. It didn't do to make enemies, whether they wore fancy clothes or miner's rags. If she'd learned nothing in her few months here, fortunes changed in a blink and it was well to keep on friendly terms with all. The bummer today might be the millionaire tomorrow.

Cassie's fingers brushed the miner's grimy sleeve, light as a butterfly's touch, enough

17

to divert his attention and, hopefully, his anger. She kept her voice level but kind. "It's simple, mister. If you want to eat at the Golden Spoon, all you need do is promise to abide by the rules." She gestured toward the board nailed to the post nearby.

"Can't be bothered to read all that balderdash." He spat a juicy wad of chewing tobacco, staining the base of the signpost.

"I'll do it for you," she offered sweetly. She closed her eyes and thought of her secret spot up in the hills, surrounded by the pine and fir, with nothing but the murmur of the wind for company. She lifted her eyelids and looked, not at the hills, nor the sign, but at Isaiah's twinkling eyes. His mouth moved silently with hers as she recited. "No spirits. No tobacco. No cussing. No fighting. No stealing. No shouting. All payment in advance. Please wipe your feet and use proper manners, or you will be asked to leave and never come back. Thank you."

She turned her attention to the prospective diner. A smaller sign also stated the day's price for the supper meal, but a lady never mentioned something as crass as money. She let Isaiah and Charlie handle that aspect of the business.

The miner scowled, bunching up his

18

beard like an angry porcupine. "I dunno if I wanna agree to all that bunkum just for a plate of burned beans."

"Suit yourself," she said.

A group of patrons pushed through the open doorway and Isaiah stepped aside to let them pass. The men tipped their hats and nodded to her, trailing smiles and comments as they filed past. "Mighty fine as usual, Miss Cassie." "When's Charlie coming?" "What's for breakfast tomorrow?"

"You'll just have to come and see for yourselves," she said.

"Will do," the last miner promised as the group trudged down the hard-packed ruts of the main street.

"Probably no food left by now, anyhow," Isaiah said to the bearded miner. "Why don't you move along?"

"Might as well give 'er a try." The man took a step. Isaiah held out his hand and glared at the stranger's boots. "I'll mind my manners." The miner groped in his pocket and pulled out his payment. He grumbled as he placed it in Isaiah's large palm, but he wiped his boots on the roped mat in front of the entrance, spat out his chew, doffed his hat, and disappeared inside.

"I'll see he don't make no trouble." Isaiah turned to follow the miner inside but

19

quickly spun on the ball of his foot and faced her. "Unless, you be needin' me out here, Miss Cassie." He drew himself up to his full size and gestured with his square chin over her head.

Cassie steeled herself not to glance behind her, but she could feel Matthew Ramsey's presence at her back and the heat emanating from his body. She'd nearly forgotten about him. *That would never do!* Not good to let her mind wander. She inched slightly closer to Isaiah. She'd made her place here by always being alert to everyone and everything in Eagle Bar. This was her chance and she wasn't going to miss out by dropping her guard.

"No, it's all right, Isaiah. Mr. Ramsey and I are coming inside, as well."

Isaiah fixed the gentleman with a one-eyed squint before he nodded and ducked through the entrance.

"This is your establishment?"

Cassie turned at the brush of fingers on her forearm. "Yes, I believe I told you that, Mr. Ramsey. Will you come in for supper?"

"Only if you'll join me," he said, dimples showing.

"We'll see," was all she promised.

He grinned at her as he carefully wiped his feet. Looking at his fine polished boots,

Cassie doubted a speck of dirt ever dared cling to any part of him. Whoever he was, Matthew Ramsey bore watching, at least until her brother Charlie returned. Charlie had a gift for seeing into the heart of people.

The name Matthew Ramsey was familiar, but there could be more than one Ramsey in these parts. What was Matthew Ramsey's business in Eagle Bar? Perhaps she'd find out for herself, but it wouldn't do to appear too eager.

"Please have a seat, Mr. Ramsey." She gestured toward an empty space on one of the benches. "I need to check on a few things, then I'll be back with our supper."

Matthew watched Cassandra walk away. She stepped into a shaft of early evening sunlight from the open door, and the rays struck her dark hair, glinting shiny as a raven's wing, demurely held in a simple bun at the nape of her neck. An older man and a red-haired stripling hung at her side, smiling and gesturing as if they were neighbors well met on a country road. She put her arm around the lad in a motherly fashion as the duo made their way to the door.

She moved through the establishment, stopping here and there to chat with diners, her unadorned blue dress a swaying oasis of fresh beauty in the bustling tent. Men of all walks and stripes moved about her like bees around a delicate flower.

Watching Cassandra, who was nearly as tall as some of the men, Matthew marveled at her command of the room, at the respect she garnered from even the roughest sort. Yet there was nothing delicate about Miss Cassandra Vincent. He'd glimpsed her resolve and strength in the alleyway. Seeing her now, he suspected she hadn't needed his help putting the burly miner in his place, but he'd do it again in a wink. Never in his most wild imaginings had he considered meeting a woman like Cassandra here in the California wilderness. He was grateful he'd been pointed in the direction of Eagle Bar. It was all beginning to fall into place. Any endeavor took determination and a quick mind. He had both in abundance. He could already smell success above the fragrance of the unwashed masses in the close confines of the camp's eating house.

He watched Cassandra disappear behind a canvas drape in the back, but he didn't mind waiting. The place was emptying fast now, as miners pushed back from the trestle tables, picked up their empty plates, cups, and utensils, and deposited them in wash-tubs at the end of the serving bench. It was all neat and orderly, in its way. Not in keeping with the eateries of Boston, of course, but a haven of hard-won civilization in the midst of mankind's degradation.

A length of flowered chintz covered the opposite canvas wall and bespoke Miss Cassandra Vincent's feminine touch and high aspirations. What had brought her to this place? From what he'd heard in San Francisco, and the little he'd observed on his journey here, she was surrounded by greed, sin, and wickedness — the lowest of men at their worst. He couldn't fathom what would make a woman of refinement linger in a man's world, but looked forward to sharing her company and finding the answer.

He jerked out of his musings as Cassandra deposited a steaming plate of baked beans in front of him. She placed a small plate of biscuits between them and slid onto the bench opposite. She inclined her head toward the meal. "Sometimes there's butter, generally not. We did have some greens, but they're gone. My Golden Spoon is a first-come, first-served establishment."

"Another one of your rules?"

Her winged brows lowered and her eyes flashed. "It may seem foolish to a gentleman like you, Mr. Ramsey, but I strive to bring a little hearth and home to myself and all who enter here."

He reached across and covered her slim hand with his. She neatly slipped hers away and tucked it in her lap. "Not at all foolish, Miss Vincent. I am most impressed by all you've accomplished here. What is it they say? 'Contact with a high-minded woman is good for the life of any man.' And I believe it."

He met her cold, dark gaze as her eyes searched his face. He wondered what she saw there — a man of honor, or a wastrel trying to atone for the past?

A solemn weight tugged at his soul. He was afraid she'd leave and that would be the end of it. *I shouldn't care. I came to save men's souls, not dabble in personal matters.* But the loneliness of being a stranger amidst strangers pressed on him more than he'd imagined. His confidence ebbed with every mile he'd traveled away from the city. He didn't fit in here.

He surveyed the room. Not a man among her clientele inspired his admiration. "Aren't you going to join me?"

"Yes, but we need to say the blessing first, do we not, Mr. Ramsey?" He detected a slight twitch of her lips.

"Allow me." He bowed his head and uttered a prayer, thanking God for not only the food and pleasant company, but his safe journey to and from San Francisco and his arrival in Eagle Bar. He was about to launch into a request for good success in his mission in the goldfields when a harsh throat-clearing abruptly cut him off.

He looked at his companion to find the one she called Isaiah standing beside her. "Sorry for the interruption, Miss Cassie."

"Not at all, Isaiah."

"I just thought you'd want to know we've closed for the night. I put up the barrier." He jabbed a thumb toward the last diner, sitting hunched over his plate, shoveling in beans like he hadn't eaten in days. "Last one eatin', but he's no trouble. Not a bad sort. Just green, I expect. Anything else you'd like me to do before I eat my supper and clean up?" The big man clapped his eyes on Matthew and his face went cheerless as a gravestone.

"No, thank you."

"I'll be around if you need me." He fixed another dark look on Matthew before he nodded and took his leave.

The black man is clearly one to be watched. "Isaiah seems a good worker," Matthew ventured.

"He's much better than that. He's a friend. He works his own claim with some

25

partners, but when my brother's out of town, Isaiah helps us out."

"Your brother?" How could her brother be so irresponsible? Matthew frowned, but at the sight of the sparkle in her eyes, he thought better of putting the observation into words.

"Charlie. He makes the trek for fresh supplies every fortnight or so. When he comes back, we have us a Hangtown Fry and eat high on the hog for a while. The miners go right wild. But toward the end, when supplies run low, it's mostly beans." She gestured toward his plate.

Matthew looked at the cooling mass in front of him and scooped a spoonful into his mouth. The hearty taste surprised him. "These taste just like the kind Cook used to make when I was a boy."

She raised one slender brow. "Cook? Are you from the South, then, Mr. Ramsey?"

"No. I hail from Boston."

"Ramsey," she murmured. "William Ramsey Shipping."

He stared at her.

Her posture stiffened and she sat straight as a schoolmarm. "First you question my presence in Eagle Bar, and now you doubt my intelligence? I *do* read the newspaper, Mr. Ramsey."

"Oh, yes . . . surely."

Cassandra Vincent didn't blink and her lips held in a stern line. Eagle Bar was full of surprises. He shouldn't be completely bowled over that, even here in the wilds of gold rush country, the Ramsey name was known. His father would be well pleased, and Matthew had to acknowledge it might help establish his place here. "Yes. We import and export, and the market on the West Coast is wide open." He sighed. "My father referred to it as a gold mine. He sent my older brother, Will, and me here to California to get the business established in San Francisco, but I've walked away from all that now. I'm here on a more important mission."

"And that is?"

"To save these wretched souls. I've decided to become a preacher in the gold-fields." He cleaned his plate with the rest of his biscuit, popped it in his mouth, and settled back with his arms folded across his chest.

"What organization sent you?"

He raised his chin in what he thought was a noble pose. "None. I came on my own. I felt the call to do something with my life, and I put my hand to the first thing that came along. My father wanted me in San

Francisco, so I seized the opportunity to travel here. Mother applauded the idea." He glanced around at the chintz-covered wall, then back into the unreadable face of his companion. "It occurs to me the Golden Spoon might make a nice meeting place for the men. A chance tent meeting changed the direction of my life, and I hope to do the same for others right here in Eagle Bar. Would you consider it?"

She was silent for so long, he felt as jumpy as a delinquent schoolboy waiting for the sting of the headmaster's ruler. Suddenly, she said, "I'll think on it. Might be cheerful for the men. I'd have to talk with Charlie. He loves a good hymn singing, if this is *truly* a proper tent meeting."

"Oh, yes," Matthew said, certain he'd won her support. And when Cassandra saw him preach, she'd likely be bowled over for good.

She put out her hand and he took it, unsure of what she intended. She clasped it in a hearty shake as firm as any man's. "Welcome to Eagle Bar, Mr. Ramsey."

"I'd be pleased if you'd call me Matthew. And might I call you Cassandra?" He held her hand for a moment longer before releasing it.

"Cassie is more fitting."

Matthew shook his head. "Cassandra is

more fitting."

"Perhaps in your world, Matthew, but not in mine, and not in this place."

He'd come here to find his place in the world apart from the Ramsey name. He closed his eyes for a brief moment. It was easy to picture Cassandra Vincent on his arm, but not in a tent city. Back home, in one of the finest drawing rooms in Boston. Cassandra would be bowled over by his mother's refined taste, but upon being introduced into society, Cassandra Vincent would be unrivaled among all the posturing, milk-skinned ninnies he'd squired in his youth.

"Ma'am." A rough voice intruded on Matthew's thoughts. He opened his eyes and the rude miner he'd confronted earlier in the alley filled his vision. The man had his filthy hand on the table next to Cassandra's.

Matthew shot to his feet and scowled. "Be about your business!"

The miner held up dirty palms. "I don't want no trouble, mister." He looked down at Cassandra. "I just wanted to thank you, Miss Cassie. I'm sorry I was so ornery before. I reckon I don't know how to keep my trap shut most times."

"You've said your piece, now move on."

Matthew shoved back the bench and stepped over to escort the man from the tent.

The man glowered as he turned to go.

"Move along now." Matthew marched the grimy miner to the door. "It'd be best if you didn't return, if you take my meaning." He held wide the canvas door.

Cassandra nearly trod on Matthew's toes as her sharp elbow knifed him in the ribs. He jerked slightly and stifled a quick intake of breath when she swept past and caught the miner's grubby sleeve in her delicate fingers. "Apology accepted, Mr. . . . ?"

"Folks call me Traveler." He tipped his hat. "Thanks for the vittles and the right-warm welcome. I won't forget it."

"You're welcome back anytime, Traveler."

Traveler skewered Matthew with one more angry glare before he strode out the door.

"You should stay away from him. He's trouble," Matthew said. "It's not worth the patronage to have louts and scoundrels like him come in here."

"He's not a lout. He's a man just like you."

"I would beg to differ. I wouldn't say we were alike in any aspect." He raised his chin and she narrowed her eyes as if taking his measure. He clenched his jaw under her obvious censure.

"Isn't Traveler one of the reasons you came to Eagle Bar with your tent meetings?"

"Well, you might say that, yes, but —"

"I'd say we have different ideas of helping folks. Good night, Mr. Ramsey." She gestured toward the door.

Cassandra was a woman. She didn't understand. Matthew held in the retort that burned within him and instead sketched a slight bow. "I'm sorry if I offended you. That was not my intent. Might I return tomorrow and we can talk further?"

"I haven't decided. Good night, Mr. Ramsey."

He opened his mouth to further argue his cause, but glimpsed Isaiah headed their way. Instead, he gave a curt nod and slipped out into the early evening air. With long, swift strides he marched down the busy street, his gaze on the back of the man named Traveler. It rankled to hear the sound of Cassandra's soft but firm voice welcoming this foul-mouthed blaggard and then dismissing Matthew's gentlemanly attentions in the same breath.

Tomorrow morning, like it or not, Miss Vincent, I will be dining at the Golden Spoon.

CHAPTER TWO

Cassie awoke the next morning to a refreshing cool breeze soughing in the trees outside the window opening of her small dwelling. She lay still for a moment and listened. A gust of wind rustled the flour sack curtain and disturbed the tiny bell suspended on a red cord from the ceiling. The soft tinkling brought a sad smile.

The sleigh bell and an old darned sock that carried her father's worn jackknife were the only things she had from him. Charlie had gotten Papa's fiddle and his Bible. Ma had been so set on leaving the farm the minute Papa was buried, she didn't take a single item excepting her gold wedding band, and on the very next day, she sold it to a tinker for cash money. Said Papa's things were no-account claptrap and we deserved better, but Charlie sneaked out a few remembrances when he loaded up the wagon.

What did it matter now? Memories did no good, particularly in this encampment. Eagle Bar was a place of today. Yesterday was as distant as the moon, and tomorrow as quicksilver as starshine.

She ought to get up and start breakfast. Miners would soon be trudging down the street, anxious to wolf down a poor bowl of porridge and whatever else she could rustle up from her dwindling stores, before they returned to the river and the hillsides to work their claims.

Cassie stretched and shivered as the cool air fell down on her. She pulled the thin blanket over her shoulders and drew herself into a ball under the warm coverlet. Soon enough she'd be cooking over a hot stove and wishing for the chill. For now, she hugged the warmth and solitude to herself for one more drowsy minute.

Morning was her favorite time of the day, when her life hovered in a pleasant place between the past and the present. She broke her rule every morning and allowed only good memories to intrude on her thoughts while she purposefully refused to think of the future — but that's why she was here in Eagle Bar. The future was coming. Each day it marched closer and she could feel it, with all its shadows, bearing down on her.

She huddled deeper under the bedclothes and blocked out the familiar qualms with her usual foolish balm: *I'll think about it come November.* Then she made the distraction complete as she said a prayer for her brother's safe return.

A shuffling outside the wall snapped her back to the realities of daily life. No doubt the chickens were stirring on their roosts, waiting for the sunrise. Ignoring the brisk chill on her bare arms, Cassie threw back the covers, dressed by lantern light, donned her boots and apron, and slipped out of the small cabin. She hurried over the short, beaten path. The smell of wood smoke, mingled with the cooking odors of a hundred meals, drew her through the back door of her Golden Spoon.

Wang Hui looked up from stirring the pot of porridge. His dark almond eyes sparkled. "Good morning, Miss Cassie."

"Good morning, Hui. I hope all is well with the Wangs." Cassie grabbed two big cast-iron spiders from the table and placed them on the cook stove, ignoring the soreness in her arm.

Hui's round face was shiny in the heat from the woodstove. "Everything is very well. Yi and Ming found butter and made spoons this morning. When I finish, I will bring back good Golden Spoon soot from the ashes in the woodstove where we melt our gold into spoons, then rub them in soot to keep them from getting stolen."

"It seems like a lot of work."

Hui tapped the side of his head and his gold tooth glinted in the lamp light. "It is the wise way. Men here have no honor. They steal from their own brother, but who would steal anybody's dirty cooking spoons?" He laughed, his ebony braid swinging back and forth. "You come and we will help you melt butter. Not safe to trust these men."

"Thank you, but I'm fine. My *butter* is quite safe. I keep it well hidden." She grinned at the little man's figure of speech for the gold they all hoped to find before the river ran dry and Eagle Bar became nothing more than a memory — a ghost town of passing greed.

As determined as any of the miners, Cassie meant to leave here with her share of riches. She and her brother were well on their way. Each trip, Charlie took their mounting stash of gold out with him. Now, with their debts finally paid, they were about to turn a new corner to prosperity. "You needn't worry," she told Hui. "No one in Eagle Bar would steal from me or Charlie. They're all our friends." She put a dollop of bacon grease in both cast-iron pans and deftly sliced up the last of the potatoes and onions.

The sizzle of frying vegetables joined the bubble of the hot gruel. Her friend scowled and his face sobered, at odds with his plump cheeks. "Friends." He shook his head and his small wispy beard flopped with the motion. "Some you *maybe* trust, but Isaiah and Wang cousins are your only true friends. More strangers come, desperate to make fortune. This is a wild place. Men lose their souls, forget what it is to be a man. Become animals, biting and clawing."

Cassie shivered at the memory of Traveler's rough hand shaking her. Her sore upper arm was a constant reminder of her brush with the violence in the mining town. She'd stared at the bruised marks his grip left on her flesh before she'd gone to bed and, in her head, repeated the only reassurance she could find: *But he's a friend now. It will never happen again.*

She pushed the fear back and stirred the breakfast fare. "This doesn't look like much, but I'll put the leavings of last night's biscuits with a little honey on top."

Hui nodded. "Not many come in the morning. They eat whatever we have, quick as breath, and are gone before their boots hit the floor."

"Just so." Cassie scrambled the frying vegetables until they were well browned. She grabbed the handle in a fold of her apron and pushed first one skillet, then the other, to the side of the stove top where they'd stay warm. She crumbled the biscuits on top and drizzled a thin stream of precious honey over the whole of it.

She crossed to the canvas drape that sectioned off the kitchen, pushed it aside, and entered the dark eatery. She quickly went about lighting the lanterns. She glanced around at the pools of light in the shadowy canvas structure, satisfied the tables and floor were clean and ready for the onslaught of morning diners.

Nothing was out of place, yet a feeling of unease stalked her every step. She picked up the slate and wrote the price of today's breakfast meal, then propped it against the door, ready to be set out front by Isaiah when they opened for the day. *All is as it should be. Everything is well. I'm a ninny, likely afraid of my own shadow.*

Cassie rubbed her aching arm and pushed aside her disquiet. She walked briskly to the long-planked table in the back and placed the tin eating utensils, plates, and bowls at the end, just as Hui popped his head out of the opening in the canvas curtain. "I will bring water, then we are ready, Miss Cassie."

Cassie frowned. That's what had plagued her. "Where's Isaiah?" Her voice sounded shrill in the empty space.

"Isaiah will come soon. Yi give him medicine last night."

"What do you mean? Is he ill?" On the nights her brother was away, Isaiah never left her alone. He always slept in the storeroom or in the small tent out back. Cassie turned to go out the back door to check on her friend.

Hui sidestepped and his chubby body blocked her path. "He is well."

"If Isaiah is well, he would not be in need of your cousin's cures. What is wrong? You had best tell me before I go out there to see for myself."

Hui sighed long and loud, tilted his head back and rolled his eyes. The rising sun bathed the side of the canvas in amber. The early morning noises of the waking camp, the clop of mule hooves, the creak of wagon wheels, the shouts of men and the tramp of boots intruded.

Cassie stepped past Hui and nearly collided with Isaiah Weaver.

"I'm here, Miss Cassie." Isaiah rushed in

the back door, a dripping bucket full of water in each hand. He strode past her and she spun on her heel and followed him as he placed the buckets in the far corner beside a dipper and a stack of tin mugs.

"What happened?" she asked.

"Nothin'. Just a mite peaked last night, is all. Fit as a fiddle now. No time for jawin'. I hear 'em out there chompin' at the bit." He barely glanced her way as he hotfooted to the front door, lifted the bar, and stepped outside. A moment later he reached inside and grabbed the slate.

Cassie shook her head. *I'm worried about stuff and nonsense.* She hurried back to the kitchen and helped Hui set out the food. The muffle of boots marching toward her signaled the end of solitude, and she turned and smiled into the dirty, haggard faces of her clientele. As the miners filed past, Hui and Cassie ladled the porridge into bowls, and with each "Thank you, Miss Cassie," she wished for a crock of butter or sweet milk to add to the fare. But with her prices down to reflect the simple menu, none complained.

The next hour was jammed with hungry men in a great hurry to fill their bellies and be on their way. Cassie kept up a cheerful banter with each one as she sought to augment the plain fare with as much hospitality as she could muster. She was convinced the combination of home cooking and a homely air kept the Golden Spoon safe from the brawling that went on in the streets at all hours.

A familiar freckled face, topped by an unruly red mop, poked out from the line of miners. Petey Fulton grinned at her. Cassie's heart went out to the orphaned boy, here in Eagle Bar with his grandfather, the pair of them trying to keep body and soul together and work a claim. The boy was rail thin, his clothes hanging off him like a scarecrow.

The man in front of Petey turned around and muttered something at the thirteen-year-old boy and gave him a shove. Petey stumbled backwards into the next diner and that man backhanded him out of line.

The ruffian looked up and Cassie met his glare with one of her own. She recognized one of the men, but not the other. "I will ask both of you gentlemen to leave, please." She pitched her voice above the rumble.

"What about my breakfast?" the first brute snarled.

"You've broken the rules of the Golden Spoon. You have forfeited the privilege to eat here." She spoke in a sharp but even tone and kept the tremor out of her voice. She wished Charlie was here. Even with Hui at her side and Isaiah to back her up, uncertainty and fear threatened to choke her. Hui's warning echoed in her ears. *More strangers come, desperate to make fortune. This is a wild place. Men lose their souls, forget what it is to be a man. Become animals, biting and clawing.* "He's just a no-account young-un." Those in line behind the contentious miner stomped their feet and a grumble of discontent arose.

"I'll show 'em the door right quick, Miss Cassie," someone offered.

Anger and preservation tamped down her spurt of cowardice. She would have no brawling in her kitchen. She raised her chin a notch. "No, I'm sure they'll see the necessity to leave on their own."

The man behind Petey stepped out of the line. "Sorry, son. Sorry, Miss Cassie."

"I hope I'll see you for supper, Elwood," she said, and was rewarded by a gap-toothed smile before he turned to the door. Muttered comments dogged his retreat.

The other offender scanned the crowd before he let out a stream of curses and skulked out the door. Isaiah would make sure he left. Her friend had a way with recognizing faces. She didn't rightly know how he managed it, but he always kept track of those who were barred from the eatery. She had no intention of inviting the odious stranger to return.

Petey sidled up to the serving table. "Thanks, Miss Cassie." The boy looked down at his boots as Hui filled two heaping bowls and Cassie filled a sack with the vegetable hash. She longed to reach out and tousle the youngster's hair, but knew it would be a sign of weakness for the boy, best forbidden in this place.

"How's your grandfather?"

"A mite poorly this mornin', but this'll perk 'im up. Much obliged, Miss Cassie." Petey gave her an ear-to-ear grin before he bolted out of the eatery with his arms full.

The uproar quickly died and as the men filed past; their rough-timbered voices talked of color and toms and the day's work ahead. Throughout the busy moments, Cassie searched the hollow-eyed faces for the bearded visage of Traveler, but the big man was nowhere to be seen. *And why should I care? He's more than likely passing through and I'll not see him again. Just like the wild stranger this morning.*

The bruises on her arm should be proof enough she didn't need to have him coming around, but the thought brought on the comments of Matthew Ramsey.

Mr. Ramsey was too high and mighty for his own good — a stuffed peacock, much too full of himself for her liking. Still, Cassie couldn't so easily shake off the feel of his strong steady hand in hers, and the way he'd treated her . . . as if she were a lady. *A woman would be safe with Matthew Ramsey by her side.* The thought rose unbidden and she dismissed the notion. *I have no cause to believe that nonsense. I don't even know the man.*

As the last few men clattered their dirty dishes into the washtub and hurried out, Cassie concentrated on the task at hand. Beans again for supper. The menu held little appeal; nevertheless she had set a goodly batch to soak overnight. She'd put them in the oven, then Isaiah would help her clean up. Hui would go off with a bucket of soot to join his cousins and work their claim. Just another day in Eagle Bar; unless, maybe today, Charlie would roll in with fresh supplies.

The happy thought put a spring in her step as Isaiah barred the door and, whistling a dirge, hustled past her, straightening benches as he moved along the far wall.

"Have your breakfast," Cassie said. Both men ducked into the kitchen and wolfed down the food warming on the stove, as fast as the rest of the serious miners. Hui was out in the dining area by the time Cassie had collected the serving kettles and pans. He nodded at her with a reminder. "If you want to melt butter, let me know, Miss Cassie. Ming will help you tonight, so I will not see you."

Cassie headed for the kitchen and Isaiah trundled by her. "Did Mr. Ramsey come by this morning?" she asked.

"He come by just as we were closin', all duded up. Didn't want to bother you, so I told him and the other stragglers they'd have to try their luck at supper." The big man kept moving, straightening tables as he strode through the room.

"Good," she said, oddly relieved.

"Didn't sit well. He knows how to kick and jaw, that one, but he's as set on comin' back as a bear on a honey tree." Isaiah threw the grumbled remark over his shoulder and presented his back to her as he grabbed the broom and continued setting the room to rights.

Cassie entered the kitchen and turned her attention to stoking the oven. To drive any thoughts of Matthew Ramsey from her head, she hummed a sweet old tune Papa used to play on the fiddle. She added the last of the seasonings, fatback, and black-strap molasses to the beans and put the crocks in the oven to bake. Then she wiped the sheen of perspiration from her face with a corner of her apron and stepped outside.

The fresh air on her cheeks was blissful relief as she rolled up her sleeves and stepped next to the wooden-crates-turned-worktable where Isaiah washed the dirty dishes. "How are you feeling, Isaiah?"

"Miss Cassie!" The big man jumped and did a quick side shuffle to hide his surprise.

She glanced up at him just as he jerked his head away, but Cassie caught the unnatural swell of his cheek. He was hurt! *How did I miss it?* Because both Isaiah and Hui had been dead set on keeping it from her!

She tugged on his sleeve, but Isaiah refused to budge. He continued to wash the tin bowls, neck bent, face twisted to the side at an unnatural angle. "Isaiah Weaver, you look at me right this minute!" Her voice remained steady, but her insides quaked. He slowly took his hands out of the washbasin and turned toward her, his face grim as a hangman's. A cut on one cheekbone and his slightly swollen and discolored left eye were a tribute to Yi's ministrations, but still they told their own story.

"Oh, Isaiah." Cassie gently touched his

45

cheek. "Who did this to you?"

He flinched from her touch and plunged his dripping hands back into the water. "Don't matter none. Won't happen again."

"Why didn't you tell me?"

He shrugged his massive shoulders and the metal dishes in his fingers clanged as the wash water sloshed at his feet. "Ain't nothin' to tell."

Isaiah was a loyal friend, but he was first and foremost her protector. Whatever happened last night, Cassie was certain it hadn't been his fault. Who would strike such a kind and good Christian man? The unanswered question scurried across her mind like a wayward rat and produced a wary involuntary shiver.

Isaiah would keep her safe from danger with his faithful, stalwart presence and shield her from the wickedness of sinful men with his silence. She ached to know the truth, but his iron-set jaw declared she'd never hear it from him. She would bide her time for now, but she'd worry the facts from some quarter eventually. The thought gave her a boost of resolve and settled her troubled mind . . . somewhat.

Cassie patted his hard-muscled shoulder. "Will you tell Charlie when he comes?"

Isaiah's eyes held a doleful shimmer. "I

might, if you'd promise you wouldn't plague him or me about it again."

Cassie quickly nodded.

Isaiah narrowed his good eye. "That ain't a proper promise."

"And you only said you *might* tell Charlie."

The big man guffawed. "We are a pair, Miss Cassie. No Jonah-gourd promises between friends."

"That's so." *And I will get to the bottom of this!*

Strong arms wrapped around her waist and lifted her off the ground.

"This is what goes on when I'm not here, eh?" said a man's voice. "Sounds like you two are cutting didoes instead of working."

Cassie shrieked and wiggled around to face him.

Matthew Ramsey stood, arms folded across his chest, glaring at the CLOSED sign in front of the Golden Spoon. He should've taken Isaiah to task and gotten inside. Instead, he'd turned like a sheep with the straggling flock of other men barred from the door. They quickly scattered off to their claims.

He'd gone back to the hotel for breakfast, but stewed as he ate rubbery flapjacks and a couple of slabs of bacon sopped in molasses. Had Cassandra given Isaiah strict orders to bar him from the morning meal? His head told him, no, Isaiah had taken it upon himself to exact a crude revenge.

His gut wasn't as convinced. Cassandra might be set on teaching him a lesson. The thought roiled in his stomach like a rotten bit of beef. Now he was back, pacing in front of the barricade, trying to work up a convincing reason to ignore the sign and seek out the proprietress. "You want I should read the rules to you, Preacher?" a man jeered from a passing wagon.

It took a tremendous effort on his part for Matthew to ignore the taunt. He bit back his response and strode past the closed eatery, but he couldn't just strut back and forth like a brainless rooster until the Golden Spoon opened for supper. He would not! He'd not be delegated to a place in the back of the line with the other men.

I'm not like other men!

A woman's scream pierced through the shouts and noise on the street behind him. He broke into a run and rounded the back of the canvas enclosure. He instantly recognized the dark hair and statuesque form of Cassandra, as a tall man lifted her off her feet. The man swung her around and her squeal was suddenly cut off by the brute's crushing grip around her waist.

Matthew grabbed the man's shoulder and spun the pair around with the force of his grip. He cocked his fist and let it fly when, from behind him, an iron hand, fast as greased lightning, clamped onto his wrist and yanked him off balance. He stumbled and glanced away from Cassandra into the fury of Isaiah's dark face. Matthew twisted around like a fish on a line. He couldn't break Isaiah's wet grip, but he did drag him toward Cassandra, where Matthew glimpsed the frown on her face.

"Should I throw him off the property?" Isaiah's voice boomed in his ears.

"Who *is* he?" the tall man asked as he casually draped his arm around Cassandra's slender waist.

"Fancies himself a preacher man," said Isaiah, "but I never knew one who could get hisself into so much trouble in one day."

"Or could stick his nose into another's business so often." Cassandra's eyes flashed.

"Hold up, there." Matthew broke Isaiah's punishing hold, straightened his jacket, pulled down the cuffs of his shirt sleeves and squared his shoulders. Since his arrival in Eagle Bar he'd had more than his fill of criticism, all of it undeserved.

He was bone tired and tired of being judged by strangers. And somehow the news had gotten 'round last night that he'd come to save souls. One and all hailed him "Preacher" in some kind of cruel jest. He'd had a snoot full of it already this morning. He glowered at Cassandra and the tall man, and crossed his arms over his chest. "I heard you scream and I was afraid you'd run afoul of Traveler or one of his kind."

They both raised one brow and it suddenly hit him — the shape of their stubborn chins, the tilt of their heads, the color of their eyes. Matthew saw the resemblance just before Cassandra said, "He's my brother."

The tall, wiry man grinned, and his eyes, so much like his sister's, sparkled. "Charlie Vincent."

Matthew felt the heat rise in his neck and creep up to his ears. *Her brother.* She'd said as much to him yesterday, but the only thing he'd kept trotting around his head was her haughty insistence that Matthew might not be a welcome patron in her Golden Spoon. No need to worry about missing her breakfast fare. She'd just served him an ample helping of crow.

He took a deep breath and extended his hand. He would not be mastered by his emotions, no matter how justified. "I'm Matthew Ramsey. I apologize for the mistake." The words stuck in his throat but he got them out.

Charlie Vincent shook his hand. "No harm done."

Matthew inclined his head toward Cassandra. "My apologies to you, Miss Vincent. You told me your brother was coming. I should have remembered." It pained him to do it, but he turned toward Isaiah as well. The black man stared him down with a face full of disgust, much worse to bear than hatred or pity. "I apologize to you as well, Isaiah. I need to learn to listen before I judge."

"Amen to that for all of us," Charlie said. His sister elbowed him in the ribs. Charlie laughed. "My sister's sharpened her elbow in my absence. You know each other, then?"

"We met yesterday," Isaiah muttered. "I'd best get to unloadin' supplies so's I can get over to the claim."

"Let's get to it. You're probably looking to unhitch Jeremiah and get him to working." Charlie winked at Cassandra. "And I've got a treat for you."

"Charlie, there's no need. We agreed that while we're here we'd just make do."

"Oh, you're going to want this one. In

truth it's a present from Abigail *and* me."

Matthew watched the brother-sister byplay and felt a tug on his heart for his own family. He might as well have gut-punched his brother, Will, when he up and left San Francisco. He'd been so all-fired determined to upend his father's plans — second best, was he? Will, as the Ramsey namesake, got all the honors. Matthew only got to tag along like a beloved but foolish pup. He was tired of it; tired of the pats on the head, tired of the "next time" promises. So when the opportunity presented itself, he'd jumped ship.

He was the one who took after their father — hardheaded and always ready with an argument. Will had barely said a word when they'd parted company. His soft-spoken older brother had requested Matthew stay on for a month or so until they got the initial business dealings squared away, but Matthew had given Will no quarter.

I'm here in Eagle Bar to save souls and that's all that matters. His conscience wasn't soothed so easily by the sanctimonious excuse. *Someday I'll return to San Francisco, apologize, and make it up to Will.*

Matthew shook off the melancholy promise and stared at the backs of his three companions. They had walked off and left him. He heard their laughter and a keen stab of loneliness lanced through him once more.

He hesitated, then spun on his heel to leave just as Charlie called, "Hey, Matthew! Cassie tells me you want to hold a tent meeting at our Golden Spoon."

Matthew pivoted and strode toward the trio standing near an overloaded wagon. As he looked into the cheerful face of Charlie Vincent, then at the scowl on his sister's face, he thought it was a curious thing. He could hold a meeting in the street, down by the river west of town, or perhaps in the Grenier, the hotel of sorts where he was staying, but he had no desire to preach in any of those locales. He wanted a pulpit in the Golden Spoon. He wanted a place at Cassandra Vincent's table.

It was foolish and prideful, he knew, but the urge to prove his worth to her grew stronger with their every encounter. If he could prove his mettle to her, he could prove it to his own father and the world.

A lady like Cassandra couldn't be forced into dancing to any man's tune. And he didn't want that from her. He wanted to win her approval and, more importantly, her regard and her friendship. He'd find a way to persuade her of his honest intentions.

A goat tied to the back of the wagon suddenly bleated and blatted, carrying on as if it was being strangled. The caterwauling grabbed their attention and struck Matthew with inspiration. He shrugged off his jacket and placed it on the branch of a nearby fir, then rolled up his shirt sleeves. "I'll help you unload." He stared into Cassandra's eyes, daring her to refuse his offer.

Charlie clapped him on the shoulder. "Good man. Cassie'll make it worth your while tonight at supper. But first we have to tame the beast." He grabbed his sister's hand and pulled her toward the black-and-white goat, twisting and thrashing to get loose as if possessed.

"This is for you, Cassie." Charlie swept an arm toward the animal as if he were welcoming royalty.

"A goat? It's half wild."

"You sound like Abigail. The goat's not that bad. I picked it up in trade on my last trip. I thought Abigail would enjoy the milk until we get our own cows, but the little devil nearly yanked her arm out of the socket when she tried to corral it. Then it kicked the pan and drenched her with milk the only time she attempted milking."

"And don't tell me. You laughed, didn't you?"

"I tried not to, but . . ."

As Matthew watched the two of them, he tried to shake off a twinge of jealousy. They'd shut him out again as completely as if they'd gone in their house and slammed the door in his face. It was like they lived in their own special world. They seemed to play off each other, able to divine each other's unspoken thoughts.

He could almost feel the crackle of energy coursing through the air around them. It was clear, in spite of her frowns, Cassandra was happy. The elegant, reserved woman he'd met yesterday was hard to recognize in this high-spirited, carefree female.

"So you brought the poor beastie here. Pray tell, bub, what am I to do with it?"

"It's a her. Her name is Nugget, fitting for gold country."

Cassandra shook her head. "Obviously, she doesn't agree."

"Oh, she'll settle down once we get her tied out back. Remember that goat we had at Rowland's lumber camp?"

"That one was tame as a parlor cat. Nugget's just this side of a wildcat."

Charlie shrugged. "She'll be worth it if we

can have some milk, maybe even some butter."

"That is, *if* I can get a hand on her." But Cassandra was already leaning over Nugget, stroking her head.

"I milked her on the trek over here. She'll be fine."

The goat calmed somewhat, under Cassandra's gentle touch, but when Matthew stepped closer, the animal rolled its eyes, bucked away and yanked at the rope. Cassandra murmured something and the creature pressed itself between her and the wagon back.

Charlie said, "How're you with taming wild animals, Matthew?"

Isaiah snorted at Charlie's question.

Matthew could handle a horse and a ship with ease, but looking into the challenging square-eyed glint of this wild-eyed goat had him questioning his next move. "I don't rightly know, but I can try."

"That's the spirit. You just saved my marriage."

Matthew cocked one eyebrow at Charlie's unexpected response.

"My intended, Abigail Callahan, told me I'd better get rid of it if I wanted to marry her. So I brought the goat here. If it doesn't work out, we can roast her up for a Hangtown Fry."

"Charlie!" Cassandra turned on her brother, hands on her hips. The goat, as if on cue, let out a plaintive bleat.

Charlie chuckled. "That's what I thought. You've come to the right place, Nugget. My twin will never let anyone lay a hand on you."

Matthew glanced from one to the other. *Twins!* No wonder they shared such a close bond and resemblance. Charlie's hair was a shade lighter. He was nearly a head taller than his sister and his face more angular, but in Charlie, Matthew saw the heart of Cassandra, and he liked what he saw.

He'd befriend the Vincent brother and sister and, in so doing, forget all about Will and San Francisco and his guilty conscience keeping him awake at night. On impulse, Matthew bent down and scooped the goat up into his arms. The thing kicked and thrashed, but he crushed it to his chest. He felt the tripping pace of its heart against his arm, and her breath whooshed out as he tightened his grip.

"She appears right taken with you," Charlie said as he untied the rope.

"Where do you want her?" Matthew eyed the animal and his wary stare was reflected in the goat's fearful, bulging eyes.

"Back here," Cassandra said. "Come with me."

Cassandra hurried up the path in front of Matthew. He'd carry this goat to the river and back every day if that's what it took to break through her cool reserve. She opened a door in a low shed, ducked in, and released a latched board. A flock of squawking chickens trundled out into a rough fenced-in yard. "We'll put her in with the chicks for now, until she gets settled."

She held the door wide and Matthew carefully brushed past, inhaling the scent of her kitchen. It mingled with the warm odor of the goat in his arms. He gently set the creature on its feet and the goat bolted over to the shadows in the far corner. Its eyes gleamed eerily in the shaft of light flooding in through the doorway.

"She'll be safe for now." Cassandra went out the door and waited for him to follow. "I'll give her a chance to get used to the place before I attempt to gentle her."

"Looked to me like you were already halfway there. The goat was clearly taken with you."

"We'll see. I don't know what my brother was thinking, bringing that poor helpless creature out here in the wilds."

He had the same thought in regards to

her safety, but he didn't voice the concern. He didn't want to ruin the thin thread of acquaintance between them. Instead, he gestured toward his soiled shirt front and noticed a missing button and a tear in the cloth where a wayward hoof had struck out at him. "Trust me, that goat is not helpless."

"Oh, dear." Cassandra nearly touched him before she jerked her hand back to her side. "I'm so sorry. If you give that to me later, I'll wash and mend it for you."

"There's no need."

"Oh, yes, I insist. It was our goat that caused the damage."

The idea of having an excuse to visit at a time when a horde of miners wasn't usurping her attention held great appeal. "Okay, and I thank you."

"I should thank *you.*"

"Not until the work is finished, I expect." He strode off to help the men unload the wagon.

As he unloaded flour and ham, crates of vegetables and fruit, salted fish and beef, Matthew enjoyed the banter with the Vincent twins, and even Isaiah's terse remarks. The work brought back the times when he was much younger, working alongside his brother and their crew, unloading cargo on

Ramsey ships. It was what his father had deemed "character building," and Matthew was glad of the experience. He noted a gleam of respect in Isaiah's gaze as Matthew hefted the last crate and, following Cassandra's direction, stowed it in the Golden Spoon's kitchen.

By the time they'd finished trucking the supplies into the half of their cabin that served as a storeroom, his shirt was soaked with sweat and clung to him.

"You're lookin' a bit more like a flesh-and-bone preacher, maybe not so scared of gettin' them Sunday duds dirty," Isaiah said as he took his leave. He gestured at the soiled smears on Matthew's once-white shirt. "I expect I'll see you tonight at the Golden Spoon."

Isaiah accepted Cassandra's hug before he and Charlie walked out to the main street together.

"Thank you again for your help, Matthew," she said. "And I want to invite you to share supper with us tonight. It'll be a fine spread."

"Thank you, Cassandra."

"Please call me Cassie. Cassandra doesn't set right, especially here."

He wanted to argue. He wanted to resort to the gentlemanly air of taking her hand

and pressing his lips to her fingers, but he guessed that wouldn't "set right" either. Instead he inclined his head. "As you wish, *Cassie.*"

"Would you care to come with me and check on our Nugget?"

The goat? It seemed an odd invitation, but he eagerly accepted. Cassie tore off a fir bough and some handfuls of tufted grass on her way to the chicken coop. When she slowly opened the door, the goat started and bolted, cowering in the far corner. As Cassie crept in, she sang to the animal and deposited the grass at its feet. She stroked its head as it took in a mouthful of food.

Matthew watched, and her sweet song wound its way into his head. He closed his eyes and listened to the lilting tune and was startled when her fingers brushed his arm.

He stepped back and held the door for her. "You have a lovely voice. Would you sing for us at the tent meeting? I mean, I'd be honored if you'd consider it."

Cassie latched the door and turned to him, her face immobile, her eyes unreadable.

What did I say? Did I offend her? Have I presumed too much? That was it! He'd make it right. It nearly killed him, but Matthew drew in a deep breath. "I know you and

61

Charlie haven't decided about the meeting. If you don't want to hold tent meetings at your Golden Spoon, that is quite all right. I believe I can hold them at the Grenier. I'm sure Zelda would be amenable to the notion, and they do have a piano, but I still hope you'll consider attending and singing for us."

"Zelda Grenier holding a tent meeting?" Cassie turned away from him and gazed at the fat white hens scratching in the dirt.

Matthew shook his head. *Fool! Why did I speak of Zelda Grenier?* The widowed hotel-and-dance-hall owner was kind, in her way, and more than hospitable, but her ringed fingers and cold blue stare bespoke of a hardened heart, not a tender one. While Zelda feigned a genteel manner to mask her toughness, Matthew suspected Cassie pretended toughness to hide her tender heart. Now he'd been fool enough to extend a backdoor invitation to this delicate soul. His mistake. The Grenier dance hall, with its clink of glasses and stink of liquor and stale tobacco, was no place for a lady.

He opened his mouth to apologize yet again, when Cassie spun on her heel to face him. "One of my chickens is gone." Her eyes flashed fire. "Someone stole one of my birds!"

62

"Maybe it got loose."

She shook her head so violently dark wavy strands tumbled out of her bun. "No, someone stole my hen and I mean to find out who!"

"Surely —"

He never got to finish. She stomped up to him, toe to toe, her brows lowered, her lips compressed in a hard line. "You may think I'm not rightly upset over a simple hen being stolen, but a thief is a thief, whether it's my chicken or your horse, Mr. Ramsey. I'll ask you not to make light of that fact."

CHAPTER THREE

Cassie marched to the kitchen, her mind in turmoil. A stolen chicken. Isaiah's battered face. Her bruised arm. And Matthew Ramsey.

Why would she mix that man into the rest of it? *Because he's trouble, pure and simple, disguised in his fine white shirt and gentlemanly manners, but trouble nonetheless.*

She'd warmed to him when he'd carried the goat for her. And when he'd helped unload the supplies, Cassie had felt . . . what? A grudging respect for the man? No, something more. She'd not admit it to anyone, not even her brother, but she liked Matthew, and the worst part was she knew Charlie did, too.

She pulled out her hairpins and inserted them between her lips. She ran impatient fingers through her hair and deftly pulled and twisted, restoring it into a neat bun before securely jabbing in the pins. As much as she cared for the Wangs and loved Isaiah, she yearned for a companion to perhaps share her quiet time of walks in these mountains, her private world that not even Charlie understood completely.

But Matthew was not that friend and never would be! Not if he laughed at her concern over the theft of her hen. *He may treat me like a lady, but he thinks me a ninny, with naught but cobwebs for brains.*

Cassie banged the pots and pans. "Zelda Grenier!" she muttered as she combined flour and lard and sorted the berries Charlie had brought this morning. "Let him have his precious tent meetings at her bar. She might call it a dance hall and a hotel but —"

"Who you talking to?" Charlie strolled in and popped a raspberry into his mouth. He squeezed one eye shut and made a face. "Oooh! Sour!"

"They'll be fine once I add them to the cobbler. The men won't care anyhow. They'll wolf it down before they taste a single berry."

Charlie lounged against the edge of the table and watched her work oats into the soft dough. "Something eating at you?"

Cassie ducked her head and beat the mixture. She couldn't look at her twin for fear he'd finagle the truth out of her. And she surely had no intention of bringing up Matthew Ramsey. But what of her decision to tell him to hold his meeting elsewhere? How would she manage to convince Charlie to do the telling for her?

"Is it the goat?"

Cassie looked into his somber face and couldn't hold back a smile. *God bless Charlie.* She couldn't waste his time here moping around. All too soon he'd be gone again. "No, it's not the goat. I actually like her."

Her brother reached over for another berry and she playfully swatted his hand. "Ouch." His fingers slipped back in and pilfered the fruit. "I knew you would." He chewed the treat and smiled. "Mmm. Must've got the only sour one in the batch. This one's sweet as my sister."

Oh, how I've missed him. "Aren't you spreading on the whitewash and gum today!"

"Only telling the truth." He swung away from the bench, grabbed the large pans and greased them. "The place looks good. Isaiah says business is hand over fist."

"What else does Isaiah say about his eye?"

Charlie shrugged and set his jaw.

She set hers. "You might as well tell me. You'll get no peace 'til you do."

"And don't I know it! I'll build a little lean-to for the goat in-between times."

"I suspected you might. Now what about Isaiah?"

"What are you thinking we'll serve tonight?"

"Beef and gravy, mashed potatoes, onions and carrots, sourdough rolls, cobbler and beans, of course, 'cause they're already cooking."

"Sounds good. Beans go with everything. Want me to fix the beef and gravy?"

She took a moment to fill the pans with berries, folded the dough on top, dusted the flour off her fingers, and turned to face him, hands on her hips. "Yes, and don't think you're going to get off telling me what happened."

Cassie pushed the baked beans to the side and slipped the pans of cobbler into the oven. She spooned some sourdough from the starter bowl and set to work on the rolls. "Well?"

Her brother sighed and it ended in a theatrical groan.

"Now that you've gotten rid of all that hot air, Charlie Vincent, perhaps you can get out the truth."

"Some of the miners got to brawling in the street last night and started beating on a

Chinese fellow. He got loose and came to the Golden Spoon. Isaiah took him in for a spell."

"And? That doesn't rightly explain his face."

"A few of the miners didn't take kindly to Isaiah's interference, but he set them straight."

Cassie puckered her brow. "Why didn't I hear anything? I should've been there to help him."

Charlie shook his head. "Good thing you weren't! You hear any hullabaloo, you grab the shotgun and stay in the cabin. Besides, Isaiah said it was just a few bums who'd had too much to drink. He sent them on their way and they won't be back."

"And what of the poor man they were beating? Where is he?"

"Isaiah sent him down to the claim. The Wangs are looking after him. That's why Yi came back and patched up Isaiah late last night."

"I don't like it, Charlie. Things are getting meaner every day."

"Isaiah says the same thing. The camp's changing right before our eyes. I've only been gone nigh on a week, but I can see it. There's more than a bushel of bad feelings building up out there." Charlie tapped his fingers on the table top. "All the more reason to have Matthew's tent meetings at our place. It'll give us a chance to spread some goodwill, and be good for business, too."

Cassie frowned. With all that was going on, they surely did not need Matthew Ramsey hitched up to their troubles. "We don't need the business, Charlie."

"Goodwill, then."

"I don't know. When Matthew talked with me, he seemed set on having it at the Grenier." Maybe "set on" was a mite strong, but Matthew *had* mentioned Zelda's place.

She studied her brother under lowered lashes. Perhaps Zelda had put the idea in Matthew's head. Cassie had seen the woman do it before to other men. Zelda Grenier always laid on the charm, thick as butter when Charlie was around; but Cassie had recognized the older woman's sly glances and the sheen of avarice in her strange, opaque blue eyes.

At least her brother's heart was safe. He might befriend everyone he met, but he was true-hearted and fiercely loyal to Abigail.

Charlie cocked one dark brow. "Zelda and a fire-and-brimstone sermon? I can't rightly picture that. Then again, she might agree to it just to cut us out of the competition, by hook or by crook, or maybe by a rousing hymn sing, eh?"

Cassie gaped at him.

"I've got eyes in my head," Charlie continued. "Zelda may be able to get anything else she wants in Eagle Bar, but not our Golden Spoon."

"It appears you've got brains in your head as well as eyes." Cassie's tense shoulders relaxed. Everything was better when Charlie was here.

He gave a mocking bow. "So what do you say? Matthew's all fired up to have his meeting here tomorrow."

Cassie could think of nothing more to say against it, yet a certain reluctance to give in to the handsome preacher gnawed at her pride. "You know we don't open the Spoon on Sundays." It was her one day to spend as she chose, roaming the hills, picking flowers, or reading the Good Book and the old *Home Journal* magazine and newspapers Abigail sometimes sent with Charlie.

"It wouldn't be any trouble, and he asked if we'd sing." Charlie's baritone broke out, filling the kitchen with the sweet melody: "Amazing grace how sweet the sound that saved a wretch like me."

Cassie joined in, "I once was lost but now am found. Was blind but now I see."

Charlie's eyes held a shimmer of tears. "Might be nice. Like old times." He took her hand and squeezed. "It'd make Papa proud. He always did love a good hymn sing."

And you're just like him with your winning ways. The familiar thought brought with it a persistent doubt. *Does that mean I'm like my mother? Maybe I'm the one in need of Matthew's sermon.*

She quelled the troubling notion and gave Charlie's strong hand a squeeze in return. "All right then, it's settled. We'll have Matthew's tent meeting here, and I'll ask Petey if his grandfather feels up to playing his fiddle."

"If he doesn't, I can play."

Zelda Grenier might have her piano, but the Vincent twins knew a little something about making their own music. The spiteful thought brought a desire to show Matthew Ramsey he wasn't the only one who could bring comfort to the lost souls of Eagle Bar.

"Hello! I hope I'm not interrupting."

Cassie jerked her head toward the open back door. *Speak of the devil.* Matthew's broad shoulders blocked out the sunlight as he strode into the kitchen.

"No, you're timely," Charlie said. "Cassie and I were just talking about the tent meeting. Are you set for tomorrow?"

Charlie made it sound like they'd been discussing Matthew. Cassie's cheeks burned. She bowed her head and busied herself kneading the sourdough. She felt a surge of pleasure she didn't want to examine too closely.

It's because I don't want to give Zelda the upper hand in this town.

The justification eased her agitation.

"Can I prevail on you to sing, as well?" Matthew leaned his substantial frame against the work table. Charlie had done the same thing moments ago, but suddenly Cassie found the kitchen cramped and overheated.

"You can't stop us." The whack of his knife cutting the beef into chunks punctuated her brother's words.

Matthew straightened and held out the soiled shirt he'd worn earlier. "I brought this over, but you really don't have to mend it."

"I'm pleased to." Cassie wiped her hands on her apron and, when she took the shirt, his fingers brushed hers. At the unexpected contact, she looked up into his blue eyes, darker than she remembered; or maybe it was due to the blue shirt he wore. The sleeves were casually rolled up to his elbows and his tanned, muscular forearm made two of Charlie's one arm. A blush rose at the disloyal thought. Her brother may be wiry as a willow branch, but he was strong as any man, stronger than most. She quickly placed the shirt on the nearby flour bin before she set the dough to rise on the shelf.

"I wondered if you might have a preference as to the hymns," Matthew said. "I'm not trying to dictate what songs you two want to sing. I thought the men might be more inspired to join in the general hymn sing if you were to lead the singing with me."

"As long as you don't ask me to preach the sermon, I'm your man." Charlie winked.

Petey Fulton dashed into the kitchen as if the hounds were at his heels, and so they were as his dog, Gypsy, trailed behind and sniffed Matthew's leg. Cassie was relieved to see Petey. The kitchen had grown stuffy and close, but he brought in a wave of fresh air.

Matthew stepped back from her worktable when the boy threaded his way to her. "Brought back your tinware, Miss Cassie, and Grandpa says thanks." Petey set the clean bowls on the end of the table.

"And how is your grandfather?" Charlie asked.

"Ready to come to the Hangtown Fry tonight." Petey rubbed his hands together. "We heard you was back, Charlie, and can't wait. Smells mighty good already."

"Petey, do you know Matthew Ramsey?"

"Yeah. He's the preacher."

"Good news travels fast in Eagle Bar." Charlie clapped Matthew on the shoulder.

"Mr. Ramsey is having a tent meeting here tomorrow. I wondered if your grandfather might come and play his fiddle, if he feels up to it," Cassie said.

"Should be a high old time," Charlie added.

Cassie looked at Matthew. He was awfully quiet for someone so enthused moments ago. "Bernard Fulton, Petey's grandfather, can play a reel likely to set your head spinning." *Just like Papa used to when Charlie and I were young.*

Matthew's face remained grim.

The dog sidled close to her skirts and whined. Cassie slipped it the scrapings of dough as she cleared off the workbench and readied the space for peeling vegetables.

Gypsy smacked down the meager treat and her tongue lolled out, waiting for more. "Is that your dog, Peter?" Matthew's voice sounded stern.

Cassie looked into his rugged face, disappointed by the reprimand she expected to come, but he surprised her by scratching the animal behind the ears.

"Yes, Preacher. This here's Gypsy. Got her pup, too, over to the claim. Name's Roman. He's a big brute. Watches over the claim. Nobody sets nary a toe on our claim lessen they want to go missin' a hand or a foot."

Cassie winced at the gruesome thought and the obvious pride in the boy's voice, but Matthew said, "How would you feel about maybe selling Gypsy?"

"You in need of a watchdog, Preacher?"

"No, not for me, but perhaps for Miss Cassie." Matthew met her questioning stare with a steadfast blue gaze. "Then nobody would be sneaking around stealing your chickens."

"Somebody stole a hen?" Charlie and Petey spoke together.

"I'm going to get to the bottom of it," Cassie declared. She frowned at Matthew. It didn't do to let others know your personal business. It was *her* story to tell *when* she chose to tell it — not before — and she didn't thank him for blurting it out.

"You can have the dog, Miss Cassie."

Cassie shook her head. "No, I don't want to take Gypsy."

Petey knelt and hugged the dog's rough

brown coat. "Don't worry. I'd likely see her every day. And she'd be more'n pleased to stay in town and eat at the Golden Spoon." He laughed as the dog licked her chops. "See?"

"I don't know," Cassie said.

"Seems like it might be a good idea. Keep you out of trouble while I'm gone." Charlie caught her eye. His solemn gaze belied his light tone.

"If you want, you can try her out," Petey said. "It'd make up for all the kindness you and Charlie give to me and Grandpa."

A shadow darkened the open door and Gypsy growled. "Thought maybe you could use these."

Traveler's rough voice sent a shiver through Cassie, as he shoved past Matthew and placed four skinned rabbits on the table in front of her.

Charlie whistled and stepped away from the stove. "Now we've got us *more* than the makings of a Hangtown Fry. This'll be one for the books. Hope you'll join us." He shook Traveler's hand.

"On the house, of course," Cassie said. *He's a friend.* Her sore arm might say otherwise, but the rabbits spoke for themselves. She heard Matthew grumble something under his breath as he left the kitchen without another word.

Matthew walked up Eagle Bar's deserted street in the early morning light. With all the hooting and hollering that went on last night into the wee hours, it was no wonder the place was a ghost town. The quiet should've lent solace to his soul, but it only spurred him on to get this day into full swing. Unfortunately, it was much too soon to set up for the meeting at the Golden Spoon, but his restless body, mind, and spirit refused to stay cooped up in his room a minute longer. He stopped and faced the quiet eatery. The slate sign advertising the Hangtown Fry was gone.

Matthew closed his eyes and breathed in the still air. Last night had been a different kettle of fish. The place was crawling and buzzing with men like swarming crazed bees. A bunched-up line of diners jostled for their places, and the mob of humanity trailed down the street reaching past the Grenier. Isaiah had stood as immovable as a granite statue, head above the crowd, ruling with an iron fist as he collected payment and allowed the miners inside only when others left. It was all very civilized, in its rowdy way.

Matthew had waited in that line, berating

himself for his late arrival, until he saw Traveler slink past the line and around the corner toward the back of the eatery. That bum was trouble, and for some fool reason, Cassie couldn't see it. She appeared to champion the lout at every turn. And yesterday when Traveler had slung the rabbits in front of her, Matthew had to walk out in order to conquer the urge to grab the uncouth stranger, twist his dirty arm behind his back, drag him away from her, and throw him off the premises.

He hadn't managed to swallow his indignation and it still burned. Last night only added fuel to his outrage when, at the Hangtown Fry, he'd slipped his place in line and followed Traveler. Just as he suspected, the filthy miner loitered at the Golden Spoon's kitchen door, and as Matthew watched from the shadows, Charlie brought him a heaping plate. The ruffian sat out there in the June night air, jawing and laughing with Peter Fulton and an older man who, no doubt, was the boy's grandfather.

Matthew knew he should've been pleased to witness Cassie and Charlie's generosity; instead he only saw the preferential treatment of a man who'd tried to hurt her — no, who surely *would* have hurt her, if he hadn't come to her rescue.

The truth of it churned in his belly and rankled like the worst sort of dyspepsia. It didn't help that he'd hoped to visit with Cassie yesterday, away from the press of miners. He'd thought of the shirt mending as a pleasant circumstance. Yet he'd only just begun to enjoy her company when the dream unraveled and half of Eagle Bar arrived to dance at her elbow in the backdoor kitchen.

Matthew took a deep breath and shook off some of the residual anger. Today was a new day, and although he hadn't succeeded in convincing himself to let Traveler be, he resolved to speak no more about it to Cassie. That woman was stubborn as a New England wild rose and just as hard to get close to without getting scratched. Nevertheless, he'd keep a close eye on the bad fellow, and when the moment came to pick the lout up by the scruff of his scurvy neck and throw Traveler out of Eagle Bar, he'd be more than ready.

"Morning, Matthew." He jerked out of his reverie at Charlie's hail. "If you want some breakfast, come on back. Cassie's done tamed the beastie and we're set to have fresh milk along with eggs and bacon. You're more than welcome." Charlie strolled past the canvas structure and joined Matthew on the street.

Caught off guard, it took his foggy brain a moment to clear. "Uh, I didn't come by to eat. I was taking a walk."

"Clearing your head for the sermon?"

Matthew nodded. It didn't hold a stitch of truth, but it sounded better than the sober reality that he'd been mooning over Charlie's twin sister.

"You aren't nervous, are you?"

Matthew stared at the slightly taller man. Charlie lifted up both palms and grinned. "Sorry!"

Matthew shook his head. He was jumpy as a frog in a sizzling frying pan, but it had nothing to do with his sermon. He'd run the words of his message through his head, and added to them every day on his trek here. It was the purpose of his coming to Eagle Bar, and he'd do well to keep his mind on his mission. Still, temptation called when Cassie's lilting, clear voice drifted out to the street.

He wiped his sweaty palms on his trousers and cocked his head toward the liquid notes hanging in the air. Surely God wanted him to include the Vincent twins in his mission. He smiled a little foolishly at the notion, but a bite of breakfast and good company would not be amiss on this Lord's Day.

"Cassie's singing in the kitchen. She always cooks better when she sings. You coming to eat, or not?" Charlie clapped him on the shoulder and hurried toward the kitchen. "It's just us today."

Matthew followed and Gypsy came out to meet him, bushy tail wagging.

Cassie stopped singing and looked up from the stove when they entered.

"Look who I found larking about on the street," Charlie said. "He didn't get enough to eat last night."

Matthew patted his stomach. "That was quite a feed. I was surprised at the amount of folks who came." *And the exorbitant price.* He'd tried to chase the disloyal thought out of his head last night, but it remained lodged like an irritating splinter in his morally outraged soul. Eagle Bar had its faults, and the Vincent twins were as greedy as the rest of the folks here, but he'd help them see the error of their ways starting today.

Cassie hummed as she scooped the bacon out of the fry pan. Her curved cheek was turned toward him, rosy and fresh in the morning light, and her hair was caught in a single braid down her back. She was more beautiful today than he remembered. When he realized he was staring, he quickly dipped his head and patted the dog.

"B'hoy, it was the best night we've ever had." Charlie grinned. "At this rate we'll need a bigger wagon to haul our gold out of here."

Matthew hid his frown of disapproval behind his fingers. In spite of their down-home charm, the Vincent twins were striking it rich as surely as any miner in Eagle Bar; maybe more so, because they took the mined gold from the downtrodden workers. Doubt wormed into his heart as he wondered again why they chose to be here. He glanced at Cassie, her lips parted, face flushed, tendrils of hair curling around her ears, her eyes shining as she shared a piece of bacon with her brother.

He'd developed a fondness for the twins and enjoyed their company. In a different place, they could be friends and go to society events together, but here? The notion that they were driven by greed didn't sit well. He didn't want to think that of Cassie, or even of Charlie. It seemed a cold reason to live and one he was dead set on preaching against. Yet, if not greed, why else would they stay in this lawless camp? Why else would Charlie put his sister in such danger?

As much as he liked the genial fellow, it

was doubtless Charlie's doing. He must have convinced his sister to come here and cook for him. Without her, the Golden Spoon might exist, but it wouldn't be crammed with miners every supper. It was not only her cooking, but Cassie herself who attracted their overflow of diners night after night.

She nudged his arm and handed him the cleaned and mended shirt. Matthew shook off the disturbing train of thought and took the proffered garment. "It looks better than the one I have on," he said and was rewarded with a small smile. "I'll put it on after breakfast."

"Then come and set. We need to get you fed up with some good cooking. I hear it takes a powerful lot of wind to deliver a proper sermon." Charlie winked at Cassie.

"Charlie! I'm sure Matthew has preached many a sermon without our help."

The banter pricked his conscience and set Matthew's stomach twisting. It was a strange feeling. A cold shaft of self-doubt chilled his soul, the first he'd experienced since he'd set his mind to the task of becoming a preacher. As they filled their plates and sat at an empty table in the quiet eatery, his confidence tumbled so greatly that he asked Charlie to say the blessing.

The twins held his hands, bowed their heads, and said a family grace. He was touched by the blend of their hushed voices and convinced of the genuine bond of their childhood faith. He'd had little of that growing up. Once he was of a size, his father was much more concerned with building his son's muscles and character through work than building his spirit and faith.

Between bites of his fried eggs, he blurted, "This will be my first."

Two sets of wide eyes stared at him as if he'd sprouted antlers and wings.

"First ever?" Cassie's soft voice didn't ooze confidence in his ability.

"Yes." He downed his milk in a gulp, hoping to drown the sudden urge to call off the meeting.

"You'll do fine," Charlie said. "It's not like you're going to be standing up in front of the president of the United States. You'll just be speaking the truth out to your neighbors and friends."

"That's right," Cassie said.

Matthew drew in a deep breath. No matter what he might think of Charlie and Cassie's lust for riches, at this moment he needed their encouragement, and they'd given it without reservation. If they believed in him, if Cassie was there to support him,

Matthew could do anything.

After breakfast, he changed into his clean shirt. The fabric smelled of strong lye soap, but he fancied he caught a whiff of her scent as well. His confidence rose with each button he fastened. Charlie's words echoed in his head. He was here on a mission and he'd be mighty sure it was a success, or his name wasn't Matthew Ramsey.

"You look like a preacher or someone about to get hitched," Charlie said.

Cassie, her hands in the wash water, said nothing, but her shining eyes gave him all the approval he needed.

Isaiah came and the three men moved the tables to the side and set the benches in rows facing toward the canvas wall that blocked off the kitchen.

"You need some kind of pulpit?" Charlie asked.

Matthew glanced around the eatery. He hadn't thought about the setup. He'd only pictured himself preaching as the men hung on every word, and came up after to shake his hand and repent of their evil ways.

Isaiah carried over the small stand they used for the tin cups and water bucket. "It ain't much, but maybe it'll do." He reached in his back pocket and pulled out a rough cross made from two oak branches wound together with a length of red string. "This'll give folks the right notion." He propped his homemade cross in a knot hole and it stood straight and small in the makeshift pulpit.

"Looks like you're set, and looks like your first converts are coming in." Charlie gestured toward a few miners straggling through the open front door.

"They're sinners hungry for the Word of God," Matthew said, and a jolt of excitement buzzed along his nerves.

"They're hungry for something," Charlie agreed. Isaiah laughed.

Peter arrived with his grandfather, Bernard. Cassie beckoned them around back to give them a late breakfast.

"I didn't see his violin," Matthew said as the benches filled.

"He probably took it to the kitchen. I'll go see," Charlie said.

"No, I'll go." Matthew hurried through the canvas drape, nervous energy driving every step. He pulled up short at the sight of Traveler standing next to Cassie. The dirty miner was shoveling in bacon and eggs like a pig at a trough.

Matthew fixed him with a stern challenging glare. "Are you coming to the meeting, Traveler?"

"Cain't abide being cooped up like some

caged hawk."

"Sorry to hear that." Perhaps now Cassie would recognize Traveler for the godless thug he was.

"You're welcome to sit out back here in the quiet and listen," Cassie said, and she took Traveler's empty plate.

Fuming, Matthew spun on his heel and rushed back into the meeting, unaware that Peter, Bernard, and Cassie followed on his heels.

"Shall we sing 'em in, Preacher?" Bernard's raspy voice at his elbow gave him a start, but, before he could reply, the older man angled his bow, tapped his toe, and nodded at Charlie and Cassie.

Matthew had planned on starting with a prayer, but as the strains of "Amazing Grace" swelled beyond the canvas walls and into the street, he clasped his hands behind his back and let the voices wind through his senses like a sweet, summer-scented breeze. Men came in and stood along the walls until nearly every seat and every space was occupied.

As soon as the last strains of the song drifted away, Matthew stepped up to the makeshift podium. He began by praying for the service, then moved on to the woes of Eagle Bar, the general wickedness of man, and those who lust for gold in particular. Someone coughed and several miners rudely cleared their throats. Matthew heard the shuffle of boots and was surprised by a gentle prod in the ribs. He glanced into Charlie's somber face. "Amen," his friend whispered. The tent erupted with shouted amens.

Matthew lifted his head, but before he opened his mouth a fellow in the back said, "When we gettin' to the singin'? I came instead of workin' my claim this mornin' 'cause I heared we was havin' us a hymn sing."

Bernard scraped his bow across the strings and Cassie and Charlie led the miners in a raucous rendition of "Rock of Ages." No one took a breath before they launched into "My Faith Looks Up to Thee."

Matthew tried not to reveal his surprise. How did they know all the words? And, more importantly, how had they figured out what song they were singing next?

Too late he realized he didn't know many hymns. In fact, he could think of only four, and even then he wasn't familiar with all the verses. Cassie and Charlie appeared to know every hymn ever written, by heart. And though it was apparent his congregants didn't know the words any better than he did, it didn't stop them from stomping their boots in time to the music and lustily singing whatever words came to mind. The caterwauling pounded in his ears.

He held up both arms and the music ended on an abrupt note. He'd sober up this crowd with a good dose of fire and brimstone. He opened his Bible and read a Scripture passage and the room went relatively quiet, except for the rustle of restless bodies. He raised his voice and expounded on the parable. He was barely five minutes into the sermon when grumbling reached his ears and several miners glared at him before they sauntered out.

"Preacher, set down and rest your windpipe. Let's hear Miss Cassie."

Matthew recognized Traveler's rough voice and whipped his gaze to the open door.

"Yeah. We want Miss Cassie." As the grumbles and rumbles from the crowd escalated, so did Matthew's voice. He felt the heat creep up his neck and, with a stern frown, finished his sentence and gestured toward Cassie, standing beside her brother.

"I'd like to say something before we sing." She pointed a slender finger at the motley crowd. "Someone stole one of my chickens."

Matthew gasped, but before he could form

a coherent thought she continued.

"I'm not accusing anyone here. In truth, I don't know who would be so low as to carry out such a dastardly deed, but I would appreciate it if the guilty party would return my property."

"Might've been et already," a voice boomed.

"I thought about that. Please return the chicken if it hasn't been eaten. If it *has* been eaten, never do it again. I'd be pleased if whoever did this makes it right. If you don't, you'll have no rest for your soul."

"Be sure your sin will find you out. She got *that* right, eh Preacher?"

Matthew glared at Traveler as the harsh jab hurtled across the room. Cassie smiled at the rough miner and Matthew's temperature shot up past the boiling point.

"If the chicken thief has eaten my bird, please leave the appropriate payment of gold or five dollars to cover the cost of my loss and heartache and, of course, the shame of thieving," Cassie continued, her sweet tone belying her stern words. "You can slip it under the washtub and we'll say no more about it. We're friends. What hurts one of us, hurts all of us. Thank you."

Heated words broke out amongst the miners. "Stealing from Miss Cassie? That's low as it gets."

"Who done it?"

"Somebody's got to know."

Matthew raised his arms for order. "Quiet! As much as I would like to recover the stolen chicken, now is not the time or place."

"Cain't think of a better one," Traveler shouted.

"Yeah, Preacher. This is Miss Cassie's place. She's got a right to speak up."

Matthew stared at the hard faces twisted with anger and mistrust. He swallowed and fought to keep his voice even and kind. "What I meant was, this is a time to worship God, not discuss chickens."

"You've been talking about sin, Preacher. Stealing's a sin, ain't it?"

"Yes, it is, but —"

"But what? Finding the sinner who stole Miss Cassie's chicken is a mite more important than another one of your long-winded prayers."

Matthew's face and ears flamed. He clenched his jaw to keep in the angry retort. He was vaguely aware of Charlie stepping close. "Maybe we ought to sing and see if they simmer down."

"Sorry," Cassie whispered to him, but she didn't look a bit abashed.

The fiddle started and the men hooted their approval. Matthew stepped back and let the song hide his frustration. At the tent meeting he'd attended, that preacher had yelled and pounded the pulpit. He'd held everyone spellbound and —

He suddenly became aware of a strange hush in the congregants. Charlie's voice faltered and stopped. Matthew looked at the twins in time to see Charlie clutch his sister's arm. Cassie held her crystal-clear solo note as she scanned her twin's face. When Charlie stared at the door, Cassie followed his gaze and her face blanched. The singing halted on her strangled cry.

Matthew frowned and glanced at the doorway expecting to see Traveler, but he was gone. In his place, stood an elegant, dark-haired woman, handsomely clad in a deep-rose dress. She looked as out of place as a white lily in a stockyard of pigs. The vibration of the last fiddle note hummed in the air.

As all eyes turned to stare, Matthew stepped forward with extended hands. "How lovely to see you again, Miss de Vere." No one may have listened to his sermon, but now the tent was as still as a room full of corpses. Only their eyes revealed a lively interest as they hung on his every word.

Her gloved fingers clutched his. "Why, if it isn't the dashing Mr. Ramsey. We meet again. I see you found your way here in good stead, and it appears you've already made a name for yourself. Well done!"

The flush up his neck roared back, but this time it came with an effusion of pleasure. "And I didn't expect you here so quickly." He was momentarily bowled over because, quite frankly, never in his wildest dreams had he expected Victoria de Vere to come to the rough boomtown of Eagle Bar.

"Did I not say to you when we dined in San Francisco, I was soon to be on my way to this very spot?"

"Well, yes, but . . ."

"But you suspected I couldn't leave the somewhat dubious comforts of the city?" Her magnetic dark eyes brightened. "Mr. Ramsey, you of *all* people should know we aren't here to collect dust in some stuffy parlor. Life is to be lived, and what better place to live it than on the wild frontier of the goldfields of Eagle Bar? I look forward to the challenge as much as you."

Her eyes flicked over his shoulder. Released from her intense gaze, he caught the hard stares and disgruntled mumbles of the sea of men surrounding them. Some were on their feet, shuffling toward the door.

Matthew was torn between letting them go and trying once more to capture their interest. He'd dispense with the distractions first. He released the woman's hands and offered her his arm. As she rested her gloved hand lightly on his forearm, he turned. "Allow me to introduce the proprietors of this fine establishment, my friends, Charles and Cassandra Vincent."

The elegant sweep of his free hand and his magnanimous words stalled as his gaze swung over the empty pulpit area. No one remained but the fiddle player and his young grandson.

"It appears the entertainment has ended for the day," Victoria said. "Might I address your congregation, Mr. Ramsey?"

The question hit his ears but couldn't penetrate the stunned buzzing in his brain. Charlie, Cassie, and Isaiah gone? Had something happened?

Victoria de Vere's voice cut through his muddled thoughts. "I have wagons that need to be unloaded, and honest work and good pay for any man who needs a grubstake or prefers a voucher to all the drinks, food, and entertainment coming to my soon-to-be-built Golden Palace."

The room rippled with the currents of deep voices rife with speculation. Matthew might not have captured their attention, but as men dropped onto the benches once more, Victoria de Vere held them in the palm of her black-gloved hand.

"How soon's this-here gold palace of yours coming to Eagle Bar?" a voice in the rear called out.

"As soon as you men get to building it. Looking over the crowd, I'd speculate it won't be long."

"What kind of entertainments we talkin' about?" a tenor voice piped up and raucous laughter broke out.

Matthew whipped his head toward the woman at his side. Surely a woman of quality like Victoria de Vere didn't mean —

"I applaud your eagerness, but we can't have much of anything until we put up the walls and roof, my friends. If you're interested in helping me get settled, see my man." She wiggled her fingers toward the back.

All heads turned to the man standing in the doorway. His sandy-colored hair was neatly parted and oiled down. He wore a maroon brocade vest and a shirt as white as Matthew's own. His beefy arms were crossed over a rugged chest and he stood, legs apart, as if on the deck of a ship.

"Mr. Logan will sign you up on a first-come basis." Victoria de Vere never raised her voice, but it commanded the attention of every man there. Benches slid back and boots scuffed the floor. The men rose as one and pushed toward the door.

Victoria laughed. "There's enough work to go around, gentleman."

She tilted her head and caught Matthew's eye. "I hope I didn't interrupt your meeting." She patted his arm. "You can be sure I'll make it up to you, Mr. Ramsey. Will you escort me back to my new property and join me later for dinner at the Grenier? It doesn't appear this establishment is in business."

Matthew nodded dumbly. Upstaged first by Cassie's stolen chicken, and now by Victoria de Vere's grand building scheme, he wasn't sure exactly *what* had transpired at his first tent meeting. He only knew it was a complete and utter failure. He'd come off as a bumbling fool. *Never again!* Nobody made a fool of Matthew Ramsey.

CHAPTER FOUR

"Maybe it wasn't her," Cassie argued.

Her usually genial brother leaned against a tree and scowled. "I can't figure how she lit here. It doesn't make a lick of sense."

They'd bolted from the tent meeting as if charged by an angry mama bear. By silent assent they'd stumbled along the narrow path up the hill behind the camp, not slowing their pace until they reached Cassie's private shady sanctuary. Only then did the words come.

Cassie kept up her refute. "Our eyes are playing tricks, bub. She'd have to look older. It's been nigh on ten years."

It can't be her. Please don't let it be her.

The thought turned her heart to jelly.

"Young or old, doesn't matter. We both know it was her," Charlie persisted. "And knowing her, she didn't come here by chance. She's up to something."

"We should've stayed put and . . ." Cassie's voice petered out. They'd skedaddled from their own place of business and now that she was sitting here, safe on her familiar rocky perch, shame and anger slapped her in the face with a distant memory. Her hand slipped to her cheek. The welt was long gone, but the searing vow she'd made that day — never to allow anyone to steal her happiness again — had vanished, too. She'd turned tail and sacrificed everything they'd worked for at the first sign of trouble.

"That's just so, but we didn't, did we?" Charlie's eyes narrowed and his brow furrowed like their papa's new-plowed field. "Says to me we need to put our heads together and get a battle plan in place before we tangle with her again."

Cassie's mind was a fuzzy ball of wool she kept winding in a single thought. *Why now?*

"Chances are she won't be going anywhere for a while," Charlie added.

"Unless she's changed. Maybe she came here to make things right." The words burned her throat like a swallow of scalding hot tea.

"Too late for that. Besides, we both know that's not true. But we're thinking the same thing, sis. She came to Eagle Bar because she heard we were here. She wants something from us. Galls me to think she'd hunt us down, stalk into our Golden Spoon, and sniff us out like a she coyote."

It wasn't a flattering picture, but more than appropriate since they'd gone to ground. *But we're not scared rabbits, not this time!* Cassie rose and gazed at the buildings below. With the wind at their backs, only an occasional blare of noise reached them. From here, all looked industrious and peaceful, yet Eagle Bar was anything but, especially now. "I'll talk to her."

Charlie stepped in front of Cassie, his tall frame obscuring her view. He grabbed both her forearms and leaned his forehead against hers as they had when they were young. "No, we'll do it together."

They weren't those mischievous twins anymore. "You can't. You've got more to lose."

"We've always stuck together and this is no different. We need each other now more than ever."

His urgent whisper told her he believed it, but Cassie knew it wasn't so. Her dear brother was getting married soon, starting a new life with a new wife. His twin sister would no longer have first place in his affections. It was good and proper, the way nature intended, and she'd not be holding him back. He deserved a happy life, much more so than any other man she knew. Charlie was good and kind and noble.

The break she'd dreaded was nigh-on here and Cassie'd best get on with it. She swallowed hard and leaned away from him to regain her resolve. "Okay, but we can't tell her anything."

"What are you getting at?"

"You know how she is. She'll twist what we say and end up taking everything we've worked for, and we're not letting her ruin us. You can't tell her about Abigail and her family." Cassie squeezed his arms.

Charlie gave her an answering squeeze. "You're right. Keep it simple. She'll get no secrets from us, I swear. We're here for a spell, trying our luck in Eagle Bar, just like everybody else."

"Yes, but we should figure out a story about what we intend to do next. Throw her off our scent."

Charlie pulled on his chin and his familiar grin finally reemerged. "Never been a problem before. Don't imagine we'll have trouble spinning a yarn or two. See if we can't keep her off balance and out of our hair for the time it takes to cash in properly."

The ideas flew between them, faster than their feet could walk as they returned to the Golden Spoon. And as each fanciful tale built on another, their steps and hearts grew lighter. It would be all right as long as they kept their distance, but first they had to confront her. *Imagine sashaying into their business as if she owned the place!* She would never be welcome in their Golden Spoon. They made the final turn in the trail and saw the man who'd see to that, faithfully standing guard at the back door of the kitchen.

Isaiah's arms were crossed against his broad chest, his face somber.

Cassie halted and whispered in her brother's ear. "We shouldn't tell anybody who she is."

"Agreed, unless she's already spilled the beans."

"You gonna tell me what's going on?" Isaiah's deep voice intruded.

Charlie clapped their friend on the shoulder. "We got ourselves spooked is all. Nothing to fuss about."

"That so, Miss Cassie?"

She almost lost her nerve. She didn't want to betray their friendship with a falsehood, so she went with a half-truth, even though the telling of it made her squirm. "We thought we recognized someone from our past, but turns out neither of us can be certain."

"You mean that fancy lady?"

"What happened after we left?" Charlie slipped his steady hand in hers.

"I followed you out and watched you hightail it up that hill. Then I snuck around the kitchen and listened."

"So, who is she?" Charlie prompted.

"Said her name was something highfalutin like 'Deverey.' Never heard tell of it. She was jawin' about buildin' some sort of place called the Golden Palace. Got all those fools out there right riled up. They went chargin' out of here like their britches were on fire, all het up about buildin' it for her." Isaiah rubbed his massive jaw. "Sounds like she means business."

"I imagine she does," Cassie murmured. "The Golden Palace, indeed!"

"Don't you worry, Miss Cassie. Nothin' she could do, nothin' anybody's gonna do, to hurt your Golden Spoon." Isaiah wagged his finger in the air. "That preacher went off with her."

"Matthew Ramsey?" Cassie squeaked out the name.

"Yes. Appeared they were acquainted. Seemed right sociable to me."

"Well, I'll be." Charlie whistled through his teeth.

"Always thought there was a whole lotta

102

whitewash on that feller, and all that wash got to be coverin' up somethin',", Isaiah said.

Didn't I think the same thing at our first meeting? Why in the name of good sense had she let herself be taken in by his fine dress and Sunday manners? Cassie's face burned.

Handsome is as handsome does. Her mother's words echoed in her memory. There were folks who traded on their looks to get what they wanted. She'd learned that lesson early on and vowed never to be one of them.

Cassie set her jaw, slipped past Isaiah, and skirted the side of their eatery. Charlie grabbed her arm and held fast, stopping her in mid-stride. "You haven't heard a word, sis." He moved in front of her, like he always did when he was set on protecting her, but this time he was in her way, barring her path to the street. A wagon stacked with lumber rumbled past behind him, but his eyes never left hers. "I know what you're thinking."

"No, you don't."

" 'Course I do. You're in a pucker. You're set on marching right down there and lighting into someone, and I don't imagine you'd be choosy as to who."

"And what's wrong with that?" Cassie placed her hands on her hips.

"Didn't say there was anything wrong with it. About now I'd like to skin the hide off a certain someone, too." He brushed his palm over his eyes. "Seems like we just decided we weren't going off half-cocked."

"I'm not."

"Looks like you've got a full head of steam to me. Only thing I can't figure is if you're after Matthew or her."

"Seems they're in cahoots, so I'd likely take on both at once."

"Hardly a fair fight. There are only the two of them." He spun on his heel and looped his elbow with hers as they walked down the street toward the Grenier. "Maybe I ought to be there to hold you back."

She hugged his arm close to her side and they ambled in tandem as if on a Sunday afternoon stroll, only on this stroll they were more than likely to meet up with the devil in some form or other. Men, mules, wagons, and horses jostled past. Snippets of shouts and conversations showered Cassie and Charlie like sparks and cinders from a loco-motive smokestack and, judging by the verbal balderdash, the sparks had already started a fire by the name of Victoria de Vere.

"So that's the name she's sporting now," Charlie muttered.

"Never mind that," Cassie snapped. "The

Golden Spoon? The Golden Palace? Don't tell me that's pure happenstance."

Their strides lengthened into a forced march.

"Charlie! Heard you were back." Zelda Grenier's hail halted their progress. Charlie pulled up and they detoured toward their competitor. Zelda stood outside her hotel, smoking a long nine. Her straw-light hair, in long ringlets, lay stiff as rope on her shoulders, spit curls clinging to her forehead. The pale, puffy skin around her eyes couldn't hide their hard, cold gleam. "You running to, or from, the fire?

"Neither," Cassie said. "Just out for a stroll."

Zelda's gaze flicked to Cassie's face for the barest glance before it fastened once more on Charlie. "That Hangtown Fry of yours was all these varmints could prattle on about this morning." She blew a stream of smoke and let out a laugh, its brittle mirth rising with the blue vapor above the noise of the street. "You come back, it's always bad for my business on the short run, but you know what I say. 'This too shall pass.' I'll be standing long after your Golden Spoon has folded up its tent and left."

Cassie gave her brother's arm an impatient squeeze.

Zelda Grenier used to be the enemy or, at the least, Eagle Bar's snake in the grass they needed to watch. Now Cassie could care less about the woman's icy stare or her pointed lack of respect for a fellow female business owner.

"That so," Charlie drawled. "Seems like there's room for both of us, at least so far."

With a flick of her lacy-black-gloved wrist, Zelda tossed the cigar butt at their feet.

Cassie watched the glowing stub, then stepped closer and ground it under her heel into the hardpan.

Zelda's harsh laugh stung her ears. "It's going to take more than that to prove your mettle this time around," Zelda said. "We've got company." Her fleshy chin wobbled slightly as she jerked her head toward the boodle and commotion across the street. "And she's the type that's all business. It takes money to make money, and she's got herself a bankroll the likes of which I've never laid eyes on, and she's roaring in like a house afire. You two won't be lasting a week after she gets her place up and running."

"I'd be more concerned about the Grenier, if I were you," Charlie said. "Let *us* worry about our Golden Spoon."

Her brother was so much better at presenting a friendly face to all. Cassie fought to match his pleasant expression with one of her own. Zelda bared her yellow-filmed teeth in a grimace that she tried to pass off as a grin. "Fair warning. Victoria's got class and mettle, something you two never heard tell of. There may be room for two business establishments like ours in Eagle Bar, but not three. And I'm not leaving. And, speaking of leaving, when you take off again, Charlie, I suspect the wolves will move in for the kill. By the time you get back, there'll be nothing left of your sister *or* your Golden Spoon, except that ridiculous pledge sign."

Charlie slipped his arm around Cassie's shoulders, but she stiffened her spine and shrugged him off. Hands on hips, she went toe-to-toe with the older woman, sucking in a deep breath to accentuate her height advantage. The scents of toilet water, tobacco smoke, and whiskey added fuel to her ire. The saloon owner twitched nary an eyebrow, her expression annoyed. Her cold gaze sliced through Cassie to the street beyond.

"You're right about one thing, Zelda Grenier. Charlie and I are nothing like you or this stranger. Sounds to me like this town can't support two *drinking* establishments, and since we're not one of them, you're the one who will be going out of business."

"Men'll starve themselves to work their claim, but they'll always allow for drink and diversions, even when they're down to their last bungtown copper. Especially miners." Zelda took a small step to the side, deftly easing away from Cassie, and looked up at Charlie. "I meant what I said. If you have a care for your sister, take her with you when you go next time."

Raucous shouts erupted from the open doors of the hotel. Zelda turned and waded into the fray, wielding her strident voice like a bayonet. "Now gentlemen, settle down! You break this place up and I'll have your hide and your gold. Owen!"

A drunk miner burst through the doorway. With Owen Cantrell's meaty fists at his back, the troublemaker was ushered out. One final shove sent the man sprawling headlong into the street. Zelda's bartender nodded to Cassie as he dusted off his hands and turned back to the dim interior.

"Let's go, Charlie." Cassie retreated from the rabble-rouser groaning on the ground nearby. Her anger seeped away, leaving her heavyhearted, her shoulders bowed in defeat. Was Zelda right? The hotelier saw Eagle Bar clearly, in all its base greed and crude passions.

At the end of the street, at the Golden Spoon, Cassie tried to steer clear of the brawling and carryings-on after the sun slid behind the mountain each day. But as much as she denied it, this place she and Charlie had chosen wasn't heaven. It was much closer to Hades, and sinking lower every day.

"Go where? Back home or down the street?" Charlie's low voice in her ear seized on Cassie's mood and claimed her attention as he locked arms with hers once more.

She glanced into his sober face. Obviously, the harridan's words had hit their mark. Zelda's caustic comments had Cassie questioning her worth and courage, but Charlie was visibly shaken as well. Should they pull up stakes and leave?

She stared at the bustle across the street and stretched her neck and back to throw off the cowardly thoughts. She looked back into her brother's eyes. The Vincents never quit on each other. Charlie needed this stake to get a new life, and she was bound to stick it out with him. "We can't go home until we finish what we came to do," she said.

"Then on we go."

They strode the short distance across the street and into the knot of wagons and men clustered in the vacant space. Two men in vests barked orders as miners labored like ants, unloading supplies. Cassie recognized many of the Spoon's clientele in the group and wondered what had enticed them to leave their claims and spend their time and strength on this gilded venture.

So many wagons, stacks of raw lumber, kegs of nails, and canvas. Cassie shook her head. *It takes money to make money and she's got plenty.* Zelda's words rang in her ears.

Cassie's roving gaze saw Victoria de Vere first, standing in a wagon bed, talking with Matthew Ramsey. She grabbed Charlie's arm and felt his muscles tense. As they watched, the woman tilted her head back and laughed, her hair glinting like a crow's wing in the June sun. The laugh was melodious as a birdsong, and Cassie smothered a shiver at the dingy memories it shook loose. The sound ended abruptly as the woman's eyes locked with Cassie's.

A moment later, Matthew jumped down and, large hands spanning her waist, easily lifted his companion from the wagon. The couple walked toward them, the woman's hand on Matthew's arm.

"May I present Cassandra and Charles Vincent," he said.

Victoria held out her gloved hand. Cassie balled her hands into fists to keep the inner trembling from showing. Charlie finally took the gloved offering and gave it a brief handshake.

"Mr. Ramsey has been telling me all about you," Victoria said.

"That so?" Charlie fixed the big gentleman with a quizzical stare. "Sounds like we need to clear up the balderdash, then."

"Sooner the better." Cassie frowned. Matthew was "presenting" them as if they were his possessions. Nobody owned them, least of all the couple in front of them.

Victoria patted the preacher's forearm. "Matthew, I'd be much obliged if you would see to the unloading of the lumber on that wagon that just pulled in. Mr. Logan and Mr. Graff have their hands full with the workers, if that ragtag bunch can be called such."

Cassie returned Matthew's stern-faced scrutiny. He'd get no sympathy or friendship from the Vincent twins. He'd forfeited both.

Matthew remained motionless until Victoria raised one eyebrow. "Charlie, Miss Cassie," he finally said, "perhaps I'll see you later."

Neither replied to the tight-lipped com-

111

ment, and he finally strode over to the work-men.

Victoria watched him go. "Persistent, that one, but it can be a useful quality in a gentleman." She turned back to the twins and perused them crown to foot and back again. The moment lasted long enough to make Cassie squirm, but she wasn't that ragamuffin six-year-old caught fishing in the creek, her dress covered in mud. When did one outgrow such childish reactions to parental scrutiny?

"You both favor me." Victoria smirked. "None of your pa's sandy, washed-out temperament. Turned out nice."

"Only on the outside," Cassie said.

"Come into my temporary office." Victoria glided past them to a tent pitched in the shade, a short distance down the street.

Charlie took Cassie's hand. They ducked through the doorway into the stuffy, dim canvas interior. "Why are you here?" Charlie asked.

"That's a fine howdy-do after all this time."

"After all this time?" Cassie parroted. "You left *us,* as I recall."

"I knew you'd be fine."

"That so?" Charlie said. "With a mountain of debts and your sickly second husband to take care of?"

"Come, now, let's be honest. You adored Edgar. Sometimes I felt like you preferred your stepfather over me, your own flesh and blood. That's why I couldn't ask you to come with me. Besides, you were nearly grown. Time enough at fifteen to be out on your own. Cassandra was as good as engaged to that Gilson boy."

Charlie's grip nearly cut off the circulation in Cassie's fingers, but she welcomed the distraction as the humiliation of the past roared over them. "The 'Gilson boy' broke it off with me after you ran off with the tinker. Guess he thought I might have the same crude inclinations. And he married my best friend while I was busy taking care of Father."

Victoria shook her head. "Probably for the best. That boy had a weak chin and, no doubt, the feeble character to match. He'd have been no match for you, Cassandra. Look at you, so fine and strong. You *are* your mother's daughter. Makes me proud."

"We're not your kin," Charlie said, grinding out the words. "You haven't answered our question. Why are you here in Eagle Bar?"

"Excuse me, Miss de Vere," Mr. Logan said. "Sorry for the interruption, but there's something you ought to see."

"We were just leaving." Charlie pushed past the stocky foreman, and Cassie dragged in a deep lungful of air.

"I'm pleased to meet you, Mr. and Miss Vincent. I'm certain we'll become fast friends." Victoria's voice cooed after them. "I'll be up to your Golden Spoon tomorrow so we can become better acquainted."

Matthew glared at Victoria's tent — the temporary office he'd helped her set up not one hour ago. Through the opening, he could just make out the hem of Cassie's dress before she moved and only empty shadow remained.

To be dismissed like a schoolboy sent off to play while the adults discussed important matters seethed in his gut like a gulp of seawater.

The bitterness worked its way quickly to his brain, burning out all other thoughts. He needn't have worried if his acquaintance with Victoria would taint his fledgling friendship with Cassie and Charlie. It appeared they were all too pleased to cut him off.

"You praying for the work to get done, Preacher?" The rough taunt broke through his mental harangue and flicked the lid off

114

his simmering anger. Matthew stalked to a nearby wagon, grabbed one end of a beam, hoisted it on his shoulder, carried it over to the growing stack piled away from the street, and flung it down.

"Ho there, Preacher, never thought you'd git those lily-white hands of yours dirty. Tryin' to impress the lady?" He turned and recognized one obnoxious clod who'd heckled him about the missing chicken at the tent meeting.

The miner's comment elicited guffaws from the other men. The back of his neck burned and he clasped his hands together to still the urge to give the half-wit a clout upside the head. He may have put his brawling days behind him, but no one got the best of Matthew Ramsey — not this oaf, and not the high-and-mighty Vincent twins.

Matthew pitched his voice to ring out above the noise. "I can best you any day of the week, friend."

Hoots and hollers surrounded him and all eyes fastened on the two men. Miners slapped their compatriot on the back. "You gonna let a preacher man show you up, Judd?"

"If you think you can keep up, Preacher, let's have at it!" Judd said.

Bets flew faster than feathers from a fox

in a henhouse. Mr. Graff rushed over. Instead of putting a stop to the ruckus, he smirked at Matthew. "You're on, Preacher." He lifted up his hands and the workers quieted. "I'll put twenty on the preacher. Who's in? Pony up." Graff slogged through the boodle, collecting names and bets.

Matthew glanced at the tent once more, but there was no sign of life. He didn't need to prove himself to these coots, but he wasn't about to back down from a bet. He turned his attention to the crowd as he rolled up his shirtsleeves. The smell of Cassie's lye soap fueled his pigheaded desire to set them all back on their heels.

Graff finally worked his way back to Matthew. "Easy money, Preacher. You set?"

Matthew nodded. He'd gotten himself into this, and he wasn't sorry. They wanted to humiliate him, fine. He'd take on all comers. They had no idea who they were dealing with, but soon he'd get the respect he deserved. It wasn't as if he was brawling, just paring the men's opinions down to size.

He sized up his competition. Judd was lanky and moved about with a quick restless stride, but he didn't appear strong. When he caught Matthew's gaze, he said, "Don't you worry none, Preacher. I'll buy you a drink with my winnings when we're done. No hard feelings."

His friends roared.

Braying fool! What Judd might lack in ability, he made up for in brashness. He looped his thumbs under his galluses and looked Matthew up and down, then ambled over to a freight wagon, whistling a tune as he leaned against the side.

Graff shouted to a driver who moved two wagons alongside each other; both were piled with hefty framing beams. The foreman got out his pocket watch. "Just in case it's close." The men laughed. "First one to unload their wagon is the winner. You've got to stack them up proper in the pile yonder. The rest of you, get out of their way. No tricks, no help. And no man here better welsh on his bet. If he does, he better leave the territory before I get a hold of him. Ready! Set! Go!"

Matthew hefted the first beam on his shoulder and set to work. His opponent was several steps behind as Matthew threw the lumber on the stack, but when he passed Judd on the way back to the wagon, Judd's grin was as cocky as ever. "It's not the first one that counts," he called over his shoulder as Matthew quickened his stride.

A rude voice rose above the miners' rabble. " 'The first shall be last and the last shall be first.' Ain't that what the Good Book says, Preacher?"

Matthew recognized the harsh tone. As disheveled as ever, Traveler stood on the outskirts, a head taller than those in front of him. The miner touched the brim of his battered hat and met Matthew's gaze. He promptly spat a stream of tobacco juice onto the ground, spun on his boot heel, and swaggered down the street in the direction of the Golden Spoon.

"Ain't that where it says there'll be wailing and gnashing of teeth?" Someone picked up the gibe and the crowd roared.

"Better hold onto them pearly whites of yours, Preacher. It's looking like you'll be gnashing 'em tonight."

Matthew swung his head around in time to see Judd dump his second beam on the stockpile and scamper back to his wagon. Matthew let the jeers fall around him as he settled in to work with a grim purpose.

By the time he could see the wagon bed, Matthew's shirt clung to his sweat-drenched chest and his bloodied hands no longer stung. His fingers and palms were numb to the wood splintering into flesh, but his shoulders and back pulsed with every step, screaming for relief. He flicked his eyes on his opponent as they both surged toward the growing lumber pile. Judd's lank hair lay plastered to his lean forehead and rivulets of sweat traced through the dust on his face, but he winked when he caught Matthew's eye. " 'Bout time for that drink."

Matthew grunted and lengthened his stride, but the shorter man quickened his step and reached the pile first, unshouldering his burden in one deft movement.

The yelling of the crowd deafened Matthew as he rushed to the wagon, but he only had eyes for his remaining two beams. If he carried both, he could win this. He struggled to balance the load on both shoulders and the men's hollers swelled. Judd hurried ahead of him.

Matthew strode after the smaller man, but immediately slowed his pace as his load shifted. He nearly stumbled while he wrestled the beam on his left shoulder and restored the balance. He set off at a jog toward the pile, but slowed to a trudge when the crowd cheered their own and Judd deposited his last piece of lumber on the stack. Judd waited. As Matthew dipped his left shoulder, Judd took the beam and placed it on the pile.

Matthew shrugged off the other as the miner offered his hand. "Guess we settled this hash, Preacher. A right fine contest.

Meant what I said about the drink later over at the Grenier." Judd gripped Matthew's sore hand in a hearty shake. "No hard feelings?" Judd's face turned solemn. "Just did it for the sport."

"None," Matthew agreed. Someone lugged over a bucket of water and thrust a dripping dipper into his hand. Matthew took a long pull, watching his opponent do the same. Men came up and clapped them both on the back. Matthew tipped the next dipper over his head, letting the tepid water fall over his closed eyes and throbbing shoulders.

"You've had your fun, now back to work!" Mr. Logan's bark tore through the boisterous camaraderie. A spurt of mob protest growled back at him. "Rest assured, Mr. Graff will see the winning bets are covered, but you'll not be getting anything until the work's done. You're welcome to leave if you like, but only those who finish the job are getting paid."

"I see you've been busy. It appears you've got some converts." Matthew jerked his head around. Victoria's husky laugh and soft perfume filled his senses, but he shook off the feminine pull. His gut still burned over her earlier dismissal. He took a step back and turned to face her.

"Very clever, Matthew," she said. "You'd never win them over at a tent meeting. Oh, maybe a handful would get in a lather, but the rest? Nothing doing. They're real men with flesh and blood needs. They only respect strength, power, and money."

He raised one eyebrow. "I don't believe that."

"Oh, you do." Victoria slipped her arm into his. "If you didn't, you wouldn't be sore over losing to that common miner."

"Judd." He spat out the name, fighting the urge to shake off her possessive touch and march over to the hotel. Trouble was, he'd look like a sore loser, and she was right. He *did* care what these men thought of him. Besides, she was staying at the Grenier, too. There was no real escape from anyone or anything in Eagle Bar.

"Judd." She repeated in a pleasant tone. "It's just as I said." Victoria looked out over the workers and gave his arm a gentle squeeze. "Now Judd is your first convert. He respects your strength. You provided the opportunity for him to rake in some money, and if you play your cards right, it's the start of what you really want. Power."

This time he flexed his muscles and pulled away, but not before she patted him on his forearm.

"I do not want power. I came here to save souls." The retort sounded petty, even to his own ears.

"And that takes power." She tilted her head and looked up at him from under her lashes. "You might not admit it, but in order to convince your fellow man of anything, you must have power over him, power he can feel but not see. Power he can see, he'll resent. Power he can feel, he'll respect, and be drawn to it like a moth to a lantern flame."

"I ought to be going." He gazed down the street. The excitement of the morning had drained away. His hands stung, his back ached, and defeat left the bitterness of a sour green apple in his throat. The Golden Spoon and his mission here seemed as distant and out of reach as Boston.

"I'd hoped you'd stay, on the payroll, of course. I know you're here for your own reasons, but a little cash to throw around might come in handy." Victoria put her forefinger to her lips for a moment. "I don't know what you believe, Matthew, but I believe it wasn't pure coincidence we met in San Francisco and again here in Eagle Bar. I believe the Lord provides, for me *and* for you. We could help each other out. You've earned the men's respect, now you have to keep it. What better way than to work with them every day? I could use a man like you, at least until I get my Golden Palace built. I plan to have it open within a fortnight."

He tried to ignore her words, but the logic lodged in his brain. Judd and another man pushed by them with keg-filled barrows. Judd grunted a greeting.

"You've got Logan and Graff," he said.

"They'll be busy with their own tasks. I've got a wagonload of Chinese coming soon. I contracted with them before I left San Francisco. They are well-versed in carpentry and other skills. They've got a few of their own to oversee the job, but I need one man who can keep all the facets of my business running smoothly. I'm here to build a respectable town. My business isn't about to be the usual ramshackle collection of boards." She tossed her head toward the seedy hotel across the street.

"Not everybody around here takes to foreigners."

"I know the lay of the land, Matthew. You don't have to protect me. Once my Chinese finish the work, some will stay to work for me, some will pack up and go. I made sure they knew about the Foreign Miner tax. I'm not bringing them here to have them jump someone else's claim. They're here strictly to work for me. Until the building work is done, I need someone to keep the peace among the men. That's where *you* come in, if you're amenable. We can discuss your terms tonight over supper. I'll make it worth your while."

Victoria turned her attention toward the work, her face flushed. Her eyes glowed with the intensity of her dream.

Matthew couldn't believe he wanted to take her up on the offer. Unloading the wagon, surveying the worksite . . . he could lead these men. He could get the best out of them and have her Golden Palace built well and in record time. His damaged hands ached, not from work but from the urge to do something he knew, something he could make a success.

"Are you still peeved about my private talk with Mr. and Miss Vincent?" Victoria asked.

Her comment toppled his castle of dreams. Matthew gaped at her.

Victoria replaced her hand on his forearm. "I would've been peeved, too, if I was a young man and had Cassandra Vincent in my sights."

"That has nothing to do with it." Matthew slicked his damp hair back from his forehead with his free hand. "I don't appreciate anyone dismissing me out of turn."

"Goodness, is that what you thought? It's the furthest thing from the truth, Matthew." Victoria's face sobered and her eyes sought his. "I didn't include you simply because I didn't want them to use their friendship with you to impress me."

Matthew wrinkled his brow. "That'd be unlikely."

"I told you, Matthew. I see the situation clearly. You've only been in town for a few days, but I see how the men look up to you. You have a character and strength that attracts lesser men. The Vincents don't have that ability. They're weak. I don't know how long they've been here, but I wanted to get to know them on their own without them trading on your character. I needed to size up the competition, you might say. Zelda Grenier is easy enough to fathom. The Vincents are a different kettle of fish, I'm afraid."

"What do you mean?" Matthew's thoughts flew down the street to the brother and sister. Snippets of memory raced past — unloading the goat, singing up a storm, ribbing each other. Maybe they were different, but weak? Never. Cassie faced up to the roughest miner without fear, and as much as Matthew doubted Charlie's sanity in bringing his sister to Eagle Bar, he had no doubts Charlie would die for her. They were family to the core. Maybe they were simply what everyone longed for. Maybe they were, as Cassie suggested, bringing a little family civility to a wild place, reminding people of home.

"They're not just here to make money." Victoria's soft statement broke through his sentimentality and reasserted his common sense.

He snorted. "I believe they are. They're not weak, and they're not here to help anyone but themselves." A twinge of remorse tweaked his conscience at the harsh assessment.

"By all accounts I hear they have a thriving business, but why come way out here? Why not build an eatery in a civilized city? Not that there *are* any west of the Mississippi." A gust of wind swept down the dusty street. Victoria hunched her shoulders and patted her hair with a careful hand.

Matthew stepped in front of her to block the rising breeze and flying debris. "You haven't seen the prices they charge for their meals. They're here for the money."

"As a gentleman of the first order, I can understand why you might feel affronted. You can look down on the foibles of your fellow man, Matthew, but in business, as in all things, it's what the market will bear. I still believe something else is driving those two. That's why I plan to dine at their establishment tomorrow evening and get better acquainted. I hope you'll join me, as you're a good friend of theirs and, I trust, soon to be a good friend of mine, as well."

"Did Cassie invite you to her Golden Spoon? Not everyone is allowed inside."

Victoria threw back her head and cackled. It took her a moment to regain her composure, and even then, she held her gloved hand to her lips to still her mirth.

Disgusted at himself for the outburst, Matthew retorted. "You find that amusing?"

"It is rich! I'm not sure about the wisdom of it as a business practice, but it tells me a great deal."

"Such as?"

"Such as, you've been a victim of their selective treatment. I take it from your terse tone, it still rankles. Don't look so dire, Matthew." She grabbed his hand in hers. "You and I both know how to see to the heart of our fellow man. If we didn't, you wouldn't be able to succeed at what you do, and neither would I. Tell me, what brought that on? I can't imagine anyone refusing to serve a gentleman such as yourself."

He wanted to deny it, shrug it off, but the urge to vent his spleen over Cassie's high-handed treatment won out. "A misunderstanding," he said. "Cassie, Miss Vincent, doesn't understand how low these men are."

"Just a babe in the woods? I got that impression from both of them."

Matthew was torn between establishing a friendship with the woman in front of him and getting through to Cassie and Charlie. They'd given him the cold shoulder earlier, and the sour expression on Cassie's face when he introduced them to Victoria said neither of them might be welcome at the Golden Spoon tomorrow. "I stepped in to save her from a particularly rough sort and she turned around and not only invited that dirty miner into the Golden Spoon, she's made him into a pet."

"And she didn't appreciate your help, I take it?"

"No, not at the time."

She raised a winged eyebrow. "Yet you had your tent meeting at their place."

"Yes, we smoothed things over. At least I thought we had." Their recent unfriendly treatment said otherwise.

"I wonder what brought that on. Was it sudden?"

Matthew flashed back to the tent meeting.

"They just up and left during the hymn sing. I thought it was because that miner I told you about, calls himself Traveler, showed up in the back and upset her, but I haven't had a chance to talk with Cassie. You came and —"

"Oh, of course. And I've taken up all of your time. How selfish of me. Please, go on and have your visit with Cassandra. We can discuss our arrangement later over supper, unless you're invited elsewhere."

"No, I promised I'd dine with you tonight."

"That would be lovely. But Matthew, one thing."

"What?"

"Get cleaned up before you go calling, maybe find a little trinket to take. It makes a lady feel special, like she's worth the extra attention."

Matthew scowled.

"I apologize. Just my motherly instincts coming to the fore."

Once in the privacy of his room, Matthew took his time washing up, combing his hair, and digging the splinters out of his hands. By the time he changed his clothes, he changed his mind. He'd let Cassie and Charlie be. Let them wonder what he was up to tonight. Tomorrow he'd breakfast at their Golden Spoon and talk with them, set things straight before he and Victoria arrived for the supper meal.

CHAPTER FIVE

When Charlie was in Eagle Bar, Cassie liked to relax in the early morning, accompanied by the familiar solace of her brother's snores, and let her mind drift along to pleasant places. Today she was worn out, way past fidgeting by four o'clock. She threw off the covers not a quarter hour later and quickly slipped into her clothing.

On bare feet, she tiptoed past her twin's cot and out into the cool, dry dawn. There was no sense pretending to rest when her brain was worse than squirrely from running in circles all night. Who could sleep with her mother's voice prattling in her ears? Although, by the sound of it, Charlie had managed to shut out not only the shock of their confrontation, but the rancorous old memories, and sleep well.

Gypsy's wet nose nuzzled her hand as she lit a lantern. The dog's eyes shone large and luminous and she tilted her head, waiting for a treat or a touch. It hadn't taken but a moment for Cassie to become accustomed to the dog's friendly presence. The animal had a knowing way about her, leaning her furry body against Cassie's leg when anxious thoughts needled her mind.

She'd never admit it aloud, but Matthew had been right. She felt safer with Gypsy around. She wasn't sure the dog would defend her if there was trouble, but in this place a growl might be as good as a bite. All it took was the notion that Gypsy *would* bite. Cassie smiled down at the dog.

Gypsy thumped her tail in response. The dog had the Golden Spoon routine down pat, shadowing Cassie's footsteps, lying patiently in the shade at the kitchen doorway, waiting while Cassie cooked; although it may have had more to do with the love of scraps than any sentiment toward her new mistress. Still, the dog was a comfort and would be a welcome companion when Charlie left again to get supplies.

"We won't think of that today." She scratched the dog's ears and Gypsy sidled closer. "He'll be here for at least two weeks." Zelda Grenier's warning crept in and threatened to crowd out her own logic.

Should she leave with Charlie on his next trip? It had crisscrossed her mind last night like a rabbit running from hounds. But it was unthinkable. The Wangs and Isaiah couldn't run the restaurant and tend their own claims, and it wouldn't be fair to ask such a task of them. If she left, it would mean closing the Golden Spoon, which is likely what Zelda had hoped for by putting frightful ideas in her head. She and Charlie couldn't both leave because it would take only one night before their unattended business was plundered. Then there truly would be nothing left of the Golden Spoon when they returned . . . not even the pledge sign.

Cassie closed her eyes and it took nothing to imagine the pledge sign, with her careful printing, nailed over a hole in the roof of some miner's shack.

Unless we leave for good.

She opened her eyes and shook her head. That would be pure foolishness. Her place was here. They'd stick it out until November and see how the travel was in the winter weather — that is, if the gold held out.

Charlie and Abigail planned to marry on Christmas Day, if her father gave Charlie his blessing. Cassie supposed she and her brother would pull up stakes for good, at least a month or so before that time. The way things were going, they'd be well set by then. She knew Charlie was ready to move on to his new life. But in her solitary moments she wondered what was next for her? Where would she go after Eagle Bar?

Heading east to start a real eatery in bustling New York? Going back to Ohio to settle on the family farm? Investing their gold in buying up potential mines? All the wild stories they'd concocted to deceive their mother held no appeal.

I'll think about it come November.

She grabbed the bucket from the hook outside the kitchen doorway and gave Gypsy's soft head one more stroke. "You'll keep the wolves at bay, won't you, girl?" The dog sniffed the air and quickly disappeared up the hill.

Cassie smiled. "My just rewards for talking to a dog."

She stepped toward the dim outline of animal pens. Work was the cure for all of it — the fear, the worry, the unknown, and the restlessness that always attacked her between breakfast cleanup done and supper cooking begun. Work would keep her Golden Spoon filled with paying customers, and work would keep Zelda and her mother busy with their own affairs and out of her business.

On her way to the rough lean-to, she hummed an old tune from her father's time, swinging the bucket as she had when a child, and unlatched the wooden gate. Nugget lifted her head, spooked at the early intrusion, her eyes big as saucers in the lantern's light. "Good morning, little one." Cassie set the milking stool on the dirt floor and plunked herself down. Her hands settled on the goat's warm teats, and the zing and slosh of milk in the pail brought another smile. The goat, the chickens, and now the dog; who would've imagined she'd have her own little farm here on the frontier? Papa would love it, although he'd been partial to Jersey cows, not goats.

The farm was the only place she'd felt happy and safe. Maybe it wasn't a place. Perhaps it was a time when she was a little girl and believed Papa would always be there to fill the small house with music and laughter.

"Well, I do declare."

Cassie jumped at the soft voice behind her, barely snagging the bucket before the goat kicked and bolted into the side of the pen. The milk sloshed over the rim and soaked into her skirt, the warm wet seeping through to her skin. She turned to face the interloper.

"I could almost believe we were back at the old farm." Victoria's low laugh bounced around the small structure, and the trembling goat crowded farther into the shadowy corner.

"What are you doing here?" Cassie brushed by the woman. "Don't forget to latch the gate when you leave." She marched toward the kitchen, swinging both pail and lantern. The sky had already lightened considerably, but she'd need the lamp in the confines of the kitchen. She could hear her mother's footsteps dogging her, but she refused to stop until she set the milk bucket and the lantern on the table.

Cassie turned, both fists on her hips. "What are you doing here, *Miss de Vere*?"

"Well, *Miss Vincent*, aren't we proper for a barefoot back-east farm girl? Butter wouldn't melt in your mouth this morning, is that it? And yet you're out milking, humming a tune just like your pa." She shook her head. "Hollis always loved his farming."

"And you hated it."

"It wasn't so much that I hated it. I just saw easier and more pleasant ways to make a living and spend one's time. Maybe you don't favor your mother as much as I thought."

Cassie shrugged off the insult and the small talk. "Why are you here?"

"Still stubborn as all get-out and you *do*

get that from me."

"I'd be obliged if you'd just answer my question and leave."

"I'm here same as everyone else, I should imagine. Hoping to strike it rich the easy way. Let the miners do the hard work and I'll provide them what they want . . . for a price. If you and Charles are any indication, I expect to do very well in Eagle Bar." The lamplight cast the left side of her face in shadow, giving her smirking lips a ghoulish cast.

"I don't care about your plans or your business," Cassie retorted. "Why are you here in our kitchen, on our property?"

"Ah, no nonsense." The other woman placed a finger beside her lips in a coquettish gesture that Cassie knew boded ill for those on the receiving end. She'd not let her mother take advantage again; not now, not ever; but she strained her ears in the direction of the cabin hoping Charlie was up. Two were always better than one when the one they were against was a conniving liar who'd sell out her own flesh and blood with the bat of an eyelash.

Victoria's smug tone didn't miss a beat. "I'd hardly expect any different from you, but as I've tried to teach you time and again, you catch more flies with honey than with vinegar, Cassandra."

"You taught me plenty, but I have no wish for flies this morning, particularly in my kitchen."

Again the husky laugh and Cassie's cheeks flamed. She faced the stove, one hand fisted in her damp skirt. "Please leave so I can be about my work. The miners will be coming by soon."

"We have time for a family chat."

Victoria placed her hand on Cassie's shoulder and Cassie spun around, shaking off the offensive touch. "We're not family. You made that clear years ago. You have no notion of who we are now and we have nothing to talk about."

"Is that so? Then why, pray tell, did you and your brother come down to my property to welcome me yesterday?"

Cassie could feel her mother's words twining around her throat like a poisonous vine threatening to squeeze out all calm and common sense. She fought to keep her reply measured and just this side of civil. "It was hardly a social call. As I recollect, *you* set foot in the Golden Spoon the minute you arrived in town. We only dropped by to tell you to leave us be. It won't happen again."

"Strange, I didn't hear either of you say that. In fact, I thought you were extending an olive branch." Her tone mellowed and the last two words quivered with a melodious shimmering note. Papa had always said Mother had a way of singing just by talking.

Silent outrage pounded in her ears and choked out any appreciation of the genteel bell-like tones. Cassie drew in a slow deep breath and forced her words to come out just as slowly. "If you didn't understand us, I'll say it now, plain as plain can be. Stay away from my Golden Spoon and we'll steer clear of you and your business."

"And Charles agrees with you?"

"Wholeheartedly."

"A shame. Neither one of my children with a lick of sense."

"We're doing well for folks with no sense."

"Oh? I'd need to see that for myself, but Matthew informed me not everyone is welcome in your establishment. Tell me. If I came to your Golden Spoon to dine this evening, would I be allowed inside?"

Cassie turned away and poured the milk into a crock. Her mother was twisting her words and twisting her innards in knots. *I'm not twelve years old this time! And Matthew Ramsey . . . what right does he have to be a tattling toady interfering in our affairs?*

"Ah, is that because you're afraid your little eatery won't meet with my approval?"

her mother continued. "Or is it simply because you're afraid of me? You always were a mite timid when push comes to shove, Cassandra. Perhaps that's why the Gilson boy passed you over."

Cassie paused at the kindling pile. She deliberately picked up a stick and squeezed it in her hand before she faced her mother once more. It did little to channel her frustration and anger. Hui would be here soon and they needed to be done with this nonsense before he arrived. "What do you know about any of it, Victoria? You weren't there. I was the one who took care of Father after you broke his heart and ran out on us."

Victoria clucked her tongue. "If your stepfather had a broken heart it was his own doing. He was the one with the foolish investments, the failed mills and the mountain of debt and ill will." Her fingers gently grazed Cassie's hand and Cassie flinched. "You'll never know how much it broke my heart to leave you. I didn't want to say this, but it's time you opened your eyes. You're a woman grown on the outside, but inside you haven't changed from that foolish girl who needed someone to take care of her. I left for *you,* Cassandra. That beau of yours had his eye on me. As long as I was around, he'd be sniffing and prowling. You didn't stand a chance. I didn't want you to lose him on account of your own mother, so I left."

Cassie reeled from the mental slap, but was grateful for it. Her mother hadn't changed, spinning her tales out of lies and cobwebs of falsehoods, swinging on either side of the gate. "Yesterday you said Myron Gilson was weak and no match for me, so I don't imagine he had a chance with you. You were a married woman at the time, although that didn't stand in the way of you running off with the first tinker who came along."

"Spilt milk, Cassandra. And no matter what you may think of him, Eli Weston was not a tinker. He was a man of great vision. But that was years ago. Let's let bygones be bygones, shall we? You were a child. You have no notion of what was happening."

"I know plenty."

This time her mother grabbed Cassie's wrist in a painful grip. "Appears to me you're trying to avoid the present, but I'll not allow this folderol to derail my purpose in coming here. I ask again, will I be welcome to dine at your Golden Spoon tonight, yes or no?"

"Come, then, if you're so set on it. We've got nothing to hide." Charlie's voice preceded him as he ducked through the doorway, his form blocking out the early-morning light. Her mother's grip slackened and Cassie wrenched her wrist free as Charlie put an arm around her, his touch warm and strong. "What about you, Miss de Vere? Do *you* have something to hide?"

Cassie dropped the stick of wood and leaned into her brother but never took her eyes off their mother.

"Two peas in a pod. You always were thick as thieves. You want to tell folks I'm your mother, so be it, but I don't think either one of us needs that particular foolishness, the whole town buzzing in our personal business. I've got an establishment to build, you've got a business to run. There'll be the right time to share our family ties, but may we both agree now is not the best time?"

Charlie whispered in Cassie's ear, "What do you think?"

"Agreed," Cassie said, "for now."

"What brought you to Eagle Bar? And don't pretend you didn't know we were here," Charlie said.

Victoria's gaze roamed over their faces. An oppressive silence filled the kitchen, in spite of a breeze stirring the canvas by the door. She stepped toward the doorway and brushed past Charlie, turning at the opening. "Is it a crime for a mother to want to see her children? I look forward to coming tonight."

Cassie kept her bare feet rooted to the ground, resisting the urge to stick her head out and watch her mother leave.

Charlie scratched his head and set about lighting the stove.

"She twisted every word, and I swore I'd never let her do that again."

"She's had a whole lot of practice at it, but we can get around her."

"How do you figure? She never answered our question." Cassie pulled out iron spiders to heat.

"Did you see her eyes when I accused her of knowing we were here? I saw a flicker of something. Fear, maybe. I can't be sure, but I think all that talk about not caring if we let folks know she's our mother was pure pipe smoke. For some reason, Victoria de Vere doesn't want anyone to know we're related. And that's her weak spot."

"I'm not sure I want anyone to know she's our mother, either."

"I agree, but it's an advantage we can use, if the occasion presents itself and we need to take her down a peg or two."

"Folks might be interested to know her as Mrs. Virginia Landsbury."

"Or Mrs. Hollis Vincent. We'll bide our time and let her think she's got the upper hand."

"But we *do* need to keep an eye on her. She's not to be trusted."

"Keep your ears open when the miners come in this morning. See what we can find out about our saintly mother."

Cassie clapped her hands. "I've got a better idea. We can go straight to the horse's mouth. I'll ask Petey if he'd be willing to hang around down there once in a while and see what he can pick up. Nobody would suspect a curious boy nosing around the building site."

"We can give him and his grandfather free meals, if he's willing."

Cassie didn't bother to tell her brother she slipped free food to Petey already, but she'd find another way to make it up to the boy.

"I am not behind?" Hui slipped into the kitchen to the sizzle of bacon hitting the fry pan as Charlie got to work.

Cassie looked up from cutting onions. "No. You're right on time. Charlie and I got up early this morning. How is everything at the claim?"

"Good. Ming leaves this morning for San Francisco with . . ." Hui dipped his head, his queue flopping forward as he dipped water from the bucket at his feet and filled a pot for porridge.

"With Yi?" Cassie asked, her eyes on the man's darting movements. Something was wrong. The Wangs were careful. They never left their claim unattended, and they never kept their gold piling up for long.

Hui placed the pot on the wooden bench and shook his head, his wispy beard swaying with the movement. "No, Yi stays. Maybe Isaiah goes." His eyes flicked over Cassie's head to Charlie.

Cassie knew the look. They were keeping things from her. *You're a woman, grown on the outside but inside you haven't changed from that foolish girl who needed someone to take care of her.* Her mother's words lanced her pride and she frowned. She didn't need their protection. Isaiah had never left Eagle Bar since they'd met him, so why now? Maybe for Ming's protection because of the beating the other day? The pieces suddenly came together in her mind. "Ming's taking the Chinese man who got beat up?"

Hui's smooth brow puckered. "He does not want to stay here after what happened to him, but good news! Another cousin is coming." Hui pushed the pot of water onto the crowded stovetop.

Hui was always the first to know the news of Eagle Bar and beyond. Cassie had no idea how he knew, particularly way out here, but the man was a human newspaper. Although more men poured into town every day, Hui, with his sharp, dark eyes and unobtrusive presence, garnered information from all who passed him by.

"Coming to help you at the claim?" Charlie asked.

"Perhaps."

"How did you hear about your cousin coming?" Cassie asked, an idea flashing like the rising sun. Maybe they didn't need to enlist Petey's services.

"From the man who leaves with Ming," Hui replied.

"Did you hear anything about Victoria de Vere? You don't have to tell me, Hui, but Charlie and I already met her and I wondered what folks were saying."

Hui sighed and hunched his narrow shoulders. "Miss de Vere is why my cousin comes. He comes with many other men to build her Golden Palace. I will try to tell him it is not good to work for her, but I have not seen him since I left China. The Wangs will talk sense to him, but he may not listen."

"It's okay if he works for the competition," Charlie said. "We don't worry about the

Golden Palace."

"Maybe you should not be so happy," Hui said. "This woman worked in San Francisco."

"You know her?" Cassie said.

He grimaced. "No, but I know some who do. She is all kind talk and pretty face, but evil designs. She is not good for Eagle Bar or our Golden Spoon."

"Don't fret." Cassie cracked eggs into a bowl. "We've sized her up and know her ilk."

"It is not enough. We will all watch and see and sleep with one eye open."

Matthew leaned against the wall of the new general store, waiting in the shadow until the line at the Golden Spoon was down to a handful of miners. Then he sauntered the rest of the way down the street and joined the late arrivals.

Isaiah was nowhere to be seen this morning. Instead, Charlie greeted diners at the doorway as if he were a glad-handing politician running for office. Good! Matthew could talk sense to Charlie before he went inside and saw Cassie.

After dining with Victoria last evening, he'd reevaluated his plan for coming to Eagle Bar. What she said made sense, and her offer of managing the workers was more than generous. He'd tell her yes today, regardless of what the Vincent twins thought of him.

Alone in his hotel room, he'd paced instead of sleeping, his mind roving over his one attempt at preaching. He had no belly for another tent meeting like that one. He'd come off as a prattling fool.

Perhaps he wasn't destined to be a preacher, but —

"Thought you would've eaten at the Grenier."

Charlie's comment jerked Matthew back to the present. The line of men had filed in and left the two of them alone outside the door. Matthew eyed the breakfast price of the day. He wouldn't pay that for the best meal Boston had to offer. The fragrance of bacon, eggs, and onions wafted between them and his stomach lurched. "No, Zelda's place isn't known for its fine cooking."

"Sorry to hear that, but we've closed." Charlie leaned his back against the pledge sign, arms folded across his chest, a thinner taller version of Isaiah but just as formidable.

Matthew had no notion why Cassie and Charlie suddenly saw him as the enemy, but he'd come here to find out. No sense tiptoeing. "You run out of food?"

"Didn't say that."

"Then what is it? Is the Golden Spoon closed, or just closed to me?"

"The last part would be about right."

"Why is that?"

"You working for Victoria de Vere?"

"Not yet."

"You staying on as a preacher, then?"

A movement at the corner of the building caught Matthew's eye. Traveler's shaggy head and face appeared, along with the carrot-top of that young boy, Peter. They walked out into the sunlight and turned. The rumble of Traveler's gravelly voice blended with the traffic on the street. A moment later a decidedly feminine hand flashed out of the shaded alley, touched the boy's arm, and Peter tipped back his head and laughed.

Maybe it had been in front of Matthew all along and he hadn't wanted to see it. Cassie and Charlie were never his friends, only pleasant-talking merchants. From now on his eyes were wide open.

He'd been wrong about Cassie being a lady and an innocent. Obviously, she preferred the base company of the mudsill. And, standing here toe-to-toe with a man he'd once deemed genial and friendly, Matthew reappraised his opinion of her brother. Charlie was nobody's fool. Matthew recognized the thrust and parry of his guarded conversation.

"I haven't decided if I want to stay on as a preacher," Matthew said. "Are you offering to hold another tent meeting here?"

"Figured you'd be setting up at the Golden Palace from now on."

"Don't see how you figure that. It's not even built yet."

"You're going to help her build it."

"Didn't say I was." Matthew folded his arms across his chest, planted his feet wide apart, and glowered. His palms, still sore from yesterday's work, mocked his casual reply. Whatever Charlie thought he knew, Matthew wasn't leaving until he took the man down a peg or two.

"It doesn't matter to Cassie and me who you rub elbows with, as long as it's not with us." Charlie's eyes narrowed to slits. "That goes in particular for my sister. Do you take my meaning?"

"Cassie is a grown woman —"

"And she's my sister. I ask again, do you take my meaning, Mr. Ramsey?" Charlie leaned forward, the planes of his face like flint.

"What have you got against Miss de Vere?"

"I'm not talking with Miss de Vere. I'm jawing with you."

"All right. What have you got against me and Miss de Vere? I've never done anything to either one of you. You don't even know me."

"We've seen enough to know."

"I came here to help folks, and that's more than I see you doing." Matthew gestured to the sign declaring the day's breakfast price in Cassie's bold print. "At least I don't put on a friendly act while I skin people alive and steal what's in their pockets."

"Maybe not, but you took up with a woman who does. Someone you knew before you came into our home and put on the preacher act."

Charlie turned and was partway through the door before Matthew grabbed his arm. "That's not true, and we're not finished here."

Charlie turned back, his lean face sober. He silently stared at Matthew's hand on his forearm until Matthew's unease grew and he released his grip. "Neither have you, Matthew. Talk this morning is, you came here as Miss de Vere's scout to get the lay of the land. The miners say Victoria's Golden Palace is going to have a mighty fine restaurant, one that'll put ours to shame. You think you can scare us off?"

Out of the corner of his eye, Matthew glimpsed Traveler and the boy trudge off to the street and part company in opposite directions. Cassie marched up and took her place beside her twin. *Why do I care what they think of me?* Matthew took in her glare, her chin thrust out, one fist doubled up in her skirt. She wanted a fight, so be it; but he wasn't about to blow up and leave without answers. He swallowed hard, but the mounting anger remained lodged in his throat.

"Trying to take us in with your balderdash again, Mr. Ramsey?" Her light tone belied her belligerent stance. "We are not the simpletons you believe. It's plain as plain can be, you are well acquainted with Victoria de Vere."

"I'm afraid it's your assumptions that are sadly mistaken. I am not a close friend of Miss de Vere, and I had no notion she was coming to Eagle Bar."

"There doesn't appear to be much future for you as a preacher, particularly if you're given to lying like that," Cassie said.

Matthew fought to keep his temper in check. Never had he met a more infuriating woman. Cassie Vincent fancied herself better than anyone else in Eagle Bar, the biggest toad in the puddle. "Not that it's any of your business," he said, "but I try to be civil with all men and women I meet, including Miss de Vere. I met Victoria in San Francisco and we had a polite discussion about my mission to the gold fields." Matthew heard his father's condescending tone dripping from his every syllable, and he relished the taste.

"You came here because Miss de Vere, oh, excuse me, *Victoria,* mentioned it? She knew about Eagle Bar. You didn't," Charlie said, his voice low and measured like a snake coiled and still but poised to strike.

Matthew flung up his hand in the space between them, backhanding the suspicions out of the way. "Maybe you haven't heard the news, but lots of folks know about Eagle Bar."

"You take my meaning well enough." Charlie's voice was calm as a millpond.

"I do." Matthew hauled in a deep breath of the warming air. Charlie and Cassie's double attack had scratched his confidence slightly, enough to allow a small weed of suspicion to sprout. He curled his hand into a fist. He yearned to grab Charlie by the shirtfront and incite him to at least show a little crack in his own self-possessed armor, but he was too sophisticated to resort to back-alley tactics. He was no Traveler. He wanted this woman, in particular, to know it. "I came to Eagle Bar of my own accord. When Victoria arrived here, I was as surprised as you."

"Oh, no, I don't swallow that one," Cassie said. "For someone who's just an acquaintance, it appears you and Victoria have become fast friends overnight."

Matthew scowled. "She's a widow in need of a man's help. I believe she's trying to make her way as best she can, by building her own establishment here. That's something you two ought to understand."

"We understand all too well. We have work to do. I'm sure you have the widow Victoria's affairs to attend to. Good day, Mr. Ramsey." Cassie dismissed him with a curt nod.

"Sorry you chose it to be this way, Matthew." Charlie wrapped his arm around his sister's waist and they disappeared through the doorway of the Golden Spoon.

Matthew's anger engulfed him. He'd tried to rein it in, but once again they'd gotten the better of him. He could let it be, walk down the street and be done with them; but he couldn't abide letting them get the upper hand. If he couldn't best them head-on, he'd find a way. Victoria wanted to know why they were here? So be it. He'd find out for her, and he'd get to the bottom of their stubborn hatred of her and of him.

He trudged a few steps, ignoring the bustle of the street. They knew something about Victoria. But what? He paused mid-step. Maybe he'd be wise not to tell Victoria all he knew. He'd keep his own counsel for now.

He set off again and strode down the street toward the work site, each long stride releasing a measure of his pent-up frustration.

By the time he stopped in front of Victoria's office tent, he was in full control of his mind and emotions. *First things first.* Whether Victoria had influenced his decision to travel to Eagle Bar or not, he was his own man. It made no sense that she would have a reason to do so, but that day over their last dinner in San Francisco, she had convinced him to come here. No matter. He'd see this through and commit his private thoughts to no one.

"Matthew." Victoria's husky voice oozed honey. She stood in the doorway, Sylvester Logan holding the flap open for her. "I'm delighted to see you. I hope you're here to bring me good news."

"Yes. I accept your offer."

"Excellent. Give me a moment with Mr. Logan, then we'll discuss how best to put your talents to use."

He stepped back and let the couple pass. Sylvester Logan barely glanced at Matthew as he proffered his arm and escorted Victoria to the construction site.

Matthew ran a sharp eye over the men arriving for work. Already a gang of them plied shovels and pickaxes, digging holes for posts. They worked with a will, and he suspected Victoria was a woman who always knew how to get what she wanted and get the most out of her laborers. He'd thought her plan of having the Golden Palace finished in two weeks ambitious, but as he looked over the workers, he reconsidered.

He spotted a familiar red-haired youth weaving his way through the stacks of lumber. Matthew grinned. "Peter! Peter Fulton!" He raised his hand and the boy trotted over. "How would you like a job? I could use a young feller like you to run errands for me."

"You workin' for her now, Preacher?" The boy jerked a thumb toward Victoria, talking with a group of men and gesturing to Mr. Logan.

"I'm going to help build the Golden Palace."

"Ain't you worried it'll hurt Charlie and Miss Cassie?"

"No, there's room enough for everyone here."

The boy squinted one eye and curled the corner of his lip, a mannerism reminiscent of his grandfather when the old man played his fiddle. "You bein' a preacher and all, wouldn't say you'd lie about it, but wouldn't say you knew for cocksure, neither."

In spite of all the goings on, Matthew found himself taking a liking to the boy. "It's true. No matter how successful the Palace is, it won't hurt Charlie and Cassie's business if they work hard to keep their customers." Why did he add that caveat? Why was he arguing with a boy about adult business practices?

"I'd a thought you'd feel like that traitor, Judas, for helpin' their enemy."

"Miss de Vere is no one's enemy. She's here just like you and your grandfather, trying to keep body and soul together." *Is that true?* Hang Charlie for planting that seed of doubt, but he'd find his answers. Perhaps the source was standing in front of him.

"And she pays well. Don't tell me you couldn't use a little extra cash. How old are you?"

"Thirteen, more or less." Peter thrust out

his bony chest, but the too-big shirt still hung off him like a tattered sail.

A twinge of sympathy tweaked at his conscience as Matthew sized up the scrawny lad. He'd thought the boy closer to ten, perhaps eleven. He was nearly old enough to make his way in the world. "You know, I was about your age when I went to sea. It was hard work but a great adventure."

The boy turned his head and glanced at the building site. "Don't appear to be much adventure here."

"In the goldfields? Anything can happen here. You can strike it rich today and make your fortune. I would've given anything to jump ship and come here at your age and pan for gold."

"Thought you said goin' to sea was a great adventure."

"It was, sometimes, but sometimes it was just a lot of days looking at waves and doing everyone's bidding."

"Sorta like here, except for the sea."

Matthew glanced over the workers and saw Victoria coming toward him. His delight quickly became frustration. He would've thought the boy would jump at the chance to earn some money, but he was nearly as stubborn as Cassie. "Yes," Matthew replied, "but in this job you can quit whenever you like. Why not give it a try? Easy money."

"I have to help Grandpa work the claim. We ain't gettin' out the color like some of the others around us. I might be able to work sometimes, but I don't want to be workin' here and missin' a big score, so I don't know. And I don't want to be workin' for the enemy."

Matthew caught the gleam in the boy's eye. *Well, I'll be switched!* He was being bilked for more money . . . by a lad. It didn't matter. He'd pay the boy, even if it came out of his own pocket. "You can use the money you earn to buy your meals at Miss Cassie's Golden Spoon. That'll help your grandfather *and* Charlie and Miss Cassie."

"Miss Cassie already gives us vittles for free, and if I paid her it might hurt her feelings."

"Hey, that's mine!" someone shouted.

"Turn it loose or I'll break every finger you got!" someone else shouted.

Matthew jerked his head toward the commotion. Two miners in dirty clothes tussled in a tug of war over a hammer. Dust rose from their boots as one swung his fist. The tool dropped to the ground when the blow connected.

"Stay here." Matthew rushed over. "You men, break it up!"

Neither glanced his way as they pummeled one another and crashed to the ground. Matthew waded into the fray, avoiding a well-aimed kick, and grabbed one man by the back of his shirt and hauled him off the other. "I said, break it up." The man squirmed in his grip like a mackerel on a hook. The man on the ground snatched up the hammer, sprang to his feet, and ran to the other side of the work site.

"Thanks a bunch, Preacher." The miner slapped at his fist.

Matthew let him go. "You're here to work, not cause trouble."

"You the boss now?"

"He's *your* boss." Victoria stepped beside Matthew and put her hand on his forearm. "You only get one warning, then you're gone. Go find Mr. Logan and he'll put you to work."

Victoria's perfume mingled with the foul breath and body odor of the man glaring at both of them. Matthew glanced at her profile, every inch a lady. Here in the goldfields, she was as fearless and capable as any man. He tried to hide his admiration.

"Ma'am." The man picked his hat out of the dust and strode off in the direction of the foreman.

"Already earning your pay, Matthew. I knew you were the right man for the job the moment I met you." Victoria gestured toward her office.

His admiration flickered at her warm words, but a spurt of suspicion quickly squashed it. Had she planned to hire him from the time they met in San Francisco? Victoria couldn't know for sure he'd come to Eagle Bar, so why did he now suspect her of something he couldn't name? "I'll be with you in a moment."

He waited until she was out of earshot and turned to the boy. "Well, Peter, do you want the job or not? I can't stand around talking all day."

"Okay, Preacher. I'll be back in the afternoon. By the by, you was right smart about givin' Miss Cassie the dog. You'll be pleased to know, Gypsy done bit Traveler this mornin'."

CHAPTER SIX

Usually Cassie enjoyed cooking the big meals with the fresh supplies Charlie brought, but today, as her hands stirred, floured, and kneaded dough, her mind was down at the other end of the street. The kitchen smelled of corned beef, boiling away on the stove, and fruit ready to be put into pies, but there was no singing or humming of Papa's beloved tunes.

"Why do you suppose she's so set on coming here for supper?"

Charlie glanced her way while cutting up rabbits. Traveler had made a habit of taking his meals with them and, more often than not, contributed fresh meat. "Been considering on the same question myself." He focused on his work. "Most likely to spy."

Cassie hunched one shoulder. "But why, bub? It's making me crazy. I know it shouldn't, but it's all I think about and it doesn't make any sense. By all accounts, she's rich. Zelda says she has all kinds of money, so why come here?"

Charlie rubbed his hands on a dish cloth. "Maybe for more gold to line her pockets, but I think it's because she somehow found out we were here and she wants something from us."

"We don't have anything. And you said yourself she wasn't in a hurry to let anyone know we're related."

"That's so. Only thing I can figure is, she has her eyes on our Golden Spoon."

"That's what I thought, too, but she's building her own grand place. What would she possibly want with our plain, canvas-covered eatery?"

"That's what we aim to find out tonight."

Petey stuck his head in the kitchen doorway, then strutted inside, his thumbs cocked under his armpits, looking every bit like a banty rooster ready to crow.

"You appear mighty pleased with yourself," Cassie said.

The red-haired youth laughed. "Been down to the Golden Palace. The preacher done give me a job runnin' errands for him. Went smooth as butter."

Charlie chuckled. "We sent the right feller to get the job done."

Cassie swatted away a buzzing fly and

covered the pie dough with a cloth. "I don't want you getting tangled up in any trouble down there, Petey. If things get bad or dangerous, you quit on the spot. We don't want anything to happen to you."

"Particularly on our account," her brother agreed.

"Don't you worry none, Miss Cassie. I been takin' care of myself since before I learnt to walk and talk. You shoulda seen that preacher. I kicked up a fuss 'bout him turnin' on you and made like I'd never work for him. He thinks he talked me around to his way of thinkin'. Grampa taught me that. Showed me how to make the other feller think he's got the better of you when all the while you got him right where you want him."

Cassie couldn't resist wrapping her arm around the boy's scrawny shoulders and giving him a quick hug. With her brother and all their friends around her, how could she even spare a single thought for Matthew Ramsey's treachery? And how could she ever doubt her safety?

Petey's eyes shone for a brief moment before she let go. He wiggled his shoulders, adjusting the baggy shirt.

"Thank you, Petey. We appreciate all you do for us." Cassie offered the boy a piece of tea cake. He chomped it down in two bites.

"Already done found out a few things," he said.

Charlie's hands stilled and he leaned an elbow on the counter. Cassie raised an eyebrow and the kitchen went silent, save for the hiss of the fire, the drone of the flies, and the bubbling meat pot.

Petey's eyes gleamed as he drew out the moment. "Got a bunch of men putting up a big tent, big as this place, maybe even bigger. Gonna have some sort of party for the miners. Miss de Vere had me stand over by Zelda's with a sign tellin' folks to come tonight, promisin' free drinks. Zelda, she come tearin' outta her hotel, chompin' on her cigar, and lit into me somethin' fierce, threatened to have Owen come out and give me a hidin' if I didn't move on."

"What happened?" Cassie's thoughts whirled. Her mother was wasting no time staking her place in town and making enemies. Zelda might not be a friend, but it never did to purposely provoke your neighbor and make enemies, particularly not in this time and place.

Petey shrugged before he snitched another piece of cake. He chewed more slowly this time, and swallowed before he resumed his story. "I just moseyed down the street in front of the General Store and there wasn't nothin' she could do to me then. But I got tired of it after a while and lugged the sign back to the construction site. They got men hammerin' and sawin' so fast it'll make your head spin. Got the floor all boarded over and other miners are workin' on puttin' up the walls already. Had some more wagons come in today as I was leavin'. More workers and supplies, I 'spect."

Charlie clapped the boy on the back. "Good job."

"I gotta go. Grampa's likely wonderin' what's become of me."

"Come back with your grandfather for supper," Cassie said.

"Smells mighty good.' Petey rubbed his palms together. "We'll be here. Miss de Vere has asked Grampa to come play at her tent meetin'."

"Tent meeting? Is Mr. Ramsey going to preach?" Cassie frowned. Free liquor and the kind of music that went with it didn't fit with preaching.

Charlie snorted and she frowned at him.

"Ain't likely to be that kind of tent meetin', Miss Cassie." Petey winked at Charlie, helped himself to another piece of cake, and sauntered out the doorway.

"Maybe I ought to go down there tonight

and see for myself what she's got going on," Charlie said.

"We both should go."

"Okay. One thing's for certain. Victoria's moving like a lightning strike. She's already set her sights on Zelda."

"Doesn't seem too clever to make an enemy of Zelda. She's got way more business clout in this town than we do."

"Maybe that's the point. Take out the competition head on. It's not such a bad thing, when you ponder on it. If they spend their time fighting with each other down the other end of the street, maybe they'll leave us alone."

"Except for tonight." Cassie returned to her pie making. "Victoria is set on coming here for supper."

Charlie flicked his elbow into hers. "You fixing to poison her?"

"Might not be a bad idea."

"Betwixt the two of us, I expect we can feed her up enough so she's more than willing to stay on her side of the street."

"How do you figure, bub?"

"It's like Petey says. We get her thinking she's got a leg up on us by coming here, and then we put the questions to her. Of course it'd work out best if Matthew tags along, and I expect he will. Appears she's got her claws into him, or else why would he have showed up here right before she did?"

"I don't like it." Cassie crimped the edges of the pie crust and, with her knife, slit the top in the shape of a tree to let the steam escape. "I don't like the idea of Matthew Ramsey prancing in here after taking us on that buggy ride about being a preacher and all. I don't trust him as far as I can spit."

"Neither do I, but I'm wondering if *he's* not the one being taken for the buggy ride."

Cassie elbowed him back with a sharp nudge. "You expecting me to feel sorry for the man?"

"Oh no, never. But Victoria, with her wheedling ways, always gets what she wants. She did it with our father and with our stepfather." Charlie shrugged. "I imagine she did it with that Eli Weston she ran off with years ago. He doesn't appear to be around anymore. Who knows how many others? All we know is, she's got a trunk-load of money she got from somewhere or someone. Matthew might be the next one in a long run of men Victoria uses to get the things in life she wants."

Cassie had to agree. Matthew might say he was a preacher, but he was a Ramsey; and William Ramsey Shipping was setting

168

up operations in San Francisco. He'd told her so the first time they met. If Cassie knew that, she could be sure Victoria knew it too. She felt a twinge of sympathy for Matthew, but shrugged it off. He was a grown man. Maybe he and Victoria were in cahoots. If not, then he'd brought this upon himself, swaggering around Eagle Bar like one of the big bugs.

Cassie stoked the stove and slipped the pies into the oven. She wiped the sweat off her nose and forehead with her apron and stepped out the doorway. The breeze cooled her hot cheeks with its soft, smooth touch. Nugget bleated, and Cassie glanced over to where the goat lay in the shade near the cabin wall, chewing her cud. The chickens scratched in the ground nearby, and their sociable clucks brought a feeling of home.

All this was theirs. Victoria couldn't change that. Cassie and Charlie had each other, and they finally had enough to clear out all the family debt. Just a few more months and they'd be free to start a new life. Charlie came and stood behind her. He placed his lean, long-fingered hands on her shoulders and kneaded away the knots.

As much as she hated to contemplate it, her brother was on the mark. Matthew Ramsey had doubtless been taken in by Vic-

169

toria; most men were, it seemed. That didn't excuse him for lying to them, and it didn't mean she felt anything but the smallest thimbleful of pity for him. She'd never trust him, but neither should she be so stubborn as to refuse him his place at a table, particularly when it could be to their advantage.

"Are you going to tell me what you've got planned?" Charlie's low voice tickled her ear.

"Likely the same thing you do, I expect. Invite Victoria and Matthew to have supper with us after the crowd leaves, and back our mother into a corner so she has to answer our questions or risk us telling all her secrets to Matthew Ramsey."

"Did I ever say I have the smartest, best-looking sister in the whole of creation?" Charlie turned her toward him and gathered her in his embrace. "I'd never let anything happen to you, sis."

"I know," she whispered, blinking back sudden tears. They held onto each other for a moment longer before Charlie let her go.

"Think I might take a walk down to the tent-raising and see for myself," he said, his voice husky. "I'll find Matthew and invite him and Victoria to come for a private supper."

Cassie stood at the back of the Golden

Spoon and watched her twin depart with long, purposeful strides. She'd felt a fierce, trembling desperation in his hug. Victoria was their mother, and they had spent their lives underestimating her. Would today prove any different?

Hui arrived and set about peeling and chopping the vegetables. They spoke of the claim and all the gossip surrounding the Golden Palace and its owner, but all the while Cassie kept an ear out for Charlie's return. As the time grew closer for serving supper, she milked the goat, left Hui in custody of the warm milk, and slipped over to the cabin.

In the dim quiet, Cassie changed her dress, breathing in the scent of fresh air and the strong soap clinging to the cloth as she buttoned it up with trembling fingers.

Here she was, a woman with a successful business, nearly in a dither over what? Some woman she barely knew. Yet they had cooked a mountain of food, as much as for another Hangtown Fry, and this foolishness would take a toll on their supplies for subsequent meals. And now she was here, wearing a clean dress and making a fuss over her hair as she strangled it into a tight bun at her nape.

There was no need to pinch her cheeks;

her thumping heart and her time over the stove had given her a rosy glow. She slipped her apron over her head and hurried back to the kitchen.

"Isaiah!" Cassie stopped short as the big man blocked the back door. "I thought you went off with Ming this morning."

"Thought I'd better stay around with all the goings-on down the other end of town. 'Sides, nobody cooks like you, Miss Cassie." He patted his ample midsection, sniffed the air, and smiled. "I been hankerin' for a piece of that raspberry pie of yours."

"Help yourself before it gets busy." Cassie brushed past him to the counter and whacked out a hefty slice for her friend. "We can sure use the help tonight." She passed him the plate and he dug a fork out of his back pocket. That was Isaiah — always a surprise, but never surprised; ready for anything.

He took a bite, chewing ever so slowly, and rolled his eyes heavenward. "I swear, Miss Cassie, tastes better than anything else on earth." He took another forkful and closed his eyes.

Cassie laughed.

"You got another Hangtown Fry tonight?" he asked between bites.

"No, but we got a pile of food, so I hope

we'll be able to sell out."

"Leave that to me. Men are already linin' up, but I'll get the word out."

"Have you seen Charlie?"

"He's out front sweet-talkin' like always, got that man that works for the de Vere woman chewin' his ear off, but he's got the price up."

"I hope it's a good one." Cassie felt like singing. All was well now that Charlie had returned and Isaiah was here.

"Oh, yeah. Charlie ain't gonna give it away," Isaiah said. "It's like last night. I'll let folks know it's more than worth it, but once I tell 'em we got pie, I don't expect it'll take much convincin'."

Hui had the clean plates set in stacks and helped Cassie load up the serving table with hot pots of food. Before they were finished, Charlie slipped in from the kitchen. "Isaiah's out front. We're gonna need all we got."

Cassie raised her brow. "That's good. I was afraid we'd cooked too much. We should've advertised another Hangtown Fry."

"Don't need to. According to Victoria's foreman, a Mr. Sylvester Logan, she's sent all her workers down here for supper and she's paying top dollar for the lot of them." Charlie let out a low whistle. "You better save out enough for our private supper after."

"I already did." She wasn't proud of her fretting over the food or the amount of time it had taken her to select the choicest morsels and set them aside — all in a vain attempt to impress a woman she hated. As soon as her mother had reappeared in her life, she'd been possessed of a mind diseased by old memories.

Cassie shook off the jitters and, head held high, walked across the empty restaurant to the front entrance and tapped Isaiah on the shoulder, as she'd done nearly every day since they'd opened for business.

Isaiah made his eyes grow wide as full moons and gestured his head toward the line snaking down the street. "Told you we'd get a crowd, Miss Cassie."

She smiled, but her gaze was on his cheek. The cut was still there, but the swelling was mostly gone and the bruise at the bottom of his eye had faded some. Isaiah had likely forgotten it, but Cassie tamped down her sense of well-being with a shovelful of caution, wary of what lay ahead.

She hurried back to the serving table, chased by Isaiah's shouted announcement and the clomp of boots behind her. "Okay, supper's ready, mind your manners."

Men wearing their scents of sweat, mud, tobacco, and, more often these days, a whiff of liquor, passed in front of her, separated by the width of the food-laden table. She talked pleasantries with those she knew and thanked those she didn't.

A growing feeling of unease built up inside her when Charlie introduced Mr. Logan with his slicked-back hair and brocade vest. The men who followed him were polite enough in their way, but all the new faces, the smell of raw wood and sawdust, and their raucous laughter set her nerves jangling. She was grateful for Charlie at her elbow, spearing meat on each man's plate, ladling out savory stewed rabbit, and joking with each miner as he passed.

Her mood brightened at the arrival of Petey and Bernard Fulton. Petey stuck his head through the canvas drape that shielded the kitchen from view. Cassie mounded their plates, and the boy grabbed them and slipped back through the kitchen to eat outside, away from the crowd. In spite of the rumble of conversation, the shuffle of boots and clatter of cutlery, her ears caught Traveler's deep voice in answer to Petey's excited chatter.

Cassie passed an empty plate down the line to Charlie and Hui. It came back loaded. She added her contribution of potatoes, gravy, and biscuit, and turned toward the canvas drape once more. A familiar dirty hand wrapped with a soiled rag brushed fingers with hers as Traveler accepted the plate with a "Much obliged, Miss Cassie."

The timepiece pinned to her bosom silently ticked away the hour. Her face ached from smiling, her stiff back protested, and her arms wearied of hashing up the metal plates with what the miners called grub. Finally, her sore wrist scooped the last bit of potatoes and gravy onto a stranger's plate and she hurried to the front door to signal the end of the seating. Isaiah sent the dwindling line of stragglers away, their stream of complaints and curses drifting down the street in the evening air.

The big man put up the closed sign and followed her through the dining area. Charlie took charge of the gold dust, coins, and paper money, and slipped out to the cabin while Cassie floated among the diners, smiling and making small talk as, one by one, the men finished their meals. Her mind was on the company to come, but she prided herself in making the Golden Spoon a haven of hospitality and, as such, always strived to keep her wit sparkling and attentive.

Matthew came in with Victoria on his arm as the last small group of men pushed back the benches and deposited their empty plates in the washtubs at the end of the serving table. Cassie wiped up the tables with a wet rag and caught Charlie's eye. He gave a slight nod and strode across the room to greet the late arrivals.

"Just in time, Matthew," her brother said. "It's nice you could join us, Miss de Vere."

"I wouldn't dream of missing it," Victoria cooed. "All the men we passed would talk of nothing else but their supper at your Golden Spoon."

"Just what we like to hear." Charlie's cheerful voice effectively hid the slight narrowing of his eyes and the razor-edged quickness in his movements. He might fool everyone else, but his twin recognized and shared the heightened awareness of danger in inviting the fox into the henhouse.

As Charlie seated the couple, Cassie hurried into the kitchen and brought out the reserved food. As she gave the congealed gravy a stir with a less than steady hand, she chided herself not to fuss and hoped it would prove decent fare — not too dry or cooled from its long wait in the warming oven.

As she set out the meal, Charlie brought

strong coffee. Isaiah and Hui bustled in the background, carting away the tubs of dirty dishes.

"My, I had no idea you did such a booming business in such a cramped space," Victoria said as Cassie and Charlie took their seats across the table from her.

"Everyone eats well at the Golden Spoon," Matthew said, and pinned Cassie with his bold blue stare.

"Did you learn to cook from your mother?" Victoria's husky voice claimed Cassie's attention.

Cassie opened her mouth but no sound emerged.

"No. Our mother up and left the family," Charlie said. "We had to fend for ourselves. Our Cassie kept house for us and our stepfather. As you can see, she's a right fine cook." He passed around the plate of meat.

Victoria selected a small piece, her eyes gleaming as she stared at Charlie. Cassie took a deep breath to clear the cobwebs of the past from her brain, but Victoria was on the attack once again. "Don't tell me you learned to do this all on your own?"

Cassie passed her the bowl of potatoes. "Charlie and I worked at Rowland's lumber camps. Mary Rowland taught me how to feed hungry men, no nonsense." Cassie raised her chin and looked her mother squarely in the eye. She had no reason to be ashamed of anything she had done, no reason to be timid in front of this treacherous woman who, once she'd given birth to them, had done nothing but dirt for them thereafter.

"Rough place, those camps." Victoria poured gravy on her meat.

"No rougher than here," Cassie said.

"Better pay this time around I expect," her mother countered.

"You take what you can get to pay the debts," Charlie said.

"And judging by the price tag for supper, you get plenty," Matthew said. At his comment, everyone swung their heads and glared at him. "Shall we bow our heads?"

"I'll be glad to say the blessing, Matthew, as it is our table," Charlie said. He bent his head and delivered a short, terse prayer, finishing with "Don't let it get cold."

Charlie's plate was as sparse as her own, with a small bit of vegetables and rabbit. Neither had an appetite for this, but neither would they back down from it.

"Debts?" Victoria picked up the conversation without dropping a stitch. "Surely someone as young and healthy as yourself wouldn't have any debts to speak of,

Charles."

"We always pay what we owe," Cassie declared.

"As do I. I hope it wasn't too inconvenient for me to send my workers here for supper? They were rather a hungry lot."

"Not at all," Charlie said.

Cassie set down her fork. "Will this be a regular occurrence?"

"I plan on it as long as I'm in the building phase. I've found you get the most out of your workers if you take care of them and feed them properly."

"Could get powerful expensive. You've got quite a crew there, with more coming all the time," Charlie said.

Victoria took a small bite of potato and chewed slowly. "The workman is worthy of his hire. Isn't that so, Matthew?"

The big man sitting across from Cassie said, "True."

"And you're a beneficiary of that as well, Mr. Ramsey?" Cassie asked.

"I am not," Matthew retorted.

"Certainly not," Victoria cut in. "Matthew is much more than just one of the hired laborers. I'm trusting he'll stay on to help me run my Golden Palace. I could use a man with his talents."

"Does that mean you're fixing on having

some revival tent meetings down there?" Charlie asked with a wide grin.

Matthew glowered at both of them, viciously stabbed a piece of meat and chewed.

"Could be," Victoria said. "But we've got a lot of work to do before we can take the time for that. Will your food supplies be a problem if I send all my men around again tomorrow?"

"No," Charlie said. "We serve until we run out of food."

"As I'm sure you know." Cassie looked pointedly at Matthew.

"Do you have investors, Miss de Vere? Or are you a wealthy widow?" Charlie asked.

"Rumors run faster than the gold dust in the river in this town." Cassie said.

"I never pay heed to rumors, Cassandra. But if you must know, I learned about investors from my dearly departed husband, God rest his soul."

"Did he invest in drinking establishments?"

"Oh no, my dear. He invested heavily in lumber mills." She pasted on a somber expression. "You said you cooked in the lumber camps? Perhaps you met him, but it would've been many years ago. He passed on a good while back and I've had to carry on by myself. How I miss him."

"It's a tragedy to lose someone you love," Charlie agreed.

Cassie clenched her teeth to stop the retort that threatened to tear out of her lips. Charlie gripped her arm. "Would you care for some pie?" she asked, instead.

"That would be lovely, but perhaps another time. Matthew and I must get back. We have a small entertainment planned for the men. As I said before, I've learned the importance of taking proper care of my workers."

Victoria stood and both men rose to their feet. By force of habit, Cassie collected the dirty plates before she stood.

"Don't you have hired help to do that, Cassandra? You look positively wilted."

Cassie scowled across the table. "I prefer honest work to provide for my family."

"You'll be an old woman before your time with that attitude. That was a lovely supper. Thank you for the hospitality. I don't know as I can spare the time away from the work site any time soon, but if I might, I'd like to buy my evening meal here and you can send it down with that red-haired boy, Peter Fulton. He works for us now."

"I'd heard as much," Charlie said, his voice sober as a country parson. "I also heard he was out on the street aggravating

Zelda Grenier for you."

"That he was. Zelda will be gone soon, I fear. The woman has no business sense whatsoever."

"Tell me, Miss Cassie, did you find your missing chicken?" Matthew inclined his head toward Cassie before offering Victoria his arm.

The nerve of the man — standing there with the enemy, pretending a personal connection they no longer shared; never *had* shared.

"Livestock missing?" Victoria's dark gaze swiveled back to Cassie.

"Nothing you need concern yourself with." Cassie looked past her mother and met Matthew's intense stare.

"As you wish. It has been my pleasure." Matthew again inclined his head and turned toward the door.

Matthew kept his voice and his tread measured, battling the urge to stride off down the street and leave his companion to fend for herself. The Ramsey family code of honor, drilled into him from birth, forbade such ill manners, particularly where a lady was concerned. And a lady she was, in spite of her inclination toward cunning. Victoria had a soft and subtle-ambush way of cutting men down, disguised in feminine smiles and wiles. He'd seen her do it with ordinary workmen, and even with Sylvester Logan. *And with me, as well.*

The thought rankled and roiled the rich supper sitting heavy in his belly. As they strolled down the street, he turned a deaf ear to the woman at his side. Victoria was set on chattering on about the Vincent twins and the fare at the Golden Spoon. He knew as well as she what had transpired. Hadn't he sat at the same table, consumed the same food, and listened to the same conversation? Although he might as well have been one of the benches, for all the heed any one of them paid him.

Matthew hauled in a deep breath of the evening mountain air, its fragrance mingled with pine, fir, fresh-cut lumber, and a whiff of smoke, mules, and axle grease — the scent of frontier industry. He needed to clear his head. He'd had enough talk for the night, maybe enough for good. He could leave here tomorrow and head back to San Francisco. There was nothing holding him back. His brother would welcome him with open arms and, at the very least, treat him decent.

Upon his arrival in Eagle Bar, he'd thought himself done with always coming out second best to his elder brother; of never quite proving to his father he was the better son to run the business; of never living down his undeserved reputation as a hothead in their eyes. Ramsey Shipping held a stake in his future, more than this dirty boomtown ever would. But could he go back to San Francisco, hat in hand, knowing he'd quit on himself twice in the same week?

"Matthew?" Victoria's usually soothing tone turned sharp-toothed and her gloved fingers pinched his forearm.

"Uh, yes?"

She stopped, forcing Matthew to halt and face her. "I thought for a moment you had abandoned me to thoughts of the sweet Cassandra." Her husky laugh couldn't quite mask the jealous ring in her comment.

"Not at all, Victoria," he replied. "The Vincent twins are the furthest thing from my mind."

The woman gave him a slow, sly smile. "Come now, Matthew. She is lovely, and you appeared quite taken with her tonight. I'm sure she noticed you had little to say, and when you did speak, it came out so endearing . . . almost like a tongue-tied schoolboy with his first bout of spring fever. And that question you asked about a chicken? I wasn't sure if it was a joke or a private moment you had shared together."

"Neither." What had gotten into him, mentioning that fool chicken? Victoria's observation stung like a slap on the cheek. If she had seen through him, Cassie had surely been laughing up her sleeve. He'd been trying to reach out to Cassie but, like everything else he did, the gambit had only served to prove him a clod and widen the rift between them.

He was done trying to please everyone else, including his new boss. "I am not a schoolboy, Victoria, although you seem intent on treating me as such."

Tonight, it had been three against one, but in spite of the verbal hiding, Matthew had learned a little something. He was now convinced, more than ever, the trio knew each other. The conversation of debts, of lumber camps, investors, father — *no, stepfather* — had been some sort of verbal sword play. No one went into that much detail yet they kept it purposely vague for no reason.

Coupled with the twins' private meeting in Victoria's tent on the day of her arrival, it was the only thing that made sense. After his first trouncing in the three-way conversation, he'd restrained himself with great effort, and as he ate, he listened and watched. Obviously, they were keeping their personal business close to the vest. For some reason, they didn't want him to know their history, but tomorrow he'd set Peter on finding out more.

Tomorrow. There was his answer. He was in Eagle Bar to stay the course, at least for now. That didn't mean he intended to grovel and eat a steady fare of crow. The sooner he got that sentiment across to his employer, the better.

"I agreed to work for you," he continued, "but not as some sort of errand boy like Peter Fulton. You say you want to use my talents, well and good. I can manage the men, the accounts, the inventory. I can even build the place for you single-handedly, but I will *not* be relegated to the role of simpleton whenever you choose to treat me so. You *do* know who I am." It was a calculated risk, but he threw the Ramsey card on the table. He had to know what she knew.

Her grasp on his arm tightened. "Oh, Matthew, I've been a widow so long I'd forgotten the passions of the young."

He opened his mouth but she swiftly touched his lips with a soft gloved forefinger. "Please allow me to continue, and then I promise you may have your say." Her finger

187

lingered, pressed against his lips, before she stroked it down over his chin and withdrew the provocative contact. "Of *course,* I know who you are. You are every inch your father's son, and more so. It was not my intent to make you appear anything but a man of industry and intellect. Surely you must know how much I value you. Since the moment we met, I hoped you'd come to work for me in this grand venture.

"A man like Mr. Logan can only be useful in certain areas. I envision you being my right arm. I simply did not want to rush you. I thought it too soon to give voice to my ambitious aspirations for you, for both of us."

Matthew stared at the woman in front of him. Keeping his expression somber, he let his gaze travel over her comely face, taking in the slight lines around her mouth that could deepen to stern grooves when she dressed down a worker; the slight coquettish tilt to her head, designed to disarm a man and silently invite him to delight in her favored affections. But they weren't favored. They were a honeyed trap she used to get what she desired.

He was well versed in the ways of the world and had seen enough of her ways to know she wasn't to be trusted. She wanted a Ramsey to work for her? It didn't quite ring true, but he'd let it be for now. He nodded, and her smile stretched wide. He might not know all Victoria's schemes, but he'd taken her measure and knew her ilk. He would not be fooled by her sweet talk or his shortsighted frustrations. If he'd felt the fool lately, it was merely because he'd been a fool on a fool's mission from the moment he set out for Eagle Bar.

"Fair enough," he said.

"I'm so glad we've come to an understanding." Victoria held out her hand in a distinctly feminine gesture. He presented his arm and she settled her fingers on his sleeve with a slight squeeze. "We had best get down to the tent before the miners turn my little frolic into a riot."

As they stepped out along the street, a rough shove struck Matthew from behind. He absorbed the blow and pulled his female companion closer, but before he could turn and address the interloper, Traveler elbowed past him. The bearded miner waved a grimy bandaged hand in his face. "Thanks to you, Preacher. That dog you were so intent on gettin' for Miss Cassie took a chunk outta me. You better hope I don't lose a finger or you'll pay."

With a shake of his fist, he would have

moved on, but Victoria lightly tapped the miner on the shoulder. "Friend, come along down to the Golden Palace tent and have a complimentary drink. We'll also have a few diversions and games of chance to cure your woes."

Traveler rudely grunted and proceeded on his way. He made a point of stopping in front of the Grenier Hotel and waited until he was sure they saw him before he stepped inside.

Piano tunes rolled out into the street as Matthew and Victoria passed Zelda's place at a more sedate pace. Victoria shook her head. "I don't predict a long life for the Grenier."

"Now that you're in town?"

"A little competition is healthy for every business. Wouldn't you agree, Matthew?"

He shrugged.

"It weeds out the incompetent and the lazy, and from my observations, Zelda Grenier is both." Victoria hugged his arm closer to her side as she steered them across the street to her property. A large group of men congregated in the street. Many more sat on the fresh-planked floor, still open to the air, of the future Golden Palace. Matthew and Victoria worked their way through the gathering crowd and a cheer rippled along their passage. The men parted as Victoria sashayed through their ranks and accepted a hand up onto the floor from Mr. Logan. Matthew stepped up and took his place on her opposite side.

"Gentlemen." The rumble of voices dropped to a low murmur. "Welcome. I hope this will be the first of many nights we'll spend together." At a resounding chorus of ribald shouts, Victoria threw back her head and laughed.

Mr. Logan held up both arms to quiet the miners.

"Gentlemen, you have active imaginations, it would seem. I pledge the Golden Palace will be a haven from your hard work and rough life of panning for gold. Even here in Eagle Bar, there's no need for deprivation. We surely can't starve ourselves of the social pursuits that make us human. I've designed my palace to be a place where you all can relax and enjoy the pleasures of life. Think of it as your home." She swept her hand in a graceful arc. "Soon we'll have walls and a roof for our gatherings, out of the night air into far more pleasant surroundings."

Matthew's eyes swept the boodle of men. The bearded, gaunt, sunburned, and dust-streaked faces were all raised, glassy eyes fastened on the charismatic woman at his side. Victoria swayed slightly, as if drunk with her power to captivate the masses at her feet. He felt her hand clutch his arm, gripping it in a talon-like clench. Did he detect a trembling in her touch? Did she know what she was doing? He glanced sidelong at her profile and she favored him with a feline smile. No fear, only a queer glow in eyes hooded in the twilight. She knew full well the power she held on to so fiercely.

She was a spellbinder, and in that moment, Matthew felt sorry for his own kind.

Victoria took a deep breath and her grip relaxed as she raised her arm high, finger pointed toward heaven. "I've received a warm welcome from all of you, and tonight I want to extend my thanks. But enough talking!" A cheer arose from the crowd. Victoria pitched her voice above the noise. "There are free drinks for everyone, as long as supplies last. Wet your whistle and come enjoy a few games of chance. This is just a small sampling of what's to come when the Golden Palace is complete."

The miners erupted in thunderous approval.

Ira Graff had set up a couple of flatbed wagons on the side. Sylvester Logan jumped down and immediately joined him. Matthew recognized a small clutch of workers from the building site, some up in the wagon beds, others lighting lamps. They had a couple of barrels open. Already men had mobbed the oasis and liquor flowed.

Victoria's low voice wormed its way into his ear, despite the din. "Can you feel it, Matthew?"

He looked into her flushed face and raised an eyebrow.

She sucked in a deep breath. "It's success! I knew the first moment I set eyes on this street, I'd struck gold!"

"Perhaps." Matthew was struck by an urge to dampen her high spirits. "But looks to me like you're the one spending all the gold. Free drinks? Free supper for the workers?"

She tapped his jaw with her gloved fingers. "Tonight, perhaps, we lose a little money, although I have confidence Chen Zhi will keep us in the black. He's one of the best." She gestured with a tilt of her head toward the tables set up under the trees out back, the gloom dispelled by lanterns, their flickering glow swaying from the branches creating a spider's web of light and shadow.

The Chinese workers had arrived that afternoon. Under Victoria's sharp eye, Matthew had helped some of the labor force set up the planks to make rough tables earlier in the day, but he'd assumed it was for the men to sit and drink. He shook his head. How could he have been so blind?

Just the other day, he should've thought it strange — first Logan, and then Victoria had allowed the work to cease while they bet on Judd and him unloading the wagons. Gaming was part of Victoria's grand plan. What she couldn't wangle out of the miner's pockets with liquor, she'd steal with the gambling.

"If you wouldn't mind, Matthew, I'd like you to mingle and make certain no fights break out and no one loses his head. I've purposely set out a small amount of whiskey, watered down, of course. We don't want anyone getting corned. I know this is not exactly up to your talents, and when we're in business I'll hire men to keep the peace, but tonight I'm sending a message."

Victoria tilted her chin toward the street. "And I see it's already been received loud and clear. *We* are sending a message, Matthew. Are you ready?"

His gaze followed hers to the trio standing apart from the boisterous patrons. Zelda Grenier and the Vincent twins, Cassie in partial shadow, watched the proceedings.

Finally, he gave his employer a curt nod.

194

"I shall be wending my way toward the tables, making sure we keep everyone happy and reasonably well-behaved," she said.

He watched her waltz through the knot of men, entrancing those she deigned to engage in conversation. He jumped down into the fray. High spirits and goodwill flowed as freely as the drink. Men slapped him on the back when he passed. He worked his way toward the onlookers watching from the edge of the lantern light.

"You ever seen such a sight, Preacher?"

Matthew spun on his heel and found a familiar face. "Judd."

His former opponent held a box supported by a rope suspended from around his neck. He tilted his head and rubbed the back of his neck. "Didn't rightly know what I was getting myself in for when I said yes."

"What have you got there?" Matthew asked.

"Long nines." Judd held up a smoke. "Cee-gars. You can have one on the house, I expect, since we're both working for the same outfit."

"You're selling them?" Matthew declined the gift.

"Yeah." Judd slipped the cigar back in the box. "It's all about striking it rich any old way we can, huh? I suspect Miss de Vere will just get richer. That's the way of it in this world. Me and you? We'll die trying to get a bit of our share."

Matthew shook his head. Victoria was at it again, reducing a man's dignity to a cheap box of tobacco.

The other man misinterpreted the gesture. "I know you're a preacher, but that don't mean you aren't entitled to a little gold now and then."

Greed. He'd preached against it in his one and only sermon, and here he was, neck deep in it tonight. His self-loathing vomited out in words. "I decided I'm not cut out for preaching. What kind of preacher works for an outfit designed to corrupt men?"

"I'm not suited to it myself, Matthew." Judd's eyes twinkled in the lantern light. "I ain't no saint, but ain't no shame in a man trying to make his way in the world. Particularly if he's doing it for a noble cause."

Matthew snorted. "I've yet to find a noble cause in this world. What's yours?"

"I wouldn't have one if I didn't have a good woman to keep me on the straight and narrow. It's my Miriam and my little girl, Rebecca. We threw in everything we own for me to come out here and make my stake, going home with a pokeful if I can, but it's slow going and I get powerful lonesome for my gals."

Matthew scrutinized the lanky man before him. Victoria had called Judd his first convert. It wasn't true, not in the slightest; but here was a man with an open, honest face, a man forthright in his friendship and noble in his cause.

Judd slapped him on the shoulder. "You're one of the ones like me. I knewed it right off. Both of us only here for a spell before we get on our feet." He gestured toward the crowded tables, the noise level rising and falling like ocean breakers. "I'm thinking about trying my luck before I leave."

Matthew sighed. "You feeling lucky?"

"Don't know too much about some of them games of chance. Ira said they got chuck-a-luck and monte. Never seen the likes of them, but I do know how to play draw poker, and Miss de Vere says I can use my pay as a gambling stake. Thought I might be able to make it into a bankroll with a little luck."

Victoria always on the prowl, taking this man for all she could, not knowing she was stealing his chance. And if she knew, would she care? *I'll see to it that she does.*

"Might not be a lucky night for you, Judd."

"How ya figure?"

"You can be sure Miss de Vere is going to get her money back for the free drinks."

Judd frowned. "You working for or against the woman?"

Matthew hadn't been convinced he should interfere, or even invest himself, in this man's noble cause, but it was done. Maybe it was because Judd called him Matthew, or maybe it was because he didn't belittle his failure as a preacher, or maybe because Judd had offered friendship without guile or strings. His was, perhaps, the only noble cause in this place. Matthew said, "Trying to do what's right, I expect."

"You think her games are rigged?"

"Can't say for certain, but I wouldn't be surprised. She brought in some professionals from San Francisco to run the tables."

"Ah. So we're working for the devil herself?"

"Temporarily."

"Just so, Matthew. I'm trying to divide my time between the claim and the building work." He rubbed his hands together. The scrub of his calloused palms spoke of honest toil and sweat. "I like building with wood. It's what I did back home. I'm not so much into the panning, but it's why I came. Why we all came. I didn't rightly know what I was in for. Green as they come, I was.

198

Now I'm here, I figure I need to get some more supplies to make my claim work, and the money from building her palace will do that for me."

Judd reached into his shirt pocket, pulled out a small daguerreotype and thrust it toward Matthew, but when he would've taken it, Judd kept a firm hold of the dog-eared corner. Matthew squinted in the low light at the family of three, standing in front of a sign proclaiming Crocker's Rooming House. Judd's grimy thumbnail moved over the woman holding the baby. "My Rebecca was just a mite back then. She's growed some since."

Judd took the picture back and stared into the still faces. "I want her to have a real home. Never had one myself. Always lived in someone else's place, worked for someone else. Me and the wife, we're gonna buy land, build our house, run cattle. The gold will disappear, but folks'll always need to eat."

Matthew clapped his new friend on the back. "You're right."

Judd mooned a moment more over the picture before he reverently slipped it back into his pocket. "Thanks for setting me straight on the gambling. I'd better empty this box, if I want to get paid. Maybe I'll see ya later."

"Yeah." Matthew remained unmoving in the milling crowd and watched Judd jostle his way through the men, talking them up, selling Victoria's cigars. He felt the familiar heat rise up in him, but this time the anger was not for himself. Judd deserved better than selling his soul for a few worthless cigars. How much would he make for this night's work? Pittance most likely.

Matthew shook off the thought, but the sepia faces of Judd's family stuck in his brain like a saddle burr. With a quick stride, he set off out of the crowd and straight to the rival proprietors standing on the edge of the street.

"Who does she think she is, coming in here, trying to steal my business with her watered-down free liquor?" Matthew caught the tail end of Zelda's diatribe before she noticed his approach and fell silent. She narrowed her eyes, hands on hips, and fixed him with a hard stare. "You here to do her dirty work?"

"I'm my own man."

"Then as your own man, you can surely find another place to hang your hat tonight and every night thereafter. For all I know, you've been Victoria's errand boy from the moment I laid eyes on you, plotting to put the Grenier out of business."

"It's called spying," Cassie said.

"It's a common problem," Charlie agreed.

Matthew flicked his gaze over the shadowed faces. The twins' eyes glinted hard as ice in the lantern light. The three of them were spoiling for a fight, and Matthew was more than primed, but however foul the mood, he took a deep, steadying breath, determined not to rise to the bait. "Think what you will."

"Matthew!" The foursome jerked their heads in Victoria's direction. She patted the arm of her erstwhile escort, a young strapping miner, and whispered into his ear before he left her at the edge of the street and turned back to the party. With little mincing steps, she crossed the short distance to join them.

"Consorting with the enemy, Zelda?" She placed her hand on Matthew's arm. "Or are you trying to steal my business partner?"

Matthew's jaw clenched as Cassie's gaze bored into him. He longed to shake off the cloying touch, but he could not. He met her accusing glare with a steady gaze. He couldn't speak out for himself, much as he'd like to. What was there to say?

Zelda didn't have that problem. "You try to throw your weight around this town, you'll regret it."

Victoria gestured toward the lively scene on her property. "I'm just treating my workers and their friends to a little hospitality."

Zelda tossed her head and snorted, "You can serve all the watered-down whiskey you like. Won't make no nevermind to me. You want a fight, you'll get one."

"Now, now, Zelda. We're ladies. Ladies might disagree, but we never fight."

"Only one I see here that might resemble a lady would be Cassie. You and I both know what we are, Victoria. I make no excuses about it." Zelda flicked the ash from her cigar.

Victoria laughed. "We're both reasonable businesswomen, then. I'll buy you out tonight." Victoria passed her a piece of paper.

Zelda held the missive close to her nose and scrutinized it before she crumpled it up and chucked it on the ground at Matthew's boots. "I won't be insulted by anyone, particularly not by the likes of you, with your fancy dress and highfalutin talk. I know exactly who you are."

"You should take it, Zelda. If you don't, you'll be out of business once I open, and you'll leave here with nothing. Don't be a fool."

Matthew pretended to watch the two women hurl insults, all the while aware of the silent twins watching. Charlie's gaze focused on Victoria, aware of her every movement. Matthew could almost hear the other man's thoughts. As one businessman to another, he bet they paralleled his own — both of them calculating how long it would be before Victoria's prophecy came true; and when the Grenier folded, would she set her sights on the Golden Spoon?

Victoria's eyes flicked toward his. It was a safe bet she'd be after the Vincent's property by summer's end. Drunk with power, she wouldn't be happy until she held all of Eagle Bar in her gloved fist.

Cassie was harder to read. At the moment, she, too, was watching Victoria, but her attention zigzagged across the street where the strains of fiddle music rose up in the mayhem.

A moment later her gaze met Matthew's. She slipped her hand into Charlie's and they turned to go.

"I'll be sending my men by for meals tomorrow." Victoria caught at Charlie's arm.

"You said as much at supper, I recall," Charlie said without turning to face her.

"I just want to be sure you have the supplies to feed them all. A hungry man is like an ornery bear coming out of hibernation. No good for anything but growling and causing trouble. I can't have that at my building site if I want to get any work done." Victoria's laugh had a shrill ring to it.

"We'll have enough for everyone," Cassie said before they walked off down the street into the darkness.

"You're going after them, too, aren't ya?" Zelda's growl brought Matthew's attention back to the stout woman. "I know why you're set on taking me down, but those two won't hurt your business none. They're not like us."

"No, but you might be surprised. Come, Matthew." Victoria held out her arm and he reluctantly linked his elbow with hers. "We have patrons to attend to. You have until tomorrow morning at ten to accept my offer, Zelda. There won't be another one."

The hotel owner snorted and sent them on their way with a few choice cuss words. Victoria laughed, and this time it was filled with mirth.

Matthew broke off from his employer and stepped into a brewing argument between two older men, but all the while his mind lingered on Victoria's comment about Charlie and Cassie. *You might be surprised?* What

were they trying to hide? He'd not leave
Eagle Bar until he found out.

CHAPTER SEVEN

"You have to admit it's good for business," Charlie said when the crowd of morning diners had finished their meals and the Golden Spoon was once again empty and quiet.

"Maybe, but breakfast used to be our small meal. Most everybody was off working their claims. Now Victoria has all those workers stomping through our place, and it's hard on the rations. At this rate we'll be down to beans in nigh on a week, and it seems like you just got here."

Cassie forced her attention on her hand and every circular motion of the wet scrub rag on the plank tabletop. She squeezed her eyes shut tight to stave off the tears. What was the matter with her? Charlie was right here and he was right.

They had more business than they could handle, more gold coming in than ever before. They'd had to turn away a fair amount of grumbling men who came late to the line this morning, and yet she couldn't shake the queasy feeling in her stomach, or the occasional flutter in her chest, when she thought of the future. Now it wasn't just about Charlie getting married and leaving. It was about their mother staying. What would she do when Charlie went for supplies and she was left in Eagle Bar to face Victoria alone?

As usual, Charlie picked up on her musings while he straightened the nearby tables and benches. "We've still got plenty of supplies and I'm not going anywhere long as Victoria's prowling around."

Cassie wondered how Charlie managed to stay so cheerful and calm? "She's trouble, but seems she's got her sights set on Zelda for now. It's like you said. If the two of them scrap, maybe they'll leave us out of it."

"Maybe." Charlie said. "But I got the feeling last night Victoria wanted us to hear her spat with Zelda."

"You mean it was all for show?"

"Can't say how much was put on, but there was something mighty peculiar going on. Victoria might've been speaking to Zelda, but she was talking to us. She had her eyes on me the entire time and she made sure I knew it."

They crossed the empty dining area to the serving table and Charlie grabbed the last half of a biscuit on the platter. He popped it into his mouth, chewed, swallowed, and shook his head. "Oh, she means to put Zelda out of business, no bones about it. But you can bet she doesn't care one whit about the Grenier. She wants our Golden Spoon. I wasn't sure of her motives at supper, but seeing her last night in the street, I'm certain of it."

Hadn't Cassie sensed it, as well? Every time they thought they were one step ahead of her, their mother found a way to undermine them. It had been true their entire childhood, so why would she change now?

Cassie scooped the last leavings in the porridge pot into a small bowl. "I figured it was too good to be true. It isn't like her to mind her own business and leave us be. A leopard doesn't change its spots. But I've been thinking, too. What can she actually do to us? She can open her own eating place and steal some of our customers, but it won't be as easy to offer them free home-cooked meals as it was to pour out free liquor. Leastwise, I can't see our mother cooking over a hot oven all day. Remember how she used to cut her finger on purpose and go running to Papa with blood dripping all over the kitchen floor? He'd make her rest and he'd fix supper."

"Rabbit stew." Charlie ran his tongue over his lips. "He made the best I ever ate."

"He had a fine hand at biscuits, too."

"That he did. But more than likely, Victoria won't be slicing any of her fingers to get out of cooking. She's got plenty of money. She'll hire people to cook for her Golden Palace. Maybe she already has. We got those fellers out back with Hui." Her brother shrugged. "Could be they know their way around a kitchen as well as he does."

"Even if she has a fancy restaurant, we'll still have miners loyal to our Golden Spoon. And if she tries to buy us out like she's doing with Zelda, even if she offered us a million in gold nuggets, I'd rather see this place burn to the ground than end up in her hands."

"Amen to that. She'll never get the Golden Spoon away from us. I promise." Charlie packed up a few leftover flapjacks and the pitcher of molasses. "You want to give these to the fellers out back, or to the chickens? No sense letting them go begging."

"Oh. They're likely colder than a wagon wheel, but might as well offer."

Cassie stuck her head out the back doorway. Hui stood toe-to-toe with a taller man he'd introduced as his cousin, Chen Zhi. They were talking over each other, rattling on a mile a minute in Chinese. The unintelligible words fell on Cassie's ears like angry bird chatter, and the picture completed itself in her mind with all the others silently watching like a bright-eyed flock of ravens.

Whatever they were saying wasn't pleasant. She'd never seen Hui angry but, as she watched, he clenched and unclenched his hands. The cousin, arms folded across his chest, was the picture of ease, but his tone was cutting as a whetted axe. Cassie stepped in, hoping to help her friend. "Pardon me, Hui, do you and your friends want more? We've still got a mite of porridge and some flapjacks going begging, but I fear they're cold."

The silence was immediate. Hui tweaked his head in her direction, his usually placid face pale and stark, slashed by lowered brows and a deep groove parting the middle of his forehead. His solemn gaze roamed over the circle of men gathered near the Golden Spoon kitchen, their dark glazed caps and bent heads looking more like a funeral than a breakfast gathering.

Chen Zhi stepped away from Hui and bowed to her. "Thank you, Miss Cassie, but we must be getting back to the work. There is much to be done and Miss de Vere is not a patient woman." He smiled at her, his clean-shaven face and shiny cheeks giving him the appearance of an innocent youth, but his perfect English, impeccable manners, and the occasional white hair threaded through his braid said otherwise.

Where Hui was a man who moved about as unobtrusively as a shadow, Zhi was clearly the leader of these new arrivals, and a man with a gleam of bold ambition in his black stare. He stood out from the group in his white shirt and brocade vest, marked, in her mind, as one of Victoria's men.

Hui's down-turned mouth suggested he suspected the same. "I must work," he said. He pressed his hands together and steepled his fingers before he gave his cousin a curt bow. He said something in Chinese and then skirted the small group and joined Isaiah at the washtubs. Charlie offered the flapjacks around, but Cassie noticed the men glanced to Zhi before they declined the leftover food. The clatter of metal plates as Isaiah and Hui cleaned the breakfast dishes, and the shuffle of the men's feet claimed her total attention.

The rough tweak on her shoulder caused her to jump nearly out of her skin. A man said, "You got no right feeding my breakfast to some no-account Chinamen."

Cassie turned toward the speaker just as her brother stepped in front of her, Isaiah right beside him.

"We have no quarrel with you." Charlie pushed Cassie back a step with a firm hand. "We're done serving for today."

"You turn me away, telling me you got no more grub, and then I come back here and find you got plenty." The man was shorter than Charlie and older, his reddish beard grizzled with gray, or perhaps just dirt-streaked. His pockmarked cheeks were stained with a purplish flush and his eyes were cloudy as dishwater gone cold and greasy. Two other rough-looking hoodlums flanked him, one with hands doubled up in meaty fists.

Hui slipped silently past her and took his place on Charlie's other side.

Cassie caught a blur of movement and glanced back. Zhi and his men glided as one, a silent flock of crows, disappearing around the far corner of the Golden Spoon.

At their defection, a cold trickle of disappointment ran over her, more for Hui's sake than anything else. She turned back to her own business and watched Hui's thin back under his tunic, straight as a sword, face forward, standing in league with Charlie. She wouldn't forget his loyalty.

Petey popped up behind the ominous trio and Cassie gestured with her head to the left, hoping the boy would take the hint to skedaddle. He disappeared in a wink.

"Seems to me anybody that's a Johnny critter lover needs to have some sense knocked into him." The irate miner stepped closer to Charlie.

"Seems to me what we do at our own place is our business. We don't want any trouble." Charlie held up both palms. "So I'll ask you to leave before you run into some."

Red beard's snort was accompanied by the tromp of heavy boots rattling up the alleyway beside the canvas-covered eatery. Traveler emerged with a roar like an avenging giant, elbowed the two men aside, muckled onto the back of the vocal one's collar, and yanked him into a chokehold. "You need to be learnin' some proper manners, Zeke, else you're not welcome here. Apologize to Miss Cassie and get back to your claim before I forget we're acquainted."

Traveler's face was as dark as Zeke's as the captured man squirmed and gasped for air.

The warning words struck a chord in Cassie's memory. Matthew had spoken similarly on their first meeting when Traveler had been the recipient of Eagle Bar justice. And now? Traveler was defending her honor, and Cassie didn't take it lightly. He could be a formidable enemy, but he'd fast become a fierce friend. They'd only known him a short while, but she knew in her heart, at this very moment, he was one to be trusted.

Traveler thrust his opponent away and Zeke stumbled to the ground. He was back on his feet, quick as an eel, but he twisted his body just beyond the bigger man's reach.

Gypsy appeared from off the hill out back and pressed against Cassie's skirts, hackles raised, her furry body vibrating with her rumbling, low growl.

"I'll have my supper tonight and you'll not be turning us away, if you value your property." Zeke ignored the flash of Traveler's fist as he quickly sidestepped and he and his companions stalked away.

"Don't you worry none, Miss Cassie. I'll catch up to him later and set him straight," Traveler growled. "But if you're fixin' on feeding Victoria's Chinamen, might be you want to send Hui and Petey down there with the food. Some folks are gettin' a mite riled up with all the new faces about." He nodded his shaggy head at Hui. "Don't have no quarrel with your kind, but there's them that do."

"I am sorry, Miss Cassie. Charlie." Hui bobbed his head and gave a slight bow. "I should not have brought my cousin here."

Charlie clapped their small friend on the back. "It's not your fault, Hui. We can serve whoever we wish, and we will."

Traveler frowned but held his tongue.

"Zhi will not be back. He is not the man I knew. Wangs and Chens will stay on the other sides of the street now." Hui dipped his head, his queue flopping against his cheek, but not before Cassie caught the gleam of moisture in his eyes. He backed away and silently resumed his task of rinsing the tin plates and cups in the nearby washtub.

Petey popped in from the back doorway of the restaurant "You shoulda heard 'im rippin' and a-cussin' down the length of the street!" Gypsy rushed forward to greet him and licked the boy's hand, tail wagging. "And where were *you,* girl?"

"I could learn her to be mean, right quick," Traveler offered.

"No, Gypsy's fine," Cassie said.

"A little growlin' won't stop Zeke," Traveler said.

"But I knew *you* would, Trav." Petey's

voice was pitched high with excitement, his freckled cheeks rosy. "Went and got Traveler soon as I saw that plug-ugly Zeke Underwood."

"Do you know those men?" Charlie stole the question on Cassie's lips.

"Those same fellers were at Zelda's last night," Petey said. "Got in a fight and broke up the place some bad. Heard Zeke, the one with the red beard, even busted Owen Cantrell's arm. I saw Owen sittin' outside the Grenier this morning, smokin' a pipe, one arm hangin' like a dead tree branch. I says, 'Hi.' He just snarled like an old bear. Got his face cut up some, too." Petey helped himself to the cold flapjacks, drizzling one with molasses before he rolled it up and took a bite.

"They must've just come into town," Isaiah said, "or I'd've seen them around."

"I saw 'em yesterday." Petey polished off the leftover breakfast. "One of 'em has a claim out by us, but the other two come in about the time all them supply wagons pulled in for the Golden Palace."

Traveler grunted. "Zeke works his claim hard. Doesn't generally come into town for nothin'. He's been here for maybe a month. Knew him from before. We fought the Mexicans together for a spell."

"So he's a friend of yours?" Charlie asked.

"Didn't say that exactly, but I'll make sure he don't do you no harm." Traveler scratched his beard. "Might go a long ways to feed him and his boys up tonight. I'll come along, see he don't make no trouble."

Charlie nodded. "A little goodwill," he murmured in Cassie's ear.

"Goodwill, or will he have us over a barrel? I don't like it, Charlie."

"Me neither, Miss Cassie," Isaiah said. "Safer out at the claims than in town, nowadays." He raised a dark, challenging eyebrow at Charlie before he joined Hui at washing up and finishing the morning chores.

"Before I saw Zeke causing a ruckus, I come by to tell you I found the one who stole your chicken," Petey announced. "He was down working on Miss de Vere's place."

"What?" Cassie gaped at the youth as he puffed out his chest. "Are you sure?"

"He said some things so I'm sure enough. Got him some coffee this morning and put a surprise in it, some jalap powder Grampa had saved. He won't be eatin' any of your chickens or anything else, leastwise not today. He run outta there holdin' his gut. You shoulda seen him skitterin' off to the woods." Petey chuckled.

"Petey, I don't want you getting into trouble like that on my account." Cassie lectured the bragging boy. He was surely picking up all the wicked ways of this place, and she and Charlie were guilty of putting him right in the thick of things. She longed to put her arm around him and keep him safe.

"No trouble at all, Miss Cassie."

"But you don't understand. It's not right to hurt other people."

"He ain't nothin' but a low-down chicken thief. Deserves what he gets." Petey spat on the ground. "Hope he loses his job down there, too."

Charlie put his hand on her shoulder. "It's over and done, sis. Don't fret. Petey won't do it again. Now we've got the dog, there'll be no more thieving and the like 'round here."

Traveler unwound his grubby bandage and flexed his perfectly healthy hand. "I made sure the news got around but, after what I saw this mornin', that dog's a poor excuse for anything more than cougar bait."

"No, she ain't!" Petey gave a low whistle and Gypsy trotted over, stood on her hind legs, and put her front paws on the boy's shoulders. The lad laughed and scratched her ears. "Gypsy's all right. Grampa and I talked her up at Miss de Vere's party last night. Ain't nobody don't know you got the most savage dog in Californy, Miss Cassie. Most folks ain't worth shucks. You feed 'em a yarn and they'll swallow it whole." Petey grabbed Gypsy's paws and did a slow dance before he released the dog. The animal lifted her nose to the air and was off, gone again up the path to the hill.

"Thanks, Petey." This time Cassie couldn't resist putting her arm around his thin shoulders and pulling him close to her side. "Are you hungry? You didn't get a proper breakfast this morning."

He leaned against her for the briefest contact before he stepped away and thrust his chin up. "I got plenty. Gotta get back down there. Big doin's. They're puttin' up walls today." Petey licked a brown molasses stain from his finger and dusted his hands on his worn, dirty trousers. "Heard they got windows and some fancy gewgaws comin', too."

"More wagons?" Charlie asked.

"Every day something comes drivin' in here. That palace is gonna be the biggest place in Eagle Bar, maybe bigger than anything in San Francisco." The boy grinned. "I'm s'posed to be passin' out cards for one free drink." He reached in his pocket and produced a deck of playing cards. "They say 'Golden Palace,' and they've been marked with a black star in the corner so Miss de Vere knows they're hers."

"Marked cards?" Charlie raised an eyebrow. "We got a little respite before supper. Might as well take a walk down to Zelda's and see what happened there after we left. Maybe take a peek over across the street as well."

"What do you hear from Matthew Ramsey, Petey?" Cassie could have bitten her tongue for asking, but thoughts of his stoic presence last night, and his defection, still stung like a mean burn from a hot kettle.

"The preacher? He's one of the ones done got the walls goin' up. Mr. Graff's got all them workers pitted against each other, right in a lather. The crew that gets the most done gets a bonus. I got a bet on it, myself. The preacher's fellers gonna take it hands down, but I'd best be hightailin' it back there to make sure they win. Don't wanna be losin' Grandpa's gold." With a cheeky wink, Petey scurried off.

"I'm headin' back to the claim. Likely have some rabbits for you in time for supper." Traveler nodded to Charlie and fingered his hat. "Miss Cassie."

On impulse she reached out and touched his hand, its crusty flesh rough as the skin of a horned toad. "Thank you."

He covered her hand with his for an instant before he stepped back as quick as Petey. "Twarn't nothin', and don't you worry none, Miss Cassie." He ducked his head and scratched Gypsy behind the ears. "Even with this worthless bag of fur and bones that calls herself a dog, ain't nothin' gonna happen to you and the Golden Spoon." He spun on his heel and left.

Isaiah and Hui followed suit a few moments later.

"You ready?" Charlie asked.

Cassie nodded. "What do you make of it?" she asked as they set off down the street. She'd traveled to this end of town more in the past few days than in her entire sojourn in Eagle Bar. She was used to staying close to the cabin and eatery in the time between breakfast and supper — doing some reading, wandering up her hill, picking wildflowers, pretending she was on her own farm enjoying a respite.

A true respite . . . wouldn't that be welcome! Maybe that was it. She didn't need to marry into a farming family like her brother intended. The way they were raking in the gold these past two days, she could buy her own plot with a little house and barn, put some gold aside for the lean times, maybe even have a hired man to help with the heavy work.

She was a woman of independent mind and sturdy stock. She knew how to handle livestock. The idea grew and bloomed in her mind with each stride they took. It carried her feet on wings, so much so she could almost feel the cushion of pasture grass springing under her feet. She looked down at the rutted hardpan street and smiled.

"What are you thinking, sis?"

She couldn't tell Charlie about the sudden lightness in her heart. She could even look at a place near to Charlie and Abigail's farm. Maybe they'd be neighbors. Her throat nearly closed, thick as sweet cream with the pleasure of the thought, but it was too soon to share the dream, even with her twin.

Her words, when they came, were low and charged with suppressed emotions. "I'm just glad we got each other. Our mother can't come between us."

"Nobody'll come between us." Charlie gave her a fierce look. "You worried about that Zeke feller?"

"No. I'm happy, bub. We've got a stash. We're not poor as old Job's turkey anymore.

Can you believe it? We can finally live our lives. No more paying off our stepfather's debts. We're free!"

"And more gold coming in every day. Can't wait to tell Abigail we can start getting our own place ready. Might even look at some cows when I go back for supplies next trip. Heard there's some for sale down Carver way."

"Maybe you could buy one or two for me," Cassie said.

"You thinking of setting up your own farm, sis?"

"Might be."

Charlie grabbed hold of both her hands and swung her around as if they were at a barn dance.

"Look at you fools, dancing in the street while this one-horse town is falling down around our ears." Zelda's harsh squawk filled Cassie's ears as the hammering stopped across the way. Zelda's shoulders were rounded, no customary cigar or bravado in sight. Her face sagged, and dust from the street etched every groove. "You're next, you know." She flung her arm toward the Grenier's broken windows. One shattered swinging door hung by a bent hinge. In the muffled din, its creaking soughed with the dusty breeze.

"But you can fix it up," Cassie said, her bright mood dimmed by Zelda's haggard appearance and the trembling in her reddened lips.

Zelda shook her head, her mussed hair draped over one dull eye. "There's no sense in going on. She's won."

"You're giving up that easily?" Charlie vaulted up the steps and into the hotel.

"It's no secret Victoria sent those men last night to destroy me."

Cassie looked over the older woman's head at Charlie's reappearance. He halted just outside the doorway and shook his head.

"If that's true, you have to fight back," Cassie said. "She's got lumber and men over there. Surely they could rebuild your hotel for you."

Charlie came down to the street. "Not a bad idea, Zelda."

"Didn't you hear me? Victoria did this, but I'll never prove it. And those brutes who did her dirty work will be back for more if I raise a ruckus. Owen said as much when he rode outta town." Zelda took in a shuddering breath and patted her skirt front with her hands until she found a long nine, pulled it from her pocket, and slipped it unlit between her thin lips.

224

"Owen's gone?"

"Asked me to go with him, but I got some business first." Zelda squared her shoulders as a raucous cheer erupted from the other side of the street. "On my way over to see if I can strike a deal with the she-devil, then I'm off to San Francisco. If you had a lick of sense, you'd be right behind me."

Cassie glanced inside the dim interior of the saloon as she and Charlie fell into step with Zelda. The familiar tables and chairs and piano were all gone. Splintered wood lay everywhere, and daylight shone through several ragged holes in the far wall.

Matthew beamed and a cheer erupted as the men pushed the second wall up and nailed it into place. Judd caught his eye from his place at the far end of the studded section. The lanky man wiped the sweat from his brow, put both thumbs in his galluses, leaned slightly back, and sent him a wide smile of his own.

At this moment, all that mattered was the building of something great, the spirit of camaraderie with his fellow men who had a mind to work. Judd had his hat back on and head down, nailing in a stay, but Matthew knew his friend was enjoying the work as much as he was, and counting on getting that bonus today. *And I'll see to it that he does, along with every man on this crew, or my name isn't Matthew Ramsey.* By nightfall, they'd have the outside walls up and boarded, the stringers completed, and the top floor planked, ready for second-story walls and rafters come sunrise tomorrow.

He glanced across the street and caught the Vincent twins and Zelda Grenier marching forward as if armed for battle. Last night's message from Victoria was a slap in the face that couldn't be ignored. Matthew wished she would just let the other businesses be, but he recognized her ruthless streak because it struck a chord in his own resolve. She was a woman who wouldn't sit quietly and wait for something to happen. It wasn't her nature.

"Looks mighty fine, Preacher." Peter Fulton stood at his elbow, grinning from freckled ear to freckled ear. "Want me to fill up the nail buckets again? Don't want the men to run out and waste nary a minute lookin' for supplies."

Matthew had seen the boy join the other gulls early this morning and place his bet with Ira. He suspected Judd had done the same, but he hadn't actually seen his new friend succumb to the lure for easy money. The wager had already accomplished Victoria's purpose. From young Peter to every man here, they worked as if possessed.

"Whaddya say, Preacher?"

"We're set for now, Peter, but I have another job for you." Matthew returned his attention to the trio rapidly closing the distance to Victoria's tent office. He pondered on the right words. "I want you to go ask Miss de Vere if she might come out to speak with me when she has a free moment, but if she's busy talking with someone else, I want you to wait your turn. And while you wait, keep a sharp ear and eye out. There are folks who might wish to cause trouble. If you think that's about to happen, you come get me fast as you can."

The lad followed his gaze and watched in silence as Charlie held the flap aside and the two women disappeared inside the tent. Charlie quickly followed. "You talkin' about Zelda? Owen and his boys lit out so there's no dirt Zelda can do to Miss de Vere, leastways nothin' I can imagine. And Charlie and Miss Cassie'd never hurt no one."

"Even so, I'd like you to go over there and make sure everything's as it should be." Matthew placed a firm but gentle hand on the boy's shoulder.

"Pshaw, Preacher, you want me to eavesdrop on 'em? Why didn't you come right out with it?"

Eagle Bar wasn't a place for parlor manners. Matthew rubbed a hand across his eyes but, when he looked down, the boy's steady gaze remained fixed on him, and the knowing smirk on the young face jabbed at his conscience.

"Ain't no shame in gettin' better acquainted with other folks, particularly from their own mouths," the boy said.

"Well, I don't want you to spy on them for my sake." *A bald-faced lie.*

"You're just lookin' out for Miss de Vere, and I'm gonna miss all they're sayin' if you keep jawin'."

"I know but —"

"Don't you worry none, Preacher. I'll listen and no one's the wiser." The boy loped off toward the tent. Matthew watched him stop near the side of the canvas shelter and bend to tie his boot.

"Matthew!" At Judd's hail, Matthew hustled back to work. No sense fretting over what the boy would do. Matthew had set it in motion. For better or worse, he'd take the blame. He tamped down the shame under the demands of the task before him, knowing he'd pay for it later with a sleepless night. Since coming to Eagle Bar he'd had more than his share of those.

He gathered the men and they pushed up the final wall, joining the building together. A crew of twelve men with sharp saws soon had posts cut, and a beam was laid across to support the stringers. Men were everywhere, sawing, nailing, enclosing the building, climbing and scurrying like spiders to put up the stringers.

Matthew spiked in one end of the carrying beam, and as he secured it in place, he watched the cyclone of workers around him. With the raw planked floor beneath his feet, it was as if he were on the deck of the *Polaris* once more with men hoisting sail, climbing the rigging, and humming like a hive of bees, each knowing his place, each doing his task and keeping the vessel on an even keel, headed on a sure and prosperous course.

"My, my, Matthew." Victoria's husky voice caressed his ear. She stroked his arm and leaned closer. "You have far exceeded my expectations. At this rate, we'll be serving drinks at the bar tonight."

"Hardly." Matthew kept his eye on the laborers, well aware of her gaze on his profile. Her presence dimmed the pleasure of the moment. For a few hours, he'd forgotten he did her bidding. Out of the corner of his eye he caught the blur of Cassie's blue skirt. He turned his head to watch the brother and sister striding down the street. Cassie glanced in his direction, but when their eyes met, she lifted her chin high and looked through him, not missing a step.

The snub brought home the unfortunate truth. It was painfully apparent they were on opposite sides. He turned his focus to the woman at his side, his gaze sweeping the area behind her, searching for Peter.

The boy was nowhere to be seen, but Victoria hadn't missed his inattention. "They'll come around," she said.

"Around to what?"

"To realizing we're their allies and friends, not their competition."

Matthew watched the stiff-backed pair march swiftly up the street. "I'm not so sure. They're stubborn as a pair of mules."

"Have some faith in your fellow man. We can, and do, get along once in a great while." Victoria laughed as if she'd told the cleverest joke.

Maybe he didn't need Peter. Victoria was opening the door, and he intended to cross the threshold and go in as far as she'd allow. "Why are you so concerned with the Vincent twins?"

"I admire ambition, much as I do in you, Matthew. I like to see it rewarded."

"But not so in Zelda Grenier's case."

"Hers was avarice, not ambition, as I imagine you well know. She'll not be bothering us any longer."

"I saw her come over with Charlie and Cassie. Looked like it was long past time for choosing sides, and they'd chosen theirs."

"Hardly. They came by to lend her their support, but the two have nothing to do with Zelda, nothing in common with her." Victoria pursed her lips. "That dreadful crone had the nerve to ask me to buy her place. It seems they had a fight over there last night. Surprising, since I could've sworn all of Eagle Bar was over here. Nevertheless, she lost her man who keeps order. Owen Cantrell? He was her right arm. Now he's gone and the Grenier, by her own admission, is in a state."

"Did you buy her out?"

"She had her chance last night," Victoria scoffed. "And she spit in my eye, but I couldn't send the poor woman off begging into the unknown empty-handed. I bought the property, gave her no doubt more than it was worth in its present state, but money well spent. Zelda is bound for the devil knows where, but she won't be bothering us any longer."

Matthew studied the hotel across the street. It had been hastily built, but it was still a serviceable building. "Some of the men could tear down the walls and we could use the lumber over here. You wouldn't have to freight in so many supplies. It would save you some money."

"Do I appear in need of finances?" Victoria put her hands on her hips and lifted her chin. "The Golden Palace will be built of all new boards. We'll make the Grenier into a rooming house."

Matthew's eyes widened. What would she need with two buildings? Eagle Bar was no San Francisco, and Victoria, with her no-nonsense business sense, surely knew that. Why dump so much money into a boomtown that would become a ghost town as soon as the last flake of gold was panned from the water? She obviously had her reasons, and he aimed to unearth every single one of them. But carefully, because his employer wasn't one to be trifled with. "Doesn't seem like most of the miners would be interested in renting rooms after they stake their claims."

Victoria patted his arm with her gloved hand. "I plan on bringing a little female companionship to Eagle Bar in a few weeks."

Matthew frowned. "I see." Why was he not surprised?

"Strictly for singing and dancing, of course. And I'll provide my girls with a safe place to stay."

Before today it wouldn't have bothered Matthew. Men and women had a right to choose their own course. But he shut his eyes for a second and saw Cassie look right through him as if he were nothing. No wonder she avoided him. As Judd said, they were in league with a handmaid of the devil.

Victoria smirked. "You disapprove, Matthew? I would have thought you'd see the obvious advantage to providing entertainment for the men. Surely you must have sought out such companionship when you were off at sea and found yourself in foreign ports of call."

"I've witnessed what happens to able seamen who frequent such places, and I've seen sailors lose six months of wages in a single night to places like yours."

"Yes, and that's what keeps your ships teeming with penniless men who need to work, and keeps these men building for me. Think how dull the world would be if we all gave up our vices and saved every penny we earned." Victoria waved her hand toward the building taking shape before their eyes.

"Work and play are all life is, and if we're clever, we get to do the pleasurable one while others do the work for us."

"These men have worked hard for you today and they all deserve the bonus."

Victoria clucked her tongue, and when he looked into her face, her eyes glittered. "That may be true, but we must decide who actually gets it. As ones well versed in the ways of the world, you and I both know there can be only one winner." She gave his arm a gentle squeeze. "And from what I see and hear, that's you, Matthew. You got your two walls up and then worked with Ira to construct a third."

"That's so, but all the men worked together to join the walls and put up the stringers."

"But *your* men had their walls boarded in before the others. Accept your due, Matthew. The men were arguing to be put on your crew this morning. After we pay out today's bonus, tomorrow they'll be fist fighting to work under you."

Three freight wagons rattled down the main street toward them. She released his arm and clasped her palms together, squealing in girlish delight. "It's here! I never dreamed we would get our supplies so quickly. I love the power money gives one!"

The drivers slowed their mule teams to a crawl and Sylvester Logan hurried out to the street, directing the first to pull around the building site toward the back where Chen Zhi and his men were building gaming tables. The second wagon held windows, their paned glass covered with wooden crates for protection. Matthew marveled at the extravagance. Would Victoria really make her investment money back, let alone make a profit worth all this labor and expense?

He glanced down at her enraptured features, her eyes riveted on the incoming freight. The woman had a sharp mind, but could it be, in her zeal for wealth, she was blind to the swift and capricious realities of frontier life?

"Look, Matthew." Her familiar clutching of his arm drew his attention to the last wagon lumbering down the main street.

A figurehead worthy of the finest sailing barque met his gaze. "The Lady of the Sea," he murmured.

"A figurehead fitting for a Ramsey, wouldn't you say?" she crowed. "I had my backer ship it from San Francisco. Ships come in there every day, and the crews abandon them for gold fever. The place is growing so fast they're ripping the boats apart and using the boards to build the city. This is just a small token of my appreciation for your help. I've told you before, the Golden Palace will be as much your venture as mine."

Victoria gestured toward the front of the building. "We'll put your figurehead under the peak of the roof, with the 'Golden Palace' sign underneath." Her gloved fingers sketched the air. "I must go supervise the unloading of the gaming cargo. There're precious and delicate supplies that Zhi and his men require to complete their work. These aren't seven-by-nine stores and I won't have Mr. Logan and his laborers manhandling and ruining it. See to the unloading of the windows, Matthew, and take care they're placed out of harm's way."

Matthew spoke to the driver and soon had a group of workmen unloading the wagons at the trees on the far side of Victoria's tent. It would make for a longer haul when it came time to put them in the finished structure, but barring any carryings-on like last night, it would keep them intact . . . for now.

The unloading of the figurehead was another matter. He and Judd and two others used ropes and a pulley and hauled the sea beauty out of the wagon bed and into the shade of the growing building. It wasn't the best solution, but it kept it handy for a future day when they could use the overhang of the ridgepole to pull it up to its final resting place. Matthew ran his hand over the carved cheek and curved lips, fingering the smooth of a million salty waves in the wood.

Peter popped up at his elbow and whistled through his teeth. "Ain't she a sight, Preacher?"

Matthew jarred from his reverie. "Where've you been?"

"Didn't want no suspicion heaped on me or you." He glanced sideways up at Matthew. "So's before Charlie and Miss Cassie come out, I skedaddled behind Zelda's and hightailed it down to the Golden Spoon. I visited with Gypsy 'til they came round, then Charlie invited me to stay a spell. I had me a bowl of rabbit stew and Miss Cassie's sourdough bread and a big old piece of pie." The boy rubbed his hollowed stomach. "I swear, Miss Cassie's the best cook on God's green earth."

Matthew clenched his jaw and reigned in his impatience. The lad knew what he was doing, dragging the conversation like a sack full of stones, forcing Matthew to bide his time or come right out and ask. "That she is." No sense wasting time. "What'd you find out, Peter?"

"I overheard plenty." The boy shoved his hands into his pockets. "But I been away from the claim for a long spell. My grandfather can't work it without me, so's I best be gettin' along. Miss Cassie done give me some vittles to take to him." He pulled out his hands, palms-up.

The boy had all the makings of a natural-born patent medicine huckster. Matthew reached into his pocket and extracted a gold coin and was rewarded by the boy's owl-eyed stare. "Wouldn't want you to disappoint your grandfather." He flipped the coin in the air. Peter deftly snagged it with one hand and pocketed it. "This ought to make up for what you didn't take from the river this morning."

"Might as well set. This'll take a spell."

Peter hitched himself up on the wagon gate and sat, swinging his legs.

Matthew pinned the lad with a stern stare. "Just give me the facts and be quick about it. I've got to get back to work if you want to win that bet you placed this morning."

Peter bobbed his head. "I like you, Preacher."

The boy would take his time, even when money was at stake, or, more than likely, Peter had already heard of Victoria's decision to reward his men with the bonus. He wouldn't put much past this quick-witted stripling. Peter would make a fine cabin boy. Maybe he'd offer the lad a position on one of the Ramsey ships when it came time to leave. Peter could work his way up. It would be a chance for a better life for him and the old man.

Peter scratched his ear. "Zelda accused Miss de Vere of sendin' those men last night to bust up her place."

Was it true, or just Zelda spewing out her never-ending reserve of vindictiveness? Matthew wouldn't put it past Victoria to help things along in that way.

"Zelda got to cussin' somethin' fierce and said Miss de Vere paid those men to steal her pile, too. Said she was poor as a church mouse and Miss de Vere better plank down the cash she promised to buy her out. 'Course Miss de Vere comes right back at her and says 'probably your man, that Owen Cantrell, took off with all your gold.' Zelda was rippin' mad, sayin' all sorts of crazy things. So Miss de Vere, she gives her what she called travel money. I couldn't rightly tell how much that was, but Zelda called her some vile names and tore outta there in a pucker. I suspect she's done gone by now."

Matthew tucked the information away and

glanced toward the building. The workers were planking the top floor; he didn't have much time to waste. "What about the Vincents?"

"Oh, they ain't going nowheres."

"Did Miss de Vere offer to buy them out?"

"Not while Zelda was there. After she left in a huff, Charlie and Miss Cassie were set to go, too, but Miss de Vere asked them to stay. Offered to help them in any way she could. It was right peculiar. Miss Cassie didn't say nothing much. Neither did Charlie. 'Course Miss de Vere was talkin' a mile a minute. She said a mouthful about wantin' to make up for the past. Said she got rid of Zelda for them.

"That set Charlie off, and Miss Cassie, too. Miss Cassie said somethin' like, 'Don't blame your cutthroat ways on us.' But Miss de Vere was nice as a sunny summer day. She kept offerin' to bring in supplies for them and help with the Golden Spoon for free. Charlie, he says he don't trust her as far as he can spit. Miss Cassie, too. Then Miss de Vere says she'll charge them a fee for bringin' in the food supplies, iffen it would make them feel better.

"Old Charlie got right riled, I could tell. He says 'You're not gettin' your hooks in us or in our Golden Spoon.' Miss de Vere's voice gets real low and shaky, like she's about to cry or somethin', and she tells 'em that was the last thing on her mind but she will need them to keep feedin' the workers." The boy stretched his neck and leaned his head back toward the cloudless sky.

"And?" Matthew prompted. *They must've said something about their prior acquaintance.*

"Mr. Logan come over and told me to fetch some nails and such for Ira Graff's men and for the Chinamen workin' out back. I didn't want to, seein' as how I bet against Graff, but I couldn't do nothin' about it. By the time I got back, Charlie and Miss Cassie were fixin' to leave so I lit outta there, like I told you."

What had they discussed while Peter was occupied elsewhere? *Plenty,* and he'd missed it. It seemed unlikely the Vincents would return, but maybe he could find a way to coax the truth out of Victoria.

CHAPTER EIGHT

The steamy kitchen reverberated with Charlie's rousing rendition of "Oh Susanna," but instead of joining in, Cassie closed her eyes, absorbed in her brother's baritone voice, so like Papa's. The June days had passed in a haze of hot sun, gleaming gold, sweat, and cooking . . . always cooking. She and Charlie had slipped down the street in last night's cool after dark and chanced a look at Victoria's Golden Palace. With the lantern light spilling through the windows and male laughter squeezing out through the open door, it looked by all accounts finished, with all the most modern fixings.

She and Charlie hadn't been there since Zelda left Eagle Bar for good and Victoria had tried to wheedle her way into their lives. What their mother hoped to gain by offering to bring in all their supplies was a tempting mystery. Charlie never wavered in his refusal to give her any toehold, but the more Cassie thought on it, the more the temptation grew. If they accepted Victoria's offer, what harm could come of it? It would only be until late fall. It would mean Charlie could stay right here at her side, singing up a storm in the kitchen. No more leaving, no more worrying while he was away.

Cassie opened her eyes and stared at his lean, strong profile as he sliced up the fatback. They were nearly down to baked beans and biscuits and, thankfully, Traveler's daily contribution of rabbits for stew. Cassie had heard grumblings among the diners about the fare last night. It was time to convince Charlie to give their mother's offer a try.

She'd nearly worked up the courage when Petey sauntered in and, with light fingers and a cheeky grin, stole a hot biscuit from the pan she'd just taken from the oven. She could never be annoyed at Petey, always popping in with his freckle-faced grin and his never-ending appetite. The scarecrow lad must have two hollow legs, because he remained whip thin no matter how many pieces of cake and pie he consumed. God bless that boy! He had been their eyes and ears for the past ten days.

Charlie finished on a long soaring note and slapped his knee for emphasis before he turned to Petey. "What's the news from down the way?"

"You ain't gonna like it."

Cassie frowned. Things had been so quiet since Zelda closed up and absquatulated. "What happened?"

"Miss de Vere herself sent me down to tell you her men are tired of beans." He wiped his nose on his sleeve and looked at Cassie, blue eyes bright. "That's all she said to tell you, but she's sendin' the preacher up in a bit to see if you don't want to partner with them and bring in fresh supplies. He don't want to come neither, heard him say as much, but Miss de Vere will do some convincin' and get her way. Seems like she does that right well."

"Yes, we noticed," Charlie said.

That news wasn't so bad. In truth, it could be the opening Cassie had been searching for. She hated to agree with Matthew about anything, but if that's what it took to convince her brother to stay, it was worth eating a little crow. "Anything else happening?" she prompted.

"Miss de Vere told the preacher to tell you she won't be sendin' any of her workers up here to eat at the Golden Spoon lessen you get fresh supplies. She thought that might bring you 'round to her way of seein' things."

Cassie shrugged. "She probably wasn't going to send any men anyhow, since her palace is built now. I imagine she'll get rid of most of the workers soon."

Petey bobbed his head, his red hair lank and shaggy, in need of a wash and a cut. "Soon's they get the finishin' touches on Zelda's old place, they say that's it for work."

"Who's 'they'?" Charlie asked.

"Some of the workers. Most are wantin' to get back to their claims, but some are gettin' ornery. They don't take to the notion that them Chinamen made the gamin' pieces and are workin' inside the Palace, runnin' the games of chance and pourin' the drinks. Some think Miss de Vere should let them foreigners go and keep on those who've helped build the place, but *they* are mostly the ones who've lost their pile at the gamblin' tables.

"The Chinamen got this little mouse that runs into a numbered hidey hole. Well, first you bet on the number and then they set him loose, seems like he knows how to go in the hole that hardly no one chose. How do you think they could learn a mouse to do that trick?"

245

"You don't waste your money on any of that nonsense, do you, Petey?"

His cheeks colored and he hunched his shoulders. "Might've seen if the mouse liked number seven a time or two. Appears he didn't."

"Now that the Palace is built, might be a good idea to stay away from it," Charlie said. "They'll take your money faster than a rattlesnake strike, and it'll be just as painful."

"You don't want to know what's goin' on down there no more?" Petey's pinched face puckered with disappointment.

"We know more than enough, and I expect Miss de Vere will stay at her end of town now she's busy with her Palace. We'll be fine up here." Cassie patted him on the shoulder. "You've been a big help to us, but we've got to let you get back to helping your grandfather on the claim. You've been running ragged from one end of town to the other. He must miss you."

"You gonna take Preacher up on his offer to get your supplies? Means Charlie would get to stay on."

Even Petey saw the good of it. Surely Charlie would, too. Cassie opened her mouth to agree as Charlie said, "No, I think I'll go, now that things are quiet. Can't have my future wife forgetting what this handsome face of mine looks like." He turned and winked at Cassie. "But I'll be back in a wink. I don't want to miss all the goings on in Eagle Bar."

So that was all there was to it. Charlie was set on leaving and she wouldn't stop him. Cassie hadn't thought about him wanting to go. It had been pure selfishness on her part to keep him away from Abigail. They were to be married soon, and she should've known her brother was pining for his intended.

"You could leave first thing tomorrow morning, bub." She ignored the clenching knot in her stomach.

"Reckon I could if you're of the same mind."

Charlie's happy face should've made her happy, too, and Cassie knew she'd made the right choice, the unselfish choice, but it did little to ease her downhearted state.

She pasted on a bright smile. "Petey, let's pack up some supper for you and your grandfather."

"We're both partial to your rabbit stew, Miss Cassie, and I wouldn't say no to a piece or two of that tea cake."

"No cake tonight, Petey," Charlie said. "But when I get back we'll have us all the cake you can eat and a Hangtown Fry."

Cassie dipped her head and fought off the sting of tears as she put biscuits and the last of the small jar of honey in a cloth sack. Charlie would only be gone a week. She should be used to it by now. He'd be back. He always came back.

As she handed the boy the food, a shadow fell across the doorway.

"Think I'll go out the front." Petey darted off through the deserted dining area.

A knock on the post outside made her jump. Charlie said, "Come on in, Matthew. No need for knocking."

Matthew ducked his head through the opening, the afternoon sun briefly striking off his blond hair and square shoulders. Cassie had forgotten what a big man he was.

"Wasn't sure but you'd be too busy for a visit." He stood stiff as the post outside, his large hands dangling at his sides.

"No, we got time," Charlie said, "long as you don't mind us working while you talk."

"What brings you here, Matthew?" Cassie asked. "I thought you took your meals at the Golden Palace now."

Matthew cleared his throat. "I do. I came to say, we won't be sending the workers up for supper anymore. The work's nearly done so they'll be heading back to their claims."

His face was somber as a gravedigger.

Cassie shot a quick glance at her twin. This wasn't the message Petey overheard. Either Matthew had softened Victoria's harsh words with his own, or he hadn't the grit to deliver them.

Matthew continued, "I know it's a mite sudden, but I hope it won't hurt your business tonight. I'm sure a lot of the men will come by on their own to eat on their way out of town."

"You think so?" Charlie leaned an elbow on the wooden counter. "We're getting low on supplies so we don't generally have as many come by when we serve the leavings."

"I think you could serve just about anything and you'd have a full house. I can't think of a man who doesn't tout your cooking and your cordiality." He nodded toward Cassie.

"That so?" she countered. "Rumors are, there were folks complaining about us serving beans and stew. Came from down your way, I heard."

Matthew shifted on his feet but looked her straight in the eye. "I'd be pleased to bring in a load of supplies for you."

Charlie stepped forward and clapped the bigger man on the shoulder. "Mighty neighborly of you, Matthew, but we take care of our own."

"This has nothing to do with Victoria. I'd do this on my own. Strictly pick up whatever you order and bring it back." He held his large palms out, calloused and tanned from hard labor.

"Much as we appreciate it, I'm headed out tomorrow, so we're all settled."

Matthew fixed them both with a sharp stare. "I don't know what your trouble is with Victoria but, whatever it may be, don't lump me in with her."

"And why not? You *do* work for her. Helped her put up that Palace, heard she couldn't have done it without you," Cassie said.

"I like to build. Nothing wrong with working with my hands."

"It's not the carpenter work, it's *who* you work for. You ought to know that by now," Charlie said.

"What do you have against Victoria de Vere? What did she do to you? And don't say 'nothing.' Any fool could see you have some kind of tangle with her from the past. What is it, Cassie? What happened between you?" He raked his hand through his hair, leaving a boyish cowlick in the back.

"It's none of your business, Mr. Ramsey. You've delivered your message. Please leave now. We need to get prepared for the supper serving." She busied herself with putting the biscuits in a large basket. In spite of his defection, or maybe because of it, she felt squirmy as a bug in the chicken yard.

"If you change your mind, just say so or send Peter down. It's been quiet out there lately, but trouble's brewing. I can feel it. You never know when some of these rowdies are going to get into it. Lots of men out there are spoiling for a fight." Matthew paused and Cassie could feel his gaze on her.

She let her anger kindle and met his piercing stare with one of her own. "Thank you for the advice, but we've been in Eagle Bar far longer than you. We know our way around." Cassie lifted her chin a notch.

Matthew broke eye contact first. "Just a word to the wise. Now that the building's done, I'll probably be moving on soon. There's nothing here for me."

Cassie gripped the edge of the table and quickly shifted her weight to hide her whitening knuckles. It was nothing to her if Matthew left. They rarely crossed paths, now that he worked with Victoria.

She drew in a deep breath and straightened her spine as Charlie brushed past her.

"I'll see you out, Matthew," he said.

Matthew Ramsey stayed on her mind throughout supper and far into the night. Just when her eyelids finally drooped and she thought she'd licked his annoying mental presence, questions whined in her skull, circling like a pesky mosquito. If Matthew left while Charlie was gone, it should make not a whit of difference to her, and yet, when Matthew said he was leaving, Cassie couldn't deny a seed of fear settling in her heart.

She tried to unearth it with the logic that Matthew Ramsey had no connection to her, no reason to look out for her well-being, but the small seed remained stubbornly buried and ready to sprout. She hadn't realized how much she relied on his stalwart presence, even if it was under the roof of the Golden Palace on the other end of the street.

But she was thrice a fool. He had no interest in staying, only in riling up old hurts. What right did that man have to presume he knew anything about them? *What do you have against Victoria de Vere?* She could still hear his deep voice sticking up for Victoria as if she were an angel. That proved he hadn't the sense of a horsefly. But in the dark suffocating moments when Charlie wasn't snoring and she had to strain to hear her brother's even breathing, Cassie's indignation couldn't uproot her growing fear.

They were both leaving her. She jabbed her feeble mind with the goads of stubbornness and independence, two traits she purported, but they were sorely lacking in the midnight hour. And at the lowest point of the night, her mother's words blew like a winter chill through the caverns of her skull: *I didn't want to say this, but it's time you opened your eyes. You're a woman grown on the outside, but inside you haven't changed from that foolish girl who needed someone to take care of her.*

How much of it was true? She didn't want Charlie to leave her, not just for this supply run, but for his marriage and life with a new family. And pile on the foolishness with her sharp pang that Matthew Ramsey was leaving as well. She swallowed the truth, and its bitterness choked her all the way down.

She didn't need anyone. She was her own woman. If Victoria could come here on her own, Cassie could, too. If only to best the woman who gave her birth and prove her mother wrong, Cassie would stay and the Golden Spoon would outdo Victoria's palace in every way.

Cassie turned on her side and squeezed

her eyes shut. She would get up tomorrow morning and get on with her life, just as she'd done every other day; but tomorrow she'd look only to herself for each decision, each action.

She was up before the rooster crowed, had the milking done, and nearly jumped out of her skin when her brother slipped into the kitchen in the predawn stillness.

"Thought I might take most of our pile out this morning. We've got a fair amount and it doesn't seem smart to leave it all here." Charlie's voice was still fuzzy with sleep.

"I was thinking the same thing. Take it all. Get off early with it, before anyone knows you're going. Let's go."

Charlie grabbed the spade and buckets. With Gypsy at their heels, they headed single file over the track and up the hill, their feet sure of the way in the morning dark. They stepped carefully around a large rock, veering off to the left on a short spur. To the familiar soft scrape of the shovel on dirt, Cassie watched the morning stars brighten and flash like diamond chips. In the dim lantern light, Charlie unearthed their growing treasure and placed it in the buckets.

"I should've brought a yoke. Is this going

to be too much for you, sis?"

She took the proffered pail and shook her head. "I can lug a mite more."

"I have no doubt, but you might feel differently by the time we get down to the wagon. It's gonna take us a couple of loads."

They worked in companionable silence. In spite of her determination ground out in the early morning hours, Cassie was already counting the days until Charlie returned. He carefully hid the stash under the false bottom beneath his feet and topped it off with a layer of dirty rags. The ruse had served them well thus far, that and the rifle he kept at the ready.

Why does this time feel different? "You be careful, bub. Keep a sharp eye out."

"Always do." Charlie finished harnessing the team and pulled her into his strong embrace. "You sure you're going to be all right with me gone?"

"I always am." She leaned into him for one last moment before she pulled back. "Get going. I'll feel a lot better when you get off from this place before anyone stirs."

"I think we can thank Victoria's palace for doing away with a fair share of Eagle Bar's early risers." He stood staring at her, his face frozen, his eyes burning.

The sensation that flashed from that

stricken look doused her in a lonely chill like they were parting for the last time. It wasn't so, but she knew her twin felt it, too. *Prove Victoria wrong — be the strong one for once.*

She worked words up from her parched throat. "I've got Isaiah and Traveler and all the Wang cousins. I'll be fine, just like always, and you'll be back before I know it."

What began as a croak rattled on with each successive word to a shrill normalcy, like priming the old iron pump at the farm. "Well, maybe not soon enough to save me from a passel of complaints about beans. Go on, now." She gave him a push and he pretended to fall against the bed of the wagon.

He rubbed his shoulder like he had when they were kids. "When did you get so strong?" he asked, parroting the words from long ago.

Cassie murmured back, "Since the day we were born and I had to protect my brother." Gypsy slipped between them, a shifting shadow in the early dawn light. The shadow turned to substance when she leaned her dusty head against Cassie's leg. Cassie absently stroked the matted fur. "Go on now, it's getting light."

Charlie scratched the dog's ears. "You take care of her, Gypsy, you hear?" He grasped his sister's hand and gave her fingers a hard squeeze before he turned and vaulted up on the wagon. "Be back soon." He slapped the reins and the horses trudged forward.

Cassie watched him go, burying her fingers deep in the dog's rough coat, clutching at the solid warmth as she blinked back tears.

The path of the rising sun skipped past her and scattered its light, chasing away the shadows and turning Eagle Bar's rutted main thoroughfare into gold. For a fleeting moment it struck Charlie's back and haloed his wagon as he rumbled past the silvered wood front of the Mercantile and the fresh raw planking of Zelda's old place.

Cassie glimpsed the second story of the Golden Palace at the far end of the street, windows shimmering in the dawn . . . or maybe it was just blurred from her tears.

She rubbed an impatient sleeve across her wet cheeks. When she looked back with clearer vision, Charlie was no longer gilded; just a glimmer of a silhouette of a man as the wagon rounded a bend and dipped out of sight on the descent to the coast.

"Work," she murmured, and the dog

cocked her head, her tongue lolling before setting off on a trot toward the kitchen. "It won't be for long," Cassie muttered, but it already felt like a coon's age.

She went through the motions of starting a fire, setting water to boil, mixing up flapjack batter and slapping together a mess of biscuits, using sourdough to stretch the meager supplies. She heard the goat bleating and rushed out to tether her in the usual space. The ground was beaten hard, and dust puffed up from her impatient steps. She hastily plunked the bucket of water down, plucked a handful of dry grass, and topped it with some green leaves from a nearby tree. "I'll see you get more later, little one," she said and returned to her work in the kitchen.

Yi slipped in, quiet as the daylight. He nodded a greeting, even as he got the pot ready for the poor man's morning fare of porridge. She wished he'd bang the spoon against the kettle once in a while like Hui, or hum a tune like Charlie, but that wasn't his way.

"How is everything at the claim today?" she asked.

"Things go well."

"For us, too."

Trying to keep the silence in her heart

from bursting into her brain and driving her insane, she hummed a snatch of "Susannah," but the tears welling in her throat extinguished it almost before it began.

"How long will you stay here?" she asked. The words were soft and small, but the question was too large for the intimacy of the kitchen.

Yi's hands stilled and he turned and looked into Cassie's face. "We talked long of this last night. We will go when the season changes."

Cassie's eyes widened. She'd expected him to give a one-word answer, then set back to work. But he tilted his head slightly and studied her. This quiet man who held healing in his hands was perhaps wiser than all of them.

"In fall, or wait until winter?"

Yi's slender fingers steepled in front of him as he left the pot untended. "It will not be when the sun steals south or when the clouds come filled with rain. The season of change is at far end of the street, but it has not come to the claims on the river. When it comes, we will be gone."

Every gentle word bludgeoned her faint heart.

"You are right," she whispered.

"Hui will speak with you before the time

draws closer." Yi touched a finger to her elbow. "And if Charlie is here, you will come with us." The slight man turned back to the stove and resumed stirring the meal in the boiling pot.

The air in the kitchen closed in around her and Cassie quickly stepped out the back door.

"Everything okay, Miss Cassie?"

Isaiah stood out back, rolling up his sleeves.

"I'm fine," she managed.

"Don't look fine. Look like you seen a haint or two." The big man hunched down and peered into her face.

"No haints, Isaiah. Leastways, only in my mind."

"Charlie get off bright and early?"

"Yes."

"He have any trouble drivin' a light wagon?"

"No." She turned and slipped back inside with Isaiah a close shadow.

"Good." Isaiah paused before he picked up the stack of metal dishes. He leaned closer. "I knew you'd be shrewd. Time's comin' to keep stores low and the wagon hitched."

Petey popped his head through the open doorway. "Charlie skedaddled?"

"Yes. We need something to eat besides sourdough biscuits, beans, and porridge."

"It don't make no nevermind to me," the boy said. "That's some fine, particularly with the milk. But I imagine if Charlie didn't come back, I'd get a powerful hankerin' for your tea cake and pie."

"He'll be back before we know it." Cassie's hearty response rang hollow after her friend's warning words, but it was too late to mope about it. When her twin returned, they would talk, and perhaps leave with the Wangs and Isaiah. Cassie gave the boy a tired smile. "You want to take some hot biscuits and flapjacks to your grandfather?"

"I wouldn't kick about it, particularly iffen there might be some milk and molasses to spare."

She packed him up a sack and he went strolling out, Gypsy at his heels, the dog's nose nearly touching the food store as it swung carelessly from his hand.

"Poor child," she said.

"He'll never be hurtin' with you and Charlie lookin' out for him and the old feller." Isaiah grabbed a large fistful of spoons.

"But we don't do enough, and his grandfather's in no position to properly care for a young boy."

"His grandfather tends to enjoy watchin' others work," Isaiah said.

Cassie was surprised when Yi nodded. "But he's not well," she said.

"Perhaps not," Yi said. Cassie leaned forward to hear the soft response, "perhaps so."

"Time, Miss Cassie?" Isaiah asked.

Cassie looked at the watch pinned on her bodice. "Yes, I expect so, but I haven't heard much of a commotion out front."

Isaiah tilted his head toward the empty dining area. "I hear some jawin' going on. I suspect that's why it's so mum."

Cassie followed the big man through the drape. She scribbled the day's price on the slate and handed it to her friend before darting back into the kitchen to help Yi set out the morning fare on the serving table.

Just another day in Eagle Bar; a day of meager meals which would bring a fair amount of grumbling, but it could also afford a chance for her to hike up the hill and read. She hadn't been alone much lately. It would be pleasant to forget about the Golden Spoon for a few moments.

Matthew stood outside the Golden Spoon, for once at the front of the line. He'd elbowed his way to his current position, but he'd been forgiven by most of the men behind him when he promised he'd never preach in Eagle Bar, or anywhere else, again. Laughter went a long way in this greed-infested place. Laughter kept folks genial, in particular when the joke was on oneself, and he had to admit it was a good joke most days.

In the moments when he could see life as opportunity and not as an unraveling sock, Matthew acknowledged the good Victoria had done him. He enjoyed the respect and conviviality of the men he worked with, and he had a genuine friendship with Judd. He wasn't fool enough to believe she'd done it to help him out, or because she wanted or needed a business partner. There was only one soul who mattered to Victoria de Vere, and once he'd come to grips with that, his guilt had eased up and his conscience settled down considerably.

She was using him as a means to some sort of end. He reckoned it had something to do with exploiting the Ramsey name or coffers to ensure her success, but he knew enough not to be taken in by her silken ways and honeyed talk.

He might be helping her establish a business and run a few others out of town, but if he didn't do it, there was a line longer than the one behind him, eager to take his place, accept her wages, and do her bidding.

He'd be lying if it didn't still gnaw at him that his choice set him at odds with the Vincent twins. He meant what he said to Charlie and Cassie yesterday, about leaving Eagle Bar. But twelve hours ago there'd been nothing more for him here.

"Got a flea in your ear, Preacher?"

Matthew turned to the miner standing behind him. "Likely so, standing here in front of you."

The comment earned him a friendly slap on the shoulder.

Isaiah pushed out the door and the men's voices lowered in anticipation. He presented his broad posterior toward Matthew, forcing him to shuffle backward into the unyielding line of bodies behind him. An uncomfortable position. Matthew's boots teetered on the edge of the small landing as Isaiah made the most of his bigness, taking his time posting the day's breakfast price.

But Matthew had fought his way here and he wasn't about to give up his position.

Isaiah turned slowly to face him, dark scowl in place. "Didn't expect to see you showin' your face around here, Preacher."

Isaiah's stalwart friendship to the Vincents

had been a growing annoyance, but he was a faithful protector. Yesterday Matthew hadn't appreciated the man's tenacity; today he was warming to it.

He didn't care for Isaiah's surly demeanor, but he couldn't fault the man's loyalty. "A man's got a right to eat." This morning he was determined to eat as much crow as Cassie could dish up, until she had no more.

"That may be so," Isaiah said, "but how's about you step aside and let these *workin'* men through to fill their bellies?"

Matthew jumped off the wooden step, sidled past the men, and sauntered over to the side of the eatery. Isaiah glared at him as Matthew settled down on his haunches to wait. "You're not going back to the kitchen."

"Hadn't even crossed my mind."

Isaiah snorted. "You best be keepin' that fact rollin' around in that thick skull of yours, or there'll be trouble."

"I intend to wait right here until the *working* men have eaten. If there are leftovers, I'd be pleased to have a plate." Matthew gestured toward the sign written in Cassie's feminine hand. "For the going price, of course."

Isaiah glowered down at him. His wide cheeks puffed out like bellows. He obviously had more words that needed to be said, but the men were hungry, grumbling and growling about the wait. Impatience won out. Isaiah turned his attention to the line of diners.

Matthew rocked back on his heels, his elbows leaning on his thighs as he took in the daily fare of Eagle Bar. A light breeze funneled off the hill and slithered through the alley, cool at the break of morning, but the day promised to be hot and dry like so many before it.

The river was getting lower and it made for talk on the street, particularly at the end of the street, at the tables of the Golden Palace. Men speculated on the chances of finding ore by digging deeper in the shrinking river bed; others brayed about the likelihood for a heavy July thunderstorm to unleash a torrent of water that would unearth hidden stores from upstream.

Matthew was bone weary of the constant squabbles, noise, and boomtown obsessions, but he was stuck here for now, and as he'd mulled over his new set of circumstances last night, he couldn't deny he was pleased with the turn of events.

He sucked in a deep breath of the dusty air, tinged with the fragrance of Cassie's baked beans, as men exited the Golden Spoon.

He had no settled idea what he was going to say to her. He hadn't spent the night plotting or rehearsing. He'd simply let the opportunity sink into his mind. Nevertheless, he was settled in his determination to push aside every protest she made against him. It might take days, but he wasn't doing much of anything else. His duties at the Golden Palace mostly involved the evenings. In a peculiar way, he was grateful for the mundane tasks of keeping Victoria's clientele genial and heading off any trouble before it started. It kept him busy enough so loneliness didn't have a chance to take root.

He took off his hat and rubbed his hand across his brow.

"We don't have nothin' left but the smell off a plate of beans. Might as well mosey back down the street where you come from."

Isaiah's gruff gloat brought Matthew to his feet. He was up at the doorway before the man could pull in the sign. "I could have a cup of tea," he said.

"Can't see you doin' that. No tea left, neither."

"All right." Matthew didn't like anyone knowing his business, but in order to get to

Cassie, he had to win over her guardian first. "How about you and I have a little jaw session." He gestured with his hat toward the river.

"Don't 'spect I have time for jawin'. With Charlie away, I need to get busy helpin' Miss Cassie."

"That's what I want to talk about." Matthew took in a great gulp of air and lowered his voice. He was throwing all his pile in on this one play, and he could only hope he held some winning cards.

"Pile on the agony all you want. Won't do you a lick o' good." Isaiah turned to go. Matthew grabbed his shoulder, leaned closer, and blurted, "Charlie asked me to help you look after Miss Cassie this time."

Isaiah shrugged off the hand but turned on his heel until they were nearly nose-to-nose. "Didn't say nothin' to me 'bout such goin's-on."

"I don't imagine I was supposed to say anything, but I didn't think I could do much good without you knowing." Matthew saw that Isaiah's eyes remained cold and dark as a January night. "You don't have to believe me."

"And I sure as shootin' don't."

"Fair enough, but I shook hands with Charlie on this, so I'm going to be around until he gets back. Just giving you fair warning." Matthew pointed toward the open door of the eatery. "We could help each other out."

"Don't see how, and I don't rightly know why Charlie would up and consort with a low-down liar."

Matthew clenched his jaw and cleared his throat. The crow went down mighty hard but he swallowed it. "You know what Charlie was up to, we both do. Eagle Bar is a powder keg. It'll only take one match to blow up this place. Might not happen all summer, could happen today. Charlie knows it, and he wants his sister safe. Simple as that."

"Ain't that simple."

"I could use your help."

"Sure you could, but Charlie and Cassie don't trust you as far as they could spit, and rightly so."

"Charlie trusted me enough to ask me to keep an eye on things with you while he's off getting supplies. I think he'd be smarter to cash it in and get out, but getting rich is a disease with most of these folks."

"Heard that sermon, Preacher."

Matthew balled his hands into fists, then forced them open to hang limply at his sides. He was worse than a dog chasing its tail and he wanted nothing more than to shoulder past the man and talk some sense into Cassie. "You can't be here every minute, and it might help to know we've got Miss Cassie protected all the time."

"She ain't gonna like it."

"She doesn't need to know."

Isaiah snorted. "You think she's not gonna know when she sees you larkin' about? She's smart as a steel trap."

"Let me worry about that."

"Isaiah!" Cassie appeared at the door.

"I was just comin' to do the dishes," Isaiah said.

"I see, but it appears you had to fend off a late diner first." Cassie gave Matthew a frown.

"Isaiah mentioned I was too late for breakfast, but I wondered if I might purchase a little milk and an egg or two." Hearing his halting poor excuse for a reason, Matthew kicked himself for not preparing last night.

"Seems to me you've got plenty of fresh supplies to eat down your way. We need to save every drop and crumb we've got until my brother gets back."

Heat crept up the back of his neck but he schooled his features into a pleasant mask. *She's smart as a trap, and I'm slower than a snail in a mud puddle.* "I'd best be leaving, then, but is there anything I can help you with before I go?"

"I wouldn't ask you if —"

Gypsy's bark ripped the door off the moment of conversation. A hurricane blast of growls and squawks slammed into them, an explosion of noise punctuated by the high-pitched inhuman scream of terror.

Cassie tore through the canvas tent, Isaiah at her heels. Matthew vaulted off the step and raced along the outside, his longer strides putting him on the scene first. He halted at the chicken yard, unable to hear his own thoughts as the birds screeched and flapped in brainless frenzy. Gypsy darted back and forth along the fence, howling. The goat's cry strangled to a gurgle as it hung from the branch of the live oak like a convicted horse thief. Its back hooves kicked in spasms and grazed the ground underneath, but its tether rope stuck fast in a snarl of bark and twigs. Each jerk of its suspended body tightened the rope around its neck.

Matthew charged toward Nugget, connecting with Isaiah's broad shoulder as both men breached the chicken yard fence and grappled with the dead weight of the choking goat. Cassie's hands came under his own as he hefted the creature. Another muscular body pressed into Matthew's as a pair of hands reached roughly over him, a sharp elbow colliding with the top of his head. He caught the glint of a blade slash through the rope as the goat flopped into their waiting arms.

He and Isaiah stretched the limp body to the ground and Cassie clawed off the remaining length of rope around its neck. She forced open its mouth and the same rough hand that had sliced the rope, grabbed the goat's tongue and blew into its nostrils.

Nugget sucked in a shuddering breath and lay there, sides heaving.

"Probably didn't do her any good, but she'll likely make it." Traveler's shaggy head nearly touched Cassie's hair as they leaned over the injured animal. The goat rolled its eyes and let out a pitifully thin cry. "Want me to carry her into the chicken coop?"

"Yes, please." Cassie struggled to her feet and Matthew gently took her arm to help her up. She glared at him, but at the miserable sight of tears running down her cheeks, he kept his steadying hand in place. She was shaking as if she had an ague, and the tremors ran from her arm to his.

"This is all my fault." She shook off his support and trudged after Traveler into the dim, low-roofed chicken coop. Matthew hovered on the outside, unsure of his place, cursing himself for letting the miner steal the moment of chivalry.

He could hear the soft cadence of Cassie's voice, crooning to the frightened animal. A moment later, Traveler ducked his head out and joined him and Isaiah, who had corralled the flapping, hysterical flock and dragged a couple of wooden crates over to barricade the hole in the rough fence.

Under Traveler's one-eyed baleful squint, Matthew picked up the length of rope lying on the ground, tossed it out of the yard and, with a couple of flips and tugs, removed the rest of the line from the tree. He swiftly coiled it up, but his hand froze when he touched the smooth cut at the end. He ran his fingers down to the other end, trying to convince himself he was seeing where Traveler's knife had slashed the goat free. He shook his head when he held the diagonal cut in his hand. The animal hadn't gotten loose on its own. Someone had been up to the worst sort of mischief.

Matthew kept hold of the rope as he stepped over the fence and out of the chicken pen. With slow deliberate steps, he walked over to the miner, grabbed him by the arm, twisted it up behind Traveler's back and marched him toward the back door of the kitchen. The disgruntled miner shoved him off, but Matthew rounded on the shorter man and shook the rope under his nose. "Seems mighty peculiar you just happening by when Cassie's goat gets hanged. Got me to thinking maybe it wasn't happenstance. What were you planning? Get in good with her by rescuing the poor creature after you were the one who almost got it killed?"

Traveler stared at him in silence for a moment before he hauled back and took a swing. Matthew saw the blow coming, ducked, took a step back, and heard his opponent grunt at the miss. Matthew raised his guard and edged closer. He'd wanted to teach the scoundrel some manners from the day of their acquaintance.

In a flash of faded-blue shirt and flying elbows, Isaiah squeezed between the two men. "Don't see how none of this would be helpin' Miss Cassie, right now." He turned accusing eyes toward Matthew. "Thought you said you wanted to protect her."

"That's what I'm doing," Matthew growled. "Step aside."

Isaiah shook his head fiercely. "We can't be turnin' on each other like a pack of low-down coyotes. Won't do no good if we want to find the one who'd do this to Miss Cassie." He balled his hands into fists and a deep flush rose under his dark skin. "Can't think of no man that low, even in these parts."

"I'm staring the culprit in the eye," Matthew said. "Step aside, Isaiah. I won't say it again."

"Fine by me, Preacher. You've had it comin' since you got here." Traveler cocked his grimy fist.

"I'll knock both your heads in, iffen I have to," Isaiah said. "Keep it down, unless you want Miss Cassie out here seein' all this foolishness." He laid an open palm on each of their broad chests and pushed.

"The goat didn't get tangled in the tree by itself," Isaiah said in a low voice. "But Miss Cassie's not to know."

"Agreed," Matthew said.

"She won't hear it from me, but I'll find the one who did this, mark my words," Traveler said.

"You mean find someone to cover your tracks."

"Get off your high horse, Preacher."

"Traveler didn't do this," Isaiah said. "We got to put our heads together and figure out what's goin' on hereabouts. You see anyone when you come runnin', Trav?"

The miner shook his head but his brow

furrowed. "I met Petey runnin' down the street, cryin' he was, sobbin' on every breath. He yelled to me, said when he come by here, he'd heard Gypsy and the way she was barkin' meant trouble. So I come on the run."

"And where's the boy now?" Matthew narrowed his eyes in suspicion.

"Said his grandfather was havin' some sort of spell. He hightailed it down the street, lookin' for medicine . . . don't rightly know. Like I says, I come runnin' here, and a good thing, too." He jerked a stained thumb toward the chicken pen. Matthew reluctantly turned his head to follow the man's gesture and saw the brace of rabbits slung in the dusty grass. "I was on my way here like I do most days. Don't recall you showin' your face around here in a coon's age, but you're here today. Mighty peculiar."

The suspicion didn't sit so well when it was hurled back in his clenched teeth, but Matthew shook it off. "Isaiah's right. I don't think we can let anyone know what really happened. It'll run all over town and get back to Cassie before supper."

Traveler glowered. "I'm findin' the no-account who did this, but I'll take it on the sly. I reckon I ought to cut up them rabbits first and set them to stew."

"I'll make sure the beans are all set," Isaiah said.

Matthew hesitated. If he wanted a place here, he needed to make one for himself. He strode toward the chicken enclosure with Gypsy at his heels, but stopped short before entering. The dog pressed against his leg and he petted the furry head. "Good girl." He stuck his head in the door. It took a moment for his eyes to adjust to the dim interior. The goat was on its feet. Cassie sat on the milking stool, stroking the animal's face and ears.

"She going to be all right?" Matthew asked.

Cassie jumped at his harsh whisper and the goat crowded into the corner.

"I expect so," came the soft reply. "I should've tied her out in a new spot this morning but, with Charlie leaving, I didn't bother. No wonder she got loose. I can see her now, standing up, stretching to get the leaves . . ." her voice broke.

"It wasn't anyone's fault." The lie came easy. The truth would be much harder to swallow when he found the culprit.

She didn't reply. Maybe she couldn't, but Matthew had a sudden flash of inspiration. "Anything I can do to help?"

"No, but thank you."

He wanted to say more, but talking was what got him in trouble on the first go-round. He slipped out without another word and walked silently past the kitchen door. He could hear the rumble of low voices inside, but kept walking toward the street. As much as it stuck in his craw to admit it, he admired the men quietly manning the kitchen.

He wove around stopped wagons, around men working, around clusters of men chewing tobacco, chewing the fat, and avoiding any sort of labor. He nodded at several hails but kept up his long stride until he reached the end of the street.

He glanced at Zelda's old place. In spite of Victoria's high aspirations, the building was little more than a glorified rooming house of fallen women, to put it politely. The Gilded Mansion was sturdy enough, but Victoria appeared to have lost interest in the building once she opened her Golden Palace. Barely gilded outside to cover up the degradation inside, it didn't appear to matter to the clientele.

Every night its "girls" were at the Golden Palace, hanging off the arm of one man or another as they plied them with drinks, and oohed and aahed over their gaming prowess. As the night wore on, they made a passing parade, one by one, back and forth across the street with a companion. Twice a week they put on a musical show with dancing and singing. It was all very civilized, just as Victoria had promised, but lately Matthew had seen signs of decay in the increasing frequency of arguments, brawls, and the ejection of dissatisfied patrons.

Like the boomtown itself, Victoria's Golden Palace was built on opportune corruption. It was only a matter of time before the corrosion of greed ate away its beams and brought about its fall. *Heard that sermon, Preacher.* Isaiah's voice from this morning echoed in his ears. Since when did he care about what folks did to each other?

It wasn't up to Matthew to change the way of things, and he was no longer fool enough to try. Only a handful of folks mattered to him in this place, and he'd do well to keep them from harm and leave the rest to their own devices.

He turned away from Victoria's recent addition and skirted her Golden Palace, quiet at this time of the day. Under the trees at the rear of the building, he foraged through the remains of boards, beams, and nail kegs. It was a credit to Mr. Logan and his men, who patrolled the grounds with revolvers at the ready, that her supplies remained untouched by scavengers and midnight thieves.

"What you up to on this fine day, Matthew?" He turned to find Judd approaching. "You ain't fixing to build another palace, are you?"

"No, nothing of the sort. It's a much smaller endeavor but, since you're here, I'd be much obliged for a hand."

"Depends." Judd took off his hat and scratched his head. "It appears I've got two offers today."

"How so?"

"Miss de Veres sent Ira down to the claim to fetch me. It wasn't like I was finding much color anyway, so I let him drag me up here. Turns out the lady herself wanted to see me."

"Victoria?"

"Yeah. She wants to put up that half-an-ark on the front of her place."

"The Lady of the Sea?" The unknown ship's figurehead had become a fixture lying propped up on the far side of the gaming hall. A scraggly patch of weeds adorned her hair, and in place of salt, dust encrusted her noble features. "When's that taking place?"

"Whenever you say, Matthew. Miss de Veres wanted to do it without you. Said she preferred it to be a surprise, but if it ain't handled proper, it could come down and crush a man. I've seen too many men die of plumb stupidity out here, and I'm not having one of them be on my conscience. Thought you and I could do it with a couple of strong hands to help, maybe in a couple of weeks or so." Judd leaned closer and his voice dropped to a soft timbre. "Truth is, I've found myself a nice little pocket on my claim. The water going down like it has, I dug into the banking and . . ." He spread his palms up and smiled. "But I couldn't let on to Ira, so I come to town for the afternoon."

Matthew clapped his friend on the shoulder. "Always knew luck would find you sooner or later."

"I was beginning to wonder myself. Now what about all this?"

Matthew took off his hat and wiped the sweat from his brow. "I'm building a goat shed of sorts." He gestured toward the far end of the street.

"For Miss Cassie? She's got the makings of a nice little farm up there. I could lend a hand for a couple of hours. Shouldn't take too long."

Matthew debated confiding in Judd, but the moment passed. Though he trusted his friend, the fewer people who knew the circumstances of the hanging goat, the better. As it was, he still had misgivings about Traveler's involvement.

"Ho! Ramsey! Miss de Vere needs to see you in her office. Pronto!"

Matthew jerked his head toward the open back door of the Golden Palace, where Mr. Logan beckoned.

"She wasn't too pleased about me putting her off for a few weeks, or about having you help hoist up the figurehead," Judd confided. "Seemed a mite peculiar to me that she thought we could do that big a job without you knowing about it. Maybe she was thinking of sending you off somewhere."

"Hurry it up!" Logan barked. "She isn't in the best of moods."

Judd poked him with an elbow. "What'd I tell you?"

"I'll set her straight and be back in a few minutes," Matthew said.

"Don't you nevermind. I'll get the rest of our goat pen pulled out of the pile and loaded on a wagon."

Matthew hurried toward Victoria's foreman.

"I expect Miss de Veres knows about this little job we're doing with her lumber, ain't that right, Matthew?" Judd's wry comment dogged his steps.

Matthew brushed by Logan as the man

muttered, "She's in her office."

Seated at her desk, Victoria's initial smile quickly sagged into a pout. "Matthew, I need you to have a talk with Chen Zhi and his boys."

"Seems to me, you usually handle all the gambling decisions."

"I do," Victoria cooed, and laid a finger on her lips.

Matthew silently groaned. She wasn't going to let him go without exacting her due. He slipped into the Windsor chair. "What is it you want me to say?" He wouldn't waste his breath pretending Victoria wanted more than a puppet.

"That is up to you. I'm sure you've had to put men in their place on your ships."

"And in what place are we putting Chen Zhi?"

She gave him a stern glare. "Cleverness is uncalled for here, Matthew. I'm trying to keep a friendly atmosphere inside the Palace. Zhi is not the problem, but he needs to keep his workers in their place. The Chinese are known for keeping their thoughts and feelings to themselves. That's why I hired them. They've been seen smiling when a man loses his pile. I've complaints they've been uppity to the miners, and this constant jabbering with each other in Chinese makes some of our patrons suspect they are plotting against them and rigging the games of chance."

"The games *are* rigged. That's why you hired Zhi, isn't it? I've heard he's one of the best."

"Matthew!"

He didn't have time for foolish debate. "I'll talk to him, but some of his men can't speak English."

"Then they'd best learn how, or shut up while they're working for me. If not, they'll be on the next wagon to the coast. Zhi is in the back room."

Matthew stood. "I'll talk to him before we open for the afternoon."

"I'll leave it in your hands. Go on, now, and take care of your business with Cassandra."

Matthew stared at her gloating face.

"You think I don't know everything that happens in this town?"

"Then you know I'm using some of the leftover scraps of lumber to build Cassie a goat shed."

"Of course."

She's bluffing. The thought roared into his head like a freight train. Only four people knew about Cassie's trouble this morning.

Victoria couldn't know about the goat hanging.

Or could she?

That thought struck Matthew like a slap in the face. There was one other person who knew about this morning's escapade . . . the one who set it into motion. "What do you know about Cassie?"

"Surely you know you're not the only one who employs eyes and ears."

"What do you mean?"

"It doesn't become you to pretend innocence or outrage, Matthew. Hiring that gangly stripling to spy on me *and* Cassie? And he's a redhead to boot. Hardly a boy one would fail to notice as he bumbles along. If it were me, I would choose one nobody would suspect. Someone who knows the secrets you whisper, then whispers them in my ear." She tilted her head, pursed her lips and paused. "If I was a woman who resorted to such behavior."

She knew about Peter? He clenched his jaw. What else did she know?

"You're a man of the world, yet you surprise me with your naiveté at times. I expect it might have something to do with your besotted interest in Cassandra. I do wish she had the intelligence to appreciate you the way I do. She fancies herself a farmer, more's the pity."

All Victoria's coyness, her barbed comments, her innuendoes swirled in his mind like chaff in a windstorm. He couldn't hold onto any one of them long enough to make sense of it all.

Finally, he tucked them away for later and seized upon the one right in front of him — Cassie. "Why would you think that? She's obviously a woman of refinement. Her livestock is necessary for her business. She's content in her kitchen, a fine hand at cooking, and she made a success of running the Golden Spoon. She and Charlie do it as smoothly as you run your Golden Palace."

"With one exception, Matthew. It takes *two* of them to do what *I* do. Cassie could not, and should not, run that business on her own. She needs her brother, or a partner of some sort."

"Seems to me no one can do it completely on their own. You've got Mr. Logan and Ira Graff and Chen Zhi, without whom I don't believe you'd be successful, especially here in Eagle Bar."

"I noticed you didn't include yourself in that list."

"I think we both know I've about reached the end of the road here."

Victoria's eyes grew wide. "Surely you

don't mean that, Matthew. We have yet to complete all the plans I have. The miners have been taking more color from the river every day. Why there's talk they're likely to hit a vein soon. Eagle Bar's just getting started, and I want us both to be a part of it. There're fortunes to be made here, and we have a stake in all of it."

Matthew got to his feet. "I'm not particularly interested in making a fortune."

"Spoken like a favored son born with a silver spoon."

He frowned and opened his mouth but she held up her hand. "I'm sure, as a Ramsey, you've heard it before." She came around the desk and touched his arm. "I apologize. I know how it stings when folks make assumptions, but it was said under the duress of thinking I might lose you. I hope you'll consider staying on, at least through the fall. After all, we still need to put up your Lady of the Seas." She squeezed his arm. "She deserves better than spending her last days lying in the dust."

Although he agreed on that one point, his irritation burned white hot behind the thinnest veil of courtesy. Ramsey silver spoon or not, he needed to get out of here before he forgot to be a gentleman. "Judd told me about the figurehead."

"I expected as much. The man is a passing carpenter, but a bumpkin in every way."

Matthew bristled. "If you mean he's an honest, hard worker and far above most of the men here, you're right. I'm honored to call him a trusted friend. Judd was right to wait on putting up the lady. No one could do it alone. With the uneven distribution of weight, it's going to be tricky to hoist it up and secure her properly. It'll take a while to set it up."

"I presumed as much, and I'd expect nothing less than the best when you're involved. Now go along with your little bout of chivalry."

She patted his shoulder, and he tore away from her and rushed to the door in need of air.

"And Matthew?"

He turned, hand on the doorknob.

"Cassandra needs more than a goat shed. Don't be afraid to help her see she needs you."

CHAPTER NINE

Never again would she tie up that goat, or any creature. Cassie didn't know exactly how to manage that vow, but if she had to keep Nugget locked in the chicken coop and bring her handfuls of green every day, so be it. When Charlie came back they'd put their heads together and figure something out. For now, the goat was safe and somewhat calm. It was hard to say if this upset would cause her milk to stop.

Cassie moved about the kitchen, surrounded by the homey smells of rabbit stew and baked beans, grateful for the efforts of Traveler and Isaiah. As she mixed together sourdough with flour and cornmeal, she silently acknowledged she should be thankful for Matthew Ramsey's actions today, as well.

When Charlie came with the fresh supplies, she'd bake a pie and ask Petey to take it down to him. Until then, she didn't have the inclination, or the time, to walk to the other end of the street and thank him properly.

Isaiah's deep, throaty tones drifted in the back door. Some days, he favored mournful songs he'd learned from his ma. Today his lamentation was in keeping with Cassie's somber mood as he put the chicken fence to rights.

His song ended abruptly as a wagon trundled up the alleyway toward their shanty.

Charlie!

Cassie ran out the doorway, knowing it couldn't be her brother. He'd left only hours ago. But who else would drive a wagon in here?

"Preacher." Isaiah's neutral greeting stopped her. Mouth agape, she stared as Matthew and a lanky-built miner jumped down from the wagon.

Matthew said, "I had some leftover lumber gathering moss under the trees. Instead of using it for kindling, I thought it might come in handy for a shed for Nugget."

Cassie opened her mouth but no sound emerged, as Matthew never took his eyes off her and never took a breath. He jerked his thumb toward his companion. "This here's Judd. He's got it in his head he wants to be a farmer. I brought him along so he can get a feel for it."

"That's so." Judd one-fingered the brim of his hat in greeting. "I've been a guest at your table for some fine eating, Miss Cassie. I'd be honored to repay the kindness a mite, if you're willing."

Cassie's gaze flicked from one man's smiling face to the other, her brain scrambling to keep up with the unexpected.

"Won't take but a minute," Judd said. "Been figuring on getting cattle, myself, but we'd need a milk cow or goat for the family. I've had a hand with cows, but never been acquainted with a goat."

He stepped closer, reached into his shirt pocket, pulled out a small daguerreotype and presented it to her like a gift. Gingerly, Cassie took the offering and looked into the faded sepia faces staring back at her. Instead of the usual sober-faced fare, the woman wore a small secret smile. Judd's lean visage was slightly downturned, as if he couldn't take his eyes off the woman and child long enough to properly face the photographer.

"Your family?" Her voice came out choked.

Judd nodded. "That's my Miriam and my little one, Rebecca."

"They're beautiful," she whispered.

"That they are," Judd agreed. "You must think me a fool or a wastrel to leave them. There're times, every day, I think that myself, and cuss myself out."

Cassie tore her attention from the picture and looked up into Judd's hawkish features, his eyes soft with a sheen of unshed tears. Miriam was a lucky woman. "I expect you're here making a stake for a better life for your family, just like the rest of us."

"Just so, Miss Cassie." Judd took the picture back and stared at the dear faces. "I want them to have a real home on our own land, nobody telling us to stay or go." He slipped the picture back in his pocket. "But come late fall, I'm going home no matter what I got in my poke."

"Charlie and I, too, I expect," Cassie said, even though she didn't rightly know where her home might be.

"I'm sorry, Miss Cassie. Me rattling on like a rusty gate hinge and you ain't got time for all this palavering." He spun around to the wagon where Matthew and Isaiah had already unloaded the building supplies.

Matthew clapped his friend on the back. "You ready to give those gums a rest and get started?"

Cassie stared at the two men and her mind flashed back to Charlie's first meeting with Matthew, when he'd been their friend. If their mother had never come to Eagle Bar, perhaps their friendship would have taken root like this one. *Perhaps.* The thought brought with it a sour truth.

"Wait!"

All three men turned to her, hammers and saws in hand.

Matthew's grin was still in place. "Sorry. I got so all-fired up with the building I forgot the most important thing. Where would you like Nugget's shed? I figure it ought to be fairly close to the chickens, but not so close to cause trouble. We're going to put up a sturdy fence, too. Probably won't get it all done today, but we can make a good start on it."

"Now who's jawing the day away?" Judd said.

Watching the masculine byplay, Cassie's heart ached for Charlie, but she pushed the longing from her and glared at Matthew. "Where did all this lumber come from? Or, more importantly, who?"

"It's just a pile of scraps from behind the Golden Palace." Cassie opened her mouth to protest but Matthew held up a hand. "Before you refuse, listen a minute."

"One minute, Mr. Ramsey." She pointedly glanced at the watch pinned to her bodice.

"These boards were left out back to rot. Victoria has no use for anything that's not new."

"That's so," muttered Judd.

"She didn't ask me to bring them. She didn't send me to you. I'm here on my own to help. You can accept that help, to keep what you own safe from harm, or you can be stubborn and refuse. Seems to me, you're a smart woman and would place the safe-keeping of your property above any personal dislikes." Matthew folded his arms across his chest, one fist clutching the hammer.

Cassie tore her gaze from his intense blue stare and looked over her "home." All she owned was here. Her future and Charlie's were tied to keeping the Golden Spoon prosperous for as long as they could. Matthew was right, but she'd never admit to it. She folded her arms across her waist and met his challenging gaze once more. "I can't accept it."

Judd sighed. "You ain't going to have me load that sorry pile of boards back on the wagon and truck 'em back down the street, are you, Miss Cassie? I was looking forward to turning my hand at a little building.

Some days the claim gets mighty lonesome and I have all I can do not to cash it in and head back to my gals. But I can't . . . not yet. This would help ease my heart some, if you'd be willing to let me work. I wouldn't say no to some dinner, iffen it'd make it set better for you."

Cassie glanced into Judd's open, honest face, and her resolve wavered.

Matthew said, "If you want, I'll go. I expect Judd and Isaiah can do a fine job without me, and I can send Petey along to help if he turns up."

"No."

The trio of men gaped at her. Their stunned expressions broke through the obstinate refusal and she held in a smile. "I meant, no, don't leave. I would be grateful for the shed and fencing, but I insist on paying for everything. And I'll give you your meals while you're here working for me."

"I accept your terms, although there's no need for it. And we don't expect you to use up your supplies to feed us," Matthew said.

Whether he intended it or not, after this morning's exchange, the barb about her supplies got under her skin. Cassie breezed past him, head held high, and strode toward the far side of the small cabin. The area had some shade and a fair amount of forage, although it was drying up under the California summer sun. "What about right here?"

"Looks fine," Isaiah said.

Looking into his wide, cheerful face, Cassie was ashamed. Isaiah spent all his time looking after her while Charlie was away, and it wasn't rightly fair or wise to make him shoulder the burden when she could help lighten his load.

"Maybe a little ways toward the hillside there." Judd interrupted her thoughts. "Might want to be able to see it from the back door of the Golden Spoon. Never hurts to be able to keep an eye on things, 'specially in these parts."

"I was thinking the same thing myself," Matthew said.

"I got some time afore we set up, Miss Cassie." Isaiah walked with her, back toward the wagon. "But if you need me in the kitchen, you just holler."

"I'm all set, Isaiah. You go on."

He hefted several boards on his shoulder, and strode off toward the other men.

Cassie paused at the kitchen doorway. She should go and check on Nugget again. All the hammering and building noise might make her all the more skittish. Cassie hurried over to the trail up the hill, plucked a handful of forage, and slipped back into the dim chicken coop. The goat lay in the corner, wide eyes glinting with the stream of sunlight when Cassie entered, but the animal got to her feet and calmly accepted the handpicked food.

Cassie absently patted Nugget's coarse, dusty coat as she listened to the male voices talking together while they worked.

She had taken to Judd, especially due to his devotion to his wife and daughter. The look when he talked of them was the same look Charlie got when he talked about Abigail. Cassie had a feeling it would never be like that for her.

Isaiah's deep tones rumbled. He said something she couldn't quite catch, and Matthew's laugh rang out. Cassie's cheeks flamed, and she ducked out of the coop, latched the door, and slipped back to the kitchen. She shouldn't be mooning about what was never meant to be. She had three men to feed, and she'd best be giving them something that wouldn't cut into her supper stores for the paying customers tonight.

She returned to her sourdough mixture, added an egg and some milk. She peeled a couple of onions and fried them up with a little fatback.

Singing snippets of old songs, she scooped out some of the tender pieces of rabbit in

Traveler's stew and set them aside. Before she fried up the dodgers, she put on some Indian pudding to boil, not fancy like a berry pie, but with a little milk it'd be just fine. She cut up some potatoes and onions to slow fry as well. She hummed a chorus as her feet waltzed across the familiar space and her hands were sure to the tasks.

As Cassie turned to get a dollop from the bacon grease crock, she swallowed her song in a gasp. Victoria stood just inside the doorway, watching her, and the older woman's melodic laugh picked up the lilt of Cassie's vanished tune.

"I didn't want to disturb you," Victoria drawled. "You looked so . . . dreamy . . . no, that's not it." She put her index finger to her pursed lips, an affectation that set Cassie's frayed nerves jangling. "I believe the word I'm looking for is *content,* if any woman can truly be content while tied to a kitchen stove." Victoria pointed at her daughter. "As I recall, someone used that very word when speaking of you earlier today."

Cassie grabbed a fistful of apron and shunted the sizzling frying pan off to the side of the cookstove. She took in a deep breath and whirled to face the intruder. "What are you doing here, Victoria?"

"Land sakes, Cassandra! If you use that tone and that toad-ugly scowl, you'll never get a man. Look at you, standing over a stove in your apron, hair like a wilted daisy, smelling of yesterday's beans, carrying on like a fishwife. You'll turn into a hag in a few years, if you don't change your ways."

Cassie squeezed her eyes shut in an effort to blot out the poisonous words that had already wormed their way into her head. This is what her mother did. As much as she tried to convince herself otherwise, Victoria's belittling ways always had the power to hurt her; but, by thunder, she wasn't going to give her the satisfaction of knowing that ever again.

She slowly opened her eyes, cocked one brow, and perused her mother from the toes of her black low-heeled boots to her maroon skirt; from her white blouse with the gigot sleeves to her matching hat tilted in a saucy manner over her left eye. Into the silence between them, the pounding of hammers and muted voices trespassed, a music of the life Cassie had chosen. It bolstered her shredded confidence like tonic. "Would you fancy me dressed like one of your Gilded Mansion hussies?"

Victoria's hand struck Cassie's cheek, quick and sharp as a scorpion's strike. It was delivered with enough venom and strength to crack Cassie's head to the side. She clutched her skirt to keep her hand from covering the stinging mark. She straightened her spine and gave her mother an icy glare. "You haven't changed a whit. Leave now. I have work to do."

"*You* are the one who hasn't changed, Cassandra. Without your brother here, you're itching to get rid of me, plain as plain can be. Afraid of your own flesh and blood, are you? Still timid, still waiting for Charlie to come and rescue you? Well, Charlie's not going to be here to do that anymore, is he? I wondered about all those supply runs he makes."

She put her hands on her hips and leaned slightly forward, but Cassie didn't budge. *Let her have her say.*

"He could come with three wagons loaded to the hilt," Victoria continued, "but he doesn't, does he? Good old Charlie, playing both ends against the middle. It's a favor to you, all his backing and filling, while he flits off to spend his time with his intended and leaves you here to do the work."

"Leave! Go back where you came from and don't return. You're not welcome here."

"Someday your precious brother won't return. When Charlie's gone, what will you do? He's chosen another over you, surely you see that. Will you live with the happy couple? His wife won't like you. In fact, she'll come to hate you and the closeness you share with your twin. If you live with him and his bride, you'll poison his marriage, and sooner than not, his wife will hate him for that and he'll hate you, too. You know I'm right."

"It's none of your concern. Perhaps I'll continue to run my Golden Spoon."

Victoria's unladylike snort filled the kitchen as she stepped backward. "Come now, Cassandra, we both know that will never be. You wouldn't last a day."

"And yet, here I am. I already do it, just like you."

Victoria wagged her finger in the air. "As you've pointed out on numerous occasions, you are not me. Might I suggest you take on a partner or, better still, seek marriage for yourself? It's the only way you'll survive Charlie's defection."

The harsh words were worse than her mother's angry slap because they had the ring of truth to them. Cassie had been haunted by the coming winter and the changes it would bring. She bit her bottom lip and let anger push out the fear. She raised her chin and glowered at the elegant woman before her. "If you're suggesting yourself as a partner, both Charlie and I would rather burn this place to the ground than have you touch one inch of it. The Golden Spoon is ours, Charlie's and mine. Regardless of what you say or think, it will remain so. Our plans are our business."

"You should marry, then. I'd hate to see my only daughter begging in the street . . . or worse."

"I can, and *do,* manage very well on my own."

"Is that why the men out back are using my supplies to help you out of your latest troubles?"

"They're being paid for their work, and I'll see you get fair price for all the lumber they use."

Victoria swatted away the promise. "Don't be a fool, Cassandra. I care nothing for those few sticks of wood. They're of no consequence except to be burned. Don't you see? You will always get the castoffs, the secondhand, because you can't stand up and demand the best for yourself. You'll always be waiting for someone to come to your rescue. I want so much more than that for you." She swooped in and grazed Cassie's cheek with her lips.

Before Cassie could pull back from the

hated touch, Victoria strolled to the door. "Get married, Cassandra. It's the only thing that'll suit you."

"It never suited you." The remark went unanswered, save for a hitch in her mother's stride before she disappeared through the door. Cassie panted in short, shallow breaths and leaned against the edge of the table. Now that her mother was gone, Cassie's legs were, too. She rubbed her temples in an effort to rid herself of her mother's cloying scent.

She tried to think. How had Victoria known about Charlie leaving today, about his upcoming marriage to Abigail? She shook her head. There were few secrets in Eagle Bar. A boom town fueled itself on gossip, rumor, the new strike, and the latest news. Why should their life be the exception?

Plenty of folks knew of Charlie's plans to wed. They'd been fools to think they could keep it from their mother's ears. What did it matter? There was nothing she could do to hurt Charlie and Abigail, far removed from the turbulent world of Eagle Bar.

Victoria's attacks on Cassie might be another story, but Cassie vowed to be a prisoner of her past no longer, to learn from this latest encounter and best her mother the next time they met; and Cassie knew there would be a next time. Charlie need not know about this.

One item hadn't come to light yet — Victoria's role as their mother. Cassie toyed with the idea of making it known around town, but to what end? She'd see what Charlie thought when he returned.

"Victoria. What a surprise." Matthew's voice drifted through the doorway. Cassie lurched to the stove, threw a couple of sticks in the wood box, and pulled the spider onto the cooking top.

She quickly wrapped the rabbit meat into the dough and pinched it tight just as Matthew strode into the kitchen. "Are you about ready to eat?" she asked, her head turned away as she focused on preparing the meal.

"Uh, yeah . . ."

She glanced over at his slow response. Matthew's head was tilted toward the doorway and it was a minute before he turned toward her with a sheepish grin. "Sorry. We can come in whenever you're ready. It smells good."

Cassie dropped the first dodgers into the pan, and the smell of sizzling crackle and the spit of hot fat filled the kitchen. Matthew stepped closer and leaned against the edge of the counter, just like Charlie and Petey were wont to do. "What was Victoria up to?"

Cassie glowered at him.

Matthew rubbed the back of his neck. "I don't want to know your business. I wondered if she was here to give you a hard time about the leftover lumber. That's betwixt her and me."

"No. It was her lumber in the first place, and I intend to pay her for it, top dollar." Cassie shifted her attention back to the dodgers. "If you'd call Isaiah and Judd, tell them to wash up, it's time to eat."

"Will do." Matthew hesitated in the door. "You look a mite rosy-cheeked. You feeling okay?" She sent him a frown, and he ducked outside without another word.

Cassie set plates on the end of the nearest trestle table in the dining area. By the time the men tromped in, she had a serving plate piled high with crispy hot dodgers, a pitcher of water, and a small bowl of fried potatoes and onions.

"Smells mighty fine." Petey slipped in on Isaiah's heels.

"Sure do." Isaiah licked his lips, rubbed his palms together and held out a chair. "Miss Cassie?"

"You sit and eat. I'll get something later."

"Oh no, Miss," Judd protested. "Come sit. Plenty here for all of us. 'Sides, we need to talk with you about what comes next. Ain't that so, Matthew?"

Matthew nodded.

The lanky miner gestured toward the proffered chair and remained standing — a gentleman in workman's rags. Cassie slipped into the seat and looked up under her lashes at Matthew. His clothes were dusty and stained like Judd's, but he wore them like the Sunday best he'd sported on the day they met. Matthew's arrogance was there in every confident gesture, yet he hadn't seemed so sure a moment ago in the kitchen. Perhaps he and Victoria had exchanged more than pleasantries outside. It suddenly occurred to her . . . Victoria, by nature, demanded men dance to her tune and hers alone. Perhaps Matthew had spoken the truth about his offer to help today, and his employer wasn't pleased he was at the Golden Spoon instead of dancing to her tune down at her Golden Palace.

Cassie looked across the table as the subject of her thoughts sat down. He nodded toward Isaiah, who bowed his head and said a quick blessing. "Can't wait to sink the old teeth into these dodgers." He passed Cassie the plate. She took one, and Isaiah helped himself to a couple before he passed it on to Petey.

"Powerful good, Miss Cassie," Petey echoed.

"How's your grandfather, Peter?" Matthew asked between mouthfuls.

"He's tolerable."

"Traveler told us he had some sort of spell," Cassie said, watching the boy shovel in the food without hardly swallowing as he sat on the edge of the bench, ready to bolt.

"He come out of it right quick. Likely something he et." His red hair flopped about his temples as he turned bright eyes on Cassie. "Nothing you made, Miss Cassie, but sometimes we get leftovers out at the claim."

"Well, I'm glad to hear he's better." She rose and fetched clean bowls and the Indian pudding, and the room went quiet save for the clink of spoons scraping the bowls.

Judd stood and picked up his dirty dishes. "Mighty fine, Miss Cassie. Thank you. This meal is more than enough pay for me."

"No. I expect to pay proper wages for all the work you've done."

"It ain't much work."

"We've enjoyed it," Matthew agreed.

Even Isaiah nodded.

"I looked in on your goat," Judd confessed. "Hope you don't mind. She's a mite skittish. I can boil down a little willow bark. Might ease her throat a mite. There're some scrubs growing over by my claim across the river."

Matthew stood abruptly. "I told Judd about Nugget getting tangled up in the rope." He caught her eye for the first time since they'd finished eating.

"That why Gypsy was barkin' something fierce this morning?" Petey stared at Cassie, his thin face sober.

"Yes, it was my fault. I tied her up poorly," Cassie said, guilt washing back over her. "She got loose, jumped up to eat the oak leaves, and got tangled in the branches. She nearly hanged if it hadn't been for Traveler, Isaiah, and Matthew."

"Nugget didn't really get hurt or nothin'?"

Cassie touched the boy's thin arm. "No, she's going to be all right."

"I'd like to help with the pen if I might, Miss Cassie."

"We could use the extra hand." Matthew clapped the boy on the shoulder as Petey followed Judd and Isaiah out the back door.

Matthew lingered behind. "I apologize for telling Judd about the goat getting caught in the tree. We got to talking while we were building and it slipped out. Isaiah wasn't too pleased."

"It's okay," Cassie said. "I don't mind him knowing. Judd's a good man."

"One of the finest," Matthew agreed. "Would you care to come out and inspect the work, Miss Vincent?"

Matthew strung out the building project for three more days, enjoying the delight he pictured on Cassie's face whenever she walked in the small building, or watched them working on the fence.

He and Isaiah added a couple of gates, and even a window opening. Judd had gone back to his claim but, true to her word, Cassie made sure he left with a full belly and proper pay.

Peter showed up at the Golden Spoon for breakfast and waited for Matthew's arrival, chomping at his elbow every day. The red-haired stripling enjoyed the building work, but shied when he was placed anywhere near the goat.

The boy was not destined to be a farmer but, as he chattered away, Matthew knew a growing desire to help Peter with his future, perhaps see him placed on a ship. Peter was an eager helper. Not much of a hand at turning out a straight cut or driving in a straight nail, but he was young and growing up right before their eyes.

Even Isaiah had warmed to Matthew's daily presence. Matthew contrived little additions to the simple project and looked forward to each day — something he hadn't done in a while.

The nights were another matter. The raucous atmosphere at the Golden Palace rose like a fever with each passing hour. Eagle Bar's street clogged with new faces and jostling, impatient bodies, all afflicted with gold fever. Word had gotten out there was a fortune to be made on the river, and irritations and tempers exploded as crowds of men squeezed in, demanding their share.

Matthew fingered the split in his tender bottom lip, a stinging reminder of his nighttime task. The card games, particularly, had taken a cutthroat turn. He'd caught an elbow last night by underestimating the strength and anger of a man who had nothing left to lose at the poker table. It wouldn't happen again.

Every night, Victoria waltzed through the throngs of men, fluttering about her gaming tables like a butterfly, oblivious to the rising tide of wrath and futility. Chen Zhi's men handled it all with unperturbable patience and unreadable faces, but, just today, Mr. Logan had sent Ira to the coast for more workers. Matthew suspected that meant not only more muscle, but more girls, although Victoria was closemouthed about the goings-on at her Gilded Mansion.

More and more, Matthew escorted men out to the street, their pockets empty, their heads filled with tarnished golden dreams dulled by cheap liquor. In the early morning hours, when he lay in bed, he wrestled with the idea of leaving Victoria's employ.

The peculiar part of it was, he couldn't quit because of Cassie. News of his leaving the employ of Victoria's Golden Palace and Eagle Bar would ruin the fragile friendship he hoped to rebuild with Cassie and Charlie.

A dozen times a day, he wondered why Charlie had asked him, of all people, to watch over his sister. It was easy to tell Isaiah that two protectors were better than one in this infernal snake pit, but it didn't satisfy Matthew's own doubts. Still, he was grateful for the opportunity to mend his fences, and he felt guilty acknowledging that, without the near tragedy of the goat hanging, Cassie would never have let him come back into her life.

He'd tried to figure out who would inflict such a heartless cruelty. He constantly searched the faces of the desperate men who

311

swaggered into the Golden Palace, his ears tuned to every complaint, every boast; but he'd learned nothing of value.

Yesterday, he'd told Peter the real story. He'd grappled with revealing what he knew to anyone outside their closed circle, but he trusted the boy. If there was one person who could sniff out the culprit, it was Peter. The youth knew his way around Eagle Bar, understood the baser motives of mankind, and knew how to play off the vices and fears of his fellow man.

Time was running out. Matthew knew solving the crime would go a long way to getting himself back in Cassie's good graces. He had one last card to play, if he chose to do so.

He paced along the outside wall of the Golden Palace, the afternoon sun casting a dark square shadow in his path, and glanced up at the building rising above him, haloed in the California sunlight. A surge of pride swelled in his chest every time he took in the sturdy lines, the plumb walls, and the beauty of a well-built business. The fleecing of men that transpired inside each night should have tempered his enjoyment of the exterior, but he couldn't deny the truth. Helping build Victoria's dream had set his eyes on the need for a course correction.

Victoria reminded him, at least once a day, of his promise to put up the figurehead. He could picture the noble Lady of the Seas, riding under the gable, looking out with disdain on those who entered. The perfect complement to the majesty of the Palace.

He picked up his hammer and added a board to his growing scaffolding. He hadn't seen Judd since they'd worked on Cassie's goat pen. Surely a sign that his friend was finding some good color.

As his hammer rang out, Matthew's mind surged ahead to a time when the gold dried up, the piano in the Golden Palace was silenced, Judd was gone to his farm, the Vincent twins to their life elsewhere . . . and what of him?

After running off half-cocked to preach balderdash to men who were of better character than he'd ever been, Matthew was at a crossroads. He could eat yet more crow and acquiesce to his father's plan of running the west coast business with his brother, Will.

He could captain one of the Ramsey clipper ships, the fastest and best-made in the world.

The idea of standing on deck, braced against the roll with nothing but ocean in all directions, fired his blood like it always had, but for how long? This restlessness within wouldn't subside with merely a change in scene, and traveling from port to port didn't hold the appeal it once had. For now, he might as well lay his hands to the task before him, building the makeshift scaffolding to support the unwieldy figurehead so when Judd came up for air, they'd be ready.

Matthew scanned the street. Mr. Logan raised a hand in acknowledgment as he drove a wagon down the way. The gentleman seated beside him had become a regular patron at the Golden Palace poker tables. Matthew's gaze barely followed the progress of his coworker. Instead, he watched for a familiar figure.

Traveler was unpredictable in his comings and goings. Matthew had kept an eye out for the prospector ever since they'd nearly come to blows. Much to his frustration, Traveler had managed to slip by him, unnoticed for days; yet he'd obviously been by Cassie's with his daily fare of rabbits and, lately, a rattlesnake or two.

Out of the corner of his eye, Matthew glimpsed the dirty hat and stained beard. Traveler stopped to put in a chew as he leaned against the hitching post. Matthew dropped his hammer and sprinted down the street, skirting the clog of bodies, until he reached the general store. Traveler squinted one eye and spat in the dirt at Matthew's feet.

Matthew gestured toward the Golden Palace. "We need to talk."

"What you likely mean is, you're about to chew my ear off."

"Won't take more than a minute." Matthew turned and retraced his steps to the scaffolding. He kept his stride purposeful, back straight, never glancing over his shoulder but straining to hear Traveler's footsteps behind him. With all the hubbub in the street, it was nigh impossible to hear one's own thoughts, let alone foot traffic.

He stopped in the shade and nearly jumped out of his skin when Traveler's voice rasped close in his ear. "I don't make it a habit to frequent this end of the street, so say your piece and be quick about it."

"I was just wondering if you'd dug up anything on Cassie's goat? I've been poking around but haven't come up with nary a scrap."

"Is that what got you the fat lip, pokin' around in somethin' ain't none of your business?" Traveler gave him a lopsided sneer.

"That's about right, but it didn't get me any closer to finding out who did this to

Cassie. Have you heard anything?"

Traveler shook his shaggy head. "Everyone's been out to the claims. 'Course that's mostly because of the color and all the new faces. Nobody's lettin' their tongue run loose these days." Traveler looked Matthew in the eye. "It's hard to get answers out of fellers when you can't spread around what happened. You can't up and say, 'You the varmint what hung Miss Cassie's goat?' " He scratched his grizzled beard. "Been listenin' to folks, waitin' for someone to brag on it."

"Me, too."

"Appears you might have a better chance at hearin' claptrap, what with all the drinkin' and carousin' that goes on around these parts."

"I thought as much but, so far, nothing." Matthew cocked his hat back and ran a dusty hand over his sweaty hairline.

"I'd like to have it cleared up a'for Charlie comes home. I'm puttin' out a trap of sorts, waitin' to see who trips it."

"What do you mean?"

"I'll let you know if I need you and Isaiah to help me catch the skunk and put him out of his misery." He glared at Matthew. "That's supposin' you got it in you, Preacher."

"No mercy on this one."

The comment earned Matthew a friendly punch in the shoulder. "Gotta git. This palace gives me the fidgets. Worse than a jail! Lures folks in and they don't know enough to leave until it's too late." Traveler spun on his heel and trudged off in the direction of the Golden Spoon.

Matthew watched him go. Any lingering suspicion over Traveler's involvement had disappeared. He still didn't trust the lout in anything, except where Cassie was concerned. The man might be crude, but there was an iron rod of loyalty in him.

Cassandra Vincent inspired loyalty in all of them. When they parted company after building the shed, Judd had mentioned his high regard for her. She was surrounded by good friends, diverse men of fidelity, peculiar in such a place. Maybe because it was so far away from civilized life. Cassie represented the wife, daughter, or mother they'd each left behind.

Matthew shook off the sentimental speculation. All that mattered was that Isaiah, Traveler, the Wang cousins, and even Peter, would fight to the death for her. He included himself on that list, even though he knew Cassie did not. And what of Charlie? He was her safe refuge but, more than that, her heart and soul. When Charlie returned, Matthew was certain the twins would have little truck for him once again.

Although Cassie pined for her brother when he was gone, Matthew begged for his absence for a day or two more, so he might spend precious moments at the Golden Spoon and reinsert himself into her life. Now that the building and fence were complete, he'd been trying to convince Isaiah he could invent little projects for Matthew to do for Cassie, in order to allay her suspicions over his presence. That would allow Isaiah to return to the river and help the Wangs work their claim, but the man was unwilling to budge from his post as Cassie's protector.

Matthew sighed and set about sawing more boards for the scaffolding. He'd nearly finished his task when Victoria sashayed around the corner and faced him. "My goodness, Matthew. You've been pounding out here for hours. That infernal banging is all I've been able to hear in my office." She swept a dramatic hand across her pale brow. "Is all this really necessary?"

"If you want us to put up the Lady of the Seas in proper fashion, I believe it is."

"And when will that occur?"

Matthew shook his head. "I can't rightly

say. Not until Judd comes into town again."

"That means you'll be staying on for some time." She placed her hand on the scaffolding, then pulled away at the rough splinters of the boards. "I'm willing to put up with this eyesore you've created, though I do wish you'd constructed it out back."

His employer's smug tone was nothing new, but it always served to irritate him. Best to overlook it. He didn't care to have a long conversation with Victoria today. "I wanted it close to the job site. No sense moving it all over creation." He rapped the structure with his fist. Good and sturdy; likely overbuilt for the task, but he'd needed something to direct his energy. "Judd might turn up tomorrow and we'd have that figurehead up in a day."

"He won't. Judd and all the miners who've been here a while are hunkered down by the river, working day and night to fill their pokes before these newcomers horn in and take their share. Can't say as I blame them." She wrinkled her nose and turned toward the busy street. "But new faces are good for business."

Matthew silently tapped his toe in the dust, but Victoria lingered. "You never did tell me what you were doing up at the Golden Spoon the other day," he said.

She rounded on him, one dark eyebrow arched high under the crown of her fancy hat. "I could ask you the same thing, Matthew."

"You know perfectly well I was working, building a goat shed. I thought maybe you came up to keep an eye on me."

"Land sakes, no. Although, both you and Cassandra could use my advice. That is, if you intend to have a future together."

"It's a little premature to go down that trail."

"You and she are already halfway down that trail, Matthew, but you're both too blind and stubborn to admit it. You could do a lot worse for yourself than Cassandra Vincent."

Matthew narrowed his eyes at the speculative gleam in hers. "I believe it was you who told me earlier this week that Cassie didn't have the intelligence to suit me, with her low aspirations of being nothing more than a farmer."

Victoria wrapped her fingers around his forearm and clamped it a pinching squeeze. He didn't wince or pull away, but focused on the beetle-browed anger eclipsing her usual coy expression.

"If that's all you heard me say, perhaps I was wrong about *your* intelligence. I believe

I said, you must prove to Cassandra that you're the man she needs, before you both turn gray and creep into your dotage, hopelessly alone."

Matthew shook off her clutch and glowered at her. "I don't believe either one of us asked for your advice." A sudden thought struck him. "Is that what you were doing at her place? Giving Cassie courting counsel regarding me?" He folded his arms across his chest and dared her to break eye contact.

Victoria tilted her head, the coquette once again in place. "If I thought it would accomplish anything, I'd give the girl an earful, but I know better. She never listens to anything I say."

"And why is that? What is it that I don't know about you and the Vincent twins? You don't work that hard at keeping a secret unless there's a dire secret to keep."

"Matthew, what an imagination you have. Must come from mooning over that girl. It's made you soft in the head."

"I knew you'd deny it, but there's something you're not telling me and I aim to find out before I leave Eagle Bar."

"Then I have no worry you'll be leaving Eagle Bar anytime soon, since there's nothing for you to discover. You'd be far better off to put your talents to work courting."

Matthew sucked in a deep breath. His tentative friendship with Cassie required kid gloves, but Victoria was a different kettle of fish. Throughout their acquaintance, she'd made a habit of alternately belittling him and bolstering him, treating him like a dull schoolboy. No longer. "You think I haven't noticed the resemblance? You're some sort of relative. An aunt, perhaps?" Her dark eyes widened, then flashed with some sort of emotion, anger maybe, before she schooled her features into a pleasant mask once more. "You can deny it if you want."

"And I most certainly do."

"But I'll figure it out for myself soon. Cassie and Charlie hate and mistrust you, *that* much is plain."

"By all accounts, they have a strong dislike for you as well. But that doesn't make you a long-lost relative."

"No." He was enjoying this foray into the unknown. For once, he had Victoria on the defensive. He reigned in his gloating delight and chose his next words with care. "I'm not a relative, but I suspect maybe I am in league with their despised aunt. It's a mighty peculiar thing. Both Charlie and Cassie were downright amiable until I took up with you. I think I might've picked up a touch of your tar and feathers without knowing it."

"I didn't search you out to have my character slighted."

Matthew bowed his head and changed tactics. "I apologize. That was not my intention. Perhaps if you told me the truth I could help."

"There is no truth to tell. We've got a business to run and more important matters to discuss than your flights of fancy. We have a problem at the gaming tables. Surely you've noticed?"

He raised his eyebrows and she clucked her tongue like a mother hen. "Of course you haven't, because you've had your mind elsewhere. I count on you to be an island of calm, forceful reason on the floor every night." She lightly touched his sore lip.

He flinched and took a half step back to put a little distance between them. "And so I am." Her personal gesture and censure pricked his pride and deflated his swell of premature victory.

"I have no complaints, thus far." She swayed closer and gently patted his forearm. "You are aware of Mr. Bowen? The dandy who arrived a few days ago, light-skinned, a quadroon or some such, I imagine, white ruffled shirt, spade beard, top hat."

"I know the gentleman," Matthew said. "He's an expert poker player."

"He's a card sharp." Victoria spat the accusation, her face rigid with indignation. "He can best any of my dealers."

"He knows the game."

"Under his fine dress and British manners, he's nothing but a scoundrel and a cheat. He's taken me to the cleaners three nights in a row, and I won't have it happen again."

"How do you intend to stop him? Maybe you could offer him a job?"

"I never hire men I don't trust," she said with a sneer, then settled into a pout. "I sent him out with Mr. Logan this afternoon as a favor. It seems Mr. Bowen wanted to go to the claims to seek out a miner who lost a goodly sum to him at the poker table last night."

Matthew fingered his cut. "I threw the man out."

"Well, you should've gotten payment before you showed him the door."

"Can't get blood out of a turnip. He was tapped out, even threw in his claim on the last hand."

"Ah! That explains Mr. Bowen's interest in going to the river. It might prove useful to us."

"In what way?" Matthew frowned. This was exactly what was wrong with his life, constantly being dragged into Victoria's squabbles and schemes, no more than a glorified errand boy. Regardless of what happened when Charlie returned, it was time to make a clean break with Victoria and move on with his life. "How does that prevent Mr. Bowen from coming to the Golden Palace and winning again tonight?"

"It doesn't. But it does give me some ammunition."

"How so?" Matthew mentally squirmed at the excited glow in her eyes. That always boded ill for someone. All the more reason to get out before he became a Mr. Logan.

"It takes but a moment to discredit one's reputation, particularly in a place like this. A whispered word here or there in the right ears and I believe our problem with Mr. Bowen will be solved tonight."

She linked arms with Matthew and nearly skipped toward the Palace door. "I'll need you and Mr. Logan to keep a sharp eye out for that miner who did this to you." Again, she grazed his lip with her finger.

Matthew fought the urge to turn his head away. "If he comes around, I'll make sure he doesn't get in."

Victoria laughed. "You talk like this is your

Golden Spoon with its silly schoolgirl rules. Oh no, Matthew. I *want* you to let him in. I intend to offer him free drinks and let human nature take its course."

"You're asking for trouble."

"And Victoria de Vere always gets what she wants. You ought to know that by now." With a twitch of her skirts, Victoria strolled like a queen through the main saloon and left him at the door.

Matthew sat down at one of the tables, steepled his fingers, and propped his head against his folded hands. The smell of stale smoke, tobacco juice, whiskey, and lingering body odor permeated the air, fostering a rancid taste in his mouth. He considered heading down to the claims, finding the miner, and warning him against showing his face around town, but he presumed the man sported a shiner and several bumps and bruises from their encounter last night and would be in no mood to listen to him, or to reason.

Whatever came of Victoria's schemes, he and Mr. Logan would handle the trouble tonight. Then he was determined to move on.

As his weary head sagged into his hands, he wished it over and done, but the ticking clock on the wall deliberately counted the moments in slow and measured beats, echoing his own sluggish heart. Maybe he should take a rest in his room upstairs.

Though his body craved respite, his mind would never allow it.

Instead of thinking on pleasantries — Cassie and the future — it was Victoria who, with her constant barrage of cunning craftiness, slammed the door on that dream and stood in his way.

Tonight's malevolent plan was just another web she had woven in order to trap some unsuspecting stranger into doing her dirty work. She used gossip to her advantage, planting seeds of mistrust, self-doubt, and fear in all she encountered. It was the secret to her success here, and he himself had fallen victim to her manipulations.

He wasn't proud of the way she could twist his thoughts until he no longer recognized them as his own. But her words inside his head banged away like a hammer on a nail until he could do nothing but listen to them. Did Victoria really know all she purported to know?

He turned his mind from the potential troubles brewing this evening to Charlie's imminent return. Perhaps he'd been approaching Cassie's problems from the wrong direction. Victoria always dangled a little information to keep him interested, but she knew more than she was telling. She just might be the key to setting things straight.

But if she was privy to what happened to Cassie's goat, how had she obtained that information?

No one in Cassie's circle of protectors would let it slip.

Victoria might know about the incident, but could she know it had been an intentional act? Could she know who'd actually done it?

She intimated she knew everything. She could best most men at her card tables. Her expression never gave away her true feelings or intent. With Mr. Logan and Ira Graff as her eyes and ears, Matthew didn't doubt the wealth of information at her fingertips — information she tucked away to use as a deadly weapon against her growing detractors.

Victoria's low, throaty intimation wormed its way through Matthew's speculation like smoke snaking around the confines of the Golden Palace. *If it were me, I would choose one nobody would suspect . . . a close friend, companion, spouse. Someone who knows the secrets you whisper, then whispers them in my ear.*

Matthew rubbed his face. *"If I was a woman who resorted to such behavior."* She had him exactly where she wanted him, like a cart hitched to a runaway horse.

Victoria's intent was to make him question those closest to him. Matthew frowned. No one connected to Cassie would have anything to do with Victoria, but her soft words yanked on his doubts.

She probably got a fair share of secrets from her girls, who likely got an earful in their profession, but such information would have little to do with the twins. Perhaps it was Chen Zhi who silently observed all the goings-on in the Golden Palace, except he spent little time away from the confines of the Palace. He and his men never fraternized with the other workers, especially since Matthew had delivered Victoria's ultimatum. They kept to themselves in a small building out back, where they congregated during the day doing who knows what.

Shadows crept in over the chairs, shrouding his feet as his coworkers shuffled in and began their nightly duties. Matthew didn't move, even as Mr. Logan opened the door and glad-handed the first patrons. He had his men in place by all doors, collecting firearms and refusing entrance to those who wouldn't surrender their gun.

A few moments later, Mr. Logan swung a chair out from the table, straddled it, and settled himself facing Matthew. "You look as poor as old Job's turkey, Matthew. You worried about getting rid of that one?" Mr. Logan pointed with his chin toward the door.

Mr. Bowen entered with one of the Gilded Mansion girls hanging off his arm. He sent her to the bar and strutted toward the tables, pausing to strike a match on his sole and light the long nine protruding from his full lips.

"Could be trouble," Matthew murmured.

"He *is* trouble. Every time one of his kind fills his pockets with winnings, he empties yours and mine. Victoria's never going to take the loss."

At his sharp tone, Matthew glanced into the other man's face and leaned forward to hear over the hubbub surrounding them as the crowd swelled and the room grew stuffy.

"You think I want to stay here in Eagle Bar, cleaning someone else's boots all my days?" Mr. Logan scowled. "You're all set on leaving soon, I know the signs. I've seen a dozen of your type drift through. You think you're too good for this, but I don't know a man alive who wouldn't chafe.

"I'm right behind you. I'm looking to score big and get myself a stake, leave this dust hole, and start my own place as good, if not better, than this one." He bent closer and laid his clenched fist on the tabletop. "Tonight is my chance. If we play this right, we come out smelling fine as a garden rose and we'll be rewarded. I'm going to see to it."

Matthew shook his head. Mr. Logan might think he knew the lay of the land, but he was only right about one thing. Victoria would line her own pockets and never take the loss. She'd never give Mr. Logan, or anyone but herself, a "reward." "I wouldn't get my hopes up if I were you."

"You just hang back and let me manage things. No heroics until I give the word, you got that?"

Matthew stiffened as he recognized the disgruntled miner from last night's altercation shoulder past Mr. Logan's men at the door. The man stomped into the saloon, swinging his head from side to side like an angry bear, his surly face distorted by a bruised cheek and black eye.

Mr. Logan clamped Matthew's forearm against the table. "Let me handle this." He levered to his feet and neatly returned the chair to its place at the table before he strode to the bar. He clapped the new arrival on the back and bought him a whiskey.

Their exchange was caught up in the eddy and flow of dozens of conversations, but Matthew didn't need to hear the words. Mr. Logan's smiling face and the next glass of whiskey, and the next, said it all. He leaned back in his chair and, with a trained eye, kept his ears open and alert to the other patrons.

As was his custom, Matthew finally forced himself to vacate the seat and stroll through the noisy room. When he glanced at the bar, he wasn't surprised to see Mr. Logan and his companion had disappeared. In spite of Mr. Logan's warning, Matthew quickly made his way to the gaming room. He reached the doorway just as the shouting started.

Mr. Bowen was on his feet. The miner held a knife in his left fist. The click of Mr. Logan's pistol stopped nearby conversation as chairs slammed back and men dove under the tables. "Preacher." Mr. Logan's voice cracked like a whip. "Take the knife."

Matthew circled behind both men and stood beyond reach of fists and elbows. He calmly held out his palm, muscles tensed and tingling, ready to pull back at the first lunge. "You ain't seen trouble 'til you've met my California toothpick," the miner said. "Here to cause more trouble, Preacher?"

"No." Matthew's stern command rang out. "Give me the knife and leave peaceably. I'll see you get it back later." He beckoned with his fingers.

The miner growled in his throat but, in one swift movement, he flipped the knife, slapped the hilt in Matthew's waiting palm and pushed past him, back to the bar.

"I'll make sure he leaves," Matthew said.

"I'll take care of it," Mr. Logan said. "You make sure everybody gets back to business."

Matthew slipped the knife into his boot and watched Mr. Bowen coolly take his seat and resume the deal. The trouble had passed with hardly a ripple in the conversation. It had been defused almost too easily.

"Where's Miss de Vere tonight?" The speaker towed Matthew to a nearby table and took a seat. The older gent, with carefully combed hair and mustache white as a summer cloud, crossed his legs and leaned back, smiling up at him. He was cleaner than most, and the glint of a gold tooth winked in the lamplight. Matthew couldn't recall seeing him around town, and the question caught him off guard.

Where *was* Victoria? She usually made her

grand entrance well before now. She was always moving through the crowd, garnering attention like a bee gathering pollen, from the very start of the evening until closing time, encouraging her patrons to spend their money.

Matthew glanced toward the stairs but the old man reclaimed his attention. "She promised me a private game of poker. She's a worthy opponent."

"You know Miss de Vere?"

"We're well acquainted. Met awhile back in San Francisco. She invited me here to see her Golden Palace." He looked around the room and whistled. "She wasn't throwing the whitewash. It's everything she said it would be."

Matthew rubbed the back of his neck, trying to shake the unease settling on his shoulders like a wet wool blanket. "I'm sure she'll be along soon." He turned his focus back to the poker table behind him, but the man at his elbow nudged his arm. "If you'd let her know I was asking for her, it'd be much appreciated. Name's Ulysses Morehead. She'll know."

Matthew gave him a curt nod, but it was too late. Mr. Logan had Bowen by the arm and was marching him toward the door. "Miss de Vere runs an honest game," Mr.

Logan announced to the whole room. "The Golden Palace has no truck with cheats."

Bowen calmly left the room. The last Matthew saw of him, he'd adjusted his top hat, paused to collect his sidearm, and walked through the door, head held high.

Matthew hurried to the bar, then glanced out the doorway to the darkened street but saw neither Bowen nor the other man. Back in the gaming room, it took Matthew several moments to search and work through the crowd, but to no avail.

Victoria was always easy to spot among the rough throng of men. She wasn't here tonight and it didn't take much to figure out why. He strode down the hall to her private office and walked in without knocking. Mr. Logan sat in the Windsor chair across from Victoria. Both had a drink in their hands.

"What did you do?" Matthew asked.

"Good news, Matthew." Victoria smirked. "Mr. Logan just informed me we will no longer have to worry about Mr. Bowen. One of the other players at his table accused him of cheating, and he knows he's no longer welcome here."

A high-pitched screech skewered the night air, hurtling in the window like a sharp spear. Matthew bolted from the room and down the hall. He pushed past idle men, leaving a path of grunts and curses in his wake. He hit the door and dashed toward the corner.

The woman's scream had dwindled to a pitiful wail. He recognized her as Bowen's escort, but his mind raced ahead. He rounded the side of the Palace and halted, his forward motion carrying him into the bottom of the scaffolding. He steadied himself on the rough boards as his eyes caught motion above.

A small group of men gathered a short distance away, hurling insults and catcalls. Mr. Bowen hung from a noose thrown over the framing Matthew had completed just hours before. Light from the Palace windows shifted in eerie shadows as the hanged man squirmed, kicking one foot. The other leg was jammed between two boards, supporting the body on his left side.

Matthew scaled the boards faster than he'd ever climbed the rigging at sea. "You there! Hold him up," he barked to the cluster of ruffians below. He grabbed the knife from his boot and slashed. The rope gave way at the first cut.

Mr. Logan and a couple of his men caught the dead weight. Matthew leaped down and grunted as his knees buckled. He was up in a flash and clawed the rope off Mr. Bowen's swollen neck.

Mr. Logan leaned over the bruised, purpled face. "Still breathing. Get him over to the Mansion, have the girls clean him up."

"Free drinks for all of you at the bar." Victoria stood next to the outside wall, her pale face stark, her eyes bright as she made the cheerful announcement.

"Matthew, go see what you can do for him." Victoria gestured toward the two men carrying the body across the street. "Mr. Logan, get some men out here. Haul this away and burn it."

"Wait." Matthew stared at her. She pointed up at the collection of boards. CLAIM JUMPER was scrawled in crude charcoal letters on the scaffolding.

"We ought to go after the one who did this," Matthew argued. "He can't have gotten far."

"Go help that poor man," Victoria demanded. "I'll send some men to search. It's not your concern. Now *go*!"

CHAPTER TEN

Cassie hummed an old tune as she grabbed the milk bucket from its nail and pranced out to the goat shed. Gypsy met her at the door, a shadow to her every movement. Clouds hung low with no fading starlight or rising sun to aid her swinging lantern, but she paused for a moment and leaned back, the light skimming the lines of the sturdy little building with its thrifty fence. The pleasure that welled up in her at the sight of it never diminished.

In truth, she loved it more each day. Although it was made by others with castoff wood from her mother, she paid for every bit of it herself. It was hers, even more so than the Golden Spoon, because she'd shared that decision with her brother. She had made this choice herself.

Her property looked like a real farmyard, of sorts. She hugged the delight of it close to her heart, where it intertwined like the bright-blue morning glories on the old wooden fence of her childhood home, with remembered sunlight of the happy life she'd shared on the farm with Papa. Cassie closed her eyes, almost convincing herself this was hers forever, that she could have a farm here and her brother would always share in their life together.

Victoria's hateful words about Charlie backing and filling to make her happy horned in on her enjoyment. As usual, her mother had planted a seed of doubt that now sprouted like a weed in the garden and cracked her perfect happiness.

She stepped into the building and crooned to Nugget as she latched the goat to the partition and set the milking stool in place. Her heart settled into a reassuring beat to the rhythm of the milk streams hitting the bottom of the bucket.

Cassie didn't need her mother's words to know what was in her brother's heart, the heart that shared its beat with hers since before they were born. "And what do you think of all this, my little Nugget?" The goat continued munching her morning feed and leaned her warm body into Cassie's bent head. "If Charlie didn't want to come back and spend time with me, he'd tell me so. We have no secrets from each other."

The only response to the one-sided conversation was a satisfied rumbling from the goat's innards, but Cassie's conscience kicked up a different story. She kept secrets from her brother to spare his feelings and guard her privacy. Doubtless, he did the same. He shared his heart and his secrets with Abigail now. Her mother hadn't been wrong about that, but she'd missed the mark when it came to the everlasting bond Cassie shared with her twin. No matter where they were, or how long they were apart, nothing, and no one, could sever that lifelong connection.

Cassie jiggled the slack udder and stripped the last of the milk from the animal's warm, soft bag. "Charlie might be back today, and wait until he sees this place."

The goat turned her head and fixed one square-pupiled eye on her mistress.

"He won't know what to make of it." Cassie set down the pail, careful not to slosh the milk, turned Nugget loose, and opened the door into the fenced pasture. The goat ambled to the opening and stood, head out, body inside, in her own contemplation of the coming day.

Will Charlie be upset that I accepted help from Matthew while he was away? The new thought skittered across her mind. She

340

hadn't exactly gone looking for Matthew's assistance, but she hadn't turned him down.

Cassie trudged to the kitchen, took care of the fresh milk and gave Gypsy a small pan of dribbles before she started a fire in the cookstove. She ruminated on the changes in her backyard and in her heart. She didn't mind Matthew coming around so much, but she had to constantly remind herself he wasn't to be trusted because he was in league with her mother.

Despite his protests, she'd seen nothing to the contrary, and Victoria, for all her interfering ways, was smug in her hold over Matthew. Nevertheless, as much as she chose to believe nothing had changed, Cassie wasn't so cocksure as she'd been a few days ago. Had her mother come earlier in the week to add salt to the wound because Charlie was away? Or had Victoria pecked away at her daughter's confidence as a ruse, in order to keep an eye on Matthew?

Her mother wasn't one to be slighted or crossed, and she would never play second fiddle, especially to her own daughter. The past had proven it so. Was Cassie's life about to come full circle? Would Matthew Ramsey suffer the same fate Myron Gilson had over a decade ago?

It had already happened, in a manner of

speaking.

Cassie slapped the biscuit dough on the counter. *Pure nonsense!* The two men weren't alike in the slightest, and she had no claims on Matthew's affections. "Nor do I wish to!"

Hui slipped into the kitchen like a shadow and hovered at her elbow. "You all right, Miss Cassie?"

"Right as rain," she snapped.

"Nothing amiss, here?" His stare captured hers. Usually, Hui bustled about with the breakfast preparations. He wasn't one to stand idle.

Cassie tried to read his placid face. Were there lines on his brow this morning that hadn't been there yesterday? "Has something happened out at the claim?"

"Yi and Ming are well." Hui turned away, claimed the large pot, and began his morning chores. "Perhaps Charlie returns today."

Cassie studied his familiar profile . . . the wispy beard and round cheeks. He carefully poured the water in and banged the spoon against the side as he dumped in the mash. "I'm hoping," she said.

"Yes, it will be a good thing when he comes."

"It's always better when Charlie's here."

Cassie tried to shake off the phantom of unease.

Isaiah staggered in, looking like a bear just out of hibernation. The big man kept his gaze on Hui, avoiding Cassie's scrutiny.

"Are you feeling well, Isaiah?"

"I'm fine, Miss Cassie." He dipped his head and dropped an armload of split sticks in the wood box.

Cassie kept her gaze upon him until he straightened and faced her. She half-expected to see another bruise or cut on the dear face. Her fears were unfounded, although dark pouches under his eyes told their own tale of too many restless nights and too little sleep.

"Did you sleep well?" she asked.

Had she imagined it, or was there a sly glance exchanged between her two friends? "What has happened?" she demanded, her voice sharp as her mind leaped into the dark and immediately seized on her brother. The roads were rutted and hard packed with travel, but the more well-traveled they became, the greater the danger of robbers and thieves lying in wait. "Is it Charlie?" Her greatest fear exploded and burst into the crowded kitchen.

"I expect we'll be seein' Charlie today, Miss Cassie," Isaiah said.

She went weak in the knees with relief, but the unease increased. "Then what is it? What are you hiding?"

"Nothin'."

The big man turned and pushed aside the drape to enter the eatery, but Cassie put a restraining hand on his arm. "Isaiah Weaver, what has gotten into you? I'll find out sooner or later. *Tell* me!"

He pivoted back to her and cleared his throat. "No need to get all riled up, Miss Cassie. Got nothin' to do with us. Had some shenanigans goin' on last night down to the other end of the street. It's a mean bunch down there these days." Isaiah took in a deep breath and blew out his full cheeks. "Lot of folks are soured on losin' their poke down to the Palace, but they go anyway. Like a fly to hoss manure, somethin' awful. It has nothin' to do with us, but we'll get our share of meanery right here iffen I don't get set up to open soon."

When Isaiah put in his words in such a hurry, Cassie knew there was more to it than he was letting on. She'd bide her time and find out the rest when Charlie came. "We'll have our share of complaining and jawing with the meanness of our breakfast. The men are getting as tired of eating the same thing as I am of cooking it."

Isaiah disappeared into the quiet dining area, and soon the only sounds in the kitchen were the clank of spoons on metal, the rattle of pans, and the creak-and-yaw as she opened the oven door.

The trio grimly sleepwalked through the next hour — the clomp of boots, the gaunt faces and dirty beards, the rough laughter and voices blended with a hundred other mornings. Cassie was grateful when the last miner left with a gruff, "Hope Charlie shows up right soon."

Isaiah barred the door and pulled in the sign. Dishes were cleaned while tables and benches were set to rights in the same glum silence. Cassie was sweeping the kitchen when Petey paraded in, bony chest puffed out, Gypsy pressed close to his side. At the sight of him, Cassie put the broom aside and hurried over, her conscience kicking her hard. She hadn't given one thought to the youth and his grandfather all through breakfast, and she had nary a scrap of food saved out for them.

Her gaze flitted about the kitchen in search of some overlooked biscuit or flap-jack, but there was nothing save the eternal bowl of sourdough starter and the smell of beans baking. "Petey, I'm sorry. I don't have anything to give you and your grandfather this morning."

"Don't have no need, Miss Cassie. You got your supplies full up." He jerked his thumb toward the outside alley. "Wagon's come."

"Charlie's here?" Her voice came out just short of a screech. She took a step toward the back door, but Petey's light touch on her arm stayed her forward motion. "What is it?"

The boy's face radiated excitement, not sorrow, and she hauled in a shaky breath. Charlie wasn't here. She could tell, even before his words confirmed her intuition. "A feller drove in down the other end of the street with a wagonful. Stopped at the Golden Palace and told me to help him unload and be quick about it. I recognized Charlie's wagon right off, Jeremiah in the traces and such, so I set him straight. He's out there now, and he ain't in a sunny mood, but what kind of fool gets crossed with thinking the Golden Spoon is the Palace?"

"Indeed." Cassie slipped past the boy and hurried outside. Isaiah stood by the wagon, beefy arms crossed over his chest. A man not more than her own age, with spectacles and stained shirt stretched over a portly stomach, climbed down from the seat. His careful movements didn't stop the angry flood of words. "I started unloading down t'other place. Waste of time. He should've told me you had two buildings."

Isaiah cast a wary glance her way.

"Where's Charlie?" Cassie asked.

Gypsy sniffed the stranger's boots, then dodged away when he spat on the ground. He muttered something Cassie didn't catch.

"Where's my brother?" she demanded.

The driver scratched the back of his head and Cassie ground her teeth at the delay. "Reckon he's back in town where I left him."

"Why didn't he come?"

"Didn't say. He sent me instead, but didn't tell me it would take so long to git here. Done wastin' my time. Think you owe me a decent wage for all I done." He looked toward Petey, who'd joined Isaiah. "Heard a man can make a fortune here. Gold everywhere."

"That's so. They're haulin' a bushel of gold out of that river ever day," Petey piped up. "But might not be nary a space left to stake a decent claim."

"I'd be a fool not to try my luck." He reached in his shirt pocket, pulled out a couple of folded papers and passed them to Cassie. "Your brother told me to give you these, but don't expect me to be helping you unload. This young feller, here, convinced me I ain't got the time. Just give me my due and I'll be on my way." He held out his gloved palm.

"Hold your hosses." Isaiah stepped in. "Charlie wouldn't have sent you without givin' you your due."

The driver's mouth popped into a thick-lipped *O*.

"What I figured. You already been paid. A feller like you wouldn't do somethin' like this for nothin'. You said your piece." Isaiah gestured with his head. "The river's that way."

Without another word or a backward glance, the stranger strode off.

"What's Charlie say, Miss Cassie?" Petey asked.

She yearned to read the missive in private, but it was not to be. Two sets of flashing eyes, two expectant faces — one dark and somber, the other freckled and alight with speculation — held her feet to the spot.

Cassie swallowed hard but couldn't dislodge the fear. With trembling fingers, she twitched open the first sheet of paper. Charlie's bold scrawl, so much like Papa's, hit her eyes. She blinked back the start of tears to bring the letters into focus.

Dearest Sis,

Don't give the fellow I hired to drive the wagon any gold. His name is Ed Freeland and he seems an honest sort, if dull. I paid him well to deliver this letter, and we shook hands on it. I'd already bought the supplies so I sent them along, too. Figured no sense in wasting them, maybe you can sell them down to the Golden Palace for a decent price before you leave.

Abigail and I were married yesterday. Sorry I couldn't wait for you to be here. Wildfire took the house and barn and her brother — most of the horses and dairy stock, too. Her pa is badly burned but, thank the Good Lord, Abigail was visiting with friends overnight and we have our Eagle Bar stake to rebuild and get back on our feet.

I'm sorry, but there's no easy way to send such sad news. Leave the Golden Spoon and come stay with us. Abigail could use a sister's comfort, as could I. Sell to our mother, if you want to. Anything you get will help, but I suspect it won't be worth the trouble. Please have Matthew bring you here. It's not safe to come on your own. Come soonest.

Love, Charlie

Cassie rubbed her forehead, trying to press Charlie's words into her buzzing brain.

"What'd he say?" Petey persisted. "I ain't much for readin' words, but you could read it to us."

Cassie had no time to make sense of it now. "He got delayed with business, but he knew we were running low on supplies so he sent them along."

"Don't seem like somethin' Charlie would do." Isaiah's scowl spurred her to refold the letter and slip it, and the unread note, in her apron pocket. Petey might swallow the partial truth, but Isaiah would need more convincing. Besides, Cassie knew Isaiah could read as well as she could. "Oh, and Charlie said not to pay the driver. It was just like you said, Isaiah. He'd already been well paid."

Petey snickered. "Always good to get the better of folks who try to get the better of you." He rolled up his baggy sleeves. "I can help you and Isaiah unload." The boy eyed the overloaded wagon and licked his lips. "Gonna have us a Hangtown Fry tonight, even without Charlie?"

"We surely are." Cassie forced a hearty note into her voice. As they unloaded flour and ham, crates of vegetables and fruit, salted fish and beef, sacks of flour, sugar, and meal, Cassie could feel Isaiah's eyes following every moment. She was grateful for Petey's nonstop chatter over the array of food.

As her hands filled with the task, her mind worked even harder. Charlie must have bought supplies before he went to visit Abigail, otherwise he wouldn't have had a wagonful. Is that the way he always did things? She realized she had no idea how that end of the business worked. She didn't know where her brother bought the food stores.

A thought flitted about her head, like a moth in the lantern light. How would she function without Charlie here? And yet she had set her feet on a path to stay. Charlie hadn't said so, but it was clear they needed all the gold they could get to help build up the farm again. How much did it cost to buy livestock and build a new barn? Again, she hadn't a notion.

"You feelin' all right, Miss Cassie? You been standin' there starin' for quite some time now."

"Just thinking."

"Lots of thinkin' goin' on." Petey popped up on her other side. "They say a man got himself hung last night down to the Palace."

"What?" The news pelted her addled brain

like a hailstorm.

"Ain't nothin'. Just Eagle Bar claptrap, most likely." Isaiah moved swiftly behind her, grabbed Petey's arm, and towed him toward the wagon. "Wagon ain't gonna unload itself."

The burden of unease, sitting on the day like the low clouds overhead, settled more stoutly on her heart, straining it to a slow, sluggish beat. Somewhere in the foggy recesses of her brain, Cassie knew Isaiah had kept last night's shenanigans from her, but it had no hold on her to truly trouble her. Charlie's news and his absence were all she cared for, and all she could manage.

Isaiah grunted in the close heat, but refused to rest until the supplies were all put to rights. "You go on to the claim now," Cassie said as he unhitched his mule from the wagon.

"I'll stay and help you cook up a proper Hangtown Fry," he said. "Folks'll be expectin' it."

"I can manage on my own. You always ride Jeremiah back to the claim after Charlie comes with the wagon."

"Charlie ain't comin,' so I'll be stayin'." Isaiah's jaw was set as stubborn as the mule's beside him. "Petey can take the mule down to the claim."

"No." Cassie put her hands on her hips and glared at both her helpers. "You go on, now. You haven't been out to the claim for nigh on a week."

"I ain't leavin."

Cassie frowned. She wanted just one moment on her own to reread Charlie's letter, and what of the unread note? Surely it couldn't hold any worse news. Her insides spasmed at the unknown. She'd never best Isaiah head-on. She turned to Petey, lounging against the wagon, idly petting Gypsy. "Petey, could you stay on?"

The boy's eyes went wide and Isaiah shook his head. "I ain't much of a hand at cookin', Miss Cassie. I much prefer the eatin' part."

"I'm not asking you to cook. I'd just like you to stay around for a spell, until Isaiah gets it into his hard head he can ride Jeremiah down to the claim and send one of the Wangs back to help me cook." She skewered Isaiah with a glare, all the while she talked to the boy. "Please," she whispered.

"Ain't right," Isaiah muttered. "But Hui and Ming could help out more in the kitchen."

"That's all I'm saying."

The big man nodded. "You stay right here

with that dog of yours, Petey."

"And I'll help Miss Cassie get started with the cookin'."

Isaiah sent Cassie a long, silent stare before he turned the mule and led him down the alley to the street. The moment he disappeared, Cassie turned on the youth. "If you really want to help me, Petey, I'd be much obliged if you take the sickle, go on up the hill, and cut an armload of feed for the goat. I usually do it, but if you take over that chore, I can get started in the kitchen right away."

Petey followed her to the shed, where she took down the sickle from the nail and passed it to him. "Might be something tasty waiting for you when you come back," she promised. "But you've got to give me some time to get it in the oven."

Petey's flashed her a big grin. "Cain't wait. Come on, girl."

Boy and dog sauntered up the path. Cassie spun on her heel and rushed to the cabin. She stood in the doorway, yanked the papers from her pocket, and reread Charlie's letter first, although she already knew it by heart. With a shaky hand, she flipped open the second missive and scanned her brother's words.

Matthew Ramsey,

I would ask you for one more favor in regards to my sister. Please bring Cassie to our farm as soon as you're able. She knows the particulars. I'll settle with you, and we'll talk when you arrive.

Thank you. Much obliged,

Charlie Vincent

What did her brother mean *one more favor in regards to my sister*? How many secrets had Charlie been keeping from her? She squeezed her fist and crumpled the paper. It would go into the fire as soon as she got to the kitchen. First, she sidled past the stock of new supplies and put Charlie's letter in the flyleaf of her bedside Bible.

She turned to go. Instead, she smoothed out the wrinkled missive to Matthew, carefully folded it, and placed it in with the other letter.

Trudging the well-worn path to the kitchen, she pulled up her sleeves. She felt peculiar — hollow, but brimming with a wagonload of turmoil. Nevertheless, she gathered the familiar tools, the flour and lard, berries and sugar. She was grateful for the mundane task of cooking all day while her brain picked apart the tangled problems of tomorrow.

She was on her second batch of pie crust when Traveler strode in with his usual offering of rabbits. "Thought maybe I could bring some fish or even a deer, later on, but I heard Charlie was back so you won't be needin' nothin' for a bit."

Cassie hesitated, but only for a second. With flour-coated hands she faced her friend. "We're always grateful for whatever you bring, particularly the rabbits. You know every supper there's never a drop of stew left in the pot." She inhaled to give herself the wind and the courage to continue. "Charlie didn't come this time. He had to stay and look after business on the coast." She got out each word as natural as breathing, but the omissions stole the breath from her.

"See you got the supplies."

"Yes, he sent the wagon with a driver."

"I'll set to work gettin' the rabbits ready." He spun on his heel and Cassie could hear his sure movements skinning the rabbits outside the back door. Petey arrived moments later, and conversation filtered into the kitchen and into her mental stewing. The ordinary pieces of the day gave her a temporary measure of peace.

"I need to take your dog for a spell this afternoon," Traveler said.

"You got a reason?" Petey said.

"Thought she might be able to sniff out the polecat that hung Miss Cassie's goat."

Traveler's voice dropped to a low growl and Cassie couldn't make out the rest of his words.

She rubbed a weary hand over her eyes. She'd almost forgotten about Nugget's near-demise. In the face of Charlie's news, it seemed a small thing, and yet, when added to their present troubles, she felt the tide of adversity threaten to sweep her under.

Matthew paced the confines of his upstairs bedroom, tapping his palm with the flat edge of the miner's knife. He halted at the window but, instead of looking down at the goings on of Eagle Bar's main street this morning, his gaze remained focused on the California toothpick. In a twist of fate, this long, sharp blade had saved the life of the man in the hangman's noose. Today it was a taunting reminder of his part in this venal affair.

He'd gone to the Gilded Mansion at first light to check on the injured man. Gertie, one of Victoria's gilded women, slumbered in a chair hauled up next to his bed. She roused when Matthew moved closer. Mr.

Bowen's shallow breaths rasped in the stuffy room, and Matthew's own breathing stuttered with the labored rhythm. He leaned over and put his ear to the man's chest. Mr. Bowen's heart beat steady as a clock, but he lay lifeless as a statue.

"Been like that all night. Hasn't moved a mite," Gertie whispered. "I've been putting cold cloths on his head and his poor neck, but not much else I know how to do." She spread her palms wide. "Maybe you could convince Miss de Vere he needs a doctor?"

Matthew left the room, knowing he had no more clout with Victoria than her kept women.

He'd returned to the Golden Palace, crept through the empty saloon and up the stairs to his room as if he were an interloper. There, he had run through the events leading to this dismal point in his life. It was past time to shove off and chart a new course. He'd known it for some time, yet he was still here in Eagle Bar.

If he'd heeded his gut weeks ago, he wouldn't have been here last night. But he'd stayed on, telling himself he wanted to finish building a great palace. He'd done that and still he'd stayed on; but in the morning light, cooped up like a penned hawk in Victoria de Vere's employ, he mentally whipped himself for dragging his feet. He could've been back with Will, working in the family business, if he hadn't been so dead set against admitting to his father he was wrong.

The barbed, bitter truth stuck in his craw. He clenched the hilt of the heavy knife in a white-knuckled fist. If he'd left when he should've, they might be burying Mr. Bowen under a crude wooden cross in the ever-expanding Boot Hill just outside of town. Instead, the poor man lay in misery, barely breathing, in a bedroom across the street.

Matthew could find no answer that satisfied his blistered conscience.

A fist hammered on the door, intruding on his inner battle. He set the knife next to the washing-up basin. He waited a full minute before he answered the clamorous rapping, gathering his thoughts, planning his next move. He wasn't surprised to find a scowling, impatient Mr. Logan on the other side of the door.

"You taken up sleeping the day away, or just hiding from the daylight? Neither one ain't going to happen today. Miss de Vere wants us both over to the Mansion, pronto."

"Any change in Bowen?" Matthew asked.

"Ain't dead yet."

Matthew strode out of the Palace and across the street, anxious to get this calamity put to rights. A disgruntled Mr. Logan jogged alongside.

Matthew waited until they reached the closed door of the sickroom at the back of the top floor before he rounded on his companion. "Did you send some men after the ones who strung him up?"

Mr. Logan sneered. "In the middle of the night, Preacher? He could've lit out in any direction. Could be laying low down at the claims, or up in the hills. You know as well as I do, there ain't no way to tell. We don't know his name. I can't put together the particulars of what he looked like, and I'm willing to bet you can't, either. He looked like a hundred other dirty prospectors, drinking their fill and dying to get rich. Don't matter much. Whoever did it is likely halfway to Mexico by now. A fool's errand to even look for him. There's no law here, and he didn't kill a man. He only tried."

"Some of those thugs in the street had to see what happened. Some maybe even took part," Matthew said.

"You wanting to rile up that hornet's nest, Preacher? Miss de Vere won't have it. Whoever did it, they're gone six ways to Sunday, and we're stuck with this mess." Mr. Logan stepped closer and jabbed his finger at Matthew's chest. "It would never have happened like it did, if you hadn't built that blame hangman's platform."

Hadn't Matthew had the same thought during the fitful night, while he twisted and turned in bed? "They could've dragged him off and found the nearest tree," he said.

"That's my point. They'd have taken him off Miss de Vere's property and he wouldn't be lying here half dead. You've got blood on your hands, and now we have to deal with it."

"You can pile on the blame anyway you like. It won't change a thing. It's over and done, and we all share in the shame of it." Matthew knocked lightly on the door and entered. Gertie sat by the head of the bed, gently bathing Mr. Bowen's face with a wet cloth.

Victoria swept into the room with Ulysses Morehead at her side. Matthew skirted the bed and stood behind Gertie to ease the cramping of bodies in the small room. Gertie did one better. She dipped her head toward Victoria, put the cloth next to the porcelain pitcher, and silently glided from the room. The door clicked shut behind her.

Victoria stood at the foot of the bed and fixed her gaze on Matthew. "I don't cotton to any infighting in my business."

"That's fine with me because I'm not part

of your business any longer."

"No, you don't get to cash in and walk away on this one, Preacher. It was your scaffolding that helped the deed along." Mr. Logan spared nary a glance at their employer but kept his gaze on Matthew and kept up his beating refrain.

"And you, inviting two men inside the Palace to foster their grudges and pick a fight, helped the deed along, too." Matthew spat out the words. "It's done."

"Not quite finished, Matthew." Victoria's voice rose to a discordant screech demanding the attention of everyone in the room. "Neither of you will be done with this until I give the word. We are *not* done here. This poor man lies at the brink of death and we bear the responsibility."

Matthew nodded. "I'll go and fetch a proper doctor."

He'd made it two strides past Mr. Logan when Victoria held up a fluttering hand. "No!" Her voice lowered to its natural smooth tones as she continued, "We will handle this ourselves. I want no prying ears or eyes in our business, and we will tell no one what goes on in this room. The rumor on the street is that Mr. Bowen survived and rode out of town, trailing the noose from his neck. We will do nothing to dissuade folks from that opinion."

Matthew didn't question her assessment, nor the accuracy of the gossip which was doubtless spread by Mr. Logan. True to form, Victoria would protect herself from any scandal, even if it meant casting aspersions on Mr. Logan and anyone else her agile mind could find.

I might've picked up a touch of your tar and feathers without knowing it. Matthew had been courting trouble since the moment he took up with Victoria de Vere. Had something similar happened to Cassie and Charlie that soured them on this woman?

"Am I bringing a doctor to Mr. Bowen, or are Mr. Logan and I taking him to one?" Matthew reiterated.

Victoria clucked her tongue. "I've always valued your persistence, Matthew, but this is not the time or place for noble gestures."

"It has nothing to do with noble gestures. You said yourself we bear the responsibility to help the poor fellow."

"A regular doctor won't help Mr. Bowen."

Matthew jerked his attention to the speaker. Victoria, too, lifted an expectant face to the man nearest her. Ulysses Morehead was obviously much more than Victoria's new escort. The tanned, handsome face, though grave, evidenced a smug set of the lips, and his eyes skewered Matthew with a shrewd stare. "I've seen it before. He's in a stupor. Might come out of it, might not . . . but it'll take more than the snake oil doctoring found around these parts."

Victoria sidestepped, as if in a waltz, linked her elbow in Mr. Morehead's arm, and clutched it to her side; a familiar gesture. Matthew suppressed a spasm of revulsion, feeling her phantom touch on his arm.

"Your main concern is that no blame be heaped on my Golden Palace," she said.

"This is only on me, is that it?" Matthew raged.

"Certainly not. There is no crime. Mr. Bowen survived the ordeal."

"He's still breathing, if that's what you're getting at, but he hasn't moved from that bed."

"Who's to say he won't wake up today? Like I said, our best plan is to wait and let it be known there was no incident at the Palace. I think we've convinced most in the crowd that it was all a hoax. Most were corned, and that helped fog their memories. If he doesn't stir soon, I'll see he gets transported to San Francisco to a doctor."

"A trip like that might do him in," Mr.

Morehead said.

"Ulysses, I know you'll soon have the matter well in hand."

"Are you a doctor?" Matthew asked.

Ulysses snickered, an obscene noise in the cloying sickroom. "I am a gentleman who knows how to get things done. Chen Zhi has a cousin who is a healer."

Matthew barely listened to the words as he studied the speaker — the gold tooth, the trimmed mustache, the aristocratic features. He hadn't recognized him last night, but listening to him now, his voice struck a chord. Mr. Morehead was familiar to him, but why and how?

"Mr. Bowen brought this tragedy upon himself," Victoria said. "But we'll see this through and help in any small way we can."

"You don't need me here," Mr. Logan said. "I'll go see to the Palace."

"You go *after* you bring the Chinamen up here," Victoria decreed. "I don't want anyone in the street asking questions."

"And send Gertie back in." Mr. Morehead's command followed Mr. Logan out the door. "Since she's going to be taking care of the man, she ought to be here to learn what her duties are."

They ringed the prostrate man in morbid silence. Matthew shook off the creeping malaise threatening to settle in his heart and brain, and pushed up the nearby window.

"We don't want him to catch a draught," Victoria said.

"Fresh air can't hurt." Matthew was surprised to find an affirming one-finger salute from Ulysses. The gesture scratched at the back of his skull, much like their old boyhood dog, Beau, pawing the back door to get out. There was something familiar in the gentleman's mannerisms. Matthew couldn't shake the faint tinkling bell of recognition, but he couldn't place him, either. "Have we met before?" he asked Ulysses.

"Last evening," came the clipped reply.

"Yes, but before that?"

"I should think I'd remember you, Matthew Ramsey. You cut quite a swath, head and shoulders above most men. I don't recall any prior acquaintance."

He knows, but he doesn't wish for me to make that connection. "Perhaps you can't remember, Mr. Morehead, but it will come to me."

"Matthew, how can you be so callous?" Victoria chastised. "This is not a parlor visit. We're here to lend aid to this poor unfortunate."

Matthew turned toward the window. Sun

glinted off Mr. Logan's oiled back hair as he stepped into the street and hustled Chen Zhi and another man inside the dim interior of the Mansion.

Ulysses opened the door at Mr. Logan's light tap and ushered Gertie in first. She scurried past Victoria and took up her vigil beside Matthew at the window.

"Stay and shut the door," Victoria murmured.

Mr. Logan snapped the lock, settled his arms across his chest, and lounged one shoulder against the closed door.

The older man with Zhi bowed to them. Without a word, he placed a bag on the small table and went straight to Mr. Bowen's bedside. His long, slender fingers skimmed over the patient's arms, chest, and neck, and finally rested on the temples of his head. He remained in that position for a time, his thin face somber, his fingers moving, pressing, his gaze fixed on the man in the bed.

Matthew's eyes widened in recognition. He was more familiar with Hui, but he'd seen this slighter-built Wang cousin, Yi, with the long dark braid, threaded with a few strands of white, serving beside Cassie when he went with his building crew for supper.

"Can you cure him?" Victoria asked, her

voice breathless.

Zhi turned to face Victoria. In a hushed, melodic voice, he replied, "I have seen this before in a revered uncle. He fell and cracked his head. No movement for many days. This is Yi. His father came with medicines, and the venerable uncle returned to us."

Yi pulled a small lamp out of his cloth bag and set it on the bedside table. With graceful, sure movements, he lit the flame and poured water from the pitcher into a large cup. From his accouterments, he produced a pinch of this and that, sprinkled them in the cup, and swirled it over the flame. A strange, pungent aroma stung Matthew's nostrils and prompted an involuntary clearing of his throat.

In silence, Yi studied his inert patient while the concoction warmed. The spectators watched, faces blank, eyes over-round. Little sounds, as they nervously shifted their feet and scratched their heads, penetrated Matthew's senses.

Yi strained the infusion into a glass container and rolled the steaming herbs into a small poultice. He tested the cloth on his wrist before placing it across Mr. Bowen's forehead. He again put his fingers on the man's temples and massaged. After a lengthy interval, he reached into his bag and procured a glass jar. He dipped his fingers into the contents, rubbed his fingertips together in a circular motion for a time, then transferred the motion to the invalid's neck, gently massaging the medicine into the raw wound and bruises left by the rope.

When he was satisfied, he nodded to Zhi, who raised Mr. Bowen to a sitting position, tilted his head back, and held his mouth open. Yi inserted some sort of whitish, shiny reed into his own puckered lips, sucked the liquid from the cup, positioned the reed in Mr. Bowen's mouth, and slowly forced the decoction down his injured throat.

Mr. Bowen made a gurgling sound, followed by a small, involuntary cough. Victoria gasped and clasped her hands together.

Three times Yi repeated the procedure and, at the conclusion, gently wiped a string of drool from the corner of Mr. Bowen's lips.

Yi positioned the pillows before Zhi propped Mr. Bowen's upper torso on the bolster.

Yi carefully packed up his belongings before he turned to face Victoria, still seated at the foot of the bed frame. His thin face serene, he humbly bowed. "No fever," he said. "This is a hopeful sign, but he is in profound sleep. I have seen this before. He may not return. He may return in body, but not reason." He tapped his own head. "This is a great mystery. No one sees or knows where he is. He cannot tell. I will leave medicine with Cousin and bring more." He bowed again and glided toward the door.

Mr. Logan straightened, braced his legs apart, and blocked the exit. "Strangest thing I ever did see. Not sure if you're trying to kill him or cure him, but it better work."

Victoria sent him a dark scowl.

"We wait," Yi counseled. "Keep him clean and propped up to breathe."

Matthew sidled past Victoria, and held out his hand out. Yi took it in a strong grip. "Thank you, Wang Yi," Matthew said. "We'll pay you for the treatment."

Yi released his handshake. "First we wait, but for Cousin there is no charge."

Matthew looked over the slight man's head and glared Mr. Logan away from the door. Yi calmly strode from the room and closed the door behind him.

"You should've insisted on giving him something, Matthew." Victoria rose from her seat. "We need to insure he doesn't talk and spread around what happened in this room."

"Wang Yi is the most honorable of all my

family." Zhi's tone was sharp. "There is no need for blood money, as you call it. My cousin will never speak of this to anyone."

"I expect you to see to that." Victoria's lyrical tone belied the sickroom atmosphere. Her skirts brushed against Matthew as she edged around the side of the bed. She bent over Mr. Bowen. "He coughed. Surely that's a good sign."

Ulysses skirted the other side of the bed and Zhi moved out of the way. "I told you the children of the Celestial Empire have their secrets of healing. I'm confident they can restore Mr. Bowen to a modicum of health, at least well enough to get him off our hands."

Zhi beckoned to Gertie and the pair silently left the room. Matthew made to follow, but Victoria put a restraining hand on his arm.

"I know you're anxious to leave, Matthew, but I must insist you stay on in my employ until this matter is resolved. You're surely aware of the danger here to all of us. You, particularly, have a stake in this, as well."

"You and Mr. Logan have made that abundantly plain. I'll stay on until this is resolved, but I won't work the floor again."

Victoria's lips twisted in ugly disapproval. "Not tonight, perhaps, but I trust a man of your *supposed courage* won't run away from trouble for long."

"I'll talk to Judd and we'll get that figurehead up for you in a day or two." Matthew swung toward the door, brushed past Mr. Logan, and marched out into the stuffy hallway. He needed some space and air.

He took the stairs two at a time and burst out into the busy street, drawing in deep breaths. His mind and stomach churned with uncertainty. If Mr. Bowen recovered, he'd be truly free, and he didn't want the promise of mounting the Lady of the Seas hanging over his head. He vowed to leave this place as soon as he could. He couldn't wait to head back to his brother and San Francisco.

"Preacher!" Matthew turned from his contemplation of the future resting place of the figurehead and met Traveler's angry glare. "Been jawin' at you for a full minute now."

Gypsy sat beside Traveler's booted feet. The prospector carried a length of rope. He took his focus off Matthew and scanned the street.

The coiled rope was a rude reminder of recent events. "What are you up to, Traveler?"

"Been tryin' to tell you. This is the rope

from Miss Cassie's goat. I been walking down the street, givin' the dog a whiff now and then."

"Last I checked, Gypsy lit into you and, for the life of me, I can't figure it, but Cassie trusts you." He scratched the dog's ears before he added, "And I reckon that's good enough."

"Wake up, Preacher!" Traveler held up a strong arm and flexed his hand. "This dog wouldn't bite a flea. She's pure worthless."

"Why —"

"Offered to make her mean, but Miss Cassie wouldn't have it. Folks thinkin' she bites might be just as good as a savage dog."

Matthew had been fooled. He stomped down the spurt of disappointment and solidly met Traveler's squinting glare. Maybe change was in the wind. At the thought, Gypsy sniffed the humid breeze.

"It doesn't seem like you'll have any luck with her running anyone to ground," Matthew said. "She may not be a mean dog, but she's not much of a guard dog, either. She's always loping off into the hills or following Peter around town."

Traveler scratched his beard. "Maybe not, but she was the only one out back there when it happened, and it was her barkin' that got us there in time to rescue Miss Cassie's goat. Critters know more about what goes on than we do. I reckon Gypsy saw, or at least smelled, the skunk that did it."

Matthew's gaze swept the bustling street traffic. "It's a long shot."

"It's worse than a shot in the dark, but I gotta do somethin'. Particularly now. Don't want any no-accounts troublin' Miss Cassie. Whoever done this is still out there and might be thinkin' up something mean to add to her woes. Can't let that happen again. All I know is, she won't be safe until we get that polecat, one way or the other. He's not gettin' away with it."

"Amen to that."

"Preacher!"

Both men looked up the street at the hail. Isaiah dogtrotted toward them, leading his mule. He beckoned toward the corner, away from the hubbub of the street. "We got trouble. The supply wagon come with the old mule, Jeremiah, but Charlie didn't come with it. Not like him."

"What?" Matthew tried to digest the news. "Why not?"

"Charlie sent Miss Cassie a note, but she didn't let on what he wrote, just said he had to stay behind to take care of business. The Golden Spoon *is* their business, so it must be somethin' bad, I figure. It's not like Miss

Cassie to keep mum like that with me. She and Charlie and me go back a coon's age."

"I'm a fair hand at slingin' hash," Traveler said. "I'll help out in the kitchen 'til Charlie gets back."

"Mighty kind of you," Isaiah said, "But Miss Cassie's some proud. She sent me away with Jeremiah, back to the claim. Says it's what I always do after we unload the wagon. I didn't want to go, mind you, but I had to get word to Hui so they can come. She'll need plenty of help with the Hangtown Fry tonight."

"Surely she won't do it without Charlie here," Matthew said.

"You don't know Miss Cassie. She'll do it, even if it kills her. 'Sides, all the men are expectin' a fry. Iffen we don't have one, they'll likely know somethin's amiss, and there's them that'd take advantage."

Matthew looked to the far end of the street, the relatively quiet sector of Eagle Bar. He couldn't see the Vincent eatery, but his mind filled in the details: Cassie cooking like a whirlwind in the kitchen.

Isaiah was right. With Charlie gone, this was no place for a woman alone. Matthew hadn't been able to convince her of that weeks ago, and he didn't expect she'd listen to him now.

The big man picked up on his thoughts. "I left Petey with her. Made him promise to stay on until the Wangs got there." Isaiah rubbed a weary hand over his eyes. "Don't like to do this, and if Miss Cassie knew she'd likely skin me alive, but I have to keep that woman safe. You said you pledged to Charlie, afore he left last time, to look out for Miss Cassie. Now's your chance to prove it. Get up there and don't leave until the Wangs or I come back."

"What if she won't have me?

Isaiah puffed his cheeks and let out a noisy breath. "You'll think of somethin'."

Traveler whacked Matthew on the back. "You can always offer to do the dishes, Preacher."

Matthew tipped his hat to the pair and hurried back to the main thoroughfare and up the street. With each step, his speculation on Charlie's absence grew. He stopped at the front of Cassie's Golden Spoon and began concocting a story — part truth, part balderdash — that she might swallow.

CHAPTER ELEVEN

Matthew Ramsey appeared at the kitchen door just as Cassie took the first pies out of the oven. Petey sat on a stool, peeling onions. She looked from one longing set of eyes to the other and suppressed a smile. Inside all folks was a tiny space where childhood lived on; and the smell of a raspberry pie, or the joy of picking a wildflower, was all it took for the heart to surrender to it.

In spite of the rigors of the morning, working in the kitchen had settled her mind to rights. She and Charlie had planned to stay on until November, and she silently resolved to do so. Surely, she could keep her Golden Spoon prosperous for a handful of months. She hadn't thought out the details, but she'd cipher out a new plan tonight. Things like bringing in fresh supplies, finding a way to give Isaiah and the Wangs the time and freedom to work their claim, especially with the river giving up its gold. Those were thorny problems she'd pushed to the back of her mind during the daylight hours.

She'd already decided on daily cooking and cleaning — straight through from breakfast to supper, working every waking moment. She was no stranger to hard work, and it would keep her from missing her brother so much. She bolstered her determination with the old dream she and Charlie had shared. With eyes closed, she pictured it — driving up to Charlie and Abigail's farm before December and giving them a golden wedding present with, hopefully, enough left over to start her on a new path.

She had already composed a note to her twin in her head, and that was foremost on her mind as she sliced two pieces of steaming pie. She needed to find a trustworthy individual to get word to Charlie of her decision to stay. Cassie was sure if she didn't contact her twin, he would come to get her, regardless of the cost to him and Abigail.

She hadn't come up with any names yet, as to who that would be. *Trustworthy* and *Eagle Bar* didn't walk hand-in-hand very often, although she was surrounded by friends she now trusted with her life — Isaiah, Petey, Traveler, the Wangs, and, though she didn't know him well, Judd had joined that list.

She passed the plated desserts to her two kitchen guests, her lips and spirits lifting.

As Matthew forked into the pie, Cassie wouldn't admit it aloud, but he was also someone she felt she could count on. After getting over the initial pique of reading her brother's letter to Matthew, Cassie allowed, for good or ill, that Charlie had not given up on their friendship with Matthew, in spite of his connection with their mother.

"Powerful good, Miss Cassie." Petey smacked his lips and pulled a mournful face as he pushed aside the empty tin plate and stared at the pile of onions. "Seems I peel one and two more take its place."

"Peter." Matthew slid his plate on top of the boy's and stood behind him, hands on his bony shoulders. "Think you'd mind if I took over peeling the onions and you went along and found Traveler and Gypsy? They were down toward the Palace, last I saw of them, and it might be timely if they returned soon."

"Surely, Preacher." Petey was up and at the door in a flash. He paused and turned to Cassie. "That okay with you, Miss Cassie? I'll be back along with Traveler right quick."

"That's fine." The response slipped out

before she had the sense to think it through. Petey was gone in a wink. Suddenly, the kitchen was too close, too hot, and too small. She caught the sparkle in Matthew's glance before he perched on the stool, picked up the knife and set to peeling onions. "You don't have to do that," she said.

"You might do well to kick me out before I make a mess of it. I haven't done this type of work since I was a cabin boy, and as much as it pains my Ramsey pride to admit it, I never gave kitchen work my heart and soul at the time. I got considerable cuffs on the ear for cutting didoes instead of potatoes but, in my boyish reasoning, I figured sooner or later they'd banish me from the galley and I'd be back on deck again."

"Did it work?" Cassie looked at the big man, hunched over the slop bucket, sleeves rolled up, gesturing with the paring knife while the onion went unpeeled in his other hand. In spite of her reticence to his presence in her kitchen, she could see him as a youth, like Petey, making his way in the world with that cock-of-the-walk attitude all boys shared.

"Can't say as it did, but it didn't stop me from trying. The sorry truth remains. I didn't learn a thing and I'm a poor hand at cooking, but with Charlie away, I'm here to help you."

Cassie frowned. There it was again, the suspicion that her brother and Matthew had decided her fate without asking her consent. "I don't recall asking for your help."

"You didn't." The reply was friendly enough, but his eyes flicked away from hers and his mouth firmed into a thin line.

"Then why are you here?"

He set the knife and onion on the bench, shifted his weight back on the stool, stuck out his long legs in the small space, and crossed his ankles. "It's a sorry tale, but I imagine I could tell it, if you can bear to listen."

"Say on."

"I ran into some trouble down at the other end of the street." He held up his palm. "You and Charlie tried to warn me, but I didn't listen. Now I'm out of Victoria's good graces, although, looking back, I'm of the notion there never *were* any good graces. I never was more than a simpleton who stumbled into her schemes, ripe for her picking. She's got her hooks into me for a mite longer, but that'll change soon enough."

"And that means I'm supposed to feel sorry for you? I don't. Not in the least."

"I wasn't hoping for sympathy, more like a place to work as far away from the Palace as a man can get in this town."

"Seems to me, not too long ago you said you were leaving Eagle Bar for good. That's a mite farther from Victoria's reach." Cassie kept up the argument to quell the small spurt of triumph mingled with admiration. Maybe Matthew wasn't such a bad sort. She and Charlie were well schooled in their mother's treacherous wiles, but other men slipped and fell at her feet, unaware they were standing in quicksand.

He cleared his throat, reclaiming her attention. "And I intend to do just that, but not yet. I agreed to help Judd put up a figurehead as a finishing piece at Victoria's palace. She's holding me to that, but I can't do it until Judd comes in from his claim. You saw that picture of his family. He deserves to make his fortune and buy his own place. And I won't ask him to leave his claim while they're pulling gold out of the river. It's a dangerous time to go off and leave it unattended."

All Matthew said had the ring of truth to it, and him talking about Judd that way softened her heart considerable, but the words of Charlie's letter clanged in Cassie's head like a peddler beating his pots and pans.

I would ask you for one more favor in regards to my sister.

What was the initial favor? Matthew wasn't telling her the long and short of it, and she needed to hear the whole truth to make sense of her brother's missive and make sense of how she should handle Matthew's offer of help.

Part of her wanted to hog up and send him packing down the road, show both men *and* her mother she could take care of her Golden Spoon all by herself. But she couldn't run this place by herself, not if she wanted to attract the usual number of customers, demand a high price for her fare, take advantage of the river's gold, and leave here with enough gold for Charlie and Abigail — and with her due, as well.

Hui slipped into the kitchen and Cassie welcomed the intrusion. She immediately turned to her friend with her waspish attitude still in view. "Hui, Isaiah is overly anxious. You shouldn't have come until the regular time."

Hui dipped his head. "Isaiah and I have not spoken. I was doing my business when I heard the wagon had come but no Charlie. Is all well?"

Cassie's eyes pricked with the start of tears, but she blinked them back, grasped Hui's elbow and steered him out of the doorway, towing him a fair distance from the kitchen before she stopped. Let Matthew think what he may. Charlie may have trusted him, but she had yet to take that step.

She glanced up at the goat shed. Nugget peacefully nibbled on the brush Petey had thrown inside the fence. Her conscience whispered, *You already let him in.* Her reason argued, *But he doesn't know that.*

"We have an old Chinese saying, 'Distant water is not quenched by nearby fire.' "

Cassie turned her attention to Hui. Suddenly aware she still clutched his arm, she ignored the heat rising in her cheeks and let her hand drop.

"I believe we may need him on our side," Hui said.

"That's the problem. I don't know if he *is* on our side."

Traveler and Petey arrived with Gypsy at their heels. "Caught the gist of it," Traveler said. "Pains me to say it, but I reckon the preacher's more honest than most. If you decide he isn't, Isaiah and me will take care of him for you right quick. 'Sides, we'll all be here workin' with you, and I'd be mighty pleased to set him straight whenever he needs it."

"Thank you, but it isn't fair to ask all of you to leave your claims and help me out." Cassie squirmed at the selfish notion of knowing she'd expected this to happen. She knew they'd offer, and she was prepared to accept their help without question, in order to get her own pile. The knowledge brought an unflattering comparison to her mother. She would not be guilty of using anyone to further her own needs.

She took a small step away from the trio and straightened her spine. She was taller than Hui and Petey. The height advantage usually bolstered her confidence. Not today. She felt small, inside and out. "I can't ask any of you to leave your claims and spend more time at the Golden Spoon, especially now, when there's gold to be had." Her words echoed what Matthew had said about Judd a few moments ago. Another reminder she was perhaps less honorable than Matthew, or all the men gathered here.

"We know what needs to be done," Traveler said. "And we're here to do it."

"I *will* pay you, but it can't compare to what you're taking from the river in a day."

"Can't speak for the rest of 'em, but I

385

don't want no pay," Traveler said, "just the meals."

"No. If you work here, you will accept proper wages. Charlie and I agreed on that at the start. If you won't take wages, I will not let you help me." Traveler opened his mouth and she glared at him until he closed it in silence. "I would be much obliged if you help me get ready for a Hangtown Fry tonight, but I want you to promise me you'll think about what it would cost you to help me out every day."

"The Wangs already know," Hui said. "One of us will be here each day until it is time for all to leave." He bowed his head. "May I speak in private?"

Petey was busy fooling with the dog, but Traveler glowered at them before he turned away and stomped toward the chicken yard.

Cassie leaned close to hear Hui's gentle tone. "Charlie is not coming back." It wasn't a question.

"No," Cassie whispered. It was a relief sharing the secret. "I need to send him a message soon, or he *will* come and he can't."

"Ming will take butter out soon. He can take butter for you and a note to Charlie."

"Thank you." The words came out as no more than a squeak, pressed between a crush of emotion and doubt.

Hui simply bowed and glided to the kitchen. Cassie watched him disappear through the back door, then turned her attention to her two remaining friends.

Traveler met her gaze, nudged the boy in passing, and both strode over to her.

"I have some onions to peel, lessen the preacher done 'em all." Petey's gloomy face lightened Cassie's somber mood.

"He wasn't too quick about it," she said. "He might've saved some for you."

"I was thinkin' the same thing."

The bearded miner gave Petey a brusque push on the shoulder toward the kitchen. Gypsy stood at Traveler's side, tongue lolling, and the man absentmindedly stroked the dog's head. "What are you cookin' tonight?"

"You've already helped with the stew," Cassie protested.

"I can do a whole lot more'n rabbit stew." Traveler's voice dropped and he leaned closer. "I'll stand in for Charlie."

She moved away at the intimate tone. "You don't have to be afeared of me, Miss Cassie."

"I know."

"No, you don't. It's my doin'. I knowed it. Happened that first time I met you and Preacher." He jerked his thumb toward the alley. "But the first time I come to your Golden Spoon, you were so kind to me, considerin' how I treated you. Been thinkin' a lot about that, what I said and did. Been tryin' to make amends."

"The rabbits."

"A poor excuse for proper apologizin', but I been out of practice at it for so long." He pulled on his beard. "Way I see it, this is my chance to make things right, and I'd be much obliged if you'd allow it."

Cassie took in the long face and the forlorn eyes. Where once they'd once been hard and bleak, they now held a sheen of tears. She suspected the big man would not take kindly to her pointing that out.

"Okay," she said. "But you need to work *your* claim, too. If the Wangs and Isaiah and Petey, and even Matthew Ramsey, help out, I insist you all spend most of the time at the river."

"There's twenty-four hours in a day, Miss Cassie, and I get more'n my fill of time at the claim, rubbin' elbows with the folks down there."

By silent accord they fell into step on the worn path to the back door. Just before they entered, Cassie stopped. Matthew's words prompted her next thought. "I hear it's a dangerous time to go off and leave your

388

claim unattended."

"They don't call me Traveler for nothin'. I ain't one to stay tied down to any place for long. Nobody with a lick of sense sets a foot on my claim. I got a few folks watchin' out for me when I'm not around."

He gestured for her to precede him into the kitchen and she suddenly glimpsed a gentleman underneath Traveler's grime and dirty clothes. She walked into her domain, the stab of Charlie's absence cutting into her at the sight of Hui in his place, busy mixing bread dough. Matthew and Petey had their heads bent over the work bench, Matthew demonstrating knife skills. Both looked up at her entrance.

"We've been putting our heads together." Matthew gave her a sheepish grin. "After the vegetables are peeled, we might be of better use cutting firewood, hauling water, doing chores, and cleaning up the place. Leave the cooking to those who know what they're doing."

"Looks like the stack of wood out back *is* a mite lackin'." Traveler followed a step behind her.

"I was of the same mind," Matthew said. "Consider it done."

"I'll be back afore supper to help set up, Miss Cassie, but I ought to go check on

Grampa," Petey said.

"Of course." Cassie was still too stunned at the cordial exchange between Traveler and Matthew to think clearly.

Matthew and Petey left without another word. As Cassie set Traveler to work making stew beef and gravy, she heard the rhythmic thump of the axe on the chopping block out back. The whack of Traveler's knife answered back as he cut up the beef.

The kitchen filled with heat and the mingled fragrances of assorted foods. As Cassie looked at the mess of meat and vegetables, desserts and bread, she felt a lurch of fear. In her quest to prove she could do this without her brother, had she used too much of their stores on this one meal?

Doubt swirled in the back of her mind, caught up in tomorrow's coming windstorm of life. She must be careful. She had no notion of who would take Charlie's place and bring in supplies every few weeks. Perhaps Ming, but he tended to stay with his own kind. Besides, it was too long a venture for him to be away from the claim. Her insides shriveled at the thought of sending Isaiah away. He was as near family as Charlie and bound to them by the past. As much as she touted her independence and her ability to run everything on her own, without Isaiah as her mainstay for the days to come, she wouldn't have the courage to even try.

"You want a taste?" She jumped at Traveler's voice in her ear. "I haven't done much cookin' 'cept scrapin' together grub for myself on the trail. Might've lost my touch."

Cassie obediently sampled a small bite from the spoon he offered. Her eyes flew wide as the savory flavors lingered on her tongue after she swallowed the meat and gravy.

"Gets a mite tastier after it sets on the stove for a bit."

"Traveler, it's wonderful! Better than anything *I've* ever made." She caught the flush of color in his cheeks before he turned back to the stove, his meaty arm immediately engaged in stirring the simmering contents of three large pots. "You're a good hand in the kitchen. Maybe better than Charlie, but we'll keep that mum," she teased. "Where'd you learn to cook like that? And why did you keep it a secret?"

He hunched one shoulder. "It weren't no secret. I just fell outta practice over the years, I 'spect. I used to cook a fair piece back. My wife was sickly for a time. She'd lie in bed, later sit in the rocker and tell me what to do."

His eyes stared through her. She recog-

nized the far-off look. Charlie had it whenever they talked of Papa and the farm.

"My Lally was a task master," Traveler
continued. "Wanted me to learn right
proper, but every time I botched the bread
or burnt the supper, she'd eat it anyway and
tell me it was the best she ever et." He
scrubbed a calloused hand across his eyes
and it drifted down to his untamed beard.
"Been thinkin' of gettin' rid of this tumble-
weed. Ain't nothin' but a dirt collector."

The glimpse of the gentleman she'd seen
not an hour ago was back, and with it, the
face of a man who had once cared very
deeply about homey things, a man not so
different than Charlie. "I didn't know you
had a wife," she murmured over the hiss,
gurgle, and boil of the coming meal.

"I don't talk about it much. It's in the past
and she ain't comin' back."

"I'm so sorry." A surge of guilt tempered
her curiosity.

"Don't be. Happens to a lot of folks. You
and Charlie don't have no ma or pa, I
'spect."

Cassie changed the subject and prepared
the dining area for what she hoped would
be an onslaught of diners willing to pay top
dollar for a Hangtown Fry. She felt a mite
greedy when she wrote the price on the

board, but she needn't have worried. The place was packed.

Matthew hustled across the street in the predawn darkness. These days he rose about the time most of the crew from the Palace was bedding down. He'd lived by the sunrise and sunset for most of his days, and it rested on his soul far better than late nights trapped in the saloon with a boodle of drunken miners.

He'd slipped easily into the new custom of helping out at Cassie's Golden Spoon. She was still a bit thorny at times, but he enjoyed the challenge. He did his best to mind his place and hide his frustration at the fierce attention of all her protectors. The poor woman was never left alone save to sleep, and even then, Isaiah always kept vigil from his tent, now pitched out of sight behind the goat shed within spitting distance of her cabin.

Only once had Matthew made the mistake of offering to relieve Isaiah for a night or two, earning himself rank disapproval from all parties. Didn't they know in a place like Eagle Bar, sensibilities and modesty didn't exist? Still, to a man and boy, they gallantly guarded not only Cassie's person, but her reputation.

He quietly entered the Gilded Mansion, crept up the stairs, then down the hall to the now familiar room at the back. He eased open the door and slipped inside. A lamp burned on the table, haloing the man in the bed. The Chinese healer was changing the poultice that wreathed the invalid's neck.

Matthew stepped closer and peered into Bowen's clean-shaven sleeping face. Gertie hovered in the background, and he wondered if she ever slept. She'd proven to be a saint in tending the poor soul, giving him broth, keeping him clean, sitting with him, even holding his hand. Matthew intended to speak to Victoria about giving her a stake for her troubles, enough so she could leave this life and make a new start. Gertrude Bremner had more than earned it.

Lately, Matthew made a habit of avoiding Victoria, but if he wanted to do right by Gertie, he couldn't lay low forever. He suspected Victoria knew his whereabouts, even at this moment, and only let him think he was his own man until she demanded he do her bidding.

"How is he?" Matthew whispered and immediately felt foolish at his hushed tones. It wasn't as if he was afraid of waking Mr. Bowen.

Yi turned to him and Matthew took in

the unhindered view of the injured man's neck, the bruises well-faded, the welts nearly gone. Yi was a gifted healer, but could he bring this gambler back from the hangman's noose?

"No better. Perhaps worse."

"I thought he was looking a bit more spritely." Even as he said it, Matthew prayed it was so. The man's peril preyed on his soul. Victoria's insistence on keeping the affair secret, her plan to nurse Bowen to some sort of health and then ship him far away, was too tempting to allow for a clear conscience. And now Yi's grave face, his caring almond eyes, stripped the whitewash off their wicked conspiracy.

"He breathes like a man who soon gives up."

"Is there nothing you can do?"

"I have done all I know. This morning I try something new."

"I hope it works miracles."

"Sometimes letting the soul go is the greatest kindness."

"Is there anything I can do to help?"

"No." Yi resumed his ministrations, reapplied the poultice and placed his arched fingers on the man's temples for a time before he packed his wares. He turned to

Gertie and bowed. "You have done well, Miss."

Matthew let Yi precede him from the sickroom and out of the building. The two walked up the quiet street together. When they reached the Golden Spoon, his companion sidestepped as gracefully as a waltz partner. "Big changes come soon. You know so. Miss Cassie knows so. When it comes, we will go. Miss Cassie must go, too, but she is like beautiful flower. If we uproot, she will wither and die. She must let go of roots here, travel on the winds of change, and plant herself in new ground. You must help her see."

Yi bowed, pivoted on the ball of his foot and strode off toward the river, not waiting for Matthew's reply.

Matthew knew Yi's sage advice was a somber reality. He watched the small, older man walk away, braid swinging in rhythm with his fluid steps until he disappeared, like a mirage, down the slope. The healer's gentle warning renewed Matthew's resolve to keep his eyes and ears open, to be ready to leave at the drop of a hat.

Cassie was in no danger for now. But he recognized the sharp wisdom of Yi's observations. Cassie had put down roots. She delighted in her backyard farm and was obviously pleased with the success of her Golden Spoon. Every night he saw her walking on air, humming a tune as she raked in as much gold as if she had her own claim on the river. He itched to speak to her about her exorbitant prices, but it was an itch he was smart enough not to scratch.

He silently padded up the alley to the back door and entered the kitchen. The lanterns burned. Cassie was bent over a bucket as she strained the morning's milking into a pot.

"Mornin'," he said, and kindled the fire in the cook stove.

"You come earlier every day."

"And I swear you must never go to bed."

"Hard work never did a body harm."

"I was thinking the same thing myself as I walked up the street." He held her gaze for a moment, unsure how much he should say. Moments like this were becoming familiar, but he still lacked the easy camaraderie she had with the others. "I like making an honest living, working with my hands, something I'd forgotten for a while. I'm grateful for you giving me the chance to make things right."

Cassie raised a brow. "Seems a mite lofty estimation when it's just chopping wood and vegetables, and hauling water."

"Gives a man time to think about what's important, and it's good to get away from the crowds."

She frowned slightly. "Let's hope you don't get away from the crowds too much. It's bad for business."

"You pack the place every day. I expect if you cooked twice as much food, you'd still sell out and have to turn men away."

"I'd rather we keep to our regular amount and have a steady setting every day, otherwise we'd run out of supplies in a week."

The kitchen was silent for several minutes save for the small patter and plunk as they went about their tasks. Matthew bent to light the fire and carefully blew on the tiny flame. He needed to be careful with his next words. The urge to offer too much, and take over some aspects of her business, was hard-as-the-devil to restrain. He stared at the small blaze crackling hungrily as it devoured the kindling.

"You aren't going to burn down the kitchen this morning, are you?" Cassie's tone held a sweetness of mirth, unloosing his reticence.

He closed the fire door, stood and blurted, "I'd be pleased to make a run for supplies, if you like."

She rubbed a hand over her eyes, but not

before he glimpsed the flicker of uncertainty.

"Tell me Charlie's route, and I'm your man. Gone and back, just like he did."

She turned away from him and gathered up her cooking wares. "I don't know."

He strained to hear the whispered words. "You don't have to decide right now. You can think on it. I can go, or I can take over someone else's duties if you want to send Isaiah or Traveler."

"No." She whirled to face him. "I mean, I don't know Charlie's route. I don't know anything about where he got our supplies. I never thought I'd need to know."

He gently touched her forearm. "I can look up Charlie, get the lay of the land, and then buy the supplies."

"No, I don't want him to think I can't do this by myself. He's got his own passel of worries."

"What happened?"

"Never you mind. I need to figure this out."

"Let me help."

"Well, isn't this something?" a familiar voice purred.

They sprang apart like guilty children caught robbing sweets from the kitchen cupboard. What was Victoria doing here — and at this hour of the day? Matthew had anticipated her cold slap of reality in pulling him back into line with her plans, but he'd never expected her to show up at Cassie's Golden Spoon.

"I guessed I'd find you here, Matthew, but it's still a sight, seeing you together. Might I assume you've mended whatever silly quarrel you had?"

Cassie stepped into the breach before he could quell his anger and respond in a courteous manner.

"Victoria, if you must speak to Matthew, do it quickly. We have work to finish." Cassie's sharp response spoke of the unhealthy effect Victoria had on most folks, leastwise those who knew her, and clearly these two women knew each other well.

"It appears you've done more than mend a quarrel. Thick as thieves. Matthew is *not* your private property. He works for *me.*"

Cassie's cheeks colored. "Matthew Ramsey is a man grown. He comes and goes as he pleases."

"What do you want, Victoria?" he asked.

"Perhaps we should step outside, Matthew." With a sly look, Victoria gestured with her gloved hand toward the back door.

"Whatever you came to say, you can say to me here. I have work to do."

"Yes, menial chores fitting for a boy like

Peter. And to think, just a short while ago, you berated me for treating you like a schoolboy."

"What goes on here is none of your business. I'll be down at your place after breakfast is served, if that suffices."

"I'm afraid that will not suffice, Matthew. I have a business to run, too. I need you now."

"I will come when I'm finished here." He turned away from her and stoked the fire, even though it didn't really need another stick.

"Very well. I see I'll have to wait on you, but don't keep me waiting long or there *will* be dire consequences."

Victoria rounded on Cassie. "I understand Charles is gone for good, something we both knew would happen. And now you've curried Matthew's favor and brought him here as a stand-in for Charles."

"Get *out!*"

Victoria stood firm. "I'm only speaking the truth. You've always had a hard time accepting what is, always lived in a dream, but this is life, Cassandra. Grow up. You want supplies, I have a wagon come in every five days, sometimes more often. Charles is gone. Others will desert you, too. I'm all you've got, girl. It's about time you owned up to it."

"Mighty crowded in here."

Three heads whipped toward the open door. Traveler blocked the entry, but his arrival spurred Matthew into action. "I'll walk you out, Victoria." He nodded to Traveler as the big man shouldered into the room. Matthew caught Victoria's elbow in a firm pinch, ushered her through the doorway, and didn't stop until they'd reached the street.

Victoria twisted out of his grasp and rubbed her hand over her abused elbow. "Goodness Matthew, what's gotten into you? You want to win Cassie? That's admirable, but don't do it at my expense."

"We are strictly employer and employee, despite the balderdash you served up when we first met. I will finish my work for you, as promised, but you have no place in my personal business."

"Now, take the one she calls Traveler. He's not a bad-looking sort. With a haircut, a clean-shaven face, and brand-new duds from the mercantile, he might even pass for a gentleman."

"He's working in the kitchen and serving up meals."

"Open your eyes, Matthew. If you think that's all he's doing, you're a fool." Victoria touched his forearm and turned on her pout. "I really *do* need you as soon as you can get away. We have matters to discuss concerning Mr. Bowen. I'll expect you in my office directly."

Matthew trudged back to the kitchen, not caring if Victoria stood by the side of street until the cows came home. He'd barely stepped inside when Cassie propelled him into the backyard. "You might as well go."

His anger and frustration spurted up anew. "She can wait until I finish my work here."

"*I* can't. I won't be beholden to that woman."

"It has nothing to do with you," Matthew argued. "I'm my own man."

Cassie put her hands on her hips. "It has everything to do with me."

Matthew took a deep breath and stared into her anguished face. A face he recognized — a more comely, younger, more delicate oval of Victoria de Vere. The slant of the eyes was more exotic, the chin more resolute, the nose more refined, but it had been staring him in *his* face for weeks. "She's your mother," he whispered.

Cassie held his gaze in silence.

The revelation poured into his brain like a pounding rain, running little bits of the past into rivulets of understanding. He mumbled, "I didn't think . . . I mean, the way she dresses and acts. I didn't think she was *any*one's mother." He shut his mouth too late. "I'm sorry."

"She's not our ma. She gave up that right when she ran off," Cassie said with a strange, hushed finality, without rancor or longing. "You might as well go and see what she wants."

"I don't want to give her the satisfaction of jumping when she beckons."

"We all do it, to our shame sometimes, but if you don't tend to her, she'll be back. I'd rather she didn't come around here again, especially with Charlie gone."

Matthew didn't want to leave Cassie, but she'd spoken the bitter truth. He needed to set things right with Victoria before he could set things right anywhere else, particularly with Cassie. "You're right. This is my own doing, getting tangled up with her in the first place. I think I know what she wants. Judd and I need to get that figurehead up at her Golden Palace. Then I'm finished down there. It probably can't happen all in one day. I'll find Judd and get it done, but I'll be back to help with supper. I promise."

She didn't acknowledge his vow, only stepped away from him and disappeared into her kitchen.

Matthew took off at a run down the street as the sun rose. "Matthew!" He halted at the familiar hail. Judd stood outside the entrance to the Golden Palace. "Where's the fire? Bet it has a name, and that name's Victoria de Vere."

The two men slipped around the corner of the building. "What are you doing here?"

"Same as you, I 'spect," Judd said. "Ira Graff came by the claim this morning, rousted me out of bed. I got the word Miss de Vere's all-fired set on getting that sea witch up today."

"It won't happen today." Victoria wasn't set on putting up the figurehead. She was set on pulling Matthew down, hobbling him like a horse with all her demands, her petty need for domination, and her threats.

"That's where you're wrong, amigo."

"I'm heading in to talk with her now."

"You can jaw at her all you want, but it won't change nothing. I was getting sick of my own company anyway. Be good to work with you again. I'll be getting everything ready. And when you figure out that Miss de Vere always gets what she wants, I'll be waiting."

Matthew stalked into the saloon and ran smack into Victoria and Mr. Logan. "I'm glad you came to your senses, Matthew," she said. "Gertie was by. It appears Mr. Bowen has departed."

"It was right after that Chinaman left," Mr. Logan said. "Wouldn't be surprised if all that foreign carrying-on isn't what killed him."

"What killed him was a noose around his neck, and we helped put it there."

"At least *I* didn't build the scaffold, Preacher," Logan retorted.

"Gentleman, save your schoolyard spat for the back alley." Victoria's command slashed through the rancid, stale air of the empty saloon like a saber. "We need to get rid of the body."

"You mean give him a proper burial," Matthew said.

"We'd do better to take him way out past Boot Hill and leave him up in the hills, let the coyotes take care of him," Mr. Logan argued.

"I don't care what you do, but I want it done *now,* before we get any more folks wandering the street and poking their noses into our business. Get a wagon, wrap him up, take him out the back way. If anyone asks, it's supplies for the Palace, but you better pray nobody asks. When it's done, come see me in my office." Victoria pivoted on her heel and sashayed across the floor.

Logan grabbed Matthew's arm. "I'll help you get him out of town, but if you want to dig a hole and pray over him, go right ahead. I ain't wasting any more effort on a dead man."

They cast long shadows as they hurried across the street. Gertie had already laid Mr. Bowen out and gathered the coverlet around him, but she stepped back when they entered the room.

"Could've covered him up." Logan pulled the blanket over the dead man's face. He motioned Matthew toward the feet and they lifted Mr. Bowen from the bed. The only sound was a stifled sob from the corner as they carried him out. Mr. Logan paused at the back door and, with one hand, grabbed a couple of grain bags. He grunted as he shoved one toward Matthew and placed his own on top of the shrouded body.

"Wouldn't fool anybody who cared to look," Matthew said.

"They better not look if they don't want to join him."

The wagon, like the grain bags, was waiting. Matthew rode in the bed with the corpse, while Mr. Logan drove them at a good clip down the road out of town. He pulled up to the knoll where a fair number of departed miners and other men now rested, helped drag the dead weight up to a spot toward the back, dropped the body, and hustled back to the wagon.

"Almost forgot, Preacher." He pitched a shovel in Matthew's direction. "Knew you'd kick at dragging him off, so I brought this for you."

Mr. Logan flicked the reins, turned the wagon, and was gone. Matthew picked up the shovel and dug into the hard, dry sod. Sweat ran between his shoulder blades, even though the morning sun had yet to throw its heat. His shirt clung to him as he drove the blade into the ground and piled the dry dirt in a heap, shovel after shovel.

He edged out a precise rectangle and worked carefully, in no hurry to get back to Victoria. Indignation flamed within him. Whoever this stranger was, whatever his life had been, he deserved the final respect of one man to another. As Matthew grappled the body into the hole, he felt a twinge of conscience at the lack of a proper coffin. He'd make up for it by planting a wooden cross, carved with the particulars he knew about the gambler.

As he filled in the grave, the muffled thuds of the caked, dry ground hitting the body made him flinch. After a time, there was only dirt piled on dirt and it became easier to bear. He capped the burial with the dry sods, bowed his head, and mumbled the familiar words of the Twenty-Third Psalm, hoping Mr. Bowen's soul would rest in peace after his untimely, horrible death.

Matthew then walked the short distance back to town, his boots scuffing up tiny clouds of dust with each step. His mind blanked on all the necessary decisions lying in wait in his brain. Instead, he stared, without seeing the lackluster withered grass, the dull film of grit on the trees, the pale blue-white sky. Not a breath of wind cooled his scorched body, and he could swear, as he entered Eagle Bar, he was walking straight into hell.

"Hold up, there!" Ira Graff's terse shout pierced Matthew's wearisome trance. Matthew took his eyes off his shuffling feet and the dry ruts in front of him, and glanced over at the Golden Palace. Ira stood at the near corner of the building, arms waving at a man driving a team with a rope attached to the whiffle tree. Matthew squinted and his gaze flew to a wiry form standing on a ladder settled next to the gable — Judd!

"Hold up!" Matthew broke into a run. The Lady of the Seas tilted at a precarious angle, a foot off the ground, a noose lodged around her carved bosom. Even at a distance, Matthew could see the danger of the misbalanced, unsecured figurehead. "Wait!"

"Glad you finally showed up, Preacher," Graff mocked.

"You can't raise her like that." Matthew eyed the block and tackle suspended under the gable end on a large spike.

"Already have." Mr. Logan appeared at his elbow. "It appears we don't need you."

Judd called down to him. "I tried to get them to wait for you, Matthew, but Miss de Vere is not a patient woman."

A small crowd of gawkers gathered across the street in front of the Gilded Mansion.

A man on a large brown gelding trotted up and blocked Matthew's vision as its rider frowned down at him and, with a voice loud as a jay call, announced, "I'm looking for a dandy, goes by the name of Bowen. Heard he was headed out to these parts. You seen him?"

Mr. Logan's hard eyes raked Matthew's face before he turned to the newcomer. "Come on over here." He gestured toward the side of the building and drew both men a short distance away from the hubbub.

"What do you want with him?" Mr. Logan asked.

"He's a cheat. I'm here to kill him, or

410

shake his teeth loose until I get my stake back," came the raucous reply.

Victoria's peal of laughter from an open window above pierced Matthew's skull. He pivoted back to the action behind him just as Ira slapped the backside of one of the horses and the team surged forward.

Matthew raced around the corner but the rope snapped taut and the figurehead jerked into the air, twisting and rocking. Judd tried to control the wildly swinging Lady of the Seas, but it struck his arm and the ladder jumped sideways. Judd gripped the sides, bumping down the rungs in a vain attempt to soften his fall.

"Hold up!" Matthew shouted, but the Lady spiraled on the seesawing rope and crashed into the upper window of the Palace. Splinters of glass and wood rained down on the street, but the scream of a horse drowned out all else. One steed reared, and the team tore down the street, the rope snaking after them like a living serpent. The figurehead shot up, hit the spike, broke loose from the noose, and dropped like an anchor. Matthew lunged toward his fallen friend, but the wooden goddess beat him. With a sickening thud, the splintering cracked wood struck Judd full across his belly, pinning him to the ground. Matthew roared into the cloud of dust, flinging himself at the pitiless Lady, but it didn't budge. He crumpled to his knees next to his injured friend, cradling Judd's head and shoulders in his arms. "Should've waited," Judd gasped. A thin stream of blood trickled from the side of his mouth. "Promise me." Matthew leaned close, his forehead touching Judd's. "Take Miriam my poke. Wish I could've seen her face. Aches something fearful."

"I promise," Matthew said. "They won't want for anything."

"It's in the privy, under —" Judd went slack in Matthew's arms.

Men rushed in, encircling the pair as they heaved the figurehead off Judd's body. Matthew picked up his second dead body of the day and staggered up the street.

CHAPTER TWELVE

Cassie stepped out of the kitchen, telling herself she was just catching a breath of air, but instead chose to walk down the alley and stand at the edge of the street. She was rewarded not by seeing the tall blond man she sought but by Petey running all-out toward her. He skidded to a stop before her, scattering grit on her shoes.

He panted hard but seemed determined to get each word out. "Been a bad accident down to the Palace."

Cassie grabbed his thin shoulders.

"That ship's head fell and done crushed a feller."

"Not Matthew!"

"No. The preacher didn't get hurt none, but he's plenty mad. Heard him cuss a blue streak at Mr. Logan and Mr. Graff."

"Who got hurt?"

"Judd."

No! Not Judd with his gentle spirit and that

picture of his family tucked close in his pocket.
"Will he be all right? Go fetch Yi." It came out as breathless as Petey's words, but even as she said it, the boy's eyes shied away from hers and he shook his mop of red hair.

"Ain't no need for Yi."

Cassie suddenly realized she was clutching the boy's shoulders, and her arms fell in a dead drop at her sides. Petey grabbed her hand and, to her surprise at the grubby childlike gesture, gave it a small squeeze. "They's comin'," he croaked.

Cassie lifted her gaze and saw Matthew, looking like a mountain of a man, parting the traffic as he trudged forward. Men stopped and stared, but Matthew marched on with Judd's body held in his arms like a sleeping brother.

Cassie stumbled toward him. "Oh, Matthew." She reached out and pushed Judd's hair away from his eyes. His skin was warm and gritty. Blood smeared his lip and chin and stained Matthew's shirtsleeve.

The cold of death stole through her and Cassie backed away. "Bring him in here." She led the way into the dining area.

Matthew laid him on the nearest trestle table and drew in a shuddering breath. Cassie touched his arm and the trembling passed from him to her. "I'm so sorry," she whispered.

"It shouldn't have happened. I should've been there."

"It's Miss De Vere's fault," a gravelly voice said, "and those others she calls gentlemen."

Cassie wheeled around.

"Miss de Vere sent me." A woman, smaller and older than Cassie, stood at the end of the table. She wore a fancy dress that was as careworn as her pinched face.

"Go on back and tell the woman who sent you that we don't need you or want you here." Cassie ignored the shimmering pain in the sad chestnut eyes, and the way the stranger's nervous fingers twisted the straight strands of her light-brown hair.

"I want to stay and help." The woman clutched the sides of her skirt. "It's guilt made Miss de Vere send me to you, but I would've come even if she hadn't told me to. That man deserves a proper burial."

Matthew said, "Let Gertie stay."

Cassie opened her mouth to argue, but the sight of Judd's lifeless body, of Matthew stooped over his friend in grief like a frail old man, stole her protest and her ire.

Isaiah and Traveler threw wide the drape from the kitchen and hesitated a moment before they slipped into the large room, Petey a silent shadow in their wake.

Isaiah came alongside the table and bowed his head. Traveler tore his gaze from the dead man to Matthew. "A couple of us oughta go down to his claim."

"I intend to." Matthew's gaze fastened on the dead man's face.

Isaiah lifted his head and gently touched Matthew's arm. "Trav's right. We need to go now."

"After we bury him." Tears streaked through the dust on Matthew's face.

"Can't wait," Traveler said. "The low-down critters down to the river will already be in there, pickin' his bones."

"Judd didn't have a partner to protect his place. They'll take everything," Isaiah said, tapping the butt of the revolver he'd taken to wearing on his hip.

"Bunch of vile scavengers." Traveler spat words like a curse.

"We'll give Judd his proper due when we come back. Come on, Preacher." Isaiah wrapped a strong arm around Matthew's stiff shoulders and pulled him away. "He's got himself a wife and child, and nobody's gonna steal the stash he meant for them."

"I'll stay and tend things here," Traveler said.

The two men trudged out the front with Petey a step behind.

416

Cassie hurried after the boy. "Bring Yi," she said softly. Petey nodded and disappeared into the harsh, unrelenting California sunlight.

"Want me to look after 'im, Miss Cassie?" Traveler asked in a low, reverent voice. "It'd be my honor."

"No," she choked.

"Then I'll go back and tend the kitchen. You gals take as long as you need."

Cassie looked into the sorrowful face of her companion. "I'll take care of Judd. You're not needed here."

"I told you I'm staying. I'll help lay him out. You'll need it. You knew him, I can see it." Her haggard face sharpened into a look as fierce as any warrior.

"Did *you* know him?" Cassie's protest lacked heart. She didn't want the stranger here, particularly in view of the woman's connection to her mother, but all her strength had ebbed and she hadn't the will to put up more than a feeble argument.

"No, but I saw him around town from time to time. His type is decent, home and wife. They don't make a habit of ever visiting with my type."

"Then why are you here?"

"Just 'cause I live at the other end of the street don't mean I ain't got a heart same as most folks." She stared Cassie in the eye with a steely glint that dared her to deny the truth of it. "I've had my times in laying folks out, my husband for one. You? Maybe your first time. It's easier when you don't know 'em or you hate 'em. Judd's a stranger I don't rightly know. It's plain you do." She flicked an index finger at Cassie's tears. "My husband, now he fit the bill for hating and not knowing, too, I guess. I'd helped my ma lay out two of her little babies, but my man was the first one I laid out all by myself. If I had known what a terrible excuse for a man he was, I'd have never got hitched. Least-wise, I got to know what it feels like when there's not breath left in a body you just jawed with at breakfast."

Cassie led the way back to the kitchen. Traveler had anticipated their needs and handed the other woman cloths and a pan of warm water. "Gonna go find a man with a pine box," he said.

The two women trudged off to the dead body. Cassie gently washed the dried blood and dirt from his face, hearing Judd's voice in her head, happy as a lark to be building the goat shed.

Her mind flittered back to her pa, not much older than this man, his lifeless body lying on their porch in his dirt-caked overalls. Their mother, in a rush to get him in the ground, grabbed a traveling preacher and buried her first husband before he was hardly cold. Cassie had held his chilly hand until the end, not ready to say goodbye, when their mother grabbed Charlie's hand and hers and dragged them from the cemetery before they had the grave dug.

Their stepfather was another matter. As much as she and Charlie had adored him, he'd lingered and suffered, as much from his unfaithful wife as from a host of internal maladies. She and her brother had laid him out in their home for two days and begged one more penny of credit from an unforgiving town to give him a proper coffin and burial. Looking back, neither way mattered. Just like Judd, those men were cold as a wagon tire and gone from her life.

But not from my heart.

"You okay?" Gertie asked.

"Yes. It brings back memories."

"Always does for me, too. You want me to go down to the mercantile and get him some Sunday duds?"

"He probably wouldn't care for the fuss, or want us to spend the money."

"Won't cost us nothing. I'll charge it to Miss de Vere."

Cassie rubbed her forehead, trying to

think. "I don't know."

"Well, he looks cleaner than most. And if your Traveler's getting a coffin, I reckon you're right. He wouldn't want more."

"He's not *my* Traveler."

"I know that, but he's your friend. Not many women can say that about all the men you got around here."

"They're good men."

"Because you're a good woman."

Noise filtered through the canvas walls. A wagon pulled up and stopped. Boots tramped up the steps and Matthew, Isaiah, and Yi arrived. Cassie looked into their tired, grim faces. Yi bowed to her and came over to the body. He took the rag from her limp hand and went to work finishing the task.

Matthew took her arm and guided her out the door where Jeremiah stood patiently next to Isaiah's wagon.

"We've been talking. I've got to tell Judd's wife what happened. I promised him I'd go and give her all the gold he saved up." He scrubbed his hand across his face. "He worked hard for all this. Never will get that farm he wanted. It's not fair."

Cassie ached to comfort him, but grief and anger emanated so strongly from his body, she dared not touch his rigid broad back.

He let out a slow sigh and turned back to her. "I want you and Gertie to come with me. Eagle Bar is no place for a woman, no place for any of us."

The thought bumped through her dull mind like a pine cone falling from the top of the tree, hitting every branch on its way to the ground. She'd dreamed about leaving a hundred times but, now that the moment was here, Cassie wasn't ready. "No," she whispered. "I'll stay."

"You can't." Some of the weariness left his tone.

"I most certainly can. I have a business to run. Not everyone was born with a golden spoon in their mouth, Mr. Ramsey. Most of us have to work for a living."

"You mean silver spoon," he retorted. "You can get off your high horse just this once. I know for a fact you've got plenty in your own poke. You've been raking it in hand over fist. How much is enough, Cassie? Look at Judd. Is it worth your life?"

"You can't judge me. You don't know a thing about me. Or Charlie."

"I know it's not safe here, and Charlie would want me to bring you back to him."

He couldn't know about Charlie's note.

"What makes you say that?"

"If I was your brother, I'd want to knock some sense into that stubborn head of yours and bring you back to a safe place where I could keep an eye on you. You and Gertie have to come with me."

"No."

"I ain't going, neither."

Cassie whipped around at the intrusion. Gertie stood slightly behind her, hands on her wide hips.

"I'll talk to Victoria," Matthew said to Gertie. "She owes you plenty. I'll see you get it. You deserve a stake to start a new life."

"Don't see that happening." Gertie twisted her hair in restive fingers. "Never had nothing. I started out, one of thirteen. Nothing but hard times and work, trying to fill our empty bellies. Hitched up with the first man to come along soon as I was old enough. Turns out he had a bunch of us girls, and got me started in his saloon on this sorry path. Life ain't changed. I ain't making the same mistake twice and jumping from this frying pan into another fire. I got nowhere to go and I ain't about to set off to somewhere with a bunch of empty promises."

"Victoria will do right by you. I'll see to it." Matthew frowned, the traces of grief replaced by a dark scowl.

"Looks to me like you got your hands full burying your friend and heading off to find his widow. Don't need any more troubles for one day," Gertie said.

"But —"

"We ain't going." Gertie glanced at Cassie. "Maybe if you come back, we'll see the error of our ways by then and return to civilization. Right now, you can't make us leave."

"Cassie, come on." Matthew grabbed her hand in his calloused clasp. "You know you need to get out of here before something worse happens."

"What's worse than a friend dying?" Cassie countered, weary of the exchange. All she wanted was to slink up the hill out back, sit in the shade far above the noise, but there was no escape. There was no shelter from the drudgery and pain of living. It clung to a body like a second skin. "There's no place that's safe."

Matthew snatched his hand away and balled it into a fist. "I've got a grave to dig." He turned on his heel and strode off down the street.

Cassie watched him go, her heart heavy and worn as a millstone.

"It's the grief talking," Gertie said.

"Women know how to cry and ain't afeared of it. Men know how to get angry. Always been that way."

Cassie slogged back inside the eatery. Through Yi's gentle ministrations and wise touch, Judd looked at peace now, as if he'd merely stretched out on the table for a short rest. She patted Yi's shoulder and continued on to the kitchen where Traveler and Isaiah were talking at the stove. "The coffin's comin' in about a half hour," Traveler said.

"Matthew's gone to dig the grave," Cassie said. "Maybe one of us should go help him."

Isaiah shook his head. "He needs to do this by himself. Best thing for us is to stay right here 'til he comes back."

But will he come back? Cassie immediately chastised herself for her foolishness. Judd's body was here. He would return, and they'd all go to the burial. Then she would calmly talk to Matthew and explain to him her need to stay here a while longer. Like Gertie, she wasn't ready to leave for anywhere else because she, too, had no place to go.

The woman on her mind hovered right behind her. Cassie could feel her presence, hear her harsh breathing, and smell the faint odor of sweat on her. "I can do some cooking, if you'll have me," she said.

"I don't know. Maybe we should close up

for tonight. What do you think, Isaiah?"

"We sure could do that, Miss Cassie, but it'd just give us time to set and wallow, and I don't know as I can stand much more of it. We have the funeral comin'. Don't imagine it'll take too long. Might be fittin' to have everybody come together to eat."

"Been thinkin' the same thing myself," Traveler said. "We already got the stew and such goin'. No sense wastin' it. And eatin' together is a sight better than mournin' alone."

The comments covered Cassie's anxious brain like a soft quilt. Doing was always better than waiting. "You're right." She stepped up to the unfinished pile of potatoes she'd been peeling. Gertie's plump hand brushed hers as the other woman silently joined in the task.

The mindless work served as a temporary balm until Matthew returned with his jarring presence, his shirt limp with sweat, stained with Judd's blood and the dirt of hard labor. He spoke in clipped sentences, barking commands as the men carefully placed Judd's body in the coffin then loaded it in the wagon.

Cassie ran back to the cabin and snatched her quilt they'd brought with them from the lumber camp. She hurried back and draped the coffin with the faded crazy quilt, and Gertie carefully smoothed the multicolored covering.

Isaiah slowly drove Jeremiah down the street; Matthew flanked one side of the wagon, Yi and Traveler the other, while the two women trailed a short distance behind.

As the solemn procession plodded their way up to the lonely hill, several others fell into step with them. Cassie flinched when her mother and her current escort crowded in and walked alongside.

As soon as they unloaded the coffin and set it next to the freshly dug hole, Matthew said a prayer and launched into a terse, brief lecture about the ills and sins they all carried. When he abruptly stopped in mid-sentence, Isaiah stepped in and recited the Twenty-Third Psalm.

The short funeral ended when Matthew said, "I'll make the crosses." Only then did Cassie notice the raw, dry dirt of another new grave nearby.

Folks drifted away as silently as they'd come. There was no widow to comfort, no gathering afterward to pay respect to his family; nothing to hold the ragtag bunch of mourners together. Mercifully, Victoria didn't linger. She laid her hand on the arm of her companion, an older, silver-haired man Cassie didn't recognize. As they strolled by on the way back to town, her mother touched her arm so lightly Cassie wondered if she'd imagined the contact.

She stood in the dusty shade under a tree, Gertie at her side, as the men lowered the casket into the hole, shoveled dirt back into the grave, and laid the dried sod over it. She'd pick some wildflowers tomorrow morning and come down alone to pay her respects to this good man.

She steered her sorrowful thoughts away from the memory of the wife and daughter she'd seen in his photograph, briefly wondering if Matthew had removed the picture from the shirt pocket or buried it with Judd — a fitting comfort against his heart.

As if she'd conjured up his presence, Matthew strode to her. "I imagine you have to get back to your Golden Spoon. I wouldn't expect you to close on a day like this." He spun on his heel and stalked down the hill.

"It's just the grief," Gertie's gravelly whisper brushed Cassie's ear as the woman linked elbows with her and gently towed her down the hill.

Cassie hardly took a breath until they were safely back in the familiar confines of her kitchen. She didn't question Gertie's help or the heavy silence that filled the hot, stuffy room.

Matthew stomped past the corner of the Golden Palace, beyond Zhi's camp house, to the small stack of haphazard boards lying in the shade of the trees out back. He quickly found what he sought, and took the wood to the small tool shed sitting off the back door of the large saloon. He rummaged for a saw, hammer, and nails, and set about constructing two crosses.

When he finished, he leaned the rough construction against the shed wall. They weren't what he wished them to be, but they were rugged and would withstand the weather. He debated whether to carve or burn the men's names in each rood, but decided to wait until he had the time and energy to do a proper job of it.

He shouldered the crosses and talked to no one on his walk out of town. The cemetery was mercifully devoid of all life. Nary a bird flew by as he drove each cross into its prospective place. Like a knife to the heart, it pained him sharply to see the plain markers, particularly on Judd's plot. He took a moment and rested his fist on the blank wooden cross piece. "I promise I'll take care of Miriam and your little girl."

He strode back to the road and made a beeline for the stable, but Ulysses Morehead stepped out from the doorway of the Palace. "Matthew Ramsey, Miss de Vere would like a moment of your time before you leave."

The man had obviously been lurking, waiting to waylay him. Matthew glanced at the upstairs windows, but the glare of the sun presented nothing but shining silver rectangles. "Where's Mr. Logan?" he sneered. "Are you taking over for him now?"

"Mr. Logan is away at the moment. I'm merely stepping in to help a friend. Like you, I'll be leaving soon."

The smooth timbre of the older man's voice grated on his nerves, but the last statement took the wind out of Matthew's retort. He stopped and gaped at Ulysses, attired in his usual vest, coat, and white shirt, despite the summer heat.

"Matters here in Eagle Bar have resolved themselves. It's time for me to move on. I'm sure you, of all people, can understand. I wish you well, Matthew." He tipped his hat, ambled across the sun-flooded street, and disappeared inside the Gilded Mansion.

Matthew glared at the open door before him. The last thing he wanted was to cross verbal swords with Victoria, but he'd be a fool not to cut his ties completely before leaving town. He trudged into the empty saloon, astonished to see her sitting at one of the round tables, head bent as she wrote with a flourish. The white piece of paper shone bright in the patch of light coming over her shoulder.

He had no doubt she'd heard the exchange between Ulysses and him moments ago. Matthew stood over her table, and when she continued to write, he decided he wasn't going to dance to her tune . . . not today. "Victoria, I only have a moment to spare. What is it you want?"

She slowly looked up, her face grave. "I wanted to offer my sincere condolences to you, Matthew. I know you thought highly of Judd."

He rested his hands on the back of a nearby chair, crushing the wood in his tightening grip until his knuckles turned white. "He'd still be alive if you'd waited for me to help him, but you couldn't, could you? You had to teach me some sort of queer, twisted lesson, and Judd, who never hurt a fly, paid the price."

Victoria touched his wrist. Matthew yanked his arm away and stepped back.

"Matthew."

"I'm leaving." He stalked to the door. He

heard her chair scrape against the floor-boards, but he would never give her the satisfaction of looking back to see if she followed him.

"Will you be coming back?"

"No." He threw the retort over his shoulder. As he stepped out on the street, he thought he heard her say, "What about Cassandra?" But he kept walking.

He picked up his horse and led the black gelding up to the Golden Spoon. He stuck his head in the kitchen door and uttered, "Isaiah." The black man heeded the call, slipped out, and upended the washtub. Matthew retrieved Judd's gold, apportioned it in his saddlebags, mounted, and wheeled his horse around.

"Godspeed, Matthew." Isaiah ducked back into the kitchen.

Matthew heard Cassie's voice, but couldn't make out the words. Isaiah's answer drifted back loud and clear, "Just come to pick up Judd's poke."

Matthew maneuvered his mount around the eatery and was on the trail out of town before he realized Isaiah hadn't called him Preacher. Isaiah had addressed him by his given name. Not that it mattered. He couldn't afford to let his mind wander backward. There were too many snares, emotional and mental, rigged to tether him to his time in Eagle Bar, and with each mile away from the boomtown, he repeatedly chastised himself to cut the ties.

He nudged the horse with a restless knee, and the black immediately stepped up the pace. He barely saw the trail as he rode hell-bent for leather, his weary body hunched over the gelding's lathered neck. At some point he felt the heat seeping into him from the horse and let it rest as he pulled aside for oncoming wagons. But the faces, the shouts, the trees, the rocks, the bobbing horizon blurred in his mind.

The sun went down and still he rode on, letting the black pick his way slowly down the trail. He awoke abruptly, slumped in the saddle, and finally stopped for the night. He didn't sleep but stared at the starlit dome overhead, thinking of Judd's widow and dreading the moment when he must tell her the truth.

At first light, he was already on the trail, driven by a fierceness to escape the guilt that clung to him. He spent the traveling hours trying to convince himself he had to move on, had to get to Judd's widow be-fore . . . *before what?* Today she and the little girl were happy, carefree, waiting for their beloved husband and father to return.

Still dreaming his dream, looking forward to the day when they would all be together, reunited in a home of their own. But that would never be, and Matthew was the one to shatter their world and kill their dream.

The thoughts pounded in his head with each beat of the horse's hooves, but he kept going. He rode into San Francisco, his weariness so heavy the rub of his clothes hurt, and the grit from the trail, caked on his hair and face, threatened to suffocate him.

As he descended the hill into town, the sun's rays hit the low clouds settling on the bay. When he mingled with the boodle and traffic, the fog of anger and grief in his head cleared like the mist over the water. In spite of the grief and frustration stewing in his heart, Matthew knew what he had to do and set his jaw in determination.

Clusters of ships' masts poked up from the harbor like needles in a woman's pin cushion. Even from this vantage point, Matthew could discern ships ready to sail from those that had been abandoned by crews infected with gold fever. The city smelled of low tide, refuse, and raw wood.

He drew in a bracing lungful of the sea-tinged air. Since the day he'd left, buildings had sprung up like a bumper crop of weeds.

Wooden hotels, supply stores, liveries, businesses catering to every whim, and makeshift tents all vied for their place in the bustling town. Everyone scrapped for their share, for the illusive fistful of gold.

That thought brought Cassie to the forefront of his mind. He couldn't believe she'd gone straight from Judd's funeral back to her kitchen, all fired up to have a Hangtown Fry and rake in more gold. Of course he'd know that about the Vincent twins from the moment he'd made their acquaintance, but their blatant greed soured his stomach.

He'd be wise to leave Eagle Bar, and all those who called it home, far behind him. As he navigated the bustling crowd around him, Matthew tried to picture himself here in San Francisco. Despite its size, blare, and uproar, it was every bit as much of a lowdown boomtown as Eagle Bar.

He rode past a canvas eatery not nearly as prosperous and clean-looking as Cassie's Golden Spoon, and even as the thought skittered across his brain, Matthew turned his eyes and mount away, earning him an angry curse from the driver of a nearby freight wagon who swung wide to avoid a collision. He wasn't going back to the gold fields. He couldn't.

Matthew wended his way down the street through a section of Sydney Town to the waterfront. New wharves, wood still dripping with pitch, reached out like felled trees into the ship-clogged harbor. He pulled up in front of a well-built structure. Its clean lines and saltbox roof conveyed a thrifty sense of longevity and purpose. The bold black lettering of *William Ramsey & Sons Shipping* declared strong New England roots and reliability.

Matthew tethered his horse, shouldered his saddlebags, and walked inside. A young man clad in white shirt and black string tie, hair slicked back, looked up through round spectacles at his entry. Matthew walked past him.

"Excuse me, sir." The thin clerk trailed after him, but Matthew ignored the elbow chaser and lengthened his stride until he reached the far door and pulled it open.

The young man rushed alongside as Matthew entered his brother's office.

"It's all right. Pay no heed to this scallywag." Heedless of the gaping clerk, Will rushed over, pulled his younger brother into a bear hug, and thumped him heartily on the back. Matthew's saddle bags clunked heavily on the floor, but his brother paid no heed. "You look more like a hard-luck miner than a preacher, Matt."

"What you mean is I look like I've been drug through a knothole."

The clerk left with a gentle click of the door closing. Matthew pushed back from the fraternal embrace and took in his brother's tanned face, light-brown hair slightly longer than usual, and his well-trimmed beard and mustache.

"Just so. You're a sight, Matt. You back for good?"

"Eventually. San Francisco agrees with you." His brother looked good, and though Matthew had left here in a cocksure hurry to run from the Ramsey shadow, he'd missed Will terribly — the irreverent laugh, the dry Yankee wit, the twinkle in his serious gray eyes.

"Not cut out for life in a rowdy boomtown, eh?"

"Maybe not cut out for life in the West."

Will stroked his beard between his thumb and forefinger. "I can't believe what I'm hearing. Is this the same brother who's always pushing me out of the way to get the first slice of apple pie, to be the first to board the ship, to be chosen as captain of the newest schooner in the Ramsey fleet?"

Matthew looked around the office, neat and trim as a ship's deck, his brother's keepsake ship in a bottle displayed on the windowsill overlooking the harbor. A painting of the coastline from the vantage point of one of the city's hills graced the far wall. He didn't need to examine the artwork to know the artist stood in front of him. Growing up, Will had a talent for painting everything from their dog's portrait to their mother's flower garden, rendered on the back fence. And a knack for building models of their father's schooners — both pursuits encouraged by their mother and actively discouraged by William Ramsey Sr. "You like it here?"

"I do. Amelia's consented to come west. As soon as she arrives, we'll get married. I've already started building us a house up on the hill. I want you to come see it, maybe make some suggestions on the plan. You were always good with that sort of thing."

Will gestured to a chair and Matthew sat, facing him.

"I'm glad you're staying. Father was certain you'd be back." Will cocked one eyebrow as he drew his chair closer and sat down as well. "I wasn't so sure, this time. You had a mean look in your eye, and lit out of here with a full head of steam. When we didn't see you back in a week, I thought maybe you'd moved on for good."

We. The word reverberated in Matthew's skull like a clanging bell, awakening old frustrations and jealousies. "Father is here now?"

"He left shortly after you did."

"What? No. What do you mean?" It didn't make sense. Matthew leaned forward and held his brother's friendly gaze. "Father didn't come with us to set up the office. He wasn't here when I left." He couldn't believe what he was hearing — didn't want to believe it, because the idea of it fueled his growing suspicions.

"He *was* here. The old fox took a ship that made it around the Horn in good time. He arrived here a full five days before we did." Will's eyes narrowed. "I thought he met with you before you left for the goldfields. He came back one night, mighty pleased with himself. I can't quite recollect, but I think that was when he told me you'd be back in the family fold soon enough."

"I didn't know he was here."

"You were dead set on staying as far away from me and the business as possible, as I recall."

Matthew gave his brother a sheepish look. "Sorry I was such an idiot."

"Seems to have worn off, leastways for now."

Matthew gave Will a playful cuff on the shoulder, then quickly sobered. "Thanks, but I can't believe Father was here and I never saw him."

"He wasn't in town for long. I thought he was set on staying and setting up the office. You know William Ramsey. He wouldn't trust anyone, not even his sons, to stir in his business without his say-so, but Father left soon after you took off for the goldfields."

Matthew frowned. How had his father been so confident of his failure in Eagle Bar, unless he'd used his wealth to buy what he wanted?

How could his father stand by and let him go off half-cocked on a fool's errand, when all his life he'd commanded complete capitulation from his son, as he did his ship's crew?

Because William Ramsey paid someone to make sure his youngest son would fall flat on his face and come back to the family business with his tail tucked between his legs.

"I only know Father was furious over your decision to leave," Will said. "But then he went off somewhere, and when he came back that night, he was in good spirits. I thought maybe he'd talked you into staying, but he never let on where he went or what he did."

"Because he was up to no good." Matthew scowled. Had it been pure happenstance that Victoria de Vere appeared in Eagle Bar on the heels of his arrival? His gut had told him a different story the moment she'd sashayed into town and scuttled his first and only tent meeting. But he hadn't listened to his gut, or Charlie and Cassie, because he'd been so set on defying his father. All he'd accomplished was being a stubborn coot who'd been duped by a woman for months, a woman most likely hired by William Ramsey to do so.

He closed his eyes and heard her honeyed tones, felt her sink her claws into his pride and hook him into building a palace. He saw the endless money she had poured into a showplace and business that would be gone when the last flake of gold was taken from the river. Who *did* that? Someone with money to burn, and someone who always bought what she or *he* wanted.

"You okay, Matthew? I've got a room down at the Gold Dust Hotel where you can rest and get cleaned up. Then I'll take you out to dinner. There's some decent food around town."

"I've got business to take care of first." Matthew shot to his feet. "You ever know a woman named Victoria de Vere? Dark-haired, tall, charming, good-looking, close to Mother's age, I'd guess."

Will rose and followed his younger brother to the door. "I don't recognize the name."

"How about an older fellow, bit of a dandy, smooth talker and has a gold tooth?"

"Gold tooth," Will repeated. "Morehead?"

"Yes, goes by Ulysses Morehead. How do you know him?"

"He stopped by here one day to pick up some money Father had wired to him. Seems honest enough. We went out to dinner and he told stories about Father and him in their younger days. The next day he left on business."

"I thought I recognized the voice, but I couldn't place him."

"I wouldn't have, either, but Morehead told me a tale about coming over to our house when we were boys. We'd just broken a lamp by playing toss in the house. We were about to run outside to hide, when Morehead came in the door and blocked our escape. Father banished us to the backyard and ushered Morehead into his private library and closed the door."

The hazy memory hovered on the outskirts of his brain, but, as he thought on it, Matthew could see a younger, brown-haired version of Ulysses Morehead, his gold tooth winking.

The boys had raced away and gone on with their play. Up until this moment, Matthew realized he'd never seen the visitor leave. But Morehead's word echoed in his recent memory. *Matters here in Eagle Bar have resolved themselves and it's time for me to move on.* Father had sent the man to ensure that Victoria was doing her job, and that job was bringing William Ramsey's recalcitrant son back into the family fold.

Matthew stooped to retrieve his saddle bags. "I'll be back in a bit and we'll chew the fat."

Will dangled the hotel room key under his nose and Matthew snatched it up. "I'm holding you to that, brother."

Matthew took his time in the hotel, cleaning every vestige of Eagle Bar from his skin and hair. When he finished shaving and had donned a fresh set of duds from the trunk his brother had thoughtfully stored in his room, he sat on the edge of the bed, head in his hands, going over what he wanted to say to Judd's widow. It sounded harsh and crude, even in the confines of his skull. How much worse would it be when spoken aloud?

His body was stiff from hours in the saddle, but he straddled his horse once more. It was easy enough to get directions and find Roper's Boarding House, set up on the beginnings of a hill with two similar establishments across the street. The difficult part was working up the courage to enter.

Matthew slipped in quietly, but was immediately confronted by a stout woman with bright blue eyes shining out of a ruddy complexion. He doffed his hat. "Good day, Ma'am. I'm looking for Mrs. Judd Simpson."

The sharp gaze turned icy as she silently perused him from the tip of his boots to his still-damp hair. "And who might you be? I run a decent establishment, not like some of the places 'round this city."

"I worked with her husband in the goldfields." He pointed to the saddle bags on his shoulders. "I've come to bring her something from Judd."

"I only have your word on that, mister." The older woman leaned toward him and planted her hands on her hips. "Why isn't her husband here, bringing it himself?"

If it was this hard with a stranger, how was he ever going to break the sad news to Judd's wife, Miriam? "My name's Matthew Ramsey, Ma'am. My family has a business down on the waterfront."

"I might have heard of you," she conceded.

"I truly did know Judd Simpson. He was a friend of mine."

"And where is he now?"

"He died in an accident a few days ago. I promised I'd give his poke to his widow and little girl."

The woman's stern face softened, and a fat tear sat on the plump curve of her cheek. "I guessed as much, but when you get the news out to a stranger first, makes it a mite easier next time around."

"I don't expect that'll be true, ma'am."

"My name's Vesta Roper. I run this place. I'm a widow woman, myself. Had to start over. I came west with my brother and he set me up here before he went out to the goldfields to try his luck. I'm half-expecting someone like you to come and give me the same sad news you're bringing to Miriam."

Matthew twisted his hat brim in his sweaty hands. Mrs. Roper dabbed the corner of her eyes with her apron. "Miriam's a right fine woman. Smart and kind. Hard worker, too. She helps me out with the cooking and cleaning, and does laundry at an establishment down the street. She should be home with her little girl any minute."

They both stepped out into the street and

saw Miriam Simpson walking toward them, holding her daughter's hand. Rebecca skipped beside her mother, her blond braids, tied with blue ribbons, bobbing in the afternoon sun.

Mrs. Roper patted Matthew's arm. "I'll take the little one into the kitchen so's you two can have a minute. Come on, Becky, I've got some warm cookies and milk for you," she called. The little girl raced ahead of her mother, darted past Matthew, and flung herself into Mrs. Roper's skirts. "You little lamb," the woman murmured. She picked up the child and disappeared inside.

Miriam stopped in front of Matthew and looked into his face. "You must be Matthew Ramsey."

"How did you know?"

"My Judd was a talker, but he was a writer, too. He wrote me letters and sent them every chance he got. He thought a lot of you."

Matthew swallowed hard, his mouth as dry as the gulch outside of Eagle Bar.

Her soft oval face turned somber. "Don't imagine you're here to deliver a letter."

"No."

"Judd's not coming back, is he?"

Matthew thought if he as much as touched her, she would shatter into a thousand pieces. "No, there was an accident. I should've been there to help him." He choked on a sob.

Miriam looked up the street, avoiding his eyes. "I can hear him now saying it wouldn't have made any difference. I know my Judd. He was a good man, didn't hold grudges, gave the world a fair shake, and mostly got a fair shake in return."

"How can you be so calm?"

She tilted her head and met his gaze, silent tears streaking down her face. "I'm not, but I had a feeling in my bones, all week, something had gone wrong. Can't exactly say why or how, but it happens now and again. I get it from my grandmother. She had the second sight."

"I promised him I'd bring you his poke. He had quite a haul the last few weeks." Matthew gingerly took her slender work-worn hand in his large grip. "I'd be glad to set up a bank account for you, if you're willing. Get you settled for whatever's next. You and the little girl will be well provided for, for the rest of your life."

She withdrew her hand and clapped her pale cheeks. "I never thought he'd come back with that much."

Matthew pulled the worn photograph from his pocket and pressed it into her hand. "He kept this in his pocket and I swear he looked at it a dozen times a day. He missed you that much and couldn't wait to come back, but . . ." Matthew's voice broke.

"He wanted that farm for us." Miriam broke into a keening wail. Matthew put his arms around her and drew her close, absorbing the sobs that wracked her thin body.

CHAPTER THIRTEEN

Cassie lifted the lid and breathed in the steam of the baking beans, the heat of the oven savage on her cheeks. She finished checking their progress, closed the oven door, and stepped out of the kitchen. She stared at the dry landscape with dry eyes. Where once the little goat shed and chicken pen had brought her joy, now they were a grim reminder of all that was lost. Judd was buried up on the hill outside of town, and no amount of early-morning visits with wilted flowers would bring him back.

She wondered how Matthew felt today, how he'd made out with his grim errand. A dozen times a day her heart went out to him and Judd's widow and little girl. It had been nearly a fortnight since he left. Cassie tried to convince herself he was busy taking care of the poor woman's affairs and helping her through her grief but, as another day passed and another, she had to accept the fact that he was gone for good. The unsettling notion nudged her melancholy toward irritation.

"Want me to start throwing together some sourdough rolls?"

Cassie started at Gertie's voice in her ear. The woman had a silent tread, but Cassie had to admit she'd been a blessing in disguise. With both Charlie and Matthew gone, Gertie's presence had helped stem the loneliness. And she was a worker, always busy, helping at whatever task needed doing without complaint.

At first, Cassie was tempted to send Gertie on her way, but the fierce fire in the woman's eyes and her stubborn determination to lend a hand in the kitchen, regardless of Cassie's cold shoulder, had stalled the words, until Cassie eventually swallowed them for good.

A wagon rattled up the alley and pulled to a halt beside the women. The driver jumped down, nodded to Cassie, and unharnessed the mule.

"What is all this?"

The young man shrugged. "Just following orders, miss."

"But who sent it?"

"Compliments of Miss de Vere."

"Take it back!"

"No can do, miss." He guided the mule

around the wagon and headed toward the street.

"Wait! I don't want this!" she called after him. "You have to take it back!"

"You want to kick up a fuss about it, go see Miss de Vere." He led the mule down the alley.

"She has no right to do this," Cassie spluttered. Not only had Victoria delivered unwanted goods, she'd had the driver take the mule, removing the means to send the hated wagon back where it belonged. She felt heat creep up her neck at her mother's obvious ploy.

Gertie walked over to the wagon and ran a practiced eye over the load. "Miss de Vere does whatever she pleases. Likely heard we're running low on foodstuffs."

Cassie scowled. "She thinks she can buy her way into everything. Well, I'll let it rot right here before I'll use any of it."

Gertie remained silent. Traveler was out hunting, promising a deer to bolster their waning larder, but with the lack of rainfall these many weeks, game was scarce. Without ingredients, there wasn't a whole lot of kitchen work to keep them busy — no peeling, no dessert baking, precious little meat, save the last of the salt pork boiling away in the baked beans.

Isaiah moseyed over from chopping wood and leaned against the wagon. "Mighty fine lookin' stores."

"You think we should use them? Let Victoria get her hooks into our business?"

"Depends."

Cassie bit her tongue to curb the scathing retort that had been boiling within her since the day Matthew left. It was meant for him, not for her faithful friend. When she spoke, the words came out sullen but not accusatory. "Depends on what?"

"Depends on if you want to close up for good and head on out of here. I expect Charlie would favor that opinion, and I'm ready to take you. If you don't, you should send one of us to get fresh supplies or buy them from around here. We're out of everything and when we have nothin' left to serve, we're out of business."

They'd been struggling to put together a decent menu for the past several days and were losing business because of it. Isaiah was right. "I'll go talk to her, but don't touch a thing on that wagon until I get back."

"I could go with you, if you like," Gertie said. "I wouldn't say nothing, but I'd be there in case she tries to pull the wool over your eyes. She's powerful good at that."

The woman's simple gesture of friendship eased Cassie's heart some. "No, Gertie, I have to do this myself. Besides, Victoria's Palace is enemy territory. I'm afraid if she sees you, she'll force you to come back."

"Miss de Vere will leave me be, long as I keep my trap shut about what goes on down to the other end of the street. Likely nobody would listen to what I have to say anyway, but she won't chance it. Go on, now. From what I've seen, you can best that old witch if you put your mind to it. Always thought one day I'd see good win out. Wouldn't that be a sight!"

Wouldn't that be a sight. Cassie wasn't so sure. With each step closer to the Golden Palace, she slowed her pace. She hesitated at the open door, empty this time of day. She'd never been inside since its completion.

"I've been waiting on your arrival, Cassandra." Victoria said from a near corner table. "Don't stand there like a ninny. Come in out of the heat. I've arranged for us to have something cool to drink."

Her mother's musical tones, laced with the usual undertones of criticism, penetrated Cassie's indecision. "This isn't a social call. I won't be staying."

Victoria poured two glasses of brown-tinted liquid from a pitcher sitting in a small basin of melting ice. "When I get in my supply wagons, I always have my drivers load a small box with sawdust and ice, strictly for my own pleasure and that of special guests. Between the trip and the heat up here, it doesn't last long, but it's worth the enjoyment of the moment." She took a slow sip of the cool drink and shuddered. "I had this made up special for you, Cassandra. It's really quite vile. I don't know as you'd remember, but I always made it for your father. He drank it by the quart out in the field, called it 'Haymaker's Punch.'"

"I remember." Cassie set her jaw, steeling herself against the softening of old memories.

Victoria took another sip and grimaced. "I see you set that Vincent jaw. It's plain you're in some sort of pique over the supplies I sent. Really, Cassandra, use some common sense. You can't run your eatery serving water and beans. Believe me, I've heard the miners' complaints every night for over a week. You were doing well, but it won't last if you don't make some decisions on your own.

"I was much younger than you when I stepped out on my own. You're still living in Charles's pocket, and Matthew was your replacement for him. Now you've driven both men away. I can't say I blame them. I was so hoping you'd get over your clinging ways and make a suitable match with Matthew. Perhaps I can help."

"I can manage my own affairs perfectly well," Cassie snapped.

"Does that mean you'll be using the supplies I sent?"

Cassie's mind whirled as she stared at her mother's tone. Had she let the woman bait a trap, yet again? One that caught her whether she walked away or stepped forward?

"It means I've come to talk business," Cassie stated with more than a thimbleful of false bravado. Her mother gestured toward the opposite chair and Cassie reluctantly took a seat.

Treat Victoria like a business dealing. Nothing more, nothing less. Sound thinking, if she could follow her own advice. Finally, Cassie said, "I'll need a listing of what's in the wagon, then we can talk about payment."

She thought she witnessed a gleam of admiration in Victoria's eyes, but it was gone in an instant. "Land sakes, Cassandra, must we quibble over whether there are twenty pounds of potatoes or fifty?"

"You don't know what's in the wagon, do you? Someone else loaded it for you. You don't have a bill of lading. You've no notion of how much to charge. That seems to me quite an unsound way to do business."

"Unlike you, I have no need to count every penny. As for business, this was never intended to be a cash transaction."

Cassie prayed she could best her mother at this duel of wits, but today it was more than that, at least to her. This couldn't be just another contest of wills. She had to face her mother and win her freedom from the enslavement of all the bad memories, all the hurt, all the criticism, all the self-doubt this woman had planted in her heart. When Cassie left the Palace, it must be on *her* terms, head held high.

She cleared her throat and did her best to clear her mind of all the cobwebs from the past. "I didn't expect you'd give me the wagon for free."

"And why not? You're my daughter and I want to help, if you'll let me. I can be as stubborn as you, Cassandra, but the difference between us is I know when to give in. You seem to enjoy cutting off your nose to spite your face."

"You don't want to give me anything. You never have. You've always taken from us, and this is no different. You say you'll give me those supplies today, but tomorrow I suspect you'll want something, and you'll remind me how you bailed me out, and if not for you I'd be out of business, and you'll ask for a piece of the Golden Spoon."

Victoria tried to speak but Cassie put up a palm. "Oh, you won't ask for it outright, you're much too sly for that. You'll pretend to help, then you'll creep in like mildew and eventually take over the whole place."

Cassie's gaze never left her mother's unpleasant face, but in her mind's eye, she wandered ahead to the time she'd leave Eagle Bar. She hadn't given serious thought to what would happen to the eatery — ovens, pots and pans, her little cabin and farm. She vaguely presumed she'd sell the property, but what if no one stepped up to purchase it?

Most of the men were miners, not businessmen. Those who ran their own business would know that if she didn't sell, she'd eventually pull up stakes and go, leaving the property vacant and unguarded. She'd seen it happen to Zelda and to Mr. Hutchins, who'd started the mercantile before she and Charlie arrived. He was long gone, and someone else had taken over the building and the failing business. Rumor was, the new owner had only settled up on Mr. Hutchins's debts, offering nothing more for taking over the property.

"Despite what you may think of me, I *am* your mother, and my life hasn't been an easy one."

"And you think ours has?"

"I know that, Cassandra. I came to Eagle Bar to make amends to you and Charles. You have no notion of how many times I've dreamed of finding my two children and becoming a family again. Don't you want that?"

"It's a little late for that." Cassie swallowed hard. All the dark emotions didn't go down, but she tried to keep her tone reasonable. "Charlie and I have been on our own for so long, we wouldn't know what to do with a mother, and I suspect you wouldn't know how to be one."

Victoria reached across the tabletop and gripped Cassie's hand in her cold fingers. Cassie stared at the unwanted contact but didn't pull away. "You're probably right, but I'm not suggesting we share a home and hearth. Months ago, you both asked why I was here. As soon as I saw you and your brother, I wanted to help you. I know how to run a business, Cassandra."

"So do we."

"Of a fashion, yes, but your Golden Spoon could be so much more. And, let's be honest, it isn't *we* anymore, its only you. I know Charles isn't coming back. He's got a new bride, a new family, and he's fallen on hard luck with the fire and all."

Cassie gasped and pulled her hand from her mother's cold clutch.

Victoria said, "I know what goes on, and not just in this little boomtown. I'm aware of your troubles. You want to rake in a pile and help your brother get back on his feet, especially after the fire. I can help."

How could Victoria have known about Charlie and Abigail and the fire? "You know where he lives?"

"Oh, yes. I thought I might drop in for a visit someday and get acquainted with my new daughter-in-law. There might even be a little one on the way by now . . . my first grandchild."

Cassie ran a weary hand over her eyes and tried to gather her thoughts. "Let's get back to the matter at hand . . . the supplies."

"Business it is, Miss Cassandra Vincent. All right. Don't be a fool. Take advantage of my supply runs, and I'll get you fresh provisions so you can have a Hangtown Fry every night. How's that sound?"

"And in exchange, what will I pay you?"

"Let's just call it an investment in my daughter's future." Victoria stuck out her soft hand and Cassie gave it a brief shake.

Cassie stood, fairly certain she'd just made a deal with the devil, but Victoria wasn't going to take advantage of her anymore. She'd run the eatery, and when the time came to leave Eagle Bar, she'd settle her debts with her mother by giving her the entire business. "On one condition," Cassie said. "I have final say on everything. You will *not* dictate anything that goes on in my kitchen or dining room."

"I wouldn't dream of interfering in the business."

Cassie's started toward the door.

"I'll send a couple of my men to unload our wagon," Victoria added.

"There's no need to trouble yourself." Cassie turned back to the woman advancing on her. Victoria was already insinuating herself into decisions. *What did I expect?* "We know how to unload a wagon, but your driver took the mule so you'll need to have him hitch it back up so we can return the empty wagon to you."

"Of course. Just send Petey when you're finished and I'll have someone come to get it."

When Cassie would have walked away, her

mother clutched her arm. "There's one more matter to discuss."

Cassie arched one brow.

"Matthew," Victoria stated.

"I don't see where Matthew is any of your business."

"With that prickly attitude, it's no wonder he hasn't returned!"

"Matthew is free to do as he pleases."

"And with that fool notion, you'll remain a spinster, with me caring for you until my dying day."

Cassie whirled away, breaking her mother's hold on her.

"I had Matthew wrapped around my little finger, Cassandra, and *you* pushed him away."

"I don't need you to —"

"Don't tell me you haven't wondered why he hasn't returned. Has it ever occurred to you Matthew might have done *more* than comfort Judd's widow? He *is,* after all, a Ramsey. Even now, he might be doing the noble thing and marrying the young widow and providing for her and Judd's daughter." Victoria leaned closer. "Doesn't that sound like Matthew? If you're not careful, you'll lose your chance with him, Cassandra."

"And how do you know I already haven't?" The words came out meek, and

Cassie immediately wished she'd kept her fears to herself.

"Because I won't let that happen. I know for a fact Matthew has not married Judd's widow. However, I can't answer as to his future intentions. Before he gets to act on any of those noble aspirations of his, I'll get him back here and I'll see to it he's yours. When we get you married into the Ramsey money, you will live like a queen."

Cassie opened her mouth but no words emerged.

"Don't pretend outrage, Cassandra. It doesn't become you. You're here, scooping up as much gold as you can get your hands on. You're just as greedy to get rich as any of us, but there are much easier ways to turn a dollar, believe me. I wouldn't be much of a mother if I didn't find you a marriage that would line your pockets."

Cassie drew back her hand and brought it across her mother's cheek. The slap resounded in the large room.

Cassie and her mother stared at each other in shocked silence, Victoria's cheek red from the slap.

Cassie stumbled backwards. "How *dare* you try to sell me like one of your Gilded Mansion girls! I'll *never* marry for money. And if you meddle in Matthew's life, I will never speak to him, or *you,* again."

She marched to the door on trembling legs but with head held high. As soon as she felt the hard ruts of the street under her soles, her gait slowed to an amble. *What have I done?* Something she and Charlie vowed would never happen. She'd let her mother get her fingers into their business and their lives. Yet, Victoria was already in their lives. How she knew about the fire at Abigail's family farm, Cassie couldn't guess.

She shook out her hand as she walked, shocked at herself for raising it to her mother. Shocked at her mother for trying to arrange Cassie's marriage to Matthew Ramsey without Cassie's consent.

Her mother had doubtless come to Eagle Bar to pilfer the Golden Spoon from them, but Matthew had appeared on the scene and her conniving nature had seen something more lucrative — sell her daughter to a rich man and become the mother-in-law in a wealthy family. If Victoria had her way, she would ingratiate herself back into Cassie's life, orchestrate her marriage, and — how had she put it? — live like a queen.

The humiliation burned Cassie's cheeks all the way to the Golden Spoon. While she was gone, Traveler had showed up with a couple of rabbits, but no big game. The men were eager to unload the wagon, and their jovial attitude made it easy for Cassie to say very little. Instead, she fed them Victoria's scheme of having a Hangtown Fry every night. Petey showed up and he and Gypsy fairly danced around the bounty in the wagon.

When the wagon bed was empty, they assembled in the kitchen for hurried preparations for the night's meal.

Only when the suppertime din was over, the cleaning done and Gertie already bedded down in the cabin, did Isaiah take Cassie aside. She told him her plans to give Victoria the eatery when they left Eagle Bar, in payment for the supplies. He remained silent, his dark face unreadable in the scattered lamplight. "What do you think?" she prompted.

"I think it's a powerful good plan, but don't you go lettin' that woman know all our secrets."

"You don't have to worry about that."

"She's right about one thing. We ought to have a mess o' Hangtown Fries, 'cause I don't think we'll be stayin' on here much longer."

"What do you mean?"

"It's gettin' downright, low-down mean out there, Miss Cassie, and I promised

Charlie I'd keep you safe and that's what I'm gonna do."

Cassie and her friends fell into a hectic pattern, working elbow to elbow, with always enough supplies at the ready. Fresh food she'd only dreamed of having appeared at their kitchen door each week.

Cooking dominated every waking hour, and the miners packed the Spoon every morning and evening. At night, she and Gertie tumbled into bed, exhausted, but then they'd talk in the darkness, saying things they couldn't say in front of the men.

While Cassie's hands turned out pie after pie, her mind turned over the future. It had been nearly a month, now, and she was sure Matthew wouldn't return. She should be relieved because it kept him out of Victoria's cunning schemes.

In her head she wished him well and could almost picture him married to the beautiful woman in Judd's photograph, holding the little girl in his strong arms. It was a lovely thought, but one she had no desire to dwell on. Instead, she thought more and more about what was ahead for her and Gertie. The men would take their gold and make a new start, but she and Gertie didn't have a plan. She wanted to give Charlie and Abigail their due, but there was more than enough for her to have her own stake.

From the very start of this venture, she'd wanted her own farm, but could she manage it herself? Would Gertie stay on and help her? Over the past few days, the notion had grown stronger. The two of them could work together. Of course, she hadn't mentioned it to Gertie yet.

Hui and Traveler whisked the hot pots and kettles to the serving table, and Cassie gave the nod to Isaiah. He opened the door and hungry men streamed in, filling the dining room with the stomp of boots, rumbling voices, and the pervading scents of sweat and liquor. Just another Hangtown Fry as Cassie greeted the stream of dirty, haggard faces and heaped on the helpings.

Back in the line, a man pushed his neighbor, and the ones in front of him stumbled forward into the food table. The jolt hit the miner just leaving the serving table, upending the mounded plate he gingerly held in both hands. Hot stew, potatoes, meat and gravy, vegetable hash, pie, and coffee slopped over, searing his pant leg, splashing onto the back of the man beside him.

Cassie, Traveler, and Hui lunged at the jarred serving dishes, trying to prevent anything from falling on the floor. Potatoes hit the ground and exploded in a white sticky mass on Cassie's dress. The room erupted in a roar of angry shouts.

Traveler grabbed her around the waist and rushed her through the drape to the kitchen. Gertie looked up from her place at the stove, her eyes wide. "Get up to the cabin and lock the door," Traveler said. "Don't come out 'til we come get you."

"But the food," Cassie began.

"Hang the food! There won't be nothin' left if I don't get back in there."

Gertie grabbed Cassie's hand, yanked her out the back door, and didn't stop moving until they were inside the dim cabin and she'd dropped the bar across the door.

"Maybe we could go back down and talk some sense into them. Bang on a pot, get their attention and offer them free pie." Cassie's voice shook.

"No. It's bad. Once they get to fighting like that, they don't care who they hit. Even decent men lose any shred of common sense. Seems they get some sort of queer pleasure out of pounding each other into the dirt. Blamed if I could ever figure it out. Tomorrow they'll be all busted up but mighty pleased with themselves."

A gunshot exploded and Gertie clutched Cassie's hand, squeezing until it hurt. Another shot reverberated, and another, and then there was an eerie quiet. After a time, boots thumped up the pathway. Gypsy barked, and a fist banged on the door. "It's okay," Petey shouted.

Gertie lifted the bar and Cassie flung open the door. She gathered the boy in her arms and hugged him tight. "Is everyone all right?" she whispered.

He nodded against her shoulder and she reluctantly released him. He showed no signs of conflict and his eyes shone bright. "Miss de Vere done sent Mr. Logan and his men up. They busted right in and cleared the place out."

"Was anybody shot?" Gertie asked.

"No, don't think so, but might be some holes in the ceiling. Once Isaiah got loose a few shots in the air, Mr. Logan pulled out his gun and said any man who didn't leave peaceably was a dead man. Cleared the place out lickety-split."

The others tromped up and Petey fell silent. Hui nursed an arm that was probably broken, while Isaiah sported a split lip and a cheek and eye already swelling. Traveler was no better, with bloodied knuckles and a deep gash in his forehead that bled down the side of his face and pooled in the neckline of his shirt.

"It's time to be movin' on, Miss Cassie,"

Isaiah said.

After they patched up the men, Cassie slipped down to the eatery — broken tables, her flowered chintz ripped from the wall and trampled, her favorite pots crushed, benches smashed, food smeared and trod all over the floor, and slashes in the canvas walls.

She blinked back tears and walked the path back to her home. Tomorrow, perhaps they'd clean up the mess; but one look at Isaiah's battered face and she knew it was over. He groaned as he shuffled into his tent. Come daylight, they would leave and, like Matthew, never return.

She and Gertie spent the hours packing what little they could salvage. Before sunrise, Cassie grabbed the shovel and a hooded lantern and hurried over the path up the hill. Despite the grisly reality of last night, she would take away a good stake of Eagle Bar gold for Charlie and herself — and mostly good memories.

She dodged around a large rock and veered to the left on the short spur. Her feet stumbled over an unfamiliar mound of dirt and she caught herself from falling when the spade she carried dug into a gaping hole. By the dim lantern light, Cassie crouched next to the fresh-turned earth.

She reached into the pit and clenched her empty fist. As she staggered back down the hill, she cried out for Isaiah, hoping against hope he had unearthed her treasure during the night.

The big man hobbled out of his tent, one eye buttoned shut. "What is it, Miss Cassie?"

"Did you dig up the stash?"

He shook his head just as Gertie joined them. The stars winked out as the sky lightened. Cassie slumped against the wall of the goat shed. It had all been for nothing.

Isaiah hauled up his galluses and shook his head in the growing light. "Don't you worry none, Miss Cassie. I'll head down to the claims and set things to right. Nobody 'cept me knew where you and Charlie had that gold and cash buried. Hui will know if someone from last night found it and stole it. We'll get it back right quick, then hit the trail."

"I'll find Traveler and we'll get the wagon loaded," Gertie said.

Cassie nodded, too numb for tears. They would find the gold. "I want Petey to have Nugget. He deserves it, for all he's done."

She and Isaiah walked, without talking, down to the river. The goat trotted behind, softly protesting now and then. "Let's find Petey and his grandfather first," Cassie said as they picked their way around tents and long toms, sluices and scattered debris, while men lurched out of tumbledown shacks, waking to another day of panning gold.

Isaiah stopped in front of a ramshackle collection of boards and pilfered pieces of canvas. A huge black-and-brown dog rose, hackles raised, growling and baring its teeth. Gypsy shot out from behind the shack and snarled at the younger dog's face, quelling its attack. The larger dog lay down by the shack but never took his baleful glare off Cassie. The goat let out a frightened bleat as a bright-eyed Petey bolted from the dwelling. His grandfather followed a step behind, leaning on a shotgun.

"We're leaving, Petey." Cassie blinked back tears. She felt responsible for the boy and wretched at abandoning him.

"Grampa and I figured as much."

"I want you to have Nugget." Cassie moved closer but the goat strained on the lead rope, screaming and bucking to get away.

"Best give her to someone else. Appears she don't take to me."

Petey rushed into Cassie's arms and the

goat broke free. "I'm sorry," he sobbed in her ear. "They didn't say we was goin' to hurt her." His choked words made no sense, but his tears did. She gently rubbed his heaving shoulders.

"You mind your tongue, boy!" Petey's grandpa yanked him away from Cassie and gave him a rough cuff on the ear.

Petey stood next to the old man, his gaze fastened on the ground.

"It was *you* done stole Miss Cassie's stash," Isaiah blurted.

"Get off my claim!" Petey's grandfather raised the shotgun and leveled it at Cassie. Isaiah dodged in front of her. Both the big dog and Gypsy surged toward Isaiah, teeth flashing, snarling and growling. The big dog lunged just as Isaiah threw up his arm and stumbled back into Cassie. She grabbed onto the back of his shirt and fought to hold herself and Isaiah upright.

"Roman!" The guttural command came from Petey. The dog released Isaiah's sleeve, and both moved back, flanking their young master.

Isaiah recovered his balance and stood with his arm around Cassie, his shirt sleeve torn and bloodied.

"You'd best go now," Petey said.

"We'll go when you give Miss Cassie what

you stole."

"Petey wouldn't steal from me," Cassie said.

"The only ones who knew where we buried your stash was you, me, Charlie, and Gypsy . . . Petey's dog."

"Noooooooo," Cassie moaned.

"I said get off my claim. The boy didn't do nothin'. You got no proof." Petey's grandpa cocked back the hammer, the click loud as a gunshot itself in the morning air.

"Leave us be." Petey's voice was rough and deep, a chilling echo of his grandfather's warning. The dogs waited at his side, hair bristled, quivering lips drawn back, low growls vibrating through their bodies.

Matthew looked out across the bay from his lofty perch on the rafters of his brother's new house. He'd been in this bustling city for over a month, working with Will, helping Miriam, but mostly up here, building on Will and Amelia's future home high on the hill. It was almost like being on a ship, the breeze rippling the water, the green island floating on the horizon like an ocean mirage.

The smell of resin and the feel of the raw wood in his hands gave him a measure of peace, but also sparked a growing desire for building his own home. Not here in the city. Someplace with room to spread out. The thought had become annoyingly persistent over the last week, and whenever he thought of his own place, it conjured up his last moments with Cassie.

The mornings were cooler now, the nights longer, the sky a sharper shade of blue. If he didn't go soon, she'd leave Eagle Bar and he might never find her again. He'd tried to put the past behind him, determined to wait it out and see if she'd get in contact with him. Now his procrastination made little sense. He'd tried to locate Charlie, but to no avail. Somehow he'd been fool enough to think he could ride out into the miles and miles of California valleys and farm country, find his former friend, and mend fences. It wasn't that easy.

Teeming crowds streamed in every day — off the boats, on horseback, and in wagons. And every day as he rode through the streets, Matthew searched the faces for a familiar tall, dark-haired man with a quick smile and an easy stride. But the truth was, he had no idea where Charlie had landed.

He'd never find Charlie or Cassie if he didn't swallow his pride and return to Eagle Bar. Besides, he needed to take the cross he had fashioned for Judd's grave and make a proper memorial to his friend. And as much as it pained him to admit it, he needed to stop ignoring the burr in his brain that kept him awake in the stillness of the night hours when there was no distraction, no work for his mind and hands.

He needed to find out for sure the extent of his father's meddling. He could either confront his father or go back to Eagle Bar and dig up his own answers. He'd kept the suspicions to himself. No need to involve Will, who knew for himself the kind of man William Ramsey was.

Matthew climbed down the ladder with the knowledge of his prospects weighing heavy on his shoulders. It was time to move. Not just move on, but strike out on a charted course for his future. As much as he loved his brother, this time in San Francisco had drilled into his bones the conviction that he didn't want to spend his life working for the family business — not even oceans away from his father, or captaining one of the Ramsey schooners. He wanted something truly for himself, built with his own sweat and blood, and if he didn't grab hold of it now, he never would.

It was quitting time, anyhow. He always went back to the office for a few hours in the afternoon to help his brother with paperwork. Matthew snatched the two crosses from the downstairs wall, waved to the workmen Will had hired, hitched his load to the back of his saddle, mounted his horse, and slowly picked his way down to the waterfront.

He'd been at his desk for maybe a half hour, spending more time looking out the window at the ships and traffic on the wharves than doing actual work. He sighed, scraped his chair back, and froze when his brother's greeting startled him from the open doorway. "How long have you been there?" Matthew rose to his feet and began pacing. "What do you need?"

"I came in to ask you the same thing." Will leaned against the door jamb. "You've been uglier than an old bear, getting more restless and moody every day. Whoever's got you, whatever her name is, you've got to go before you drive yourself *and* me crazy. It's not that I don't enjoy your company, and you're a tolerable partner, but we both know this job takes the heart out of you. I've seen you up at the house. When you swing a hammer, you're a different man. Amelia and I can't thank you enough for the work you've done on the hill, but you and I both know it's time. Are you thinking of going back to sea?"

"No, I don't expect so, but thanks." Matthew strode to the door and clapped his brother on the shoulder.

"Any time you need a kick in the seat of the trousers, drop by. And Matthew, if you ever want to work together, or want to come stay in that house you've been building, there's always a place for you here."

"I know."

"Godspeed." Will's voice followed Matthew out the door and brought the echo of Isaiah's voice in his memory. It *was* time to go back.

He mounted his horse and rode straight over to Mrs. Roper's boardinghouse. He'd hardly tethered his horse when the door burst open and Becky raced out and threw herself into his arms. He caught her to him, whirling her around and lifting her high into the air, and was rewarded by her delighted giggle.

"I had a feeling you'd be dropping by today," Miriam said from the open door. "Come on in and sit, and join us for supper."

Matthew set the little girl on her feet and she wormed her small hand into his, tugging him toward the rooming house.

"Becky, go on in and see if Mrs. Roper

476

needs you to help her get the table ready." The child obediently flitted past her mother and disappeared inside.

"You're not staying, are you?" Miriam said.

"No."

"Becky's going to miss you something fierce. You've been good to us, Matthew."

"I'll be back," he said, surprised at the tug on his heart. He untied the cross he'd carved and held it up.

Miriam gently ran her finger over the letters of her husband's name. "Right nice, Matthew. Judd loved working with wood."

"Yes." The word came out choked and he cleared his throat. "I'm going to take this marker up to his grave in Eagle Bar. I didn't have a chance to make a proper one before I left. If you'd like to come, I'll take you and Becky."

Miriam smiled as tears ran down her cheeks. "No, I want to remember him here, the last night we spent together, sitting under the stars and looking out toward the hills, dreaming. The morning he left, he twirled me and Becky around, and he was fair to busting with going off and making our fortune." She wiped her wet face with the hem of her apron and turned bright, moist eyes to his.

"I could give you and Becky a berth on a Ramsey ship, take you anywhere in the world."

"I know. You've been more than kind, but I've pondered on it long enough. We'll stay put and throw in our lot with Vesta."

"But you don't have to work, Miriam."

She caught his hand and squeezed it gently before letting it go. "Don't you think I figured it out? You added to my Judd's gold."

Matthew didn't insult her by denying it. "I promised him I'd look out for you."

"And you have. I appreciate all you've done, but I'm set on staying. I like this city, the sea, the hills, the sunshine. It's going to be a wondrous place once it gets done with its growing pains. Vesta and I are thinking of buying the property next door. Partners we'd be. It's not the farm Judd wanted, but we came west together to buy our own spread, and Becky and I will have a place of our own. I think he'd like that."

"I expect he would." Matthew turned to hide the sadness welling up in him, and looked out over the buildings crowding the streets.

Miriam touched his arm. "What about you, Matthew? You're not happy here. Will you stay in Eagle Bar?"

"No. I don't know for sure where I'm headed after, but whenever I'm passing through San Francisco, I'll drop by to see you and Becky." He tied the cross on the back of his saddle. "Goodbye, Miriam."

"Godspeed, Matthew." Her lilting voice followed him down the street. The next morning, he gave a final look to the growing city by the bay and silently wished both Will and Miriam well as he turned his back to the water and faced the rising sun.

He rode into Eagle Bar near sunset three days later. He'd been slowed by a rock in his horse's front hoof. The bruise wasn't enough to hobble the animal, but bad enough to prompt him to get off and lead as much as he rode.

He was tempted to plant Judd's cross, and the smaller one he'd packed for Mr. Bowen, but the day was nearly gone. He scratched the three-day beard on his jaw and looked toward the small cluster of buildings ahead. He could hear the rumble of voices tumbling from the open door of the Golden Palace as he walked past.

He pulled his hat low and quickened his stride. Would Cassie still be serving supper, or would Isaiah have turned away the hungry, disgruntled miners who'd lined up too late? He decided he'd come in for supper, then hobble his horse out back for the night. If all went well, he'd convince Cassie to come back with him within the week.

He'd thought of little else during his time on the trail, turning the conversation over in his head, hoping he'd get an imaginary Cassie to agree with his plans.

He hurried up the street, noting the new livery and smithy, the expanded mercantile, and the unfamiliar faces. As he approached the eatery, his gaze raked over the men wandering in and out of the dining room doorway. *Where's Isaiah?* His thoughts flashed back to his initial meeting with Traveler accosting Cassie in the alley, and he broke into a run.

Matthew halted at the hitching post, its raw, yellow poles fragrant with pitch. He tethered his mount and hurried inside. The saw of a fiddle and a rinky-tink piano added to the raucous atmosphere of men's ribald shouts as a group of five women sashayed up on a platform where the serving table used to sit. They began to dance, and the heat and noise in the room rose. Matthew pivoted away in disgust, taking in the sawdust-covered floor, the bar set up in front of the dingy canvas wall where Cassie's bright chintz had once hung, and the hazy smoke-filled air.

He didn't see Gertie and didn't recognize any of the fancy women. He strode forward, nose-to-nose with one of Mr. Logan's men, whose hand rested on the revolver on his hip. The guard stepped aside as Matthew pushed through the drape to the kitchen area.

A slender young man dressed in store-bought clothes siphoned beer out of a keg.

"You, there!" Matthew barked.

As the boy turned toward Matthew, his hand jerked. Beer splashed on the tabletop and foamed on the floor. The boy hit the tap and stemmed the flow.

"Peter? Peter Fulton?" Matthew took in the trimmed red hair, darkened with oil and slicked back like Mr. Logan's. The boy looked grown up. Matthew hadn't been away that long, had he?

"Preacher! What are you doin' round these parts? Everyone said you were gone for good."

Matthew's gaze roamed over the bottles and kegs of liquor. The cookstoves were gone. Only the worktable remained with the stains of berries, carrots, and lard marking its former use.

"Where's Miss Cassie?"

"She's gone. They all up and left."

"When? Why?"

The boy licked his lips, grabbed a rag, and sopped up the spill on the wooden surface. "Had a fight one suppertime, lots of men brawlin', bullets flyin', holes in the canvas. Made a right wreck of things. Isaiah got walloped. Traveler, too, and Hui busted his arm. Cain't say what would've happened if Mr. Logan and his men hadn't showed up when they did. Mr. Logan says he'll shoot 'em dead if they don't clear out, and they got gone right quick after that."

"What was Mr. Logan doing up here?"

"I ran and got him, but he was right close. Miss de Vere likes me and Mr. Logan to keep an eye on things for her."

Matthew shook his head. "Miss Cassie wouldn't allow it."

"After you skedaddled, Miss Cassie got all her supplies from Miss de Vere. When Miss Cassie left, Miss de Vere took over the place."

"And you work for her now." Even as the last word left his mouth, Matthew's stunned brain cleared. Peter had told him the truth. Victoria had told him the truth. He'd just been too dense to listen. Peter Fulton, this boy everyone trusted, was as much a poker-faced gambler as Mr. Bowen had been. Victoria's voice from months before echoed in his skull: *Hiring that gangly stripling to spy on me and Cassie, too, I take it? And he's a redhead to boot, hardly a boy one would fail to notice as he bumbles along.*

"You've worked for Miss de Vere for a long while now."

It wasn't a question but the confirmation came in a quick duck of the boy's head. "I got to get back to work."

"Just one more thing, Peter." Matthew stuck his head out the back door. Cassie's chicken yard stood empty, the fence broken down, white feathers quilted around the base of the tree. An old newspaper and several tin plates littered the ground. Gypsy and a larger dog lay near the goat shed, gnawing on bones. "What happened to Miss Cassie's chickens and goat?"

"She took the goat along with her. It appears my big dog, Roman, likes chickens. Didn't know 'til he'd busted up the coop and it was too late." Peter fussed with the keg.

"I saw your grandfather out front playing his fiddle. You both look good. You living in Miss Cassie's place now?" It was a guess, but not much of a stretch to imagine this as Victoria's reward to her loyal spy.

Peter's face turned hard, his skin paled, and his freckles stood out like pepper on a bowl of chowder. Matthew glimpsed the emerging features of a cold-blooded, selfish man. "A feller has to live somewhere. I told you, Miss de Vere wanted us to live here to look after Miss Cassie's interests." He scowled. "Miss Cassie's got Charlie. I always knew she'd be all right. Grampa and I got to look after ourselves the best we can. I got to go, Preacher."

Matthew slipped out the back door into the fading light. How could he have been so blind? Peter had bamboozled all of them and sold out to the highest bidder.

As he retrieved his horse, Matthew looked up at the sign, slightly askew but still sporting the Golden Spoon moniker. The pledge near the door was stained with layers of tobacco juice and mud. Cassie's daily pricing slate was shattered and mixed with broken glass.

He borrowed a lantern and shovel from the livery for a hefty fee and the promise to stable his horse there for the night. He took his time planting the crosses on the hill, telling Judd about his wife and daughter.

It was full dark when he returned to the stable and, for more money, secured a place to lay his bedroll for the night. He didn't bother to wash the dirt off his hands, but strode back to the last place on earth he wanted to go.

Matthew entered the saloon of Victoria's Golden Palace along with a small group of men. He glimpsed Mr. Logan leaning on the bar, but kept the crowd between them. In his absence, Victoria had expanded the gaming room and poker tables, doubtless achieved when she moved the dance show up to the Golden Spoon. Alcohol flowed like spring water.

Matthew ran a practiced eye around the large room and spotted at least eight of Mr. Logan's men working the floor, holsters on, armed and ready. Not so different from what he'd observed at the Golden Spoon. Victoria wasn't taking any chances with her investments, old or new, it seemed.

He cautiously mingled with the miners, waiting for the opportunity to slip past Mr. Logan and make his way to Victoria's office, but suddenly he saw her slowly descending the staircase. He sucked in a deep breath. He should've known. Victoria always made her nightly appearance, talking up the men, pretending to gamble on her own games of chance and encouraging the miners to drink and enjoy themselves.

Matthew had witnessed her success, night after night, but tonight he wanted to talk with her in private and he was doubtful she'd honor his wishes. He threw back his shoulders and caught Mr. Logan's surprised look as he strode through the room and proffered his arm to the elegant woman in the maroon gown.

She hesitated a moment, her features stiff, her gaze sharp on his face, before she placed her black-gloved hand on his forearm and squeezed.

"I need to talk with you in private, Victoria."

She gestured with her head toward a corner table. Mr. Logan had left his place at the bar and preceded them. With brusque efficiency, he rousted the four men sitting at the table and they shuffled off to the bar.

"In your office."

"Nonsense, Matthew. You know I like to spend my nights down here among my guests, making sure they feel welcome."

"It won't take long."

She shook her head and her dark hair brushed his shoulder. The scent of lilac water mingled with the pungent odors of unwashed bodies, urine, liquor, and tobacco smoke. "If you insist on speaking in my office, I'm afraid you'll have to wait until I'm available."

He propelled them toward the empty table. "I take it you're available now, if I join you at your table."

He escorted her to the table, pulled out a chair, and helped her into it, every inch the gentleman, before he claimed the opposite seat. He would play her game, but only for a time. He needed information and he knew he needed to best Victoria's cunning to get it. His pursuit of his father's involvement could wait. "Do you know where Cassie is?"

She fluttered her fingers in Mr. Logan's direction. "My, my, Matthew. You've been off gallivanting for nigh on a month of Sundays. Now you come in here, all in a lather. That's a fine howdy-do after all this time."

"I've been up to the Golden Spoon and talked with Peter Fulton."

A saloon girl delivered a bottle of wine and two glasses and filled them with an unsteady hand. Victoria waited until the woman left, then took a sip. "I expect Petey told you Cassandra and her compatriots packed up and left lock, stock, and barrel."

"Not quite lock, stock, and barrel," Matthew countered. "It appears you ended up with the lion's share of what once belonged to the Vincent twins. How'd that come to be?"

"Hold your horses, Matthew." Victoria leaned back and sipped her wine. "I swear, you weren't always this cantankerous."

"I'm tired of your twaddle, Victoria. You understand full well what I want to know."

Her laugh pierced his eardrums. "I assure you there is nothing wicked going on here." She patted his hand and he quelled the urge to recoil from her touch. "Quite the contrary. You abandoned Cassandra. Charles abandoned Cassandra. What was the poor woman to do? She came to me for help. We reached an agreement. I furnished all her supplies and let Gertie go down there to help her. She had a Hangtown Fry every night and raked in a pile. With my help, she made her fortune. When she left, I naturally took over my share of the business. If not for my timely rescue, there would no longer be a Golden Spoon."

"Far as I can see, there *is* no Golden Spoon." Matthew silently digested the spoon-fed drivel. What had really happened? Peter was as cagey as the woman seated across from him. Cassie would sooner go to the devil before she'd go to her mother for help. *Her mother.*

For the first time since Matthew's return to Eagle Bar, he smiled. He would bait the bear in her own den. "It appears to me, you finally got what you came for. You stole the Golden Spoon from your son and daughter."

Victoria's eyelids fluttered, but if he'd hoped to shock her, Matthew was disappointed. "Cassandra told you I'm her mother? I'm glad. I waited until she was ready. I suspected she would confide in you once Charles was gone, but you and she are wrong about the rest of it. I came to *help* my children. Cassandra was flighty when she was a girl. She has no real notion of the hardships I faced and the reasons I was forced to leave. Charles knew better, but those twins were thick as thieves. He'll always take up with his sister, even if it means going against the one who gave him life, his own mother."

"Did Cassie go to stay with Charlie?"

"I expect so, although I told her not to. Him with his hands full, a new wife, and rebuilding after the fire. Having a sister larking about isn't going to foster good relations with his bride. I tried to explain this to her, but I imagine she'll settle in and test her brother's loyalties. Soon enough, Cassandra will be moping and carrying on when she sees Charles has replaced her."

"That doesn't sound like Cassie." Matthew couldn't stop his quick defense.

"I always knew you'd be the right man to handle my daughter."

"Where *is* Charlie's place?" He fought to

keep the desperation out of his voice.

"Why, I thought you knew. Is that why you came back, Matthew? To go in search of Cassandra? I'm *more* than willing to help. Charles has a spread outside of Indigo Springs, northwest of San Francisco." Victoria lifted her chin. "Although, that was *before* the fire."

Indigo Springs. Matthew had what he needed, but now, with any luck, he'd get the rest of what he sought.

Victoria inclined her head toward the bottle and Matthew refilled her glass. She looked at him through lowered lashes and sighed. "My Cassandra always needed her brother. I expect she's discovered the painful truth by now, that Charles doesn't need her. She's likely brokenhearted, lonely, and in dire need. Might even up and take off on her own. But just because she's got a trunk full of gold, doesn't mean she's safe. I'd hate to see some mean-spirited man take advantage of her. She's too trusting."

"That could be said of all of us. We all trusted Peter, but he was always working for you, wasn't he?"

"That boy is smart as a whip. A credit to his grandfather. Nobody will ever get the better of either one of them. You can be sure I've rewarded him for his diligence."

"I heard as much. I took a gander out back at Cassie's old place." Matthew nodded. "They seem to have made themselves to home."

"I didn't think Cassandra would mind. She always was partial to the boy, and he *did* help build that goat shed."

Enough about Peter. It was time to strike his last blow. "What about my father? Don't tell me William Ramsey's money didn't build your Palace."

"I would never insult your intelligence, Matthew. Your father gave me a stake. I make no secret of it."

"But my father would never invest in this venture for anyone but himself. You came to keep an eye on *me,* to make sure I returned to San Francisco."

"The Golden Palace was always a means to an end. I have no intention of spending my life in this one-horse boomtown."

"Then why are you still here?"

"Because, unlike my daughter, I knew you'd be back." Victoria stood and leaned toward him, her hands on the tabletop. "I expect you're disappointed in me and your father, but parents do what they can for their children. Your father is merely looking out for his son, just as I look out for my children."

"You mean you want to meddle in our lives."

"We only want you to be happy." She came around the table, hooked her arm in his, and drew him to her side. "Unlike your father, I don't see the harm in young men sowing wild oats. I take it the Ramsey family isn't permitted to do so, but I wanted to give you a chance at that, Matthew. That's why I hired you. Not to spy on you for your father, but to show how you didn't need your father's approval to find success. This isn't a task I sought out. William Ramsey approached me through a mutual acquaintance."

"Ulysses Morehead," he said, so disgusted he could barely spit out the name.

"I see you've already pieced together the transaction quite nicely. You *are* clever. The moment you and I met in San Francisco, I knew you were a man of noble character. I hate to say this, but my daughter has always been a source of disappointment and blighted hope, so much like her father. I know you care for her, and I thought you were the right man for her, but I care for you, too, Matthew. You're much too good for her."

Revolted at the woman beside him and sickened by his father's duplicity, Matthew gave her a curt bow, spun on his heel, and broke away from her without another word.

"I hope I'll see you again when I return to San Francisco." Victoria's voice chased him out the door.

He slept little, angry at himself for being a fool, angry at himself for being angry at a selfish woman who would never understand. As midnight spun toward dawn, his mind spun over the betrayals, and his suspicions wouldn't rest. It would be just like Victoria to abuse her daughter in a vain attempt to trick Matthew into going to Cassie's rescue. He was certain half of what he'd learned tonight was whitewash and pure lies, but did it matter?

In the morning, he traded his lame horse for a fresh mount. He gave Judd a final tip of his hat on his way out of Eagle Bar. He traversed the familiar trail at a good clip, but not in desperate haste. Regardless of his father's treachery and Victoria's cunning plots, their lies and schemes amounted to nothing now. Victoria was right about one thing — he didn't need their approval. He'd cut loose the ties that had hobbled him. Cassie was with Charlie. She was safe, and he needed the time and the miles to figure out what to say to her.

He still hadn't figured that out when he

stopped at a place in Indigo Springs, cleaned up, and got directions to Charlie's spread. A short while later, he rode past the blackened skeletons of a grove of trees up to a small house. The fresh lumber gleamed under the California sun. It had been built a slight distance from the charred rubble of what must have been the original home. He heard voices and the ring of hammers as he dismounted.

Matthew walked slowly toward a barn under construction when the slam of the door behind him, followed by quick footsteps, caused him to halt and turn around. A young woman with chestnut curls approached. She had a plain face, but sparkling eyes and a friendly smile.

"Matthew!" He spun back around at the familiar hail and stared into Gertie's delighted features as she hurried toward him. "I knew you'd come," she said. "James, it's Matthew!" She turned and ran toward the barn.

James? Matthew followed more slowly, aware of the young woman walking at his side.

A moment later, Charlie appeared, followed closely by Traveler. Charlie said, "I knew you'd come, Matthew. Glad you're here." He strode forward and clasped Matthew's hand in a strong grip, and pounded his shoulder with the other hand. "Matthew, this is Abigail, my wife."

Where is Cassie? At that moment, Nugget tore around the corner of the house, bleating. She ran toward them, stood on her hind legs, and planted her front hooves on Charlie's back. He shrugged her off but reached down and gave her head a rough pat.

Maybe Peter hadn't been playing as fast and loose with the truth as he'd feared. If Cassie had her goat and her fortune, all was well. Perhaps now she'd be ready to hear what he had to say.

"This goat is a demon," Charlie said.

"I told you as much, but you brought it on yourself when you got her," Abigail teased.

"I need *Cassie* to tame the beastie." Charlie's lean face suddenly sobered. "Are you going to bring Cassie back home, Matthew?"

"I thought she was here with you."

"Who told you that?"

"Your mother."

Charlie grimaced. "Never believe a word that woman says."

"You don't know where she is?"

"I do and I don't." Charlie groaned. "You

know my sister. Stubborn as Isaiah's mule. She's with Isaiah somewhere in the Oregon territory, and I expect she'll try to get him to leave her there."

"But why?"

"It's where we came from. The lumber camps. It's where Cassie learned to cook for the men. Come on into the house." Charlie wiped his sleeve across his brow. "Abigail's made some switchel. Mighty refreshing in this heat."

Matthew stood rooted to the spot and watched the couple, Charlie's arm still around Abigail's waist as they strolled toward their new home.

"About time you showed up, Matthew," Traveler said. "If you'd showed up sooner, you might've saved Cassie a heap of trouble."

"James." Gertie rested her hand on the man's arm.

"James?" Matthew echoed. "What happened to Traveler?"

This man in his neat work clothes, short hair, and clean-shaven face, bore little resemblance to the gruff miner he had met in Eagle Bar. But the woman on his arm, in her blue calico dress, looked like a farmer's wife, her cheeks rosy, her smile genuine. Both Gertie and Traveler had been changing before his eyes, just like Peter.

"I picked up Traveler along the way, somewhere."

"But it's James now," Gertie insisted. "I'll go help Abigail. You boys come along when you're ready."

"Gertie has a kind heart," Matthew said, at a loss to why she'd abandoned them out here in the yard.

"Ain't no denyin' that."

"She's a good woman."

"Too good for the likes of me."

"You mean you're moving on and leaving her, *James*?"

"Like you did Miss Cassie?"

The man might have changed his name and his ways, but he still knew how to get under Matthew's skin. "Seems like you left her, too, or else she'd be here with Charlie."

"Don't you think I tried? When we left Eagle Bar, I swore on my wife's grave I'd deliver her safe right here, as if she were my own sister."

Traveler had a wife? "What happened?"

"Cassie wouldn't have none of it, and Gertie took her side. Powerful hard to fight against a woman, and two like them? Impossible." He looked down at his boots. "Now you're here, I expect you'll bring her back and I'll be movin' on."

"I thought you and Gertie might —"

"You thought wrong!"

"Look, just because she had a rough past doesn't mean you have a right to look down on her and abandon her."

"I ain't abandonin' her." He balled his hands into fists at his sides.

"Seems like it to me."

"I'm leavin' so she won't get tangled up with me."

"You're too late."

Both men startled at Gertie's sudden re-appearance.

"Told you before, woman, you can't be sneakin' up on a man like that. Ain't healthy."

"I was hoping Matthew would talk some sense into you."

They'd obviously been around this bush more than once, and Matthew was certain he had no desire to be privy to their argument, but Gertie shook a finger at both of them. "You men think you know everything. You don't know nothing. James thinks he don't deserve a second chance."

"Stop, Gertie!

"He had a wife and a son."

"Left them behind me, just like my name," he muttered.

"He has a boy a little younger than Petey,

lives with his wife's people. His wife died in childbirth."

"*Stop,* woman!"

Gertie rubbed his stooped shoulders with a gentle hand. "It's all right."

"No, it ain't. Been nigh on ten years now, and it'll never be right." He raised tortured eyes to Matthew. "I wasn't there when she needed me. Wasn't s'posed to have the baby so soon, so I went off to help a neighbor buy some cattle and left her all alone. When I come back, she'd been dead a while and the baby was wet from head to toe. He'd cried himself to exhaustion, didn't even wake when I picked him up and took him to his grandparents. I buried my wife that night and lit out for nowhere.

"I couldn't stay. I couldn't face my boy. He favored my wife, even when he was a little mite. Had her blue eyes and smile." His voice broke.

"But I always sent money for him. He went to school, and with what I got minin', I'm thinkin', he might even go on to one of those colleges back east. If he doesn't take after his no-account pa."

"You ought to go see him," Gertie said softly, her eyes wet.

"Best I don't. He's used to things the way they are. But I check up once in a coon's age. He's doin' well. He's a good boy."

"A boy needs to know his pa loves him," Matthew said "You've protected him his whole life. He deserves to know that. He might want to be like you. He could do a lot worse. What's his name?"

"James." The response was barely a whisper.

"You coming?" Charlie called from the house.

"Can you tell me how to find Cassie?" Matthew asked after they'd settled on the trim porch.

"I expect she's up to one of Rowland's lumber camps. He had three, maybe more now." Charlie wrinkled his brow. "We worked there for a spell after our stepfather passed. Edgar, our stepfather, packed us up and we made it out to the wild west coast in the thirties. Cassie and I were young and thought it was a great adventure. And poor Edgar was trying to keep the woman he married happy. He didn't know our mother. She was never happy, no matter how much he gave her, but he tried."

Charlie drew in a shuddering breath, his hand gripping the rough rail, clearly in the throes of the past. "Edgar saw gold in those forests of giant trees, and convinced his banker friends back east, along with the settlers up north of here, to invest in his sawmills. He was too soon. He didn't count on how hard it'd be to get the trees out. Wasn't like it is now. No roads, no men to work the rivers, no logs to market. He foundered, and the money went. But if he could see it now! It's just like he dreamed. Cassie's gone back there to work."

"I heard she had a pile when she left."

"You don't know?" Gertie said.

"Victoria?" Matthew scanned the sorrowful faces of the group. *Taking her daughter's property and all her earnings.* He should've done more than just beat his gums at the woman.

Charlie rubbed his eyes and sighed. "No, it was Petey. Leastways, that's what we think."

"Isaiah figured it out," Traveler said. "The goat was scar't of Petey. The boy said somethin' 'bout helpin' Logan string it up."

"What? That doesn't make sense," Matthew said. "Why?"

"Don't rightly know, but the boy played us all for fools. That dog of his knew where Cassie and Charlie buried their stash. Near as we can figure, Petey used the dog to lead him to it. He up and stole it because he knew Cassie would be leavin'."

"I'm going back and wring that little

weasel's neck," Matthew ranted. "He and his grandfather, living it up at the Golden Spoon. I should've known."

"No! Ain't none of us going back there," Charlie said. "Cassie said so herself. She had Traveler . . . I mean, James, deliver a note, said she didn't blame Petey. Said we had a good run, but maybe we were meant to work for our bread. My sister loved that boy. I don't think she wants to believe he did it. And she's right. Long as we've got each other, it doesn't matter if we're rich or poor. We're more comfortable with poor, seeing as how it's been that way our whole lives. All I want is my sister safe. I'm asking you to bring Cassie home, Matthew."

"I will. I made you a promise in Eagle Bar, and I'm here to see it through. Just point me in the right direction."

Matthew headed north the next morning, trailing a packhorse with supplies, Charlie's firm handshake lingering on his mind. He chafed as the days of riding turned into weeks, barely noticing the passing land-scape. But when the trail cut through the ancient green forests Charlie had men-tioned, Matthew felt the cool begin to seep into his dry bones.

The dim sunlight dripping through the massive trees lent a sacred air to the place.

He moved from one lumber encampment to another farther north, said to be the Rowland camp. Matthew rode in one early afternoon, the branches dripping from a morning rain, the forest's silence broken by the rhythmic undercurrent of saws, punctuated by shouts and axes biting into solid wood. In spite of his weary body, he stopped in front of a long, low log structure and vaulted from his horse. He opened the door and laughed when he saw the familiar face of a man sweeping the dirt floor.

Isaiah Weaver turned his head at the sound. "She's in the back, Matthew."

A sudden wave of uncertainty rushed over him. "Can you ask her to come outside? Maybe don't tell her I'm here?"

"Will do."

Matthew ducked out the door and waited, leaning on the hitching post. A moment later, he heard the door open behind him and her light footsteps suddenly halting. He strode up to her, held out his hand, and waited. Cassie stood in a shaft of sunlight, chin raised, looking off into the trees.

She slipped her hand in his.

Matthew stared out at her world and saw the masts of schooners, the logs of a sawmill, the walls and roofs of a town, and the fine, satin-smooth boards of a home and cradle.

ABOUT THE AUTHORS

Born and raised in coastal Maine, sisters **Sadie and Sophie Cuffe** bring the strength of a living sisterhood to their writing, as well as the spice of differing perspectives on everything from cloud formations to classic lyrics. They've written for numerous magazines and newspapers, and authored over twenty novels and novellas, including *Blind Man's Bluff.* They run a small farm in Unorganized Territory and bring jane-of-all-trades life experiences to their novels. They write squarely to the heart of real women and men who aren't twenty-something, don't wear a size two, and who prefer boots and flannel to high heels and neckties. And they've spent quality time on horseback in cowboy country, riding the South Dakota plains. Contact them at sscuffe@yahoo.com or Facebook: Sadie and Sophie Cuffe.

Printed in the USA
CPSIA information can be obtained
at www.ICGtesting.com
JSHW081349020923
47716JS00002B/6